Summer on Sag Harbor

ALSO BY SUNNY HOSTIN

Summer on the Bluffs

I Am These Truths

Summer on Sag Harbor

A NOVEL

SUNNY HOSTIN

WITH SHARINA HARRIS

WM

WILLIAM MORROW

An Imprint of HarperCollinsPublishers

SUMMER ON SAG HARBOR. Copyright © 2023 by Asunción Hostin.
All rights reserved. Printed in the United States of America.
No part of this book may be used or reproduced in any manner whatsoever
without written permission except in the case of brief quotations embodied
in critical articles and reviews. For information, address
HarperCollins Publishers, 195 Broadway, New York, NY 10007.

HarperCollins books may be purchased for educational, business, or sales
promotional use. For information, please email the Special Markets Department
at SPsales@harpercollins.com.

FIRST EDITION

Designed by Bonni Leon-Berman

Library of Congress Cataloging-in-Publication Data has been applied for.

ISBN 978-0-06-299421-9

23 24 25 26 27 LBC 5 4 3 2 1

*This book is dedicated to Mr. William Pickens III,
the unofficial mayor of Sag Harbor Hills, who began
summering in Sag Harbor in 1946. Thank you, Mr. Pickens,
for being the first person to introduce me to SANS and
welcoming me to be a part of the community. You are missed.*

CHAPTER 1

"THE FATHERS"

February 2021

The day of reckoning had come. A polite but firm phone call from the estate attorney at Cravath, Swaine & Moore forced Olivia Jones to face the sins of her godfather.

It had been nearly a year since she discovered the truth about her godfather's involvement in her father's death, yet the betrayal still burned.

On the cold February morning before the meeting with the attorneys, Olivia sought to reconnect with her godfather by visiting his storage unit—the perfect place to honor his request to read the last letter he'd ever written to Olivia.

Olivia had a keen memory, but it was on days like this that she cursed it. It was etched in steel, her godmother Ama's quivering mouth, wet brown eyes, the tremor of her pale beige hands when she slid his letter across the table, pleading with her to read his last words.

When Olivia ignored Ama and the letter, it was as if she could hear Ama's heart breaking—like cracked ice splintering bit by bit until it exploded. Ama, rarely vulnerable, spoke life to Omar's confession beyond the grave. At the time, Olivia couldn't bear the admission. She ran away from her beloved sanctuary in Oak Bluffs.

If she was honest with herself, she never stopped running.

Now clutched in her hands was a worn white linen envelope. The letter felt like a featherlight bomb. She regarded the envelope carefully, she didn't move, her breathing careful as she sat stiff in silence—a little lost, possibly melancholy.

At least the Prussian blue velvet wingback chair was comfortable. It was the type of furniture one would not expect in the middle of a storage unit in New York City, but on a Restoration Hardware showroom. Her godfather must have known Olivia would need the cushioned comfort as she sat cocooned in the collected memories of her father, a man she'd never really known, who'd died when she was just a baby.

Omar Tanner, her late and ever-efficient godfather, had seen to every detail. When she first visited the room last year, her head spun from the opulent details. It was no ordinary storage facility, but rather a vaulted studio apartment where the likes of Gates, Bloomberg, and Buffett could rest assured their clients' possessions were well-attended and personally seen to by housekeeping—where time and temperature had no impact on their property.

Her attention lingered on the gorgeous black-and-white photos framed and hung along a wall. She recognized the headshot of her father in his police uniform—the same photo still sat on the mantel in her mother's living room.

She crossed the room to inspect photographs she'd never seen. There was one of her father as a child and a boy who looked so much like him, sitting on a beach. From the blue Monte Carlo parked behind them in a lush grove of trees, she guessed the picture to be from the early 1980s. There was another picture of a young girl dressed in her all-white Sunday best. The photos were like an open door to a family she'd always wondered about. Olivia's mother, Cindy, always deflected her questions about her father and his family when she was growing up, but Olivia knew that there must be more hiding behind her mother's many silences.

When she reached to pick up another framed picture, a loose photo wedged between books tumbled off the ledge, right into her hand.

The picture captured a smiling Black family—two boys, a younger girl, mother and father, posing in front of a house on a beach.

She flipped over the photo and found what looked like a thin, feminine scrawl.

Jones Family Vacation
Sag Harbor, 1982

She held the picture tighter, her head spinning from a truth she'd always known. Many times she'd wondered about her father's family, but she'd been too afraid of her mother's reaction to ask.

Olivia slipped the photo into the small crevice of her Hermès clutch. She'd think of her long-lost family later. It was time to read Omar's letter. Holding her breath, she opened the envelope and unfolded the stiff paper.

Dearest Olivia,

If you're reading this letter, I have passed on. It's hard to imagine a world in which I'd ever be apart from you girls much less Ama, but I guess life is about greeting a series of obstacles that seem impossible to surmount with grace. I love and admire all three of you girls. I know a father—even a godfather—isn't supposed to have his favorites, but Olivia . . . you are mine. Like me, you've had to bloom where you were planted. By now I hope you know just how strong you are.

Ama and I know this well, and I hope that in time, you'll come to see the truth of your strength, your beauty, and your value.

I'm not sure exactly what Ama has told you, so I'll start at the beginning.

I was one of the first Black men to make Partner at Cravath, Swaine & Moore, as you know, and I was often the only one in many spaces. There were certain tasks that fell to me at the firm, including recruiting Black law students for summer internships, diversifying our client base, and making the business case as to why our communities and people were worth investment. I believe that was some of my greatest work. However, during my time at the firm, we took on an unusual case, an embezzlement suit involving someone raiding the pension funds for the New York Police Department's union. We were representing the union, and although I was aware of the case, I wasn't working on it directly. When they called me to take a statement from the whistleblower, I knew that this person must be Black.

The whistleblower, a young, tall, proud, brave, Black police officer named Chris Jones, was your father. Within a few minutes of meeting me, he pulled out the sweetest baby picture of you, and I could tell just from the way he talked about you that you gave his life meaning. I'll never forget that he said that you were his whole world, and I hope that you'll never forget that either. His entire face lit up talking about you, like a man in love. He said that he wanted a basketball team filled with Olivias. He wanted more of you. He loved you so very much.

As you can imagine, this was a very high-profile case, and your father did both a very honorable and dangerous thing by deciding to reveal the truth about who was stealing money from the pension fund. Soon after I met your dad, one of the white partners at the firm invited me to Hilton Head, South Carolina, to a partners' trip, one I had been excluded from for years. I was desperate to belong. In retrospect, I realize that I needed affirmation from the white men in my firm—validation that I was good enough. He invited me to get information about the whistleblower, because his friend was the one facing embezzlement charges and serious prison time. So, in a moment that I have regretted for the rest of my life, I let your father's name slip from my lips.

Shortly thereafter, Chris Jones was murdered. I knew immediately I was to blame.

Your father was a stand-up man who did the right thing. I wished I had told you the truth, but the years passed, and it never seemed like the right time. I hope that you'll forgive my weakness in not giving you a chance to make up your own mind. I wanted to be your knight in shining armor forever.

I know you are an independent woman, making a name for yourself in this world. But what is important is to do what makes you happy. I've set aside the better part of my estate for you. When you're ready, I have a team set up on the legal and accounting sides to handle the transfer of the assets I left for you in a trust. This includes a home in my beloved Sag Harbor.

Though I'm in no position to make such demands, I humbly request that you spend at least one summer in Sag Harbor before you make a decision to sell. It's not only a place I love, but a place where your father spent his summers as a boy, a place where Ama and I celebrated anniversaries. I believe it can become your home. To rest, recover, and be in peace with our kind of people.

Although I'm not there with you, know that you are never alone. You are protected by the angels who watch over you, both your father and me. Know that your father and I will walk alongside you, too. You are beautiful, my Olivia, inside and out. You deserve all the love.

Always,
Omar

With trembling fingers, Olivia carefully folded the letter into thirds. The simple diamond from her fiancé, Anderson, cuffed her ring finger. She stretched and wiggled her hand. It was a perfect fit—Olivia had gone to a jeweler for a resize. She didn't love the engagement ring, but she appreciated the gift and even more, the meaning of commitment behind it.

Now Olivia wondered if she would have to resize her life again for a gift she wasn't at all sure she wanted.

A house!

Squeezing her eyes shut, she debated the merits of skipping the meeting with the attorney and hiding in her apartment.

"I'm no coward." She opened her eyes, her attention drifting to the wall of memories.

It wasn't just Omar's beloved Sag Harbor. This place belonged to her father, too. She smiled shyly at the photos, though her head nod was firm.

She would go to the place that made her father smile, eyes nearly shut, mouth wide open and laughing like someone cracked a joke instead of yelling "Say cheese" toward the camera.

After leaving the storage facility, Olivia called the law firm to confirm her imminent arrival. But Omar, as usual, had something specific in mind. Among more paperwork handed over for Olivia to sign had been a simple pamphlet that read: "The History of SANS: Sag Harbor Hills, Azurest, and Ninevah." Upon opening it, she found a real estate agent's card secured by a staple inside the flap, as well as another name jotted inside.

Joel Whittingham. Unofficial Mayor of SANS.

No number or email. Just the man's name, and his unofficial designation, as if that were enough.

"What are you up to now, Omar?"

CHAPTER 2

WELCOME TO THE NEIGHBORHOOD

May 2021

The moment Olivia Jones started her first job as an analyst at Goldman Sachs, she'd vowed to never take the bus again.

Four years of riding the Megabus nearly every weekend as an undergrad at Cornell made her all but allergic to buses.

But the path of least resistance for a day trip to Sag Harbor had been the Hampton Ambassador.

Orange sunrays spilled across the sky, just barely touching the Vanderbilt skyscraper as Olivia hurried past Grand Central Station for the fifteen-minute walk to the corner of Fortieth Street.

Though Anderson offered, it had been too early in the morning for a five-minute drive. Besides, Olivia wanted the brisk walk since she'd missed her morning run. What's more, she needed to walk off the nervous energy that covered her body like a second skin the moment she discovered her inheritance—not only a house but possibly a community in Sag Harbor.

In the three months since, she signed papers, met lawyers, her financial advisor, and finally multiple discussions with her fiancé about spending time to wait out another wave of Covid. When the vaccinations became available to the public, she decided to make the leap and visit the summer home.

She'd timed her arrival early with fifteen minutes to spare. Olivia, painfully punctual, hated the idea of being late even more than she disliked the idea of inhaling a stranger's breath on a public bus. Though between the vaccination and double masks, she'd done as much as she could to protect herself and others. Thankfully city officials had taken every precaution when it came to masking—from thoughtful spacing in open areas to leveraging technology for contact tracing. Her fellow citizens had also done their part in mitigating the pandemic, and it warmed Olivia's heart when she witnessed small acts of kindness, like supporting bodegas and mom-and-pop businesses. It was all too easy to shop ecommerce sites for groceries and goods, but New Yorkers took care of their own.

A few minutes after Olivia arrived at the stop, a few other passengers formed a line behind her, in various states of dress from pajamas, tank tops and shorts, to summer dresses and casually expensive blouses and slacks. Olivia worried that perhaps she was overdressed in an aquamarine vintage print Pucci dress.

A few days before she modeled several options in front of Anderson, eyeing her outfits more keenly than a judge on *Making the Cut*. She wanted Whitney, her real estate agent-slash-neighbor-slash-HOA president to take one look at Olivia and feel confident that she would be an exceptional addition to their community.

Olivia whipped the long, ankle-length dress around, revealing her spiked metallic Louboutin sandals. The dress was more than a dress, but rather protection from old insecurities of growing up in a small two-bedroom apartment in Queens. She wanted to belong. She realized, after listing the pros and cons of following Omar's directive, that her life had stalled.

Her godsister Perry had reunited with her husband and had a newborn baby, Libby. Billie, her other godsister, was the lucky new owner of Ama's home in the Bluffs, where they'd spent summers together since they were young. Now Billie was happily boo'ed up there with her wife, Dulce.

And then there was Olivia.

If she deigned to let her feelings have their way, she might allow herself to feel a bit adrift. But Olivia was stoic and suspicious of anything that resembled melodrama. She drew her gaze away from the station and tried to take her mind off the memories she'd shared with the Oak Bluffs crew. It was time to replace the steady anchor of rituals with Ama, Perry, and Billie—like summertime shopping in the city before jetting away to a full summer in Oak Bluffs after Memorial Day.

There would be no watching fireworks comfortably on the Vineyard's lawn. No nights of whispers and wine with her godsisters. Though sadness snaked at the pit of her belly, she rubbed her stomach and took a fortifying breath.

She would make new summer friends, new routines, new rituals, new memories.

The bus pulled up five minutes before it was scheduled to depart.

Olivia waited her turn to flash an app that included her seat assignment—two seats, third row from the front—she'd purchased both seats for extra room and peace of mind. She then walked up the stairs clutching the Chanel tote bag where she'd tossed wasabi edamame, bottled water, and a few books. Near the front of the bus were wrapped snacks and water rather than the wine amenities they'd advertised on the website. But then again, most services had been modified during the pandemic. Olivia breathed deep, smiling with relief that the bus smelled like Berbera mist rather than the peculiar Megabus eau de humanity.

Once the bus departed, she tried to read a book on women in leadership, but it didn't hold her attention. She dozed off for a bit and when she woke up, she noticed the bountiful, but naked trees lining the highway and signs for Ronkonkoma, and then Westhampton, Hampton Bays, and Southampton.

As the bus chugged along the Long Island Expressway, Olivia took a selfie of her profile against the bus window while the bare trees rushed past. She was a terrible selfie taker but this one came out well. Her freshly coiffed hair hit her shoulders in loose curls the way she liked it. She sent it off to Anderson, her fiancé, before she could overthink it. He insisted on photo documentation of the journey since he had to stay in the city for his comedy show.

Seconds later, he responded reliably with a crazy tongue emoji and heart eyes. Olivia snorted at his silliness and replied with a lone red heart.

Before Olivia knew it, the bus pulled onto Sag Harbor's busy Main Street. Olivia slow-blinked twice, reminding herself that she was indeed in Sag Harbor and not Oak Bluffs. Though Sag Harbor was only a hundred miles away it seemed as if she had traveled back in time. Quaint shops housed in classic white clapboard buildings, some intermixed with red bricks, reminded her of old schoolhouses. Signs from shoppes, to restaurants, and even a liquor store hung like flags above the awnings, with fonts reminiscent of the early 1900s.

A Black woman standing in front of the American Hotel, who Olivia immediately recognized as Whitney Parks, waved her hand in the air.

Olivia nodded, smiled, and walked toward the gorgeous real estate agent, who looked even more stunning in person than the photos Olivia had pored over online. She clicked on picture after picture of Whitney, who had the look of a Barbie doll with café au lait skin, long hair, long lashes, and a picture-perfect smile. Many photos included her handsome ex-basketball player husband at fundraising galas for Black museums and colleges, including one where the *New York Times* described Whitney as the "stalwart president of the Sag Harbor Homeowners' Association." Olivia admired

Whitney's fashion choices—Duro Olowu at the Studio Museum in Harlem's fiftieth anniversary gala, Sergio Hudson at the Met Gala, Christopher John Rogers at the United Negro College Fund's spring fling.

Her flawless fashion choices also drove Olivia to look her best. Once she spotted the floral silk midi tea dress that gave her the look of a vintage Hollywood screen queen, Olivia knew she'd made the right choice.

Still, her knees wobbled, and her stomach roiled like a topsy-turvy boat at sea. That familiar sensation had been well established over the years—the same feeling she had the first day of private school, the first day of college, and the first day at Goldman Sachs.

Olivia always looked the part—wore the right clothes, said the right words, but she'd wondered if they could see her courage, as flimsy as plastic, beneath her wavering smile.

Olivia clenched her jaw, and just managed to stop herself from rolling her eyes. At twenty-eight she should be well past these feelings.

Whitney dropped her waving arm, replacing the distant greeting with an up-close and personal smile. Her hazel eyes, more green than brown, exuded intensity. Whitney lifted her chin and narrowed her eyes just *so*, focusing them like a camera lens, soaking in, and sizing up. But then a smile broke through, equally as intense but warm as the sun.

"Welcome to Sag Harbor!" Whitney greeted.

Olivia's shoulders dropped an inch. "Thank you. And . . . thank you for agreeing to meet me."

The realtor waved her off. After they both confirmed their vaccination status, she'd volunteered to pick her up and drive Olivia to her new home.

"I'm just up the road, parked near the Whaling Museum."

"Oh!" Olivia bit her lip after the chirpy excitement leapt out.

Whitney let out a loud laugh. "It's wonderful. I highly recommend you pay a visit."

Olivia nodded. She'd read online about Sag's history as a whaling town that brought Blacks, Native Americans, and European immigrant seafarers and their families together in the early eighteenth and nineteenth centuries.

"Oh, and you must tell me where you got your dress. You look gorgeous," Whitney complimented once they arrived at her car.

"It's Pucci. A wonderful vintage boutique in Soho started deliveries during the pandemic." Like many other consumers during the pandemic, she opted to buy things online. She wore the same designers, and she knew her size. If for some reason a piece didn't fit well, she got it altered by her tailor.

"Well," Whitney started once they'd buckled their seat belts. "Luck is certainly with you. Look how the sun decided to show out for you after an entire week of drizzle and fog. Before we go to the house, shall I take you for a little tour?"

"Sure," Olivia agreed. Though she was eager to see her new home, she'd at least seen the images online. She could wait another hour.

Whitney rolled back the roof of the car. When Olivia inhaled, the scent of freshwater hit her nose.

She'd done her research about the area, including reading articles about the elite Blacks who began building a vacation home community in the Hamptons in the 1950s and the interracial community who'd populated the area in the 1800s. Olivia zoned out a bit while Whitney chatted away, allowing the view of the water to wash over her.

The bay, with its calm blue waters, didn't remind her all that much of Oak Bluffs.

Good. She nodded more to herself. Olivia needed something completely different, something new, something that didn't remind her of what she'd lost.

And what better way to do it than to establish new roots in Sag Harbor?

Olivia listened as Whitney told her about the three neighborhoods that were now a landmarked historic district. When Whitney drove the car away from the cove, Olivia tugged her attention away from the enrapturing vistas and played the role of doting new student, nodding along as Whitney told her stories about Main Street's highlights, the beloved bookstore, and an ice cream shoppe.

Whitney drove along Hampton Street, and then turned onto Eastville, pointing out the AME church.

"I would stop," she glanced at her watch. "But I think we should get you into your new home . . . then brunch before you leave." Whitney winked.

Whitney turned down a few streets, a quick right, left, right, and so many other turns that Olivia felt she couldn't easily replicate. The neighborhood was a maze and it seemed by design.

With her nose a mere inch away from the window, she absorbed the neighborhood with modest homes that lined the neat street. Olivia's idea of Sag Harbor had been different, flashier.

There were few people out on the streets, and the homes were not overtly fancy. Most were unassuming, one-story homes, with second and third stories hidden behind trees and ivy. Freshly cut lawns lay beneath a thin layer of dew from the morning's rain showers. The wide, paved streets were perfect for bike riding and easy driving. Olivia, who rarely drove, would likely dust off her license out here.

"Be prepared to fall in love," Whitney warned as she parked on the side of the street.

They quickly exited the car. Olivia shifted her weight from side to side, waiting impatiently for Whitney to open the door to the gray clapboard house on Ninevah Place. She noted the preserved boxwood wreath that hung on the freshly painted front door as well as the matte black door knocker and monogrammed doormat with her last name "Jones" that adorned the entrance.

Secretly delighting in the detail, tendrils of warmth poured over her. Someone clearly took care of her home during the five years it waited for Olivia.

When the door finally sighed open with a gentle push from Whitney, Olivia walked in and found herself at a loss for words. The generous foyer and mudroom opened onto a living room with bleached wood floors and a wall of glass doors that stretched the entire twenty-five-foot length of the house. She walked inside, eyes wide, eating up every delicious detail of her home. Pulling out her phone, she remembered to snap pictures for Anderson.

Outside was an in-ground pool covered by a tarp, a BBQ grill, and a patio that could comfortably seat at least ten guests. Just past the low hedges that encircled the backyard were steps that led down to the beach. And beyond the beach was the bay and its blue waters.

Whitney pointed out other features of the home—central air; radiant floor heating in each of the three bathrooms and the foyer; airy, ten-foot ceilings in the four bedrooms, including one that could be used as a nursery or a guest room depending on your pleasure and life stage.

Olivia trailed behind her, admiring the elegant décor that gestured toward both the area's nautical themes and the Black art neither too gaudy nor competing for attention. Whoever decorated her home knew her style, selecting timeless and powerful pieces. If she were to guess, someone hired Doreen Chambers to decorate her home.

"Has it always been this way?" Olivia blurted her questions before the realtor waxed poetic about freshly painted walls.

Whitney dropped her pointing finger and spun around to face Olivia. "Been what way?"

"Decorated like this."

Whitney blinked and nodded a few times. "Y-yes. As far as I remember, it was decorated a few years ago by the older gentleman who left this home for you."

"Omar." Olivia uttered his name around the knot in her throat.

"Yes. Him. He seemed like a delightful man and I'm very sorry for your loss," she sped past the condolences. "He oversaw the decorations and art. He'd asked for my recommendations for local art galleries."

"Was there a . . . woman with him?"

Whitney looked up at the ceiling as if her memories lived there. "Not the first few times. But once or twice. And then his wife if I recall correctly. She's come here once before to hire cleaners. They come once a month to dust and whatnot. The lawncare is managed by Mr. Whittingham."

The unofficial mayor. Olivia nodded, her mind processing, spinning, accepting. Whitney's voice faded away, replaced by the whooshing sounds of the bay in her ears. Both Ama and Omar had been involved. Everything had been organized just like her childhood, meeting her godsisters, summers on the Bluffs. She even wondered if meeting Anderson had somehow been staged. Her emotions seesawed between appreciation and annoyance.

Whitney tapped her shoulder. "Ready to go outside?"

"Yes." Olivia stood in front of the wall of glass doors that led onto the backyard, enjoying the view of the bay's calmer waters. The proximity to the water was at least one way in which this home was better than Billie's house on the Bluffs.

Her seesawing emotions finally landed on appreciation. Overcome by a sense of rightness that she never felt before, of being planted exactly where she was meant to be, the tension inside her shoulders, inside her heart, melted away. This was not just another place to rest during the summer, but a home where she could write a new chapter of her life, to build a family with Anderson.

Olivia took one last look at the bay, and then she turned to Whitney, who was busy shutting the blinds and turning off the lights. "You're right. I am in love."

"Of course you are." Whitney smirked. "Oh, before I forget, I have a special delivery for you." Whitney hustled to the kitchen pantry. When she opened the door, she pulled out a series of newspapers—including the *Wall Street Journal.* "I don't know of anyone under the age of fifty who reads newspapers anymore."

Olivia did and this was all Ama. Her hands itched to roll out the paper and read the *Journal* in forty-five minutes in the methodical way Ama had taught her at the kitchen table in Oak Bluffs—market news first, then two headline articles, and finally, a lifestyle piece so that she didn't transform into a finance automaton.

"Oh, and this is for you as well. The cleaning crew handed this over to me last week."

Inside was a small envelope, the size of a wedding or baby shower invite. She'd received a few dozen of these bite-sized invites over the past decade. Olivia immediately recognized Ama's feminine scrawl.

"Do you mind if I step outside?" Olivia lifted the envelope.

"How about you stay here, and I leave? I'll be waiting in the car." Whitney rushed outside the home before Olivia could nod her assent. Olivia's knees became liquid. She slid onto the chair near the kitchen table, and with the beautiful view in front of her, she read Ama's words.

My dear Olivia:
Bravo, brave girl! I am so proud of you for reading Omar's letter and accepting your inheritance. By now I am sure you've put the pieces together for my and Omar's master plan. We wanted all our girls to have a home of their own. As much as I would love to say this gift is from us, Omar saw to every detail—from searching

for the right home, finding the perfect view, and later, filling your home with things he knew you'd love.

Though it's not the Bluffs, Sag Harbor is such a special place. Omar and I spent many magical days and nights there from celebrating to healing. When Omar told me his plans for you, I was overjoyed. Because this place, darling girl, is somewhere you can strike out on your own, as you were always meant to do. This is where the past and the present blend. A place to build a family as I know is your heart's desire, and a place to grow your legacy.

Even though I am far away, I do expect an invitation to visit.

Be bold, find new friends—heal—just as I and Omar have done standing on the shores of the bay. I love you, my darling beautiful girl. I cannot wait to see what you'll do with this gift.

Always,
Ama

P.S. Omar may have left you this house, but I have gotten to know your neighbors. I think you'll have a fun summer. Be open to new people and experiences.

Olivia closed the letter, the ache in her heart growing as she remembered Ama's location in the south of France.

Though Ama seemed impossibly far away, the letter made her feel closer—closer than a text or even a call.

Olivia wasn't sure what Ama had meant about having fun—she didn't imagine much happening in this historic and sleepy neighborhood, but she did look forward to exploring and would make an effort to meet new people.

Away from Ama's shadow, she would be her own woman and make a name for herself—just as Omar had envisioned. Olivia knew she could find a home here. All she had to do was grab the brass ring.

CHAPTER 3

NEW BEGINNINGS

June 2021

"You're staring off into space again." Anderson whispered in Olivia's ear.

With the light streaming from her wide bay windows, and the sound of water gently lapping against the smooth, sandy beach, she knew she'd made the right decision to summer in Sag Harbor.

His forearm wrapped around her waist.

She gave his arm a quick squeeze, but her fingers lingered, tracing along his forearm. After a year and a half together, she knew the feel of every muscle in his body. Strong and corded. Comforting and warm.

With his free hand, he handed her a cup of coffee, handle-side first.

Ama had sent her special blend and Anderson had tried his best to perfect the ratio of dark roast, chicory, and whipped cream. Olivia took the deep coffee mug swimming with too much dairy.

Inhaling, she pretended to soak in the aroma but really took a deep fortifying breath before drinking his unique concoction.

"Mhmm."

"Good?" His whisper was more curious than seductive. She understood that he always wanted to be a better version of himself.

"Delicious," Olivia lied with great enthusiasm. "But," she turned to place the mug on the counter and snuggled closer into his embrace. "I'd rather taste you."

That wasn't a lie. The man was delicious in every way—his taste, his smell, his looks.

Anderson had the appearance of an action-hero—a lean but muscular build, with cheekbones that could cut diamonds, and ridiculously deep blue eyes that challenged anyone to peek into the windows of his soul. Chris Evans had nothing on this man.

But it was his smile that moved him to the top of the class. More than once, Perry had called it his cat-that-ate-the-canary smile.

Olivia disagreed and said, *"He's not the satisfied cat . . . I am. Because the pleasure is all mine."*

She dipped her nose into his chest, no matter the season he smelled like summer—bergamot and sunshine—perpetually warm, never cold. She rarely ever had to guess at his feelings, even when he was slightly cross.

Olivia licked his lips. "I'm glad you're here," she whispered against his mouth.

Another truth.

It'd come as a surprise that Anderson had not wanted to spend the summer in Sag. He'd crossed his arms, his eyebrows lowered, forehead creased more than she'd ever seen on him as she nervously babbled about the history of Sag Harbor and her gift from Omar. But eventually Olivia convinced him there were plenty of residents who needed rides and food delivered and that this would be a romantic getaway while the city continued to recover from a second summer of the pandemic. Vaccines had begun rolling out late last year, but the country was still mostly sequestered, opting to dine in instead of eat out. Now they were two weeks into their romantic getaway, having arrived just after the Memorial Day weekend. Anderson, unlike Olivia, who had never met a stranger, rarely stepped outside to interact with neighbors. Since they'd arrived there was a dull pain that shot from her neck to the base of her skull. Sometimes it flared whenever she noticed his poor mood.

Anderson squeezed her bottom. "I want to be wherever you are."

She wrapped her arms tighter around her human anchor. They hadn't been together long yet he became an essential part of her life. His words and presence were like chamomile lavender tea on a cold winter night.

"What's on your agenda for today?" Olivia asked.

"Writing. Research, then off to the office." Anderson laughed.

Olivia just managed to let out a rusty laugh. The "office" he referenced was his beloved Prius in which he delivered groceries and goods to their neighbors.

"Sounds like a busy day." She kept her voice light, opting for peace instead of judgment. She wanted to be a supportive partner. But a small part of her, one that started off no bigger than a seed but then like a flower bloomed, feared that his career choice as an artist would tear them apart.

Olivia stepped out of his arms and looked at the time on the stove. "I've got a client call at ten. I'm making a smoothie then I'm going for my jog."

While Olivia moved around the kitchen to grab supplies for the smoothie she'd drink after her jog, Anderson connected his phone to the Bluetooth speaker in the kitchen and to Olivia's utter annoyance turned on his podcast.

Podcasts, as well as news and documentaries, were the "research" portion of his job. He said that he was "self-employed," by which he meant he was writing a screenplay and streaming hours of stand-up specials and films and other materials as "research."

Olivia pointed to the juicer and mouthed "Sorry" to Anderson when she pressed the lid.

She was not at all sorry.

The mechanical whirl from the blender gave her a thirty-second reprieve from the current events podcast that blasted from the speakers installed in the ceiling. The hosts argued about the protests sweeping across America sparked by George Floyd's murder a year ago. It wasn't that Olivia didn't care—she'd spent many restless nights thinking of the fatherless daughters, widowed husbands, and brothers who would never see their sisters again.

What she didn't like about this podcast hosted by two white guys, is that they wanted to jump to solving the problem without examining the root cause. Police brutality, discrimination in the housing market and workplace, and outright racism were some of the driving factors as to why Black Americans hit a fever pitch.

Olivia released the lid. Anderson grinned and thankfully didn't turn the podcast back on.

When they first moved in together, Olivia had been surprised by Anderson's voracious appetite to learn and consume content. He called it his "study time." He enjoyed all forms of media—radio, podcasts, television, and documentaries ranging from scandals to pop culture to brain science. Some topics bored Olivia to tears and he had an adorably annoying habit of blaring his shows through Bluetooth speakers. After a gentle recommendation from Olivia to transition his learning endeavors into a solitary practice by gifting him AirPods, he mostly listened through those.

Even if she could no longer hear it, she knew when he found something fascinating. Effortlessly sexy, he tilted his head to the right, his sandy brown curls falling down on his forehead just above his eyes. A stillness settled over him and he took on the look of a living sculpture.

There were times when he would pause a video, cross his arms, tilt back his head, his perfect even white teeth denting his lips. The man was eye-candy and on many occasions when she couldn't temper her hormones, she climbed on top of him and made use of his teeth denting soft places on her body.

Anderson, seated on a high-back bar stool, leaned away from the island counter, his feet shod with leather thong shoes that had not only seen better days, but better decades. Anderson had embraced the beach culture of sandals, cargo shorts, and short-sleeved shirts, though it was more Tommy Bahama than relaxed, quiet elegance.

Olivia covered his cheek with her hand and leaned over to give him a kiss.

He squeezed her waist on the way down.

"Go back to sleep. I'll be awhile."

"I'm not sleeping after that kiss." The corners of his eyes crinkled. "I just got an idea from the episode. I'm going to email my agent and then get ready for my show."

Just recently some comedy clubs had reopened and a few gigs had slowly rolled in. It was another argument from Anderson as to why they should stay in the city. They'd come to an agreement that he would focus on big gigs and would stay in their apartment in the city if he had any back-to-backs.

Olivia stepped outside and stretched. Mornings now found Olivia running her daily four-mile loop around SANS. Her body tingled, ready to get started. But when she opened the door, her neighbor, an older Black woman, shouted, "Hey, there!"

The woman waved at her, not only in greeting but motioning Olivia to walk the distance to her neighbor's home.

Olivia held in her sigh. She desperately needed the quiet of the morning, she needed the sting from the wind to ground her, she needed distance between her and . . . everyone. She had not kept her promise to Ama on attempting to make friends. Between the move and passive-aggressive discussions with Anderson about their temporary residence, Olivia had been too tired to socialize.

Olivia smiled wide and waved back, while her manners pushed to the surface, overcoming her irritation.

She followed the paved path that led to her neighbor's stout porch, and lingered near the bottom, not sure if her neighbor wanted her to come any closer. But the woman waved her on.

"I don't bite."

"I'm sorry I don't have my mask, but I'm vaccinated. I'm Olivia Jones."

"Ruth Brooks." The older woman waved a hand. In the other hand, she held a stitched square cloth. "I'm *not* vaccinated," she replied with hard edges to her voice. "And don't give me that look, young lady. My son lectures me enough as it is. I'll get it in a few months or so. After I see how it affects everyone else."

Olivia fixed her face to neutral but remained standing in place. Though she didn't know the older woman, her sentiment regarding the mistrust of the vaccination didn't come as a surprise. Many Black people had been verbally opposed to the vaccine and with the history of inhumane experimentation like the Tuskegee Study of untreated syphilis in Black men and the fact that Henrietta Lack's cells were taken without her knowledge, Black people were understandably cautious.

Olivia believed the vaccine could and would save lives and she'd been grateful when Cindy, Ama, and her godsisters hastily replied "Of course" when Olivia badgered them about taking the vaccine.

But that didn't mean she'd be disrespectful to an elder who felt differently.

"A pleasure to meet you, Mrs. Brooks."

The woman tilted her head, smiling. She seemed to approve of Olivia's formal greeting.

Mrs. Brooks looked to be a little north of seventy, the same height as Olivia, so perhaps she may have been a little taller when she was Olivia's age. Freckles smattered the apples of her tawny cheeks. Her stylish, loose salt-and-pepper curls brushed her shoulders. Her hair had a healthy sheen that made Olivia jealous. Earlier in the pandemic, she'd forgone her beloved relaxer and opted for oils and popular shampoos. A year later, and dozens of YouTube tutorials, Olivia still did not know how to style her hair. And now with her daily runs in the bright unencumbered sunshine (courtesy of flat beaches and zero skyscrapers), did the dozens on her damaged hair. It was her secret Black-woman-shame that she didn't know how to manage her curls.

Travis, her stylist back in New York, occasionally made house calls, but certainly not for someone, even a friend, who lived a hundred miles away.

Olivia smoothed her hair, as if that could suddenly fix a mane that hadn't been touched by a professional in months.

"I've been wanting to meet you, young lady. Only time I see you is when you're flying about the neighborhood."

"Flying?"

"You run so fast, it's like you've got wings. I thought you were a fairy!" While Mrs. Brooks stared and giggled at her, Olivia began to overthink her athleisure wardrobe of spandex pants, and a razor-back dark green tank top that nipped in at her waist.

"Hmm. You're no fairy."

"I'm not?" Olivia asked, suddenly offended but not entirely sure if she should care.

"Yes. Fairies are petite and cute. You, my dear, are too tall and too gorgeous. Your husband is a lucky man."

"Oh." Olivia stared down at her shoes. "We aren't married . . . yet."

"Really? He's cute," she teased. "Not as handsome as my son, just so you know."

"We're engaged." Olivia flashed her ring finger. "But Anderson and I would welcome the opportunity to meet your son."

Mrs. Brooks laughed and coughed a bit. She patted her chest, humor sparking her coffee-brown eyes. "Aren't you polite."

Her mother and Ama would box her ears if she were anything but. Instead, Olivia demurely shrugged off the compliment.

"You could've told me to mind my business."

"There's no need for that. I'm not offended, I promise," Olivia replied truthfully. She cleared her throat, determine to change the subject. "So . . . what do you have there?" She pointed at the material in Mrs. Brooks' hands.

"I'm a quilter. I'm making something for my granddaughter." Her voice was seven-layer-cake rich when she mentioned her granddaughter. "I'm missing her something awful these days. It's tempting to go ahead and get the shot. That's the only way my son will let her come see me." Ruth looked up and away. With her lips turned down and her eyes dim, she was the picture of loneliness.

Mrs. Brooks sighed. "I'll let you go fly now, but don't be a stranger. Now that I know you're nice, I'd love to show you my quilts."

"I'd like to see them," Olivia said with enthusiasm and pulled out her phone. "May I have your number?"

Mrs. Brooks chuckled. "You can just come on over and knock. If I'm busy, I won't answer."

"It's always good to have a neighbor's number," Olivia replied. Besides, she didn't want to set the tone for someone popping by her home—even if she lived a few steps away.

Mrs. Brooks shooed her like a fly. "Next Wednesday. Six p.m."

"I . . . guess that works," Olivia said with her phone in hand.

"See how easy that is?" she snorted. "You young people live and die by your phone. See you next week." She turned away before Olivia could argue about the phone number exchange.

After meeting her neighbor, Olivia cruised past the houses on Hampton Street and the movie theater and shops on Main Street, then past the AME church and cemetery. She saved her favorite part for last, leaving her cooldown for a walk up the wide-open stretch of beach that led to her house. Before going inside, she stood still for a moment and faced the beach. She inhaled and exhaled, letting the warm air with just a smattering of salt fill her lungs. Eyes closed, she lifted her head toward the sky, catching a small breeze that teased her curls. She grinned at the sun, dropped her head, and opened her eyes, though her smile remained. The run had transformed her mood from tense to upbeat. This was all hers, she thought as she turned to admire the spectacular view of the bay from the deck. This much beauty made all her hard work well worth it, and some of the heartache, too.

When Olivia's mother had asked if she wouldn't be lonely in the new house, she'd informed her mother that Anderson would keep her company. Olivia knew that her mother was old-fashioned and didn't approve of any couple, even one edging their way into their thirties, living together before marriage. Cindy hadn't had much to say about Anderson or their arrangement, only a cryptic warning.

"Come see me and come live with me are two different things," Cindy said with a finality that dared her daughter to question her wisdom. Back then, Olivia sighed loudly and found an excuse to get off the phone. But now, several weeks into their new living arrangements, she was seeing things from her mother's point of view.

It wasn't that Olivia regretted her decision. It all seemed heaven-sent—Anderson loved Omar's favorite musical artist. He was one of those people who looked at life as a fun challenge—like levels to be cleared in a game, badges to be earned but at the end everyone could win.

Olivia, who was used to getting her own way and following her own mind, found herself alternately perplexed and soothed by her fiancé's easygoing, affable nature. She liked that outlook and genuinely wished she embodied that fresh perspective.

Not to mention he made her feel like no man had done before: beautiful and accepted. She wasn't too expensive or too cultured or too ambitious.

Or too dark, the monster in her head whispered.

Even with the good that bonded them, there were differences

between Olivia and Anderson that became more obvious once they lived together. Olivia was a morning person and a creature of habit, up by six, out for a run by six fifteen, at the dining table by seven to eat breakfast and scan news articles before she tucked into a day of work. Anderson was a night owl, prowling the house in the small hours of the morning.

He'd gone back to bed while she ran, likely tiring himself by two or three a.m. listening to a podcast. Yes, curiosity about the world was sexy but being partly employed was not. She winced at her unkind thoughts, but she couldn't seem to stop them from mounting in intensity.

It was easier to ignore the facts of how Anderson made a living when they didn't see each other every day, much less live together. But it was only a matter of time before that wasn't possible anymore, only a matter of time before residents would discover that her fiancé was delivering takeout. She shook her head just thinking about it and headed upstairs to clean up.

Olivia was about to step into the shower when she slipped and fell. She rubbed her tailbone, and groped around the bathroom floor for the offending item—a dirty pair of Anderson's blue boxer shorts. The cleaners, who were scheduled to arrive tomorrow, couldn't come soon enough. In the meantime, she picked up the boxers and walked back to the bedroom, where she dropped them onto Anderson's side of the bed an inch from his face. He didn't move. It was petty, she knew, but no amount of asking politely if he could pick up after himself had helped.

As Olivia waited for Anderson to wake up, her list of complaints about him stacked up in her mind. There were the Richard Pryor albums he listened to seemingly nonstop and laughed at with an abandon that made her uncomfortable. She still wasn't comfortable with a white boy laughing at these jokes, couldn't get over the feeling of being laughed at herself. And then there was that he didn't wear shoes on the beach or the patio, which meant he was constantly tracking sand into the house.

Is this what Omar meant when he encouraged her not to settle for anything less than the love she deserved?

Anderson finally stirred awake and pulled the fabric away from his face. He grabbed Olivia firmly by the wrists and tried to lure her back into bed. She considered it briefly, and then surrendered, deciding that she had some time to spare for a quickie. In the bedroom, Olivia had no complaints about Anderson. He was a good lover, generous and versatile. He also had a beautiful body. While she heard folks moan on social media about the weight they'd put on from snacking between Zoom calls and commuting to their kitchens, Anderson was still as fit and sexy to her as he ever was, and Olivia was determined to keep herself slim enough to fit into a single-digit size.

Olivia was grateful that she and Anderson shared the solid, common ground of desire for one another. As Anderson kissed her and then they made love, Olivia forgot that she had fallen, forgot that she had a full day of work ahead of her, and let go of the list of Anderson's faults that she'd been compiling. For a brief moment, before the rest of the world and her responsibilities came into the play, Olivia enjoyed the feeling of being lost in the sensation with Anderson. For now, that was enough.

CHAPTER 4

THE REAL HOUSEWIVES OF SANS

June 2021

The next day, Olivia went into town and purchased a picture frame from a craft store.

She placed the photograph of her father and family on a small table in the living room.

"There. You have a place here, Daddy." She spoke to the indelible image of her father, young and alive and surrounded by family. His arms slung around the boy who strongly resembled him. His brother, likely. His twin? Maybe.

Same height, almond-shaped eyes, mouth wide, but her father had grown into his face. A cute kid, but a beautiful man. Olivia looked just like him.

Then there was her mother, Cindy. The way she looked at Olivia, eyes narrowing while pointing her bony finger to accompany the critique of Olivia's posture, her size, her skin—as if examining corporeal imperfection.

"Stop wearing bright colors. You know it doesn't look good on you." When Olivia grew up there was an obvious societal preference for light- and brown-skinned women—from magazine covers to commercials. But it hurt like hell that her own mother had bought into the lie that not all skin tones were beautiful. At least, that is what Olivia assumed.

Those memories often warred with ones of Omar and Ama.

"There she is, Miss America," Ama sang whenever she caught Olivia strolling downstairs on her way to one of the many activities on the Vineyard. On many occasions, Omar stopped reading his newspaper, moving it aside to give Olivia his full attention. How she wished she could see him again and hear him call her his beautiful girl.

On second thought, he'd called Perry and Billie his beautiful girls as well, so maybe she wasn't so beautiful after all. But most of all, with Omar, there had been absolute acceptance and love.

Back then, Olivia noted with the precision of a field researcher whenever Ama and Omar had given compliments. Though they weren't overly abundant, they gave compliments often enough to notice a pattern. There were none she could identify. No matter the hairstyle, clothes, or colors she wore, it had not changed their opinion.

In fact, the color of clothes they'd purchased for her summers at Oak Bluffs and for the school year had always varied.

As a child, it confounded her because someone, either Cindy or Ama and Omar, had told a lie.

Regardless, she looked like her father, which meant there were people out there, maybe his brother or parents, who would be open to getting to know her.

"I'm going to find my family," she swore to the picture of her father.

She smiled at the photo and returned to the kitchen to finish preparing dinner—her simple but classic salmon and pesto pasta dish—and thought that it was possible she'd cooked more in the last two months than she had in her entire life. Just as she opened a bottle of wine, a ritual when cooking dinner, the phone rang. Olivia reached for the yelping phone on the wall. It'd been so long since she'd heard an actual telephone ring that she didn't recognize the noise at first.

"Hello, Olivia Jones speaking," she said, defaulting to her mother's formality.

"Hi there, this is your neighbor, Addy Weston. My friend Whitney Parks mentioned you finally claimed the old Tremont house. I thought I might call and welcome you to the neighborhood."

"Why thank you, that's so generous of you to check in on me."

"Don't mention it. We take care of our own out here. Anyways, what are you doing this weekend?"

"We were just planning to go get some materials for the house, then putter around a bit."

"Oh. There's a we?" she asked like a schoolgirl talking about a crush.

"Yes, me and my, um, fiancé."

"Your *um* fiancé? Or your actual fiancé?" Addy asked. Olivia felt a twinge of nervousness as she was transported to the start of every female friendship she'd ever forged, the heady mix of apprehension and excitement which was not unlike falling in love.

"He's my fiancé. Anderson."

"Oh, great. And what does he do, may I ask?"

"He's a stand-up comedian. And a writer," Olivia added swiftly. She omitted his rideshare work. She figured that was a topic best discussed another time, or never.

"Oh," Addy said. Without even seeing her face, Olivia could tell that it had dropped in disappointment. "Well, you won't be out too long before other eligible prospects start crawling out of the woodwork."

How forward. At least when Mrs. Brooks had asked about Anderson, she asked teasingly and with a smile.

"I'm good," Olivia replied, a bit sharply.

Addy paused, and Olivia projected her thoughts into the silence.

The doorbell rang and Olivia turned slightly to face the door. She moved toward the door until the short cord of the phone yanked her back. She covered the phone with her hand and replied. "One minute."

She wanted to yell for Anderson, but she would need a bullhorn to pull him out of his sleep. "Sorry, there's someone at the door," she said to Addy.

Someone she didn't know. Maybe Mrs. Brooks? She'd need to install a Ring security system so she could vet unwanted visitors.

"You can answer, if you want."

"No, no. Anderson will get it," she lied. And if not, that would teach whoever popped by to find her phone number like Addy and call first.

"Well, then. If you're available, I thought I'd invite you and some of the other girls for drinks at Kara Warren's house. We're having a kind of party. Think of it as a toast to the end of spring. Or a pared-down version of the usual summer opening parties."

"Of course. That'd be lovely," Olivia forced herself to say. She longed to spend time with anyone that wasn't Anderson, but the thought of putting on real clothes and talking to an entirely new group of people filled her with a certain amount of anxiety. "I'm looking forward to it," she lied. Just as she was mumbling thank you, she heard the dial tone, and was grateful for an end to their conversation.

She hurried to the front door, but the person who knocked had vanished. On her step stood a gray-and-white planter filled with lilies. A card-size note had been propped against the planter.

Dear Olivia:
I'm so sorry we haven't met in person. I've been out of town, visiting family and, much to my disappointment, Whitney served as my proxy. I've waited nearly five years to meet you. If you don't mind slowing down for an old man like me, I'd love to take you for a walk. In the meantime, please enjoy the peace lilies.
—Joel Whittingham

The name Omar had scrawled in that brochure. In the haze of the inheritance and move, she'd forgotten about Joel. And like Omar's note, there was no number or address listed; no tangible way to get in touch with this mystery man.

She picked up the potted flowers, and then placed them on the side table in her living room. She stared at the peace lilies and laughed without humor when she realized the irony. The SANS community were an oddly friendly bunch who would likely not allow Olivia much peace.

After dinner, Olivia poured a second glass of wine and dialed her mother's number. Asking Cindy for anything—an opinion, a favor, or her time—had never been easy. But this was important. Part of the reason she stayed in Sag for the summer was to track down the Jones family and perhaps make inroads to form a relationship.

"Hello, Olivia. What can I do for you?" Cindy greeted her as if she'd only met her yesterday.

"Just calling to let you know that we're still settling in."

"Hmm. So, you went to that place? With Anderson?"

"Anderson is a part of my life now. He's permanent," Olivia recited in a robotic voice. She'd told her mother this before and wasn't interested in repeating herself.

"And how will he work from there? How will he support the household?" The inflection in her voice signaled to Olivia that she needed to pivot the conversation.

"His career allows him flexibility. And either way, you've taught me to take care of myself, which I have done."

Cindy let out a breath.

Olivia visualized her mother's tight shoulders relaxing. "You're right about that. Don't get me wrong, he seems like a decent guy, just a little unsteady. In marriage, you almost always experience unsteady. But I'm sure he'll find his way."

Olivia's mouth dropped open wide enough for a family of flies to fly in. Cindy rarely ever gave sound advice about relationships, let alone marriage.

"Hello?" Cindy asked after awkward seconds of silence.

Olivia nodded, though her mother couldn't see her. "Y-yes, I'm here. I agree. Anyway, the home is beautiful, and the community has been welcoming."

"Good for you." This time, Cindy went silent.

"I'm so glad I found it."

"No. Omar found it. You followed. As always."

"I thought you liked Omar."

Or at least respected him. Cindy had said it many times. Regarding Cindy's feelings toward Ama, she seemed a little jealous of her godmother. Olivia suspected she wanted the life that Ama had, but she ended up a widowed and single mother.

"I liked Omar." The lightness to her voice returned. "I just don't think it's proper that a man who isn't your kin bought you a home."

"I've known him most of my life. He was like a . . ." her voice lost steam. "Like a father to me."

"But he wasn't."

"I'm told my father's family summered here." Olivia took advantage of the subject change to talk about her father.

Cindy harrumphed. "Sure, they did. In the summer. Memorial Day until Labor Day. Lord, I missed your father something awful during that time," her voice shook.

Olivia leaned forward, piqued at her mother's rare vulnerability. "Did they . . . do they have a home here? My father's people, I mean? Maybe you visited—"

"No. Never."

"Why not?"

"What's with all the questions, Olivia Charlotte Jones?"

"I . . . no reason. I just wanted to know more about my father's family."

"You've always been a curious girl. But now isn't the time," she warned in a heavy voice.

"Mother, please. I'm not asking for a lot."

"Yes, you are. More than you know. And let me tell you something, little girl. The Jones family are nothing but a den of vipers, especially that brother of his."

The need to ask for his name burned on Olivia's tongue. But her mother was on a roll and not to be interrupted.

"I don't know how your father rose above that mess, but he did. He was a good man. And I won't let you stomp on his memory by spinning up those devils back into our lives. Not when we worked so hard to get away. Now I don't want to speak of this again. Do you understand?" her mother breathed heavily over the phone.

"I do," Olivia answered, weakly.

"I'm late for a meeting with friends. We'll talk later. Goodbye."

Before Olivia could respond, Cindy ended the call.

Olivia stood from her seat and returned to the house. First order of business included another glass of wine. Second, she wanted to look at the picture. To prove to herself that Cindy's assertions about the family—her family—were false.

She stood in front of the photo, studying a group of strangers. From the picture, they seemed harmless enough. Mother and father had been smiling. The three children, one of which had been her dad, smiled brightly. Even their eyes looked happy. Much happier than Olivia had as a little girl. Perhaps it was a misunderstanding? Cindy was a young mother, and she imagined emotions ran high, especially if they hadn't been married, which she suspected they hadn't.

A marriage license. That's a start! And a death certificate. An obituary. Surely her father's family had been mentioned. She'd have to subscribe to one of those family tree websites. That could help her search, too.

"I'll just have to ask my new neighbors about the Jones family," she whispered to herself.

☼

When Olivia arrived at Kara's house on Saturday afternoon, she'd walked for twenty minutes, during which she got lost no less than three times, trying to follow her phone's GPS directions. It was as if the families in SANS really didn't want to be found by interlopers. If you didn't know how to get where you were going, you shouldn't be there, anyway. Olivia stood outside the house for a moment, charmed by the unassuming cottage.

What she loved most about Sag Harbor was that the wealth there was understated. The focus was less on houses that dazzled in their grandeur and more on the friendships and family relationships that bound one, two, three, or more generations. At least, that is what Whitney had told her when she handed her the keys to her home.

Olivia had already reached many of the professional and financial goals she'd set for herself at the beginning of her twenties, and when she was being honest with herself, she knew it was time to pivot away from the dogged careerism that had defined this decade of her life. Now that she had a place in the city and a house on the beach, plus the trust that Omar had left for her, her thoughts wandered more and more toward legacy. First, she wanted to know more about the generations that preceded her, and maybe, if she was lucky, to leave something worthy for those that followed.

Makeup compact in hand, she quickly dabbed away the dewy moisture on her face. She hadn't perspired very much thanks to the towering trees that provided ample shade. Then she smoothed down the white tailored shirt whose wrinkles she'd tried to steam away in the shower. She patted down the bespoke Sergio Hudson mohair poncho that she'd worn instead of a coat on the warm spring day. Olivia's Christian Dior tote limited-edition handbag, which she had stalked for no less than six months, at one point putting a daily call into her Bergdorf's stylist, was slung casually over her shoulder. Olivia took a deep breath in and then rang the doorbell. She waited for what felt like an eternity for someone to answer. When no one did, she realized the door was open, and let herself in. She walked down the hallway that was filled with family photos, including some sepia ones that looked like they dated from the nineteenth century.

Olivia heard several voices inside. Instead of rushing toward the peals of laughter that rang out like church bells, she found herself transfixed by an image of a man in a white T-shirt and khaki trousers, standing next to a girl who must have been his daughter. The girl proudly held up a fish that was no less than twice the size of her head. The joy between father and daughter was palpable. The few things her mother had shared about her father was his love of fishing. He'd once even brought Olivia and Cindy along, but something funny must have happened because her mother laughed and slapped her thigh when she recalled the memory.

"I told him not to bring you on that boat. He insisted anyway, so I came along to help. He learned a lesson that day."

Olivia stored the vague, funny memory away as if to stockpile food for the long winter ahead. She cherished the memory, though she couldn't recall it. The important detail she hung on to was that her father had loved fishing. It was a comforting thought that he got the chance to share his hobbies with his daughter before he died.

"I see you found the picture of me and Daddy. You must be Olivia."

Olivia smarted a bit at the easy way "Daddy" fell out of the speaker's mouth. She turned to the voice and found a tall, thin woman who was the picture of grace, with impossibly perfect skin and a full afro that fanned out from her head and touched her shoulders.

"Guilty as charged," Olivia said, extending her hand. "And you are?"

"What a pleasure it is to not be known immediately out here, you know?"

Olivia nodded as if she did know. New York was the city of anonymity.

"I'm Kara Warren."

"Like the artist?"

"Yes, in fact. And you, my dear, are a quick study. Do you collect art?"

"I wouldn't call myself a collector just yet. But I have a few favorite artists, and Kara Warren is one of them."

"Something about those silhouettes and jigaboos turns you on, huh?"

Olivia laughed at Kara's boldness. She liked people who could cut through things to see and say what's true. It's what made her good at her work, and she looked for that quality in the small group of friends she held close. "I think the work is unforgettable and . . . brave," Olivia added.

Kara held an unflinching mirror to the status of Black America, often blending elements of past and present, showing the viewer that nothing much had changed.

Some of her art was heartachingly painful, while her other works were so jubilant you could taste the hope leaping from the canvas. To Olivia, hope tasted effervescent, citrusy like candied lemons dipped and rolled in brown sugar. She couldn't remember the last time she tasted hope.

"Isn't that what we go to artists for, their bravery? My father always said that's why he enjoyed surrounding himself with artists, why he collected their work. Just to know and remember that even as he made safe choices like his father and his father before them, there were people out there risking it all."

"Your dad was a collector?"

"Is. He'll be out later in the summer. Just us vagabonds for now. If you like, I'll give you a tour of the house and the art later."

"I'd like that," Olivia said.

"Good. Now, let's get some liquor in you. God knows we all need it."

Olivia followed Kara as they walked past the living room with its double-height ceilings and cream-colored stuffed sofas to outside. The backyard looked similar to her own—a spacious red-brown deck that overlooked the beach. The view was breathtaking, but Olivia's attention was drawn from the shoreline to the women lounging in varying states of repose.

"Ah, the new neighbor made it!" Addy exclaimed, her voice brassy and a bit loud. Olivia looked around and calculated that they were all already at least two glasses of wine in. She had some catching up to do.

"Thank you so much for having me," Olivia said. She patted her bag and realized that she should've brought something with her. Ama would be mortified. She prayed her faux pas would go unnoticed, or at the very least, forgiven.

"Of course, love. Consider us the welcome committee," Addy said as she sidled over to the bar cart that was arranged with an impressive array of wines. Olivia noted Addy's striking resemblance to Perry with her fair skin and hair that looked like it was straightened by a blow dryer and not a relaxer. If Olivia's sharp eye still served her, Addy was a size six and caramel complected, thick enough in all the right places and trim where it mattered, with dainty hands and feet. In her nervousness, Olivia reached back to her old habit of sizing up other women's skin color and was not surprised to find that her own skin was the darkest in the room.

"What's your pleasure?" Addy said. "Are you a wine person?"

"I like to drink wine, but I can't say that I know much about it," Olivia said. She sat under the retractable umbrella on the long-cushioned bench. Though it wasn't unreasonably hot just yet, the wine paired with the sun would soon make her feel like a baked clam.

"Stick with me, kid. You'll go far," Addy said, pouring a glass of Belle Glos Pinot Noir.

"Far down the road toward becoming an alcoholic," Whitney Parks said, stepping through the screened doorway.

"Whitney!" Olivia exclaimed. "It's so good to see you," she said. Olivia had never been happier to see someone she barely knew. Whitney was the real estate agent who gave her the keys to her home, but they hadn't spoken much since she moved out to Sag. Whitney went in for one of her big hugs and this time, Olivia welcomed it.

"I wanted to surprise you and to congratulate you again on moving into the old Tremont house. I think that's more than worthy of a toast," Whitney said, raising her glass as Addy hastily opened another bottle of Belle Glos from the bar cart.

"Yeah, I just had to meet the person who finally claimed that beautiful place. Folks have been trying for years to figure out the owner," Addy chimed in. "Meanwhile, Whitney has sold four houses this month. And all my girlfriends have been blowing up my phone since the city shut down. I guess everyone has the same idea. If you have to weather the continuing storm of the Rona, might as well be somewhere beautiful, right?" Addy smiled, seemingly satisfied with the pop of a newly opened wine bottle.

"Cute bag," Whitney said as she took a seat on the bench next to Olivia. She turned Olivia's purse around, admiring it from various angles.

"Oooooh," Kara cooed. "How many weeks did you wait for that one?"

"Five months, almost six. I stalked that bag!"

"I know that's right!"

Olivia smiled, pleased that her purse had served as a beautiful ice breaker for this well-established friend group. She peered at the spread of bacon and cheese crostini, stuffed mushrooms, and various sweet treats.

Addie tracked Olivia's attention. "Please, grab a plate. I also opened a Malbec. If you like it, I suggest pairing it with the berry Brie." She pointed to the individual-sized skillet filled to the brim with blackberries and Brie cheese. "If you're a Zinfandel lover, try the strawberry ricotta bruschetta. Oh! And the—"

"Honestly, Addy, just let the woman eat what she wants," Kara lovingly snapped before sipping her wine.

"Sure, but if she wants to be basic like . . ."

Kara's mouth popped open. "Like who?"

Addy snorted. "Like you."

"Please." Kara rolled her eyes. "I've traveled the world, dined with the rich, famous, and shameless. From the boujee to the bourgeois." She elegantly waved her hand in the air as if painting a picture.

"Yes, I'm a sommelier; I know these things. Olivia here strikes me as having a complex palate. One who appreciates the explosion of flavors."

"As well as color and textures," Olivia added as she swirled her glass.

"Don't tell me you're not only beautiful but you can throw down in the kitchen?" Addy asked in a faked annoyed voice.

Olivia nodded like the Duchess of Sussex. "In my mind, I've won every season of *Top Chef*."

"Well okay then, Ms. Martina Stewart." Addy snapped her fingers.

Olivia laughed behind her hand.

"Now that I somewhat know your taste, the Malbec and berry Brie pie it is." Addy winked. "You'll thank me later."

"I'll thank you in advance," Olivia said, as she accepted the glass Addy prepared.

"Let me be your wine sherpa, new chica," Addy crowed.

Olivia felt transported back to her first informational tea when she pledged a sorority in college. She had that same feeling now, that she was being judged on everything that came out of her mouth and every detail of her outfit. She worried, as she often did, that she'd come up short.

"Speaking of taste and flavors, tell us about that fine-ass white boy you got holed up at the Tremont house. Cheers!" Addy said, lifting her wineglass into the air.

Whitney choked on her wine, while Kara leaned over and swatted Addy's knee.

"That fine-ass white boy has a name and it's Anderson Edwards. He's my fiancé. We met in New York City. He, too, has excellent taste in food, wine, and women."

"Good taste, indeed. I see he likes the sistas."

A lick of anger flared. Tipsy or not, she wouldn't let a stranger imply that he had a fetish. Before Olivia could formulate a cool thought, Kara saved her from a well-worded strike.

"Go easy," Kara admonished her old friend. And then, to Olivia, "She bites, but I promise she's not rabid."

"What'd you say, Kara? Remember that I know all of your business," Addy said. "I've been knowing you since the days of . . ."

"Box braids," Kara said, and sighed.

"Lest we forget, I have pictures of your *Poetic Justice* moment to prove it," Addy said.

The statement was a testament to the longevity of their friendship because box braids were back in style again.

"Speaking of being all up in my business, I have to tell you all that I finally started Dr. LaGrange, and it really has done wonders for me," Kara said.

Olivia looked over at Kara and noticed that her eyes were glassy, possibly from the liquor or from real sentiment. It was hard to tell. Olivia took the reprieve and hoped the audacious Addy wasn't as verbose and curious about her fiancé while sober.

"That head doctor you've been trying to get us all to see?" Addy rolled her eyes.

"Head doctor?" Olivia asked quizzically.

"Kara started seeing this new therapist. Before, you could barely get Kara to tell you why she likes her favorite flavor of ice cream. And now she's calling me to talk my ear off about her attachment style." Addy threw up her hands in mock surrender and turned to Olivia. "Lord help us. I'm glad you're here. We certainly need all the help we can get."

"I don't know about you ladies. But I must admit that after nearly a decade of living out of a suitcase, I'm flummoxed by being grounded. It's unsettling, you know," Kara said. Olivia wondered what truths lurked behind Kara's wet eyes. She shared some of Kara's feelings about being undone by so many sudden changes in her routine, but she was surprised to witness this much vulnerability so soon. But maybe that wasn't a bad thing? She'd been accused many times that she rarely showed emotions.

Olivia squared her shoulders as if adjusting her emotional armor and clutched the stem of her wineglass.

"Shall we make a toast?" Whitney interjected, effectively shifting the strange mood.

"Ohh, let's," Addy agreed.

When Whitney picked up her wineglass, Olivia found herself taken aback by the size of her wedding and engagement rings. Somehow, she'd missed them when Whitney showed Olivia to her new home.

The diamonds on Whitney's ring finger sparkled in the afternoon light. In all her years around the fiancées and wives of finance execs, it was the largest she had ever seen. Like gravity, something pulled at her to glance at her own hand. She eventually gave in, the sting of jealousy hit her cheeks and prickled her neck.

"To friendship. And to an early start to summer," Whitney said.

Olivia took a sip of the Argentinian Malbec that Addy poured for her. The wine was so smooth and rich on her tongue that she was almost ready to forgive Addy for her snarkiness.

"So, apparently, Olivia's white boy is a comedian. Is he funny?" Addy asked.

The wine soured on her tongue.

"He is, in fact," Olivia offered a stiff smile. "I've seen him do his stand-up routine a few times, and he always kills it." Smugness, pride as well as six ounces of wine warmed Olivia. It dawned on her she might have this pleasure more often if she stopped hiding him.

"That's wonderful. I always felt lifted watching Charles play. There's something about seeing someone you love doing what they love. Nothing beats it," Whitney said.

Olivia still couldn't really get over the fact that Whitney was married to *the* Charles Parks, a #1 NBA draft pick and one of the last hopes of redemption for the New York Knicks, a team she continued to love in spite of her good sense.

Addy opened her mouth, her eyes on Olivia, as if preparing to ask another nosy question.

"What about you, Addy?" Olivia blurted the question like a game-show contestant. "Do you have someone special?"

Whitney snorted. "She collects men like Pokémon cards. Gotta catch them all."

"Hey, now!" Addy protested but laughed into her drink. "I'm good at sharing."

She winked at Kara who grinned back at her friend.

Kara waved a hand. "Enough about men!"

Whitney nodded. "Here, here. That's what I'm trying to escape.

Anyways, we're just glad it's one of ours that took the Tremont house. It's important for us to have the means and to use them to continue our legacy," Whitney said.

"Personally, I don't care if the folks who buy houses in Sag Harbor are Black or white, just as long as their money is green. I certainly didn't decide to live full time in East Hampton, believing race was a thing. People are my thing," Addy said.

A sentiment she could afford to have with her skin tone, Olivia thought unkindly. The first impression for dark-skinned women was their skin. Olivia lost count of the times that, upon meeting, people treated her with derision, contempt, or suspicion. She had to claw herself out of a preconceived hole not of her making. Addy not believing *race was a thing*, when it smacked Olivia in the face daily, was woefully ignorant on the low end of the scale and absolutely absurd on the high end.

Whitney reached over to give Olivia's hand a friendly squeeze. The jury was out on Addy, but if Olivia could talk with Kara about art and Whitney about love and basketball, she'd be all right.

Maybe they could help her figure out the mystery behind her own family origins. She felt comfortable with asking at least two out of the three neighbors.

"Have you ladies ever heard of the Jones family?"

Whitney snapped her finger. "Yes! Darren and Shameka? Beautiful couple, they just had a baby."

Olivia opened her mouth to dispute, clearly, they were too young, but started to ask about them but stopped, maybe they were cousins. Olivia took a sip, readying herself to disclose personal information. "Do you know of a Chris Jones?"

Kara shook her head this time. "Is he our age?"

"No. He is . . . was . . . about twenty years older."

"I don't know that man," Addy whispered.

"Is he your relation?" Whitney asked.

"Yes." Olivia drank more wine.

Whitney tilted her head. "Was he a resident?"

"No. But he regularly summered here with his family as a child in the eighties and early nineties. Two brothers, a sister, mother, and father. They visited from Memorial Day to Labor Day to visit my aunt and uncle."

"What are their names?" Addy asked.

"I . . ." Olivia winced. "I don't know. I'm afraid I'm operating in the dark. I just know my father's name, though it's quite common."

"You could hire a private investigator?" Kara suggested.

"I could." Olivia nodded. Or she could call Ama. The woman could find a four-leaf clover in a field of green.

She shook her head. The taste of sweet wine rushed up her throat. She just managed to swallow.

No. She wouldn't call Ama. Not when her father's death had been caused by Ama's former husband. It was unnecessarily messy.

Olivia didn't like mess. She dealt with it too often in her childhood and had zero tolerance for it in her adult life. Not when she could make her own choices.

"Mr. Whittingham is your man," Whitney told her, nodding as if satisfied. "He knows everyone and remembers even the most obscure detail."

"How can I reach him?"

"Don't worry. He'll find you," Kara answered while the rest of the women, excluding Olivia, burst out in laughter.

"All right." Olivia lifted her eyebrows, drank more wine, and let the conversation move on from her mystery family, knowledge of which she wasn't quite ready to share with the world.

By the time she left Kara's house, Olivia's head was spinning, both because of the three glasses of wine she drank and Kara's house and art tour. Olivia learned her father's home, that changed hands only three times, passed down from one successful Black man to the next. On Kara's tour, Olivia admired pieces by the self-taught artist Thornton Dial that were so vibrant that the figures felt like they would come alive and dance off the walls. In the upstairs bedrooms, Olivia saw what her mother would call a beautiful-ugly portrait of a Black woman with a blond weave by the artist Henry Taylor and five watercolor paintings by Christopher Ofili. She'd seen the Taylor and Ofili paintings in museum shows, one at the Studio Museum in Harlem, and another in an Ofili retrospective at the New Museum. She was sad that she'd missed seeing more of Dial's work at the outsider art show at the MoMA and said so. When Kara seemed impressed by her knowledge, she was happy but seeing works of this quality in someone's home was disconcerting. The tour left her filled with a confusing mix of awe and envy, and an acute sense of her own smallness.

Kara walked Olivia to the front door to say goodbye.

"Hey, Kara . . . would you mind sharing the number for the doctor you mentioned?"

"Doctor?" Kara asked. "Oh, the head doctor, Vivian! Of course. Just let me get a piece of paper and a pen to write it down for you. I'm sure my dad has paper and a pen somewhere in here," Kara said, pushing open the door to her father's study. It was covered wall to wall in books and art and featured a shag rug that would have been tacky anywhere else but was somehow charming there. "I have become something of an evangelist for self-care and a devotee of Dr. LaGrange. She is just everything. Spelman undergrad, Harvard for med school, Columbia for residency, so she can do talk therapy and prescribe meds, too. Her hourly fee makes you a little nauseous at first, but she really is the best of the best, and is worth every penny."

Olivia nodded and stuffed the paper with Dr. LaGrange's phone number into her purse. As she walked home, she considered the additional details she'd gleaned about her neighbors. Addy and Kara had known each other since childhood, and theirs was the third in a series of friendships between their families, the first forged by their grandmothers who threw bridge parties on Sag, the second by their mothers who wrangled their children on Havens Beach and got them through the best private schools in the city. Addy and Kara had shared more than one boyfriend during their teen years, including one infamous guy named Slade who they'd warned Olivia to stay away from. They knew just about every resident, a few notable visitors, but unless there were cute guys around their age, they didn't know the families who occasionally visited for the summer. If she were to solve the mystery of the Jones family, then she would have to get to know her neighbors from previous generations.

Whitney and her gigantic wedding rings had arrived in Sag Harbor in the late nineties as her husband's basketball career wound down. Despite a rocky start, Whitney eventually endeared herself to everyone with her commitment to the Sag Harbor Homeowners' Association, working her way up from secretary to president, due in no small part to her persistence and unbeatable red velvet cake. Addy was led by her passions for wine and *la belle vie*, while Kara's career as an artist and independent curator allowed her a freewheeling life full of travel and art.

To Olivia, who had doggedly climbed up the corporate ladder at her firm for the last decade, it sounded suspiciously as if Addy worked as a sommelier not because she had to, but because she wanted something to keep herself busy and in the mix. Whitney's real estate hustle seemed to be less about earning dollars and more about her vision for Sag Harbor, her commitment to holding the line against gentrification. Olivia wondered what her life might have been like if she'd made different career choices, because her parents were wealthy or because she'd married well. She wondered if it was too late to change course in the life she'd begun charting, how much effort it'd take to turn the ship around and align her work with passion instead of practicality. Maybe that was something Dr. LaGrange could help her figure out.

Despite her earlier reservations about bonding with neighbors, she was glad to be welcomed into this new fold, to have a social anchor for the uncertain weeks and months that lay ahead. By the time she arrived home, she still felt warm from the wine and company, and was thankfully too tipsy to do her usual post-social routine of overanalysis—finding fault with everything she thought, said, and did. For now, it was enough to look up at the moon, which seemed to hang lower in Sag than it did in the city, to lean into the notion, as whimsical as it was, that she could reach up and touch the stars.

CHAPTER 5

A BEAUTIFUL DAY IN THE NEIGHBORHOOD

June 2021

Olivia woke up surprised and happy on Sunday morning to a text from Whitney Parks.

WHITNEY: So wonderful to see you yesterday for wine. What's on the agenda today?
OLIVIA: Not much for me. My routine now is man-work-house, rinse and repeat. Why, what's up?
WHITNEY: I've been remiss on my welcoming committee duties. Sunday drive later?
OLIVA: I'm in.
WHITNEY: Perfect. I'll pick you up at 2.

Olivia spent way too much time deliberating about precisely the right outfit to wear. Months of Zoom calls had habituated Olivia to crafting outfits just from the waist up—impeccable makeup, tasteful blouses, and jewelry, all thrown over pajama pants and rabbit slippers. She could barely look at a heel. Last night, she'd worn a low heel to Kara's house and her feet were still on fire. She worried that perhaps she'd overdressed in a Chanel jumpsuit and slides, but she could see that Whitney had put some effort into her outfit, too, when she pulled up a few minutes after the scheduled time in front of Olivia's house. Olivia noted the peak of Whitney's fedora as she sat in the idling vintage Mercedes convertible. Most of the old-timers on Sag had less showy cars, but Whitney was a law unto herself.

"Well, don't you look like a vision in pink?" Whitney whistled as Olivia climbed into the passenger side of Whitney's Mercedes and sank into the buttercream leather. "Aren't you glad that we didn't waste this perfect weather sitting inside? And now let me show you the real history of Sag Harbor."

"Yes, please!" Olivia said, and she meant it. She looked down at Whitney's Chanel sneakers and a shoe bag tossed into the backseat and was glad that she'd chosen flats. Just because going out was rare didn't mean you had to look terrible when you finally did. In fact, the rarity of it these days called for more attention, not less.

Olivia's idea of the Hamptons had always been different, flashier. As Olivia noted the modest homes that lined the neat streets of Sag Harbor, she relaxed a bit and tried to imagine herself spending summers here like her father and family had done. She'd only been to the Hamptons once before visiting SANS. One summer weekend nearly eight years ago, she stayed in a room in a sprawling mansion with a gaggle of white girls who were also first-year analysts. They shared the difficulties of the first, intense years at the firm before one by one, the other women fell victim to the suburbs, emerald-cut eternity bands, the Mommy thing, or all the above.

When Olivia had mentioned her Hamptons jaunt back in the day to her beloved childhood best friend, Tanya Greaves, Tanya had warned Olivia that she wouldn't like it. Tanya grew up with Olivia in Montclair, New Jersey, and was on the infinitesimally small list of girls who Olivia's mother approved of, a list that could be counted on one hand. Tanya's family decamped for Sag Harbor every summer the moment school let out and she'd invited Olivia to join them for a weekend for as long as Olivia could remember. Tanya just barely concealed her hurt that Olivia rejected her invitations to Sag for years in favor of the Vineyard and then became caught up in a scene in East Hampton that Tanya didn't care for.

Olivia learned her lesson quickly, as that initial introduction to the Hamptons was a disaster. It was the first and last time Olivia went on vacation with people from work; experience had taught her to draw firmer, clearer boundaries between business and pleasure. That weekend was flashy, full of hedge-fund-bro-packed mansions so large one might just as easily mistake them for nightclubs whose new age beats, and sweaty, privileged kids, were carbon copies of the clubs in the Meatpacking District that Olivia found so distasteful.

Olivia listened as Whitney recounted an extensive genealogy of Sag Harbor's impressive Black families. They were a veritable who's who of Black America. Olivia listened to Whitney's stories about the famous poet Langston Hughes writing, partying, and drinking more than a bit too much right in the backyard of the Tremont's house that was now her own. And then there was the late Colin Powell whose statesmanlike presence quieted the rooms he entered before his smile broke the ice. There were the more recent visitors— Fortune 500 CEOs, college presidents, doctors, wildly successful artists, TV personalities, and one billionaire who was named every summer season's most eligible bachelor before he'd settled down with a white woman to the collective groan of the single ladies on Sag.

Whitney pulled up in front of a wide, two-story, brown clapboard house with three steps and a perfectly manicured lawn. The house looked familiar, but Olivia wasn't sure why.

"This is the Greaves' house," Whitney said reverently as she silenced the car's engine.

"Ahhhh," Olivia said. She rolled down her window to snap a picture of the house that she'd seen in photos at the Greaves' immaculately kept home in Montclair and on Tanya's social feeds. She'd text Tanya later, but Olivia's heart felt full of joy in finally seeing the home that her friend and her family deeply loved.

"How'd you remember that I'm friends with Tanya Greaves?"

"I'm in the business of remembering people's business," Whitney said slightly ominously as she started the car again.

"Well, if that's our rich legacy, this is our uncertain future," Whitney grumbled as she gestured to a construction site just past the Greaves' house. From what Olivia could tell, where an entire block of homes once stood, the foundations for a massive mansion now loomed. The steel beams and white Tyvek tiles were arranged in a kind of snaggle-toothed smirk. The logo of a real estate developer, ASK Properties, was emblazoned in block letters on the wood slats that surrounded the construction site. The name of the company sounded familiar, but Olivia couldn't recall where she'd heard it before. "Behold the gentrification of Sag Harbor. If we let them have their way," Whitney intoned like a weary game-show host.

Olivia watched as a hardness that she hadn't glimpsed before settled into the corners of Whitney's mouth.

"Look at this. An entire hot mess. You know what their slogan is? ASK us about selling or building your home. How stupid is that?"

It wasn't stupid, but clichéd. Olivia nodded in solidarity anyway.

"They've been here, stuffing up people's mailboxes with flyers. Then there's this slick-looking white boy. Out here shucking and jiving and harassing these good folks by convincing them they can't afford to keep up with the rising property taxes. So they convince them to take the money and run."

Whitney sounded like a prizefighter as murmurs of her scrappy childhood in the Bronx slipped into her speech.

Ama had warned Olivia that while Whitney and her husband were beloved stewards of the Sag Harbor community, Whitney was rough around the edges when she got worked up. "Passionate" was the word Ama used, and because Olivia had known Ama forever, she knew that "passionate" was Ama's code word for "'hood."

As Whitney went on and on about how ugly the new mansion would be, an eyesore and a blight on the cherished Sag Harbor community, Whitney sounded less like a polished basketball wife who sold real estate on the weekends because she was nosy and wanted to be all up in people's business, and more like she wanted to save Sag Harbor and keep it unapologetically Black.

She sounded like she was itching for a fight.

As she drove, Whitney continued to air out her hard feelings. "Before we know it, we'll be seeing ASK Properties on every other block. It's bad enough what we're starting to see with all the new people out here. Take, for example, what happened on the beach in Ninevah last summer. Every time I think about it, it takes me all the way back to the days when I used to tell girls to meet me at the corner of Joy and Greenfield. This is the time I call 'B.C.' by which I mean before I found Charles, when I wasn't afraid of messing up a manicure or clogging up these pores with Vaseline, if you know what I mean."

Olivia nodded, although she wasn't entirely sure what Whitney meant. Between her childhood in Jersey's suburbs and summers on the Bluffs, Olivia was sheltered. She rarely raised her voice, and certainly had never been in a proper fistfight. Olivia watched with interest as Whitney pulled her car into the parking lot of the public beach in Ninevah. She couldn't understand what was getting Whitney so riled up that she was even breathing harder, but Olivia was certainly curious.

"Want to take a quick walk on the beach?" Whitney asked, although her question was rhetorical. Whitney was already halfway out of the car and sloughing off her sneakers and socks as she spoke. Olivia smiled as she'd realized that she'd misread Whitney's shoe bag in the convertible's backseat. Instead of pulling out the pair of heels that Olivia suspected was inside the bag, Whitney slid on a stylish pair of flip-flops.

Olivia wanted to demur, knowing that her Chanel slides were anything but sand-proof and waterproof, but she went along. They walked silently for a bit, trudging through the sand on the empty beach. Just beyond the public portion of the beach, a series of gorgeous, understated homes rose about two hundred feet from the shoreline. While the water reminded Olivia a bit of Oak Bluffs, the water in the bay was calmer, more like river water and less like the gray waters on the Cape. She wanted to ask Whitney how Sag connected to the Long Island Sound, and if this was freshwater or saltwater, but Whitney was clearly on a mission from which she would not be easily deterred.

At the penultimate house, before the sand continued as far as Olivia's eye could see, Whitney stopped and blew out a hard puff of air. "You see this?"

Olivia wondered if it was a trick question. Her eyes focused on the house which stood out among its peers with its expansive wall of windows on the first floor, an infinity pool, and a deck that suggested the house was a hotel or one of the lavish summer escapes she'd seen on Nantucket.

"No, this!" Whitney said, calling Olivia's attention to the staircase that led down from the deck to the beach.

"Oh, okay," Olivia said. She hadn't seen steps like this leading from any of the other houses to the beach, but she wasn't sure why it mattered.

"This is yet another example of white folks trying to encroach on our legacy and do the absolute most. Or the least, as it were."

Olivia shook her head in mock outrage—she still didn't understand what was so upsetting about it all.

"If you'll notice, all the other homeowners use the public access that leads down to the beach, or hidden stairs that were put there some fifty-plus years ago when these properties were first built, and that have served everyone just fine since then. But no, these white folks decided that they just had to have their very own stairway to heaven, tearing away all the reeds that keep the waters back and protect our homes from the elements. We asked them to cease construction immediately when we saw it. They hired a lawyer to fight us. As if we aren't lawyered up with some of the best firms in the city from Teddy at Paul Weiss to our girl at Skadden. I told the owner when I saw him at the farmer's market that if he insisted on making changes to his home that threaten the historic nature of the Sag Harbor community, we would fight him with all the resources at our disposal. He didn't know what to say to that. And by the end of the weekend his lawyers called ours to say that they'd decided not to pursue legal action. As if they would've won if they tried. Now it's just here rotting, a staircase to nowhere."

Olivia understood Whitney's argument, even if she didn't agree with it entirely. Clearly, what looked like just a set of steps to an outsider meant much more once you knew the history of Sag Harbor, how hard the families had worked to establish the community, and how committed they were to maintain it. As it was, Olivia had only been there a month, and Sag Harbor was already feeling like home. She could see how and why you could become protective of a place this beautiful.

As Olivia and Whitney made their way back to the car, Olivia looked up longingly at the huge, ornate building that she'd somehow managed not to notice looming over the other end of Havens Beach.

"What's that? Such interesting architecture," Olivia said, shading her eyes and tilting her head back to get a better view of the three-story structure.

"Oh, that's the convent. Formerly the home of the baron Edward Havens, who the beach is named after. And then it became a finishing school for girls run by the Catholic Church. Rumor has it that this was a place where girls could come to have their babies discreetly, to spare their families the shame of a child born out of wedlock. But you didn't hear that from me."

"Wow. Now that's a story," Olivia said.

"It is, isn't it? If Havens Beach could talk, the stories it would tell. It's hard to imagine it this early in the season, but later in the summer this place is hopping. This place has seen the beginning of childhood friendships, romances, business deals. This beach has seen it all. In a way, the nuns are the least interesting part."

Olivia let everything Whitney said wash over her as they trekked back to the car. She noted, with a small sigh of relief, that somehow her slides had emerged from the impromptu walk on the beach unscathed. What Whitney told Olivia about the threats to the sanctity of Sag Harbor was not news to her. Olivia overheard conversation at the Greaves' last Christmas party that suggested Sag Harbor's formerly tight-knit community of Black elites was being threatened by developers who preyed on vulnerable, elderly homeowners. If the gossip was to be believed, some children, grandchildren, and great-grandchildren of the original Sag Harbor families had fond childhood memories of Sag, but apparently these memories weren't fond enough to motivate them to hold on to their family property. It was the same story in so many formerly predominantly Black neighborhoods in the city—from Bedford-Stuyvesant to Harlem. Olivia was far from a revolutionary, but the years of Tanya's summer stories and now her up-close view of Sag Harbor had convinced her that the place was a gem, and that the word of its value was out well beyond the Black elite who'd called it home for more than half a century.

"You never know what the power of a committed few can do in the face of the apathetic many," Olivia said. Once the words were out of her mouth, Olivia couldn't say exactly where they came from;

she hoped she hadn't committed herself to a stance she couldn't support later.

Olivia breathed in the fresh air and reflected on how far she was away from the life she'd left behind in the city, and yet how content she felt. Olivia watched Whitney wave at a figure up in the distance. Once they got closer to the lot, Olivia could see a gentleman dressed in a polo shirt and sharply creased khaki pants, the garbage picker in his hands at odds with his presentation. His snow-white hair formed a halo around his head. He paused his cleaning as they neared. When he smiled at them, Olivia remembered something her old teacher often said, which rang true: if people did what needed to be done, the world would be a better place.

"Olivia Jones, I'd like to introduce you to the unofficial mayor of Sag Harbor, Mr. Joel Whittingham."

It's him!

Olivia power-walked to close the distance, eager to meet the mystery man.

"We finally meet, Mr. Whittingham," Olivia greeted while offering her hand.

"I've been looking for you, Olivia Jones."

Mr. Whittingham took one of her hands and sandwiched it in between his own. It wasn't a hug, but it was warmer somehow. "We've been waiting for you to claim the Tremont house."

Olivia nodded. "It took me some, um, time to get things organized. But Omar, per usual, wanted things done in a certain order. But I'm here now." Olivia had said the statement carefully, studying Mr. Joel Whittingham's face to see if he would respond or react to Omar's name.

Mr. Whittingham nodded, smiling, and it seemed as if secrets sparked in his warm brown eyes. "Welcome home."

Olivia had so many questions. She sighed, disappointed that Mr. Whittingham didn't immediately reveal the nature of his association with Omar. Not to mention her eagerness to ask about her father's family.

But as Olivia finally noticed Whitney's attention darting between them with a curious gleam in her eyes, Olivia realized she wasn't entirely ready to address their odd relationship. His silence on the matter was the right move.

"I hear you give those folks in finance a run for their money."

"So I'm told," Olivia said. Twenty twenty-one was Olivia's year. She'd already been featured on some of the best and brightest and top "30 under 30" lists. If Ama had taught her anything, it was that false modesty was a sin. Ama hadn't made it as far as she had on Wall Street pretending to be less outstanding than she was.

"How is Amelia doing these days?" Mr. Whittingham asked.

Still no mention of Omar, but he would get around to it, she supposed.

"She's doing well. Traveling a bit."

"Oh, that's right. She's with Carter Morris, an old running buddy of mine."

Olivia smarted a bit at the mention of Carter, the man Ama took up with some years after Omar passed. It wasn't as if Ama was cheating on Omar, but it was still hard for Olivia to open her heart to Carter.

"He told me to look out for you. But someone already beat him to it." He winked. "I told him you are in expert hands in this community."

"And who is this somebody?" Whitney finally broke into the odd conversation. "Do I know them?"

Olivia wrestled with a smile. "My fiancé, I suppose."

Mr. Whittingham was beaming now. Olivia didn't know why, but she found their exchange entirely funny and endearing.

"I've been coming up short on my unofficial mayoral duties with everything going on," Mr. Whittingham said. "But I don't let anything stop me from my daily walk on the beach. The doctor says that the best thing I can do is get my thirty minutes of exercise in, so I figure I can accomplish my sports and community service in one fell swoop. At my age, you have to do everything you can to help yourself," Mr. Whittingham continued.

"Now you and I both know you aren't a day over fifty," Whitney said, patting Mr. Whittingham on his shoulder. "I am glad to see you out, though. You know I am behind on my welcoming work, too. I was just taking Olivia around to give her a sense of Sag Harbor—the insiders' tour—and that's well overdue," Whitney said.

"Well, we are all out here just doing our best in extraordinary times. I promised our dear friend I'd keep an eye on you," Mr. Whittingham said. "And I aim to keep my word. I'm so glad to finally meet you, but I can't wait to get to know you."

Olivia was touched by his sincerity. "Thank you, Mr. Whittingham. That's awfully kind of you to share."

"If I remember things correctly, the Tremonts left their concrete chess table in the backyard. I hope you wouldn't mind having me over for a game one day?"

"I play a little chess," Olivia started, thinking fondly of the games she played with Omar. "I'd never turn down the offer of good company."

"This is the guy you want on your side. He's a gracious winner, too," Whitney said, beaming at Mr. Whittingham as if he were her favorite uncle who visited once a year.

"Then I look forward to your first move," Mr. Whittingham said to Olivia with a conspiratorial chuckle as he set off on his walk.

Once they were in the car, Olivia and Whitney watched the water and Mr. Whittingham for a long moment before they pulled off.

Whitney broke the peaceful moment. "Do you and Mr. Whittingham know each other?"

Olivia buckled her seat belt, then shook her head. "I don't know him, but he seems to know me."

Whitney didn't respond for a while until she simply stated. "Okay."

"Okay?"

"Mr. Whittingham is the unofficial mayor of Sag Harbor. He knows where the bodies are buried, but he's too polite to resurrect them, if you know what I mean." Whitney tapped her long and bedazzled manicured fingers on the steering wheel.

"If he likes you, then it means that you are good people."

The compliment, sweet and warm, filled her up like a mug of Ama's famous hot cocoa with vanilla bean marshmallows.

Whitney let out the world's longest sigh. "We need good people. We need to fight for our neighborhood."

The warm feeling from the compliment fled. Olivia enjoyed Sag Harbor. Curiosity about her family had driven her to accept Omar's gift, but she'd stayed because of the serenity and security of her beach home.

But fighting? How could she fight for something when her mind, body, and spirit were at war with her past?

Olivia nodded and smiled, all the while staring ahead. She wasn't ready to fight anyone else's battles, even for oddly charming neighbors.

She needed to get her head on straight so she could eventually return to normalcy—to life before the truth bomb.

When Whitney pulled up to Olivia's house, she quickly slid out of the car and waved goodbye. Moving forward, she would limit friendly neighborhood excursions or parties. Not until they understood that Olivia Jones was no one's hero. She wasn't even her own.

CHAPTER 6

A SPECIAL DELIVERY

June 2021

After the SANS exploration with Whitney, Olivia noted the time. She had exactly one hour before her weekly call with her godsisters.

The house was quiet. Anderson's car was missing, which meant he was out making deliveries. Olivia mentally crossed her fingers and toes that none of the good people of SANS recognized her fiancé.

She just wasn't up for another conversation about Anderson's career, nor about their plans. It was very unlike Olivia. Her very career hinged on present and future analysis.

Presently, she wanted a bath. She hurried to pull the materials she needed, a towel warmed from the dryer, the inflatable neck pillow and the star of the show, the Laura Mercier Ambre Vanilla Honey Bath crème that her godsister Perry had sent in a welcome home care package.

The scent of vanilla bean, honey, and brown sugar rushed her senses as near scalding water filled the freestanding bathtub. Olivia was grateful to the Tremonts or Omar for updating the *owner's* bathroom suite, *not* the *master suite*, as Whitney had corrected her. She said real estate agents no longer used the outdated term.

The tense muscles around her neck and back considerably relaxed after she immersed herself in the water. She elevated the ambiance with music from her phone, selecting Tiwa Savage, a Nigerian artist that she and Anderson had discovered on NPR's Tiny Desk concert series on YouTube. The singer's smooth, ethereal voice was just what she needed to wind down.

The phone beeped and dinged a few times, indicating an email and text messages. She ignored the interruption and enjoyed the rest of her Sunday soak. Olivia nearly drifted off to sleep when the music stopped playing, replaced by the digital chimes of her ringtone.

It was time for the godsister FaceTime chat. A few months into pregnancy, Perry had conference-called Olivia and Billie and tearily asked if they could talk more often. The intensity of Perry's feelings surprised Olivia. She'd initially chalked it up to pregnancy hormones. Perry had her best friend Layla, after all. Olivia could never quite understand their friendship, especially whenever Layla, a white woman, insisted loudly that she was not only Black but blacker than Perry.

Though it annoyed Olivia, and drove Billie up the wall, both had decided to simply ignore Perry's obnoxious friend.

Olivia grabbed the fluffy towel, quickly dried her body from head to toe, and answered the ringing phone.

"Sorry, ladies," Olivia greeted.

"Well, hello to you. Did we interrupt you and Anderson's sexy times?" Billie's chirpy voice carried over the phone.

"No." Olivia wrapped the towel around her body. "Why would you think that?"

"For one, you're breathing heavily," Perry replied. "Secondly, you haven't turned on the video. And thirdly, you sound odd." While Billie's voice pepped, Perry's voice petered. Olivia figured it was the tone of a new mom, even one who adored her baby girl.

"No, I had a soak in the tub. I used the products you shipped. It's delightful."

"Isn't it?" Perry quickly agreed.

"So . . . how is Libby Amelia?" Olivia dutifully asked.

"Beautiful. Brilliant. She's up to one hundred words now. Most children her age say about fifty words."

"Wow," Billie said with the same level of enthusiasm one would have for drying concrete.

"Oh, hush, Billie," Perry snapped.

While her godsisters bickered, Olivia slathered on body lotion and capped it with her seaweed extract oil. She pulled on the sleeveless peach silk pajama short set.

"Bah, you know I love her. Where is my genius toddler, anyway?" Billie asked.

Olivia clicked on the video icon. "Yes! It's been too long."

Damon, Perry's husband, must've been in the same room because no less than three seconds later, the very wiggly Libby sat in Perry's lap.

"Say hey to Aunt Billie and Aunt Olivia," Perry said in a sweet voice.

"Bebe, Lilo!" She clapped and waved.

"Hello, sweet girl." Olivia blew kisses.

Billie made funny faces much to Libby's enjoyment. There was no question as to who would receive the fun aunt title.

Libby hopped off her mother's lap and Perry moved outside to the balcony. Her late mother's home, now Perry's, was truly beautiful.

"Okay, we're alone now," Perry intoned. "Mental health check. How is everyone?"

"Only blue skies over here." Billie chatted about the new recipe Dulce had concocted. She causally dropped that they were considering taking the next steps in adoption or considering a sperm donor. Perry clapped, clearly excited by the prospect of giving baby Libby a cousin.

Olivia experienced twin emotions. On one hand, she was extremely excited for her godsister, but on the other, she was jealous. Billie was the wild child, the one who would likely never settle or have a family. Olivia was the staid one. Career first, then relationship, and then kids.

Olivia swallowed her jealousy and pasted just the right level of smile on her face.

Next, it was Perry's turn as she lamented how her body would never be the same. Billie and Olivia told her she looked amazing, which was the absolute truth. Billie advised her not to fall prey to the toxicity of snapback culture.

"Olivia, you've been quiet. How are you and Anderson?" Perry asked.

"Better yet, how are *you* doing?" Billie asked. "You've had a lot of changes, too."

"Anderson and I are . . . solid, I think."

"You think?" Billie responded.

"He's just . . . struggling here. He's a friendly guy but lately he's just hasn't been around. He shoots over to New York a lot for his shows and auditions."

"Well, to be fair, he didn't exactly want to move to Sag Harbor. That was your idea," Billie reminded her.

"That was Omar's idea," Olivia muttered under her breath. It didn't really occur to her until she got the brochure that he'd planted the seeds in her father, Chris Jones' shrine. She couldn't believe Omar was masterminding from the grave.

"Yes, well, you followed his directive," Billie agreed. "So cut Anderson some slack."

"I . . . guess. I just hope he isn't with someone . . ." Olivia cut herself off when she saw Perry's lip quiver. Olivia silently berated herself for the thoughtless comment, knowing Perry was still tender after discovering her husband's infidelity, which led to her own.

Perry cleared her throat. "Don't jump to conclusions. Weren't you just telling us last week about how you both needed a breather?"

"She did," Billie confirmed. "And not to mention there are so many relationships that are strained from Covid. He probably needs space, just like you."

"I don't know why," Olivia said with a pout. "I'm a joy to be around."

Her godsisters went silent until Billie cackled. "Did you crack a joke, Olivia Jones?"

"No. I am a joy. Ask my neighbors." Olivia segued into all the neighborhood events she'd been pulled into, and how she planned to pull back.

"We've known you since you were a preteen. We don't need testimonials." Perry laughed. "Besides, your neighbors sound delightful. Don't be afraid to be open and make new friends."

They chatted for another half hour. Because they were Ama and Omar's Girls (Billie had even named their group chat "A&O's Girls"), they all had to-dos. Billie would reach out to someone Perry recommended for a fertility consultation. Olivia and Perry also advised their younger godsister to discuss who planned to carry the baby should they go the sperm donor route. Earlier in the conversation, Billie breezily said that they planned to decide by way of the game rock, paper, scissors. She said it jokingly, but both Perry and Olivia were unsure. You could never tell with Billie.

Perry's to-do was to find an open weekend for her and Damon to get away. Both Billie and Olivia volunteered to babysit at their home. Perry had settled on Billie and Dulce since they were considering children.

Finally, the godsisters tasked Olivia to lean into her new community and to have a conversation with Anderson about her insecurities.

Once the conversation ended, Olivia worked on her to-dos straightaway by calling Anderson. It went straight to voicemail.

"So much for our deep talk," she muttered, ending the call. If she left a message, it would not be nice.

She sighed and found text messages from Mrs. Brooks and Addy, and a new email from Dr. LaGrange.

She checked the email first. Before she'd gone out with Whitney, she'd submitted an appointment request through Dr. LaGrange's website. Based on the email the doctor had a last-minute cancellation and opening for tomorrow morning. She wanted to confirm if that worked for Olivia and, if so, to visit the website to fill out paperwork for insurance. After thanking the doctor, she confirmed her availability.

Next, she checked Mrs. Brooks' message, a brief text to inform Olivia that she had fallen ill with a cold and would need to reschedule their meeting. Olivia expressed her sympathy and promised to reschedule. Then she made a mental note to make her neighbor chicken noodle soup.

She finally opened the text from Addy.

ADDY: Does this white man belong to you?

"Belong to me?" Olivia noticed an image attached to the text. It was a picture of Anderson, dropping off food at Addy's front porch, smiling and waving at the camera.

"Dear God. Not her. Anyone but her."

Olivia sat on the chair near the window, waiting for Anderson to return from his . . . excursion. Yes, that is what Olivia would call it. Most partners would experience relief at the confirmation that cheating was not involved.

But of all the places and of all the things to be doing. And to add insult to injury, Addy no doubt got those checkmarks that confirmed Olivia had read her text. She couldn't even pretend it'd been sent to a wrong number. Olivia knew the neighborhood would buzz about the white boy who delivered food. There was nothing wrong with making an honest living, she reminded herself.

At half-past nine, Anderson opened the door and let himself in. He fumbled around in the dark until Olivia turned on the lights.

"What are you doing?" Olivia whispered, the thread of anger evident in her voice.

"Good evening, Olivia. Nice to see you, too."

"It's no longer evening." She pointed to the window behind him. She crossed her arms and straightened her posture in her chair. This wasn't a conversation to slouch. She would need all the steel in her spine.

"What is this about?" Anderson bypassed the key rack mounted on the wall and tossed them on the counter. "You know I'm working."

"You didn't answer your phone. You're always gone, either somewhere around the island or jetting off to New York." She included the latter to add more substance to her anger.

"All roads lead to . . . work." He leaned against the counter.

"Do you . . ." she licked her lips, struggling to find the right words. "Look, you are such a talented person. I love your sets and all, but do you have to do the Uber Eats thing?"

"U-Uber Eats thing?" He pushed off the counter, walked toward the table, but he didn't sit. He just stood, his body and anger towering over Olivia.

His eyes transformed from the surface of the ocean when the sunrays strike sea, to murky depths on the mysterious deep blue.

"I'm a comedian and actor. Sometimes . . ." he thrust his hand through his hair. "If you want to live an extraordinary life, you've got to make certain sacrifices. But you wouldn't know anything about that, would ya, sweetheart?"

"What does that even mean?"

"You've lived a charmed life. The best schools, great neighborhood. Hell, your godmother, Amelia Vaux Tanner, is the wolf of Wall Street. She practically paved the way for your success."

She nearly corrected him with "witch," but she'd hated that extremely reductive term used against her godmother. "You think one Black woman is enough to make the road smooth?" This time, she stood. "Do you understand the number of times I've had to get in early, stay later, prove myself over and over to my bosses, my team, my clients? For the longest time, I wouldn't add my face to my email icon because I didn't want anyone to have preconceived notions before meeting me. And hell, we won't even talk about the colorism I've experienced in and outside of corporate America. And—"

"I'm sorry." Anderson grabbed her hands. "I'm sorry. I was . . . was out of line. I didn't mean it."

Olivia took a shaky breath. "Then why did you say it?"

"Because you're ashamed of me and that hurts. I want you to be as proud as I am when I walk by your side. I don't want you to scan my clothes or check my shoes."

Olivia opened her mouth to deny the accusations, but she couldn't. She was at a loss. No, she was ashamed to be so class conscious. She, after all, was the beneficiary of Ama and Omar's goodwill. Otherwise, she'd be living a straightforward blue-collar life and likely wouldn't have been exposed to a career on Wall Street.

"I'm . . . I'm sorry." Her head drooped with shame.

He squeezed her hands.

"As far as Uber Eats, well . . . that's not exactly what I do."

She gripped his hands tighter, determined not to jump to conclusions. She hadn't raised her head to look at him yet. "What is it you do?"

"A few weeks ago, I swung by the pharmacy, and noticed an older woman. She was jittery, nervous as all hell, and I asked if I could help her. She said that she was scared to pick up her prescriptions.

She still didn't feel safe because she wasn't able to take the vaccine because of a medical condition."

"Oh."

"Yeah. So, I took her number, told her maybe I could figure something out. Spoke to Dave Danvers. He owns the pharmacy. Made a few calls and long story short, I'm a one-man show to deliver groceries and meds to the elderly."

"Ohhhh." Olivia wanted to smack her head.

She didn't want to be the bad guy. The one who judged a book by its cover, yet she'd done the very thing she'd accused others of doing.

"I'm a mess, aren't I?" She finally lifted her head, a storm gathering in her eyes.

He dashed her tears away. "You've worked hard for what you have. You like what you like. I'm just damned lucky you love me."

"I'm lucky, too."

Anderson blushed, pulling her into a hug. "Who outed me anyway?"

Olivia pushed back. "Oh, umm, Addy. She's a sommelier. She snapped a picture of you."

"Ah. She's the one that looks like Rashida Jones. Yeah, I delivered something to her grandmother, I assume."

Olivia smiled. "That's the one. How'd you know?"

"I noticed the picture. I just . . ." Anderson blushed again. "I thought she . . . might have had a crush on me. I didn't think she took the picture to make fun."

Could she feel any lower? Yes. Yes, she could. "Don't worry about Addy. I'll handle her and anyone else who has something to say about my brilliant comedian, actor, Good Samaritan fiancé."

"You can add screenwriter to the list, too."

"Ah, yes. You're still working on that screenplay, right?"

"My third script. My agent is shopping my second attempt."

"Oh?"

"Yep. With everyone at home, streaming television shows and movies, producers in Hollywood are hungry for content. He thinks I've got a good shot."

"That's wonderful, Anderson. Absolutely wonderful."

"You're wonderful," he countered, as if she would disagree.

"You know, I told my godsisters that very same thing today. They laughed."

Anderson laughed, too. "I would like to show you just how wonderful you are." He slipped his hand under her shirt. "Will you let me show you?" His thumb dragged over a peaked nipple.

"Yes," she hissed. He dropped to his knees, parted her thighs, and slid between her legs with a practiced ease.

While Olivia whipped the silk camisole over her head, Anderson had taken off his shirt, revealing his ripped torso.

Olivia lightly scratched her fingers down his defined abs until she reached his waist. When she unbuckled his belt, Anderson pulled his pants down.

"Do you want me?" Confidence had replaced his hurt tone.

"Yes." Her eyes lifted from his abs to his eyes. They were no longer stormy but clear, a cerulean blue.

"I want you so much."

He breathed heavily at her confession.

"Come closer," she demanded.

When he complied, she feathered kisses over his chest, his stomach, pouring into him her passion and her sorrow.

He felt it, she knew he did, because he stepped back, lifted her head to meet his eyes.

Olivia swallowed. "Anderson, I'm so sorry, I—"

"Stop thinking. Just feel."

"I don't know if I—"

Anderson yanked her from the seat, his corded forearms circling her back and, with the other hand, tugged her shorts past her waist and down her legs.

Olivia was just barely able to kick them off before Anderson cupped her bottom. She hopped him—her long legs clenched his waist, arms clasped around his neck. A sexy, full-bodied hug.

In seconds, he lifted her higher into the air and swiftly entered her.

She sighed at the sensation—a velvet hammer sliding into silk.

Firmly rooted inside of her, they stared at each other. He looked at her as if he could see her desires—a fire in need of stoking.

He pulled out slowly, his eyes dark and dangerous and just a little hazy, as he walked them back against the table.

He dropped her carefully onto the tabletop, wrapped her legs tighter around his waist and inched even deeper inside of her. Olivia arched her back, breasts pert, neck exposed. He braced her waist, his fingernails sank into her flesh as he drove into her again and again, a series of thrusts, hurried, feral, unleashed.

His skin flushed as he released a growl.

His even white teeth bit into her fleshy bee-stung lips, serving slow, erotic kisses while he kept the frenzied pace.

It was an odd, sexy dance. Olivia's breath quickened, the sensation of being contained by his hands at war with the wild abandon, the openness of orgasming in the kitchen. She was hot—hot all over—yet she shivered as she scaled up her climax.

"A-anderson."

He didn't answer, verbally. He impaled, eyes shut tight, lost in the sensation.

All she could feel, all she wanted, was him.

Anderson opened his eyes, shuddered, her name on his lips. He groaned low and hard, his eyes becoming clearer with each jet of release.

He smoothed her hair away from her forehead. Somehow, he found the strength to carry her upstairs to their bedroom.

By the time Olivia cleaned herself up and readied for bed, Anderson's eyes were closed. She quietly slid under the sheets and scooted over to wrap her arms around his waist.

She couldn't sleep. Guilt sat firmly on her conscience. Why did she care what Addy, or anyone thought of her fiancé? He made her feel loved and safe.

He was a stand-up guy, honest to a fault—something she desperately needed. Especially when every detail of her life—summers with Omar and Ama, even her relationship with her godsisters—had been heavily crafted by her godparents.

She sighed. She was really looking forward to meeting with Dr. LaGrange on Monday. They had so much to work on. One, her insecurities. Two, her trust issues. Her heart flopped down to her stomach. That was the difficulty of therapy. She would have to expose and explore things about herself she likely didn't understand. Anderson grabbed her arm, startling Olivia. "I may not be what you envisioned as your dream man," he said in a deep, sleepy voice. "But I love you, Olivia Jones. Never forget that."

By the time Olivia gained her composure, he rolled over and went back to sleep.

His confession hadn't warmed her heart. It drove her out of bed, downstairs into the kitchen to make her neighbor Mrs. Brooks a large pot of soup. As she chopped carrots, celery, and bought the broth to boil, she thought of Anderson's sleepy declaration. She thought of Omar's wishes.

Sometimes even Olivia teetered on whether Anderson could be her knight in shining armor.

But what troubled Olivia, why she stirred ingredients for homemade chicken noodle soup well past midnight, instead of lying in bed with her arms wrapped around the man who loved her, was simply this: Why didn't Anderson believe he was her dream man?

CHAPTER 7

THE PHONE TREE

June 2021

The next morning, Olivia texted Mrs. Brooks that she would drop off a canister of soup on her porch. Although she'd cooked a gallon of soup, she didn't want her neighbor to lift the heavy pot. On a small recipe card, Olivia left simple heating instructions and a get-well message. Next, she kindly asked Whitney for Mr. Whitting-ham's number and address. Tomorrow, she would find him and ask questions about her father's family.

She didn't wake up for her morning run. She'd slept in until seven thirty, logged into work early to make up for the time she'd miss while she attended her therapy session. Or rather, *doctor's appointment*, which is what she'd messaged to her boss for her last-minute request to miss most of the morning. Thankfully, her company didn't monitor their team's whereabouts, but Olivia had always felt compelled to explain. According to her mother, Cindy, you should never feed into the stereotype of CP time.

Ama had a different approach. For clients and your boss, arrive early. However, if someone needed a lesson with respect to who holds the power, one could use a strategically late arrival for a power play.

"*It's like smoked paprika, cher. You only need a dash for flavor and show. Nothing more.*"

Today she would arrive early for Dr. LaGrange. She carefully selected her wardrobe, which include an oyster pearl silk blouse, high-waisted khaki shorts with tan and black Chanel ballerina flats. Olivia stared at herself in the mirror, ensuring she conveyed someone emotionally secure, who needed just a little guidance to get back on track.

She arrived twenty minutes ahead of schedule, filled out a new client questionnaire with topics ranging from vaccination status to favorite foods to anything Olivia found triggering—sights, sounds, smells. After she completed the form, Olivia handed the clipboard to Dr. LaGrange's assistant, who introduced herself as Molly, and then she sat in the overstuffed loveseat until someone called her name.

Olivia gripped her knees, focusing on the harp-like music playing over the speakers. It was barely audible, but still it soothed. Olivia organized her thoughts, determining where to start. Cindy, Omar, Ama, her father?

Maybe she could start in chronological order, which meant discussing her father. "But I don't know him," she whispered, shaking her head.

No, Olivia could start from the earliest memory, which meant her mother. But she wasn't up for discussing Cindy. Just the thought of her mother's nitpicking and, on occasion, outright disdain, made her head pound.

"She's ready for you."

Olivia startled at Molly's voice and jumped from her seat. She stepped through the doctor's office door. When she looked around, she was . . . underwhelmed at the décor.

No art, no personal pictures, just muted earth-tone colors. A large desk stood near the massive bay windows. While the office décor was nonexistent, the view was breathtaking. Her office wasn't smack dab in the middle of the busy town, like most of the restaurants and shops. It stood apart, a standalone building within walking distance of Havens Beach. The window had been propped slightly ajar, but not fully opened.

Dr. LaGrange looked the part of patient head doctor in her early thirties, but with her background and credentials, she had to be at least mid-to-late forties. She wore smart black wireframe glasses and a black shirt with pink and turquoise beading. Her gorgeous ombre brown curls sat atop her head in a pineapple-bun hairstyle. In her ears were silver studs.

The desk blocked Olivia's view of her pants and shoes, but she could tell the doctor had style.

"Welcome, Olivia."

"Thank you. You have a wonderful view."

"It's my daily treat." The doctor pointed to the small table with two cushioned seats. "I'm so sorry. I usually offer water, coffee, or tea, but we'd like to minimize contact. So, it's six feet away, with the windows open, even with the vaccine. I hope you don't mind." She asked, though the windows were already opened.

Olivia sat. "Not at all."

"Excellent." The doctor nodded her thanks. "Now, Olivia, tell me why you're here?"

"I added it to the questionnaire but my . . . I've had a challenging year outside of the pandemic and its negatively affected me."

"Was there a specific event or a series of instances?"

"I . . . well. That's complicated."

"Why is it complicated? Can you break it down into smaller parts?"

Olivia nodded. *Chronological order it is*, she thought to herself.

Olivia started with the death of her father, how her mother, Cindy, didn't really seem to love her, but rather tolerated her existence.

She told Dr. LaGrange about Ama, but she withheld her name as well as Omar's. She finally told her about Omar's gift and how she ended up in Sag Harbor. The entire exchange took about fifteen minutes. She wasn't used to talking about herself for so long.

Olivia took a deep breath. "That's most of it. Oh, and I have a fiancé." Olivia glanced at her slim wristwatch. "Maybe we can talk about him another day."

"If you'd like." Dr. LaGrange smiled.

"So . . . what do you think?"

"What do I think?"

"What's going on with me? Do you think I suffer from depression? Anxiety? Kara mentioned you prescribed medication if needed."

"Olivia?"

"Yes?"

"Deep breaths. We are going to take this bite by bite. I want to circle back to your mother."

Olivia's body locked. "What about her?"

"Can you tell me about your strongest memory from childhood in relation to your mother?"

She reclined back in her chair until a memory surfaced.

Olivia had been twelve years old. It was the first day of school and only the second summer she had visited Ama and Omar. She'd returned home happy and giddy. Ama and Omar weighed down her bags with new clothes. Her mother, Cindy, had inspected each article of clothing, seemingly disappointed to find nothing wrong. She turned to her, looked at her head.

"I'm tired. But you've got to do something with that hair."

Olivia had fingered her fuzzy braids. Cindy grabbed a pillow from the sofa and set it on the floor. It took hours for her mother to unbraid her hair, wash it, dry it, and then Olivia's most hated task—the hot comb to straighten her hair.

But Cindy had done it, and five hours later she looked at Olivia and frowned.

"How do I look, Mama?"

A strange look crossed her face—sorrow, anger, defeat. Olivia recognized the emotions now, though she didn't back then.

"You look like . . ." she shook her head. "You'll do. Don't wear anything too bright." She waved Olivia off and shuffled to bed.

She recounted the memory back to Dr. LaGrange. "She took a lot of time to do your hair. Did she complain?"

"No." Olivia shook her head. "She's not a heavy complainer. She gets the job done and my mother . . . well, she's always made me feel like a task to be checked."

"You asked your mom how you look. Why do you think she struggled to answer?"

"She doesn't think I'm beautiful."

"Has she ever said you weren't?"

"No. She once told me I was pretty when Omar took me to the father-daughter dance. For prom, she didn't like my red dress. But trust me, she doesn't think I'm pretty."

"I'm a person who believes that beauty isn't something to be celebrated. Yet"—she shrugged—"you are conventionally beautiful."

She said it in such a straightforward, scientific way Olivia nearly believed it to be true.

"Any guesses why your mother thinks this isn't the case?"

It was on the tip of her tongue to mention her skin, but she hadn't any evidence. Doctors, whether head or heart, lived in facts. "No idea."

"Do you look like your mother?"

"No." Olivia laughed. "Cindy is brown-skinned, a little shorter than me. Her hair is usually in braids or wigs now. The only thing we have in common are our figures." With a Coke-bottle frame—small waist, proportional hips, and well-endowed chest and behind, Olivia was the literal definition of "she got it from her mama."

"But what about your face?" Dr. LaGrange motioned her hand

over hers. "You can still look like someone, but with a different skin tone."

"I look like my father." Olivia grabbed her phone, zoomed in, and leaned just a little closer to show Dr. LaGrange the picture she snapped from the storage unit.

"Why yes, you do. Like he spat you out."

"Does he look familiar to you?" Olivia suddenly pivoted.

The doctor shook her head. "I didn't grow up here. I moved here about three years ago. Why do you ask?"

"I'm looking for his—my—family. The Jones family used to summer here a few decades ago. I'm looking for relatives—aunts, uncles, cousins. Maybe even my grandparents. Cindy thinks I should leave it alone. I suspect my father's family was not kind to her."

Something unlocked in Olivia's mind.

She snapped her fingers. "Do you think that's why she doesn't like the way I look? Because I remind her of my father?"

"I'm not entirely sure if she doesn't like how you look. She hasn't called you ugly."

"Not straightaway, but contextually, yes."

Dr. LaGrange nodded. "It's something to ask your mother. That's the only way you'll know."

Ask her mother? Dr. LaGrange would amend her advice if Cindy Jones ever darkened her door.

Olivia shrugged. "That's enough about my mother. I want to talk about my father and godfather."

"If you'd like to move on, we can."

"You don't think we should?"

"I think we should talk about things you find important."

"Don't get me wrong, my mother is important, but . . ."

"Yes?"

"I'm really upset about my father and godfather. I should focus on them."

"Because you feel more for them."

Olivia nodded. "Yes. I mean, no! I love my mother."

"This is all confidential. You're safe here." Dr. LaGrange's voice went deep and smooth.

Olivia nodded.

"You can breathe now."

Olivia exhaled noisily. "Sorry, I, um, may have overreacted."

"Don't apologize for how you feel. It's obvious you have lots of feelings for your mother. And perhaps some things your mother has said, or rather has *not* said, affected your feelings about yourself. This could even influence the way you dress, the car you drive, even your partner."

Olivia snorted. "My mom doesn't dislike Anderson. Well, she doesn't like the fact that we're living together."

"How long have you two been dating?"

"Sixteen months," Olivia stated proudly, as if rattling off the age of her toddler child.

"Were your mother and father affectionate to each other?"

"I don't know, but I assumed so."

"Why?"

"The pictures. The way my mom looks when she speaks about him. She doesn't talk about him often, but when she does, it's like she has hero worship. Her eyes get wide and then . . . then she tears up. Starts crying."

Once Olivia had walked in on her mother clutching a picture of her and her father. He looked much younger, fifteen or sixteen, if she had to guess. Her mother wore a white tank top and jean shorts. Her father, a bright orange polo shirt, khaki shorts, and orange-and-blue Nike sneakers. Cindy had been horrified when Olivia walked in and shouted at her to leave.

That was another powerful memory. One she'd nearly forgotten.

At the top of the hour when the session came to a close, Dr. La-

Grange walked to a hip-level cabinet, pulled out a notebook and handed it to Olivia.

"I'd like to see you twice a month. Can you commit to that, Olivia?"

"Yes." She nodded.

"In between our sessions, I'd like for you to journal about your day."

"Are there any key points I should include?"

"Just write for now and make a note of how you feel. It doesn't have to be a novel. Just happy, sad, angry, confused. You can even draw an emoji if you'd like."

"Will you read my journal?"

"I would like to. It'll help me, help you. However, if you only want to keep it to yourself, you most certainly can."

"I . . ." Olivia licked her lips. "I'll have to think about it." She grabbed the notebook and thanked her. She stared at the bright pink notebook. "Are all of your notebooks this color?"

"No."

"Hmm. Is this a test? What's the goal?"

"The goal is to process your feelings and to be aware of your emotional mindset. You work on Wall Street, correct?"

"Yes." Olivia recalled she added her occupation on the form.

"Think of this as a way to benchmark where you are. Then we'll work together to set a good pace to achieve where you want to be."

"It seems practical," Olivia said and nodded. "I didn't think this would be practical."

"What did you expect would happen?"

"Crying," she instantly said, thinking of Kara and her onset of tears with a virtual stranger.

"Give it a few more sessions," Dr. LaGrange said with a smirk. She lifted her eyebrows when Olivia didn't respond.

"I'm joking. You set the pace and we will align on expectations. You're the driver and I'm the GPS to make sure you don't get lost."

☀

When Olivia returned from the appointment, she found Mr. Whittingham sitting on the front porch of Mrs. Brooks with a bouquet in hand.

Yes. I'll kill two birds with one stone today. Though she needed to log back into work, the therapy session made her feel productive in terms of regaining control of her life. And right now, she very much wanted to learn about her family. Mr. Whittingham seemed to hold the keys to the kingdom of SANS.

After she parked her car, Olivia stood near her porch and waved.

He didn't smile or acknowledge the greeting. He looked lost.

"Mr. Whittingham?" Olivia asked.

He stared ahead as if he couldn't hear her call.

Something isn't right. She hurried across the yards, her steps quickening as she took in the tears on Mr. Whittingham's face.

"Hey there." Olivia gave him a small smile. "All okay?" she asked the question, though she instinctively knew his answer.

He shook his head.

"She's gone." He exhaled. "Ruth is dead."

Olivia kneeled and reached for his hand. "You found her."

He squeezed her hand. "Her son called and asked me to check in. She hadn't answered his phone calls. Didn't answer mine either. I found the spare key and I—" he waved a trembling hand toward Mrs. Brooks' home. "I found her in bed, weighed down by so many quilts, but she was still so cold."

"I'm sorry." Tears streamed down Olivia's face. Although Olivia had spoken to the woman only once, Mrs. Brooks made a strong impression.

"Me too. She was a fine woman. Garrett will be devastated." He stood, patted his pockets. "I need to call him."

"What can I do?"

"Give me two hours to take care of Mrs. Brooks and call Garrett. Then call Kara, Whitney, and Addy. They'll gather what we need and get the community situated."

The wail of an ambulance filled the street. He looked at Olivia, startled.

"I'll do that." She stood, her hands still in his. The ambulance pulled into the driveway.

Sunlight softened the pulsing red-and-white lights from the ambulance.

His eyes drifted to the paramedics rushing to the porch, a gurney and a medical kit that looked like a toolbox in hand.

He glanced nervously at the duo. When the screen door opened and slammed, he looked straight ahead. Olivia followed his attention across the quiet street where flowers bloomed and bees buzzed. It was an unreasonably beautiful day; just as it had been when Omar passed.

She wondered about what the weather had been when her father died.

"What's that?" Mr. Whittingham asked.

"Oh, I . . . must have said it out loud. Just wondering about the weather and my father . . . it's complicated."

"He liked books," Mr. Whittingham stated.

"Who?"

"Your father."

"Oh, Omar. Yes, he loved—"

"Not Omar, your father. The Jones boy."

Olivia's eyes widened. "You knew my father?"

"Yes, I did. Didn't want to tell you like this." He turned his head to face Olivia. "They had kinfolk just down the street. Aunt and uncle never had kids, but they loved their niece and nephews. The first summer they came to visit, the family had gone to the beach, but he had an upset stomach, so he stayed behind. They asked me to keep an eye out for him and so I did. He said he was fine, but he didn't want to go outside. He wanted to go to the library and asked that I drive him." Mr. Whittingham smiled. "He liked *Encyclopedia Brown*, but I told him to read a detective series by Walter Dean Myers. Every week I took him to the library."

Something that sounded like the ocean whooshed through her ears.

"Two hours," Mr. Whittingham said, ending the strange revelation. His voice, light and worn, drifted like the breeze.

Olivia wanted to know more, ask for more, like the names of her aunt and uncle. But now wasn't the time. She would take that walk with Mr. Whittingham as soon as possible.

"Two hours," Olivia squeezed his hand and smiled, attempting to anchor him.

He squeezed her hand again. Olivia had taken it as a signal for his readiness. She dropped his hand and took a few steps to the left, clearing a path for the paramedics.

He smoothed the wrinkles from his short-sleeved button-up shirt. "Thanks for being here. Thanks for helping me get out of—"

"That's what neighbors are for."

Only when Mr. Whittingham disappeared into the house did she leave the front porch. She went into her empty house. After fixing herself a cold glass of water, she finally let the tears fall again. She cried for Mrs. Brooks. She cried for Omar and her father.

Olivia reached for her phone and took a deep breath, pressed the contact card of someone she hadn't reached out to in a long while.

"Well, hello, cher. I sure have missed you," Ama's voice shook with emotion.

Olivia sniffed tears. "I miss you, too."

"Why are you crying? Do I need to straighten out any of the fine folks in Sag Harbor?"

Olivia laughed while shaking her head. She told Ama about Mrs. Brooks and how in a few hours she would call to inform Addy, Kara, and Whitney. Olivia gave Ama the *Reader's Digest* version of her and Anderson's relationship.

She didn't mention therapy. She wasn't ready for the questions about why she needed to do so just yet.

The conversation eventually moved on to Ama who'd been cruising the Mediterranean with Carter. Olivia detected the careful way Ama referenced him, as if too many repetitions of Carter's name would be triggering. Today, Olivia was grateful. The rawness of death sat on her skin like a fine sheen.

"I'm sorry I haven't called you, Ama." She was also sorry she hadn't taken her calls. She just hadn't known what to say. She was still ashamed of her reaction—of the cruel accusations she'd lobbed to Ama about Omar.

"Maybe I should come for a visit. We could stay a few days and I can head down to New York to visit with Perry and the baby."

"No, Ama."

"Well, fine then." Her voice had gone small.

"It's not that I don't want you to come. I know you're having a wonderful time. You and Carter deserve more time together. Besides, hold off on New York for now. There's still a surge."

Maybe there was a surge here. Mrs. Brooks had cold-like symptoms. She could have died from Covid for all she knew.

"That's fine, cher. But I will visit soon," Ama insisted.

"I'll see you soon. But not too soon."

"Fine, fine. Eat well, stay hydrated."

"You, too."

She harrumphed, as if someone Olivia's age couldn't dish advice. "Take your vitamins and don't work too hard."

Don't work too hard? That was a first for Ama. Maybe Carter and his bohemian ways had a good effect on Ama.

"It's been two hours, cher. Time for you to call your neighbors."

"Oh." Olivia glanced at her phone. She smiled when she realized Ama had distracted her for two hours, despite the different time zone.

"I guess I need to contact them." Olivia swallowed the rising lump in her throat.

"Yes, call. You will not text the news. That's tacky. Omar and I did not raise tacky girls."

"I'll call everyone."

"Good. Goodbye for now."

"Goodbye. I'll call more often," Olivia promised.

"I'd like that. I love you," Ama said before she hung up. She didn't wait for Olivia to return the sentiment.

Olivia took a deep breath and made the first call to Whitney.

CHAPTER 8

BEAUTIFUL STRANGER

June 2021

It had been three days since Mrs. Brooks died.

Three days since Mr. Whittingham shared details about her father's childhood.

Three days since she dared step outside and distract the mourning SANS community.

According to the neighborhood gossip, Addy, Mrs. Brooks had died from complications of Covid. She'd gone to the hospital at the onset of her symptoms and had informed her son of the diagnosis a few days later.

Olivia didn't wear black or cry since the day she died, but she wasn't a monster. She wouldn't joyfully jog outside while the community reeled from the impact of Covid. For many residents, it had finally hit home. And like any small-town whodunit mystery, everyone had placed blame on the grocery store, the restaurants, even Mrs. Brooks' beloved craft shop.

But Olivia could see beauty in their community, too. From the safety of her home, she spotted the potluck dishes, the cards, and flowers. She suspected Mrs. Brooks' son had returned home, but she wasn't brave enough to face a stranger's grief.

She could barely manage her own.

Today she compromised with her restless body and jogged before sunrise so that even the early risers would miss her routine.

"Not early enough," Olivia muttered under her breath when she saw Mr. Whittingham chatting with someone near the shore. She couldn't see the face of the man who spoke to Mr. Whittingham, but from what she could gather, he had an attractive profile. No one could miss the stranger's height. He was taller than Mr. Whittingham, who stood at six feet. His fitted shorts stopped along his knees, revealing thick thighs. Though the main attraction had to be the way his shorts cuffed nicely around his backside. The blue-and-white-striped shirt, rolled up at the sleeves, revealed nicely corded forearms. Olivia slowed down to a walk and stretched. Sticking to the shadows, she attempted to creep away, but Mr. Whittingham waved and in a booming voice said, "Hello, neighbor."

The guy turned around to face Olivia.

Oh.

Oh.

Olivia couldn't turn away from the view. It was like the sand had congealed around her feet, rooting her in place.

It may have been the way his onyx skin gleamed under the rising sun—like someone had smoothed tiny, crushed diamonds over his skin. Or the way his dark eyes, the color of black coffee no sugar, no cream, locked on her.

He smiled—small and sad, but still devastatingly gorgeous. The dark beard didn't camouflage the deep dimples near his mouth.

He stood inhumanly still, quiet. Olivia liberated her feet from the sand and slowly walked over, all the while this strange, beautiful man stared back at Olivia as if he'd been gobsmacked.

Mr. Whittingham cleared his throat. "Let's make introductions, shall we? Garrett Brooks, this is Ms. Olivia Jones. Olivia is new to the neighborhood. Garrett is Mrs. Brooks' son," he said to Olivia. He pointed to her house behind them. "Her home is right next to your mother's . . . to yours now, son." Mr. Whittingham's voice trailed off. A look of sorrow robbed his bemused expression.

"Hello, Olivia." Garrett nodded.

Her stomach pitched at his delicious voice.

"You made my mother soup."

"I did. I'm so sorry for your loss. She talked about you and your daughter, but I only met her once. She was going to show me her quilts."

"Oh, really? Hopefully, it wasn't anything too embarrassing."

"Not at all," Olivia shook her head. "She said you were handsome."

"Handsome?" he asked, a gleam in his eyes.

Now why did I say that? "Yes, and um, that she missed her granddaughter," Olivia rushed on.

Garrett looked down, nodding. "Yeah. Zora misses . . . missed her, too."

"What do you have on your agenda today?" Mr. Whittingham asked Olivia.

"I think I'll go into town today," Olivia fingered her hair. "I'm looking for some natural hair products." Dr. LaGrange's comment about Olivia shaping herself to what her mother preferred had sat on her psyche. After some self-reflection, Olivia realized she changed the way she dressed around her mother. She never wore bold colors, and her hair was always pin-straight.

Today, that would change, and the first challenge was to take care of her hair in its natural state.

"I'm not sure if you want a recommendation from an old man, but I recommend Abeja Apothecary hair care." Mr. Whittingham spelled it out for Olivia. "I know the creator, Bea. She's got her products in the grocery store."

"Oh, wow, I'll have to give that a try. And the owner lives in SANS, too?"

"I'll share her information after I catch up with Garrett here."

"Oh, yes." Olivia turned her attention to the Chocolate God in front of her. "I'm sorry again. I'm, um, just over here if you need anything. Bye now." Olivia waved and jogged away, her heart beating wildly as if she were still running through the neighborhood instead of a light jog to her house.

When she entered the house, Anderson stood by the window, a mug of coffee in hand.

"Oh, hey." Olivia turned to close the door and settle her beating heart.

"Who's the guy talking to Mr. W?"

"Oh, he's Mrs. Brooks' son."

"Oh," he said before taking another sip of coffee.

"Yeah. You'll probably run into him and his daughter."

"He's not married?"

Olivia had looked at his hand and did not notice a ring, nor an indention.

"I . . . didn't ask for his marital status. I just expressed my condolences to him."

"You seemed to chat for a long time." His tone was faultless. But there was something about the line of question, the way he crossed her arms and furrowed his brow that made Olivia feel like his questions were leading to a setup.

"Yes. I told Mr. Whittingham about my plans to try something new with my hair. He suggested I go into town. He's popping by after he's done with Garrett."

"Garrett?"

"Mrs. Brooks' son, Anderson. What's up with the interrogation?" Olivia pressed.

"I don't like the way he looked at you."

"How did he look at me?" Olivia's voice pitched high because of Anderson's astute observation.

"Like you were made for him."

"Don't be ridiculous," Olivia huffed. "And besides, you must have darn near perfect vision to see from such a far distance."

"I'm not being ridiculous. He was facing me, and when he noticed you—"

Three quick knocks on the front door stopped Anderson from finishing his words.

"That'll be Mr. Whittingham." Olivia narrowed her eyes at Anderson. "That is, if you'll allow me to have a man inside."

"Oh, c'mon, Olivia."

"Mr. Whittingham," she greeted her neighbor, who now wore a N95 mask over his face.

Mr. Whittingham stood on the porch, looking over her shoulder, and waved at Anderson. "Hey, neighbor."

Anderson must not have seen him because he stomped up the stairs.

"S-sorry. He must not have seen you."

"Oh, that's okay. We'll catch up next time." Mr. Whittingham gave Olivia a winning smile. "I wanted to see if you were up for a drive later today. If so, I can show you around, maybe even introduce you to Bea."

Olivia clapped her hands. "That would be wonderful." Maybe she could get tips and tricks, as she had no idea what to do with her hair. And, of course, Olivia was desperate to ask him questions about her father.

"I would love to get some advice from her about hair care routines."

"Now, I must warn you. Bea isn't the friendliest. Don't get me wrong, she's got a heart of gold. But she doesn't warm up easily to strangers. So we can swing by her storefront to see if she's there. If not, we'll have to catch her later."

"What are her hours of operation?"

He shrugged. "She's into many things. She has her own apothecary operation, so it just depends on the day."

That's frightening, she thought. Instead, she said, "That's interesting."

"She's a little hippy dippy. Smart. You'll like her, I think."

"Well, I look forward to meeting her and maybe if we have time"—Olivia cleared her throat—"I . . . I would love to talk to you about my father."

"Of course. That's the real reason I came by. Well, that and I saw your fiancé through the window. Just wanted to make sure everything's good," he asked in a blink twice if you need to be saved tone.

"Everything is great," Olivia lied, her voice neon bright. "Well, I need to get ready for the day. I'll see you at noon. Where should I meet you?"

"I'll come to your house. A beautiful young lady should never have to wait on someone."

Olivia smiled and said her goodbyes. While she completed her daily ablutions, Anderson sat stone silent on the edge of the bed.

She wet her toothbrush, and before brushing, she broke the ice. "I'm meeting Mr. Whittingham at noon. He wants to introduce me to someone who creates hair care products."

Anderson stood and walked behind her. They both faced the mirror. Surprising her, he pulled her close into a hug.

"So I'm an asshole."

"Mhmm."

"A jealous one."

"All signs point to yes," Olivia agreed, with a smile on her face.

"Can I make it up to you? We can go out to dinner."

"Really?" Her eyes brightened in the mirror.

Anderson abhorred walking around town, and since they lived in SANS they hadn't gone out to eat. She understood not wanting to go inside, but they'd both been vaccinated. Besides that, some restaurants had adjusted their setting for outdoors. It was a stark change to the guy who walked with her for blocks from his comedy show in New York back to her home.

Anderson nodded. "Yes, my love. Wear something pretty."

"Please. I always wear something pretty."

"You do. How about seven o'clock tonight?"

"Perfect."

Olivia took special care of her appearance for her meeting with Mr. Whittingham. The entire time, she argued internally why she felt the need to look exceptionally nice for a tour about town.

The red open-collared silk shirt would've been too much for a drive and possibly a stroll down the beach, not to mention the potential for heat and sweat that could appear on the unforgiving material. Instead, she opted for a pink ruffle-collar maxi dress.

The dress flowed just above her ankles and dipped at the neckline, hinting at her ample cleavage but not enough to raise eyebrows.

Anderson's eyebrows, of course. Not Garrett's.

When flashes of Garrett came to mind, she squashed it down like an unwelcomed bug. Was he movie-star attractive? Yes. But so was Anderson.

Anderson was the one who bent down on one knee and professed his love. He's the one who adjusted his life in New York City to move out to Sag Harbor.

And he deserved much better. Not an unfair comparison to a virtual stranger. But the way Garrett stared at her like she was a mermaid who sprung out of the sea onto the shore had been unsettling.

If she were being honest with herself, the reason she felt unsettled was that it wasn't one-sided. If she were the mermaid, then he was the dashing prince waiting to be saved.

She blushed at the thought of Mr. Whittingham bearing witness to the fireworks between her and Garrett and she prayed he didn't think less of her in that moment of weakness.

Mr. Whittingham arrived just as she changed from her house slippers to a colorful Respoke espadrille heel platform. She hurried out the door and met him in his car. Olivia greeted him after she opened the passenger door.

"A young lady should never have to rush outside. I would've liked to have rung the doorbell."

"My apologies. I'm just . . . excited to talk to you again. I'm excited to meet Bea, too." Olivia had quickly googled the no-set-hours entrepreneur and was intrigued when she found a simple landing page with hundreds of testimonials praising her products.

There was no picture of her on the website, no biography, just ingredients and pictures of flowers and herb gardens and beehives.

They drove in silence at first, until Mr. Whittingham offered a compliment. "You look absolutely stunning today. Pink is your color."

Olivia blushed. "M-my color?"

"Yes. My late wife, Carole, had your same complexion. She looked good in any color, but when she wore pink, red, yellow, white . . . whew! It was like a spotlight shone on her from the heavens."

Olivia rubbed the back of her neck. "That's um . . . very kind of you to say. Thank you."

Her neighbor dropped his smile. "Don't tell me you don't know how to take a compliment."

"No . . . I can absolutely take a compliment."

"I know you can. You did when I first met you and mentioned your job. You soaked it right in because you knew your worth."

"I do," Olivia quickly agreed.

"Does that beau of yours compliment you?"

"Anderson? Absolutely. I never want for compliments with him. It's just that . . . in the past, a certain someone said I didn't look the best in bright and bold colors, and I think it has taken a toll on me," she replied in a diplomatic tone.

Not to mention all the backhanded comments she'd received over the years.

"You look good for a dark-skinned girl" had been an oldie but goodie, tossed like a delicious treat from the young and old. Or, *"You look like a dark-skinned Barbie doll."*

The you look gorgeous or nice compliment without the descriptor of dark skin had been rare.

"Hmmm. Well, that person must not have the sense the good Lord gave them. I've seen you in bright and bold colors."

Olivia nodded. She needed to work on validating herself. The other day, when she told Anderson about her thoughts on changing her hair, she held her breath, expecting him to say something cutting.

He hadn't. He just smiled and said she looked beautiful no matter how she styled her hair.

"So where are we off to?" she asked, effectively changing the subject.

"I want to see if Bea is home. If so, I'm happy to make introductions. We can shoot for the grocery store if her little storefront isn't open."

"Where is it located?"

"Her home is about a two-mile walk to the end of Havens Beach. The old convent."

"Oh! It's the place Whitney pointed out the other day. I can't wait to meet her."

"Now again, I advise you to approach Bea with caution. I tried to call ahead but she doesn't really use a phone. She won't take kindly to our tracking her down. She's a little prickly and very private."

Olivia nodded. "Absolutely. If her shop isn't open, I can purchase her products at the grocery store."

Mr. Whittingham parked near the curb on the street. "There it is." He pointed to the white-and-green three-story cottage-style home. They got out of the car and walked up the sandy pathway leading up to the home.

Olivia had expected a compound with darkened windows. But instead, it was a stunning cliffside home with a large wraparound porch along the main floor. There were too many large and opened windows to count. Olivia immediately recognized the French-style mansard roofs, which typically belied living quarters, likely housing the unwed Catholic girls.

"It's beautiful."

"It is." He nodded. "But it doesn't look like Bea has opened her shop. We can swing by the store."

Though Olivia nodded, she stood rooted in place.

"Can you tell me about my father? My real . . ."

"Oh, yes. He went by CJ back then."

Olivia shook her head. "I had no idea."

"Mhmm. He shortened his name the second summer he visited Sag Harbor. I think he was around nine years old. Oh, he was so funny. Every day, he wore a name tag and in big red letters: CJ. He was a twin."

"I thought so!" Olivia said, remembering the photo.

"Well, he always wanted his separate identity. He hated it when folks mixed them up. But if you knew them, you could easily tell them apart. CJ was taciturn, even as a child. He liked his own company unless it came to the ladies."

"Really?" Olivia scrunched her nose. That hadn't sounded like the man her dad's old friends had talked about. They claimed Cindy was the love of his life, and he was the life of the party. Maybe he'd changed as an adult.

"What else?"

"He loved music. He played the trumpet and piano. While his twin—"

"What's his name?" Olivia wanted to know her uncle's name. She had a feeling Cindy wouldn't readily share the information.

"Gosh, I can't remember his name." He cleared his throat like he had a humongous lump in it. "Chuck or Cameron . . . something like that. Started with a C. I'm afraid I wasn't as close to his brother."

"Do you have a picture or . . . any documents I could reference?"

"Absolutely. I'll get that to you." He grinned. "You remind me of him."

"Really? Because I look like him?" Olivia knew she wasn't the life of the party, but she didn't love the idea that people thought of her as reserved.

Mr. Whittingham shook his head. "You keep things close to the chest, but you care. It's all in the eyes."

"My eyes?"

"You've got lots of stories in there. And so many more to be told, Olivia."

Olivia didn't ask what he meant by that. She looked straight ahead and then asked, "Where is Bea's storefront located?" Olivia didn't spot a retail area.

"Sometimes she sets up a booth in the driveway."

"A booth?"

"It's like a lemonade stand. But for hair."

"Oh. And you . . . know someone who uses her products?"

"Kara and Addy, as far as I know."

Olivia raised an eyebrow. From the few encounters she'd had with her neighbor, he seemed to have the ear of all the neighbors in SANS. But Olivia found it hard to believe he knew their hair routine. Olivia guessed her face look incredulous because Mr. Whittingham laughed.

"Addy catered the launch party for Bea's hair care line. All the ladies brag about the quality of her products. She's something like a wizard when it comes to creating natural remedies, like tonics, medicines . . . you name it."

Olivia laughed. "Back in the day, they would've called her a witch." The term reminded her of Ama's notorious epithet, the Witch of Wall Street.

"I'm not a witch."

Olivia jumped, clutching her chest.

A woman stood just a few yards behind Olivia. The woman seemed to appear out of nowhere.

She didn't look as angry as the tone of her voice.

"I . . . I didn't mean you are a witch. I was simply commenting about—"

"Someone you don't know."

She looked over Olivia's shoulder. "What are you doing here, bringing strangers to my home?"

"This is Olivia Jones. She's new in town and I told her about your Abeja line. Olivia, this is Bea."

Bea. Olivia noticed that no last name was given. From the way she stood, legs spread apart, arms folded, well to be fair, she held glass bottles with what looked like honey. Bea looked to be in her late thirties with cheekbones as sharp as diamonds, perfectly round lips, and golden skin. The baseball cap covered a head full of two strand twists that hung past her waist. The bill of the battered baseball cap was pulled down so low that Olivia could barely see the top of her face, but it did nothing at all to block her beauty.

Bea sighed. "I sell most of my products at the grocery store now." Her voice was much softer and reverent when she addressed Mr. Whittingham.

"Yes, but we just wanted to see if you were selling today. Answer hair questions and all of that."

Bea rolled her eyes. "C'mon. I've got some things out back."

Olivia and Mr. Whittingham followed Bea, who walked at a brisk pace toward her backyard.

"Guess I'm getting my steps in," Mr. Whittingham said and winked at Olivia.

Suddenly, Olivia wasn't as excited to meet the infamous Bea. When Olivia rounded the corner, her disdain for Bea was eclipsed by her stunning yard. Rows of perennial herbs including lavender and white sage covered the yard. The highly aromatic smell of mint hit her before she noticed the small, spiked leaves. She led Olivia and Mr. Whittingham up four steps into a sunroom. Rows of white cabinets and amber-colored bottles of all sizes were neatly lined on the shelves.

On the counter below were bottles of Everclear grain alcohol and another bottle of hundred-proof alcohol that Olivia couldn't easily identify by the plain blue label.

"I'm not an alcoholic. It's for tinctures," Bea whispered while reaching for blue bottles out of the lower yellow cabinet.

"Tinctures?" Olivia asked.

"Chamomile. Gingko, Milk thistle."

"O-okay." Olivia nodded, though she was out of her element. Though no one would mistake this for a professional lab, it had all the makings of one with a homey feel including an unfinished slab of wood that stood alongside the wall. Just below the pristine white cabinets were shelves painted yellow with a mixture of flowers, swirly designs.

It was very whimsical. But the woman who stood in front of Olivia—her eyes cast low, tattooed arms, tank top, shorts, and combat boots—didn't strike Olivia as whimsical. She had the look of a doomsayer with a bunker and ten years' supply of dried-out food beneath her house.

Bea handed her three light blue bottles.

"Is this good for transitioning hair?"

"It's good for your current texture. You use chemicals, right?" She spat out the word "chemicals" as if Olivia worked for a power plant that dumped toxic waste in the local river.

"Yes, but I haven't relaxed my hair in months."

"Good for you." Bea pumped her fist, but it wasn't done sarcastically. "You'll need this deep conditioner," she said point to one of the bottles. "It's good for keeping your hair hydrated. Lots of goodness here like jojoba oil and green tea." She then pointed to the taller bottle. "Leave-in hair oil. You really will need to use this to stop breakage." She pointed to the last bottle. "Co-wash. We'll wait for the hair milk. And let's see . . ." she tapped her finger on her bottom lip. "I'll give you a bottle of shampoo, too. No sulfates, of course."

"Of course." Olivia surveyed the bottles Bea had placed on the counter.

"I'll grab you a bag." Bea pulled out a blue recyclable bag from under the cabinet.

"Thank you," Olivia said as Bea stuffed the bags. "How much do I owe you?"

"One hundred and twenty-five dollars."

"Do you accept credit cards?" Olivia reached in her purse.

"No."

She paused reaching for her wallet. "Any sort of payment apps?"

"No. Cash only here. You could use other flexible payments at say . . . the grocer."

Olivia clapped her hands. "So sorry, but I don't carry cash."

"I thought you were a bigwig finance person?"

"I am. And yet I don't carry cash. May I come by later to pay you? I don't have to take the products now. I can return later—"

"No. Take it. I'll come to your place for payment."

"Sure . . . I'll give you my address."

She waved Olivia off like a pesky fly. "I'll find you."

Mr. Whittingham waved as he hustled outside. "I'll be seeing you, Bea."

"I suspect you will," she answered with a smile.

"Don't be a stranger now," Mr. Whittingham said. "Come into town every once in a while, or else I'll get a new walking partner."

Olivia shook her head as she followed Mr. Whittingham outside.

Once they returned to his car, she let out a long sigh. "That was nice of her to trust me to pay her back."

"Oh, well, there's no real reason not to. We all know each other well. We trust our neighbors."

"She trusts . . . me?" Olivia highly doubted his statement.

"She trusts me, therefore that trust extends to you." He nodded. "What are your plans for the evening, young lady?"

"Anderson wants to take me out to dinner."

"Oh." Mr. Whittingham laughed.

"Why the laugh?"

"Oh, I think Garrett just brought out the competitor in Anderson."

"I'm not some prize."

"You aren't a possession, but make no mistake—you are a prize."

Olivia looked at the passing scenery in the window.

"Would you like a recommendation?"

"For tonight? I would love it."

"You're young, beautiful, and smart. SANS is a great place to discover who you are. That's what your father did . . . from a kid to an adult, he took time for himself. You should do the same."

Olivia crossed her arms. "That's not the advice I was looking for."

Mr. Whittingham smirked. "Fine. Bell & Anchor has great oysters and tender scallops."

"That's better."

CHAPTER 9

A TOAST TO THE GOOD LIFE

June 2021

Olivia had not taken Mr. Whittingham's advice because Anderson had already made their date reservations for DOPO La Spiaggia, a small Italian restaurant. It had been a perfect choice for a romantic evening out in town, and it had been one of the few restaurants Olivia hadn't ordered to-go in the past few months. The veal shanks in the osso buco were cooked to perfection. When Olivia asked for a wine recommendation that paired well with the veal, Anderson had jumped in before the server could speak, and recommended Barbaresco, a delicious dry red wine.

"Our sommelier recommends the Bruno Giacosa Falletto, sir. Would you like to try?"

Anderson nodded and the server poured a sample into his glass.

"Rich, earthy, full-bodied." Anderson stared deeply into Olivia's eyes. "It's very good."

"You know your wine," Olivia complimented after sipping her glass of wine. "I remember when I met you, that I couldn't even get a glass of rosé."

Anderson flushed. "That's because my gig was in a hole in the wall. One day I'll perform all over the world and you know what that means?"

"What does that mean?"

"No more shitty wine for you."

Olivia laughed. "The drink was subpar but the company . . . top notch." She lifted her glass toward him, toasting to his success.

The delicious wine and meal mellowed her mood. They were back to Olivia and Anderson of old, good wine, good conversation, and amazing chemistry.

After finishing dinner, Olivia suggested they walk off their food. Anderson smiled, with a glint in his eyes that conveyed he'd rather "work out" back home.

Olivia squeezed his hand. "You know, we've never really strolled around the shops before. And I could really go for a sorbet." It was a warm and perfect summer night. She didn't want it to end.

"Sorbet?" Anderson sighed. Olivia frowned because it was so very unlike him.

"Well, if you don't want to, then—"

"Okay, sure. Where is it?" Anderson scanned the area.

"Right past the ASK office." Olivia pointed at the pink-and-blue wooden sign suspended above the door.

Anderson groaned. "Why don't we pick some up from the store?"

"It'll only take five minutes." Olivia looked around, as if someone had followed them.

"What are *you* looking at?" Anderson asked.

"Just checking to see if we have paparazzi tailing us. You don't seem comfortable around here."

"Well, I . . ." His ringing cell phone cut him off. Anderson's eyes grew wide when he saw his agent's name flash across the screen. "It's Drew." He lifted a finger. "One sec."

Olivia nodded. When she turned around to give him a modicum of privacy, she noticed a father and daughter, hand in hand, skipping into the ice cream parlor. The father bent his head low to listen to the young girl. Olivia smiled. The little girl waved and yelled, "Hello!"

Olivia looked around, making sure she was the person the little girl addressed.

As the father straightened his body froze as if tendrils of ice were locked inside him.

Garrett.

He looked as if he just stepped out of work in a pressed periwinkle shirt, khakis, and loafers. Last time she'd seen Garrett standing under the sunrise, but he looked no less handsome under the bright lights scattered along the street.

The stuffy summer air cocooned Olivia's body but looking at Garrett shot bolts of lightning beneath her skin, slicking her skin with sweat.

Is it a fever? She touched her forehead but it felt cool to the touch.

Olivia fanned herself, as if to waft her desire into another direction.

Garrett stared at her unflinchingly, while his daughter tugged his hand and yelled hello even louder.

He didn't look awestruck this time.

He even shook his head a little, gave her another small *pained* smile, and topped it off with a neighborly two-finger greeting.

The osso buco felt like solid gold plates in her stomach. She cradled her abdomen and did an about-face turn toward Anderson.

Her fiancé grinned and mouthed, "Good news." Anderson covered the phone with his hand. "My screenplay's been green-lit."

"Really?" Garrett's disappointed face vanished and was replaced with Anderson's excited face.

"Yes. Lots of details. Hate to cut this short, but could we do dessert later?"

Olivia nodded, but then stopped. "I really want that sorbet. You go home, I'll grab a rideshare."

"Rideshare? Are you . . . are you sure?"

"Yes. Of course. When you get home, chill the champagne. We have lots to celebrate."

Anderson bent down and kissed her. "Love you. Talk soon." Anderson turned and hurried down the street.

When Olivia turned around, Garrett and his daughter had disappeared.

Olivia hurried down the street and into the ice cream parlor. Garrett and his daughter stood in the line with their desserts in hand, ready to pay the cashier. He had a simple vanilla cone dipped in chocolate fudge. His daughter had a cup of ice cream. Olivia couldn't make out the flavor due to the mountain of rainbow sprinkles.

"Look, Daddy. It's the pretty lady."

"Yes. There she is." His smile spread in an easy, practiced way.

"Hi, Garrett." Olivia's voice didn't waver, and she was glad. She hoped he didn't think she followed him. She wanted the sorbet and to give her fiancé space to plan. Nothing more.

"Hello, Olivia." His warm voice covered her like honey butter.

She rubbed her arms, as if she could wipe away the imagined sensation.

"And who is this gorgeous young lady beside you?"

"I am Zora Alice Brooks." Her two front teeth were missing, giving her an adorable lisp.

"What a powerful name, Zora."

When Zora nodded, her braids curled at the tips, bounced with the motion. "I'm five years old." She raised one hand and wiggled the fingers for Olivia to count.

Olivia bent low, pretending to count Zora's fingers. "Very nice. Five is such a fun age."

"Thank you, Miss Olivia." She picked her up spoon and scooped up ice cream. "Want some?" she offered.

"No, thank you. I'm going to order a lemon sorbet."

"Good choice," Garrett agreed. He leaned over and whispered something to the girl behind the counter, who giggled into her hand.

"We're going to sit in the corner over there," he pointed to the small table with four chairs. "If you and . . . your guy want to join us?"

"It'll just be me tonight. And y-yes, that would be lovely. Just give me a moment to order."

"Of course." He lowered his head, licking his ice cream. Olivia peeped at the pink flickering over the chocolate ice cream cone.

The erotic maneuver lit her up like lightning in a summer storm. Olivia turned around, squeezed her eyes shut, fortifying her jolted body. She didn't realize she'd been fanning herself, until a teenager girl said, "I know, right?" She cheesed from the counter.

My goodness, Olivia would not give into her hormones like the child in front of her. Olivia squeezed her fanning hand into a fist. "It's just hot in here."

"Really? We keep the shop around sixty-five degrees."

Olivia cleared her throat. "Well, the air from outside is making it hotter," Olivia replied hoping the girl in front of her would shut it.

The girl snorted and whispered, "No, that dude just made it hotter."

"I'll have the lemon sorbet, please. One scoop, in a cup."

The teenager dropped her smile. "All right then." She rolled her eyes and rolled out the sorbet. "Anything else?"

"No, thank you." Olivia pulled out her card.

"Oh, the hot dude said he would pay for you. No worries."

"Oh, that's okay. I'd rather pay you now, in case he forgets . . ."

"That's okay. I'll remind him." The teenager smiled before she turned her back to Olivia.

When Olivia turned around, his eyes were already on her. She lifted her cup and toasted him, as if it were champagne instead of sorbet.

When she arrived at their table, she thanked him.

"You're welcome."

"How are you . . . holding up?" Olivia asked after she settled into the open chair near Zora.

"Not great." He glanced at his daughter, who happily swung her legs, while eating her ice cream. "She was a great mom. She held me together when Dana, my late wife, died."

"I'm so sorry." Olivia had meant it. He'd lost his wife and now his mother. She studied him—not as a woman deeply attracted to a man, but as human being whose pain was evident.

"Distract me," he requested suddenly.

"W-what?"

He slowly scanned Olivia. "Tell me about yourself."

Olivia chuckled. "You haven't heard everything between Addy, Whitney, Kara, and Mr. Whittingham?"

"I'm not interested in their interpretations. I've always been more of a primary source, man."

"I'm twenty-eight years old."

"Not as fun as five."

"Fewer bills for sure," Olivia giggled.

My God, I'm giggling. She scooped up more sorbet and let the cool of the lemon flavor settle the heat stirring inside of her.

"For sure," he agreed, before licking ice cream from his cone.

Chocolate from the fudge lingered on his tongue, and she wondered what it would be like to be on the receiving end. She stuffed more sorbet in her mouth, closed her eyes, counting to five.

People count when they have anxiety and dirty thoughts, right?

"I don't know if we have enough time to talk about me."

He looked down at his classic, round silver watch with a sapphire face. "How about ten minutes?" he tapped his watch.

"I like your watch." She'd considered buying something similar for Anderson as a Christmas gift. "Do you mind sharing the brand?

It's Swiss, right?" The sapphire-colored crystal fabrication led to her assumption. Olivia reached out to get a closer look.

Garrett flipped his hand to block the watch. "I don't want your guy wearing the same thing."

"I would never—"

"Ten minutes to tell me all things Olivia. Tick tock of a watch you'll never see up close again." From his stern tone, she could tell he meant it. Though the curve of his lips softened the steel in his voice.

Garrett set up a tablet for Zora, who happily played an interactive learning game that included numbers and the alphabet.

They talked and Olivia told him the typical things she did for her nine-to-five. She said nothing about Anderson or therapy or Omar and Chris or Cindy.

But she knew deep down, he would listen, and he would enjoy doing so. Maybe it was his relaxed stance, leaning in, occasionally eating his ice cream so it wouldn't melt into a puddle. Or the way his eyes never left her face. He seemed enraptured by her background, smiling at stories of her summers in Oak Bluffs. Sometimes he broke the lull of conversation with a joke or a smile, when Olivia scrambled mentally to keep things light and upbeat, but then dark memories invaded her thoughts.

"Surely it's been ten minutes."

He leaned far away and looked at his watch.

"Oh, stop it. I won't sneak a peek."

"Oh, yes you will. You are still the same girl who took photographic evidence of her godsister sneaking out." He threw the story she shared about her younger godsister back in her face.

"I didn't share it." She only threatened to share it, if Billie didn't teach her how to swim—something she didn't know how to do because Cindy didn't want to deal with her hair.

"It's been twenty minutes."

"I've distracted you enough. It's your turn to tell me about your-self, please."

"Me?" Garrett pointed to his chest. "I'm boring."

"I doubt it. Okay, fine, tell me about your work. I get at least ten minutes, too."

He smiled before responding. "I'm a real estate attorney. I live in Ridgewood, New Jersey."

"I've heard of it, but I've never been there."

"It's not far from your beloved New York, a train ride and trans-fer, but my wife liked the quiet. She needed the quiet in the end." He nodded as if to convince himself he'd made a good choice.

"And the schools?" Olivia asked, happy to return the favor by pulling him away from the dark.

"Top notch. Zora is excited about kindergarten."

"I'm soooo 'cited." She looked up from her game and wiped at the ice cream mustache around her mouth.

"And you'll make a lot of friends," Olivia said.

"Mhmm. Lots and lots and lots because I'm nice."

"And then you'll get to spend summers out here. What a lucky girl." She directed the last comment at Garrett.

"Well . . ." Garrett shrugged. "I'm thinking about selling." He polished off the rest of his cone.

"Selling?"

"To ASK."

Olivia gasped and immediately regretted the gregarious reaction. But goodness, Whitney would be gutted. "You haven't told Whit-ney, or Mr. Whittingham, I presume?"

"Oh, no. Whitney would kill me."

"I've heard ASK has been fairly . . . aggressive. Not to mention they're gentrifying the area." Thankfully Olivia hadn't received any of the flyers her neighbors had often complained about.

Garrett nodded. "The area is changing, and I hate that—"

"And it will continue to change if we keep handing over the keys to our community."

"Who's getting our keys, Daddy?"

"No one right now, baby."

He lowered his voice, whispered, "I'm comfortable, financially, but I have to worry about retirement vehicles, about Zora's future and my current mortgage. All on a single income. Sure, Mom left a little something, but I'd like to save that for college or . . ." he stopped speaking. Something weird came over his face.

"Or?"

"A wedding."

"What if she doesn't want to get married?"

"Then she can use it for a home."

"She already has a home, nestled in a lovely community and life-long friends," she argued, thinking of Addy and Kara.

"You're very passionate, Olivia Jones."

Olivia was steady and staid—the perfect personality for a financial wizard. Which is why no one said that of her, not even Anderson.

But Garrett wasn't Anderson. She needed to put some distance between them—to allow her infatuation to cool.

"Just doing my job. Whitney would have my head if I didn't defend the homestead. Listen, I . . . realize that we don't really know each other, but instead of selling to ASK, be thoughtful in who you sell to . . . perhaps another family who would appreciate the community."

"I will. I promise."

"Pinky promise?" Zora looked up at her dad.

"Sure."

"Ms. Olivia, he needs your pinkie." Zora wiggled in her chair.

"All right." Olivia lifted her pinkie while Garrett scooped it with his own.

"I, Garrett Brooks, pinkie swear that I'll be thoughtful about selling."

"If you decide to sell. And of course, you won't sell to ASK if you can manage it?"

"I . . ." he frowned. "Those weren't the original terms set."

Olivia shrugged. "In for a penny, in for a pound. Now what say you?"

"I say I do. I mean . . . I will."

Olivia tried to remove her finger, but he tightened his around hers. "While I have your hand, can you help me out with the Fourth of July fundraiser?"

"What's that?"

"I'm not sure but Addy and Kara roped me in to hosting it at my house. We could use your skills."

Olivia smiled. Whitney likely suspected his plans to sell the home, which is why she foisted the fundraiser on him.

She pretended not to know, and asked, "What skills of mine do you need?" Olivia narrowed her eyes.

"Your smile."

The heat inside of her broke out into a boil. "Garrett, I—"

"Why are you holding my fiancée's hand?"

Olivia snapped her head around to find her angry fiancé looming over their table.

CHAPTER 10

THERE GOES THE NEIGHBORHOOD

June 2021

If Olivia had superpowers, she would disappear at the snap of her fingers. Unfortunately, she lived in the real world and Olivia couldn't avoid her fiancé and gorgeous next-door neighbor's confrontation.

Though it didn't help that she still held Garrett's finger.

Anderson pulled their hands apart, replacing Garrett's hand with his own. "We're leaving." He tugged her hand, attempting to steal her away like a child in the throes of a tantrum, and in front of little Ms. Teenager, who had a phone clutched in her hand, aimed at the unfolding scene.

In an ice cream parlor, of all places. Oh, yes. The most embarrassing moment to date.

She yanked her hand back. "Anderson, stop."

A wildfire blazed across Anderson's cheeks. "You were just holding his hand."

Garrett stood so fast, his seat toppled. "You need to calm down."

A nasally sniff followed be a loud wail froze the adults in place.

Zora's brown eyes swelled with tears. "I . . . I'm sorry. I told Daddy to pinkie swear Ms. Olivia." Zora tearfully confessed it. "Daddy wants to get rid of Granny Ruth's house and Ms. Olivia told him no and . . . and the only way to keeps a secret is to pinkie swear it.

That's what Granny said but now she's gone." Another wail ripped. Her body was tiny, but her lungs were mighty.

"Sweetie, I . . ." Garrett shot Anderson a lethal look, then returned his attention to his daughter. "I don't want to get rid of anything. Daddy's just weighing his options. I'm sure Ms. Olivia's friend—"

"Fiancé," Anderson corrected.

"I'm sure that man didn't mean to yell."

"No, I didn't." Anderson gave Zora a tight smile. "I'm sorry. Please don't be afraid of me. Enjoy your ice cream, okay?"

Olivia tugged on his elbow. "Let's go."

After they left the parlor, Olivia allowed herself ten paces, ten seconds to breathe, ten seconds to let time and distance swallow the swell of anger.

"How dare you?" Olivia stopped walking. She leaned closer and then hissed, "How. Dare. You."

"Open your eyes. He wants you, Olivia," he said, smacking his palm with the back of his hand. "And the asshole is making moves in front of his daughter."

"He's not making . . ." Olivia looked around, noticing whispers and stares pointed in their direction. "We'll talk at home." Her voice was markedly lower. She would not make another scene with Anderson.

Olivia slammed the car door and raised a hand when Anderson attempted a conversation. "No, we're not talking. Not in town, not in the car, not in the yard, inside *my* home."

The five-minute drive felt like five hours. The tension between them was so thick, she couldn't cut it with a hacksaw.

Anderson made a beeline to the living room.

Olivia grabbed the champagne from the bucket, poured it into a champagne flute, and sucked down a third of the glass. The bubbles had just passed her throat by the time she finished the entire thing.

She grabbed the bottle and another glass before joining Anderson on the opposite end of the couch.

Olivia closed her eyes and exhaled. "Congratulations on selling your screenplay."

Anderson opened his mouth, seeming to hesitate. When Olivia offered a dry smile, he replied with an unsteady, "Thanks."

"From what I understand, it had to be optioned first?"

Anderson winced. "A production company reached out a little before I met you."

Olivia bit her lips. That had to have been almost two years ago. This entire time he'd said nothing, as if it weren't a huge deal.

"Why haven't you said—"

"These things fall through all the time and I . . . I didn't want to be one of the hundreds of guys in New York who say they've got something optioned, but nothing ever comes of it."

She stared at him in silence, managing not to shout the obvious—no matter the reason, he should've told his fiancée.

Finishing a screenplay and securing an agent was a major accomplishment and something to celebrate. Yet he'd kept her in the dark.

Is he keeping other secrets? Does he really love me?

She clenched her jaw, determined not to voice her thoughts. Determined not to let the power of gravity pull her self-esteem any lower.

Tucking her hands behind her back, she calmed her chaotic thoughts.

"Did you know this is the first summer I haven't been with my Ama and my godsisters?"

Anderson shook his head. "No," he answered quietly.

"I'm twenty-eight years old and every summer, Ama made sure I cleared my schedule: three weeks with no work, everyone at my job knew June and July were off the books for anything major. Every Christmas and Thanksgiving holiday, Cindy insisted we spend it together. You've met my mother. Can you imagine the two of us stuck in a room with too much food and a ten-foot Christmas tree?"

"Your mom is . . . interesting for sure." Anderson's voice is much more relaxed. He grabbed the champagne bottle and poured into the empty flute Olivia had left on the table.

"Omar may have bought me this house." Olivia waved a hand. "But I'm making it a home. Omar may have left a card with Mr. Whittingham, but I'm cultivating the friendship. And sometimes, I think Omar helped me find you during a time that I desperately needed someone." Olivia's voice dropped to a low whisper. "But I won't allow you or anyone to make demands on my life. Not when I'm so close to figuring out what I need."

Olivia stood. "Please enjoy the rest of the champagne. I'm going to bed . . . by myself."

"What about what I want?"

Olivia shrugged. "From my point of view, it seems like you've done exactly what you've always wanted to do."

"No, what I want is to get out of here. And when are we leaving, Olivia? It's nearly July."

Olivia shrugged. "Summer officially ends in late September."

"I don't want to be here forever, Olivia," he enunciated each word, as if his avoidance of town and self-imposed isolation by way of Uber hadn't been obvious enough.

Forever? The thought never occurred to her, yet the idea of making this jewel of a place her permanent home didn't scare, but rather excited her.

"I'm not in the mood for champagne. I'll sleep in the guest room tonight."

Olivia, still mute, only nodded.

She stood while he climbed the steps, never once turning back. Never once apologizing for his behavior. The little girl inside her, stuck in a tower, trapped in fear, waiting, and wanting and needing a good guy to take her hand and lead her away, retreated further inside the castle.

"There's no such thing as a knight." Something cold snaked inside of her—colder than Cindy's stare froze and shriveled her insides. It wasn't her heart, but something intangible.

Hope, maybe? Hope for an extraordinary love like her mother and father. Like Ama and Omar. Like Billie and Dulce.

Or maybe those relationships weren't that extraordinary. Maybe they endured because they didn't give up on each other—they put in the work.

Hope and dread, pain and wanting, spun in a blender, but the ingredients didn't mix.

She couldn't make sense of anything, couldn't figure out the right answer, or the right path to follow.

Dr. LaGrange's sage words popped into her head. *"If you write how you feel, the clarity will come."*

Olivia grabbed her notebook and, just as Dr. LaGrange asked, documented her day. Within the margins, she noted how she felt.

Earlier in the day, she'd been hopeful about their date. But when she saw Garrett, she felt something light her from the inside. What's the best emoji and expression for fireworks? It was far better than a smiley face.

Now, recounting in her journal what had happened, she felt mortification. Again, much more complicated than a frowning face.

"What a mess." Olivia flipped through her journal, determined to find her last moment of happiness. A part of her wanted to extract her diary, add it to an excel spreadsheet and crunch the data into a business intelligence tool to understand the trends.

A tool wasn't necessary. She could clearly see through the flip of a page. She was happiest walking with Mr. Whittingham or at girl's night with Whitney, Kara, and Addy. Or during Sunday phone calls with her godsisters.

Lately, there hadn't been any smiling faces with Anderson. He hadn't been around enough to make her smile.

With time, could he be this infamous knight in shining armor? Resentment stirred in her stomach at the thought of the term. It was as if Omar had planted the seed and it germinated within her thoughts.

She slammed the journal closed. "This is ridiculous."

Omar isn't here, but Anderson is.

Anderson took her to view the storage room Omar had created. He'd even dressed in all black to convey the seriousness of the event.

Anderson served the community by helping the elders with their groceries and medicines.

Anderson held her as she cried over Omar's lifelong secret.

Most importantly, he thought she was beautiful. He told her all the time.

"He's a good guy. This is just . . . a rough patch." The excuse wafted toward her like perfume. Olivia stuffed her damning journal into her purse and grabbed the champagne and glasses—this time the champagne coupe glasses.

She marched upstairs and found Anderson furiously texting someone on his phone. When she stormed into the guest room, he turned over his phone and tossed it on the nightstand. Olivia stared at him for a moment, wanting to demand he tell her who he'd been texting. But her poor reaction would be as bad as his, and that would solve nothing.

"Congratulations . . . again." She offered him a glass as if it were an olive branch.

He stood and took the glass. "This is driving me crazy."

"What is?"

"I'm miserable."

Olivia flinched. Sure, they'd had some tense moments these past few weeks, but she thought Anderson was happy. She hung her head, waiting for him to air the laundry list of her undesirable qualities.

"I should be on top of the world celebrating with my fiancée, but I'm jealous and I feel stupid for my reaction. But I am jealous, Olivia. I can't help how I feel."

"What can I do to make you feel better?"

"Stop seeing him."

His simple request tasted toxic. "He's my neighbor, Anderson."

"*Our* neighbor, Olivia. I'm willing to try if you are." He laughed, but she knew his genuine laugh because he laughed often. This wasn't ha-ha funny. This was guttural.

"That's not something to joke about, Anderson. I like it here. You really embarrassed me."

"When did I embarrass you? Was it the Uber Eats deliveries? The no shoes?" He exhaled hard, his voice going steely. "Or the fact that I'm white."

"No, Anderson. You attempted to drag me out of a very public place and in front of a little girl. When she recalls a relationship, that scary scene may very well be top of mind for Zora, and I hate that."

"I know. I . . . hate that, too."

"I'm here toasting you. I'm trying to celebrate you, in vain. You are determined to stay in a poor mood."

"I don't like this."

"Don't like what, Anderson?"

"You're making me out to be the bad guy."

"No, I'm not. This isn't about being good or bad. I'm simply asking that you try in this moment to be proud of your accomplishments. I'm asking that you drop your jealousy."

"I'm sorry." Anderson sighed. "I know you aren't a fan of food and drinks in the bedroom. Can you give me a moment and I'll meet you downstairs?"

Olivia glanced at his phone. "Are you texting your agent?"

"Um, yeah. Still nailing down contractual details." His tone was tense and tight.

He's lying. I know he's lying.

Olivia's heart ached. She rubbed at her chest, hoping this wasn't the beginning of their end. "Okay, Anderson. I believe in you."

His eyes flared at her statement.

After returning downstairs, she quickly grabbed her notebook and made a note of her feelings.

Sadness, deep abiding sadness.

Ten minutes later, Anderson came down, glass in hand. They toasted and drank. They did not look at each other. And when they finally went to bed, they did not make love.

Olivia's attraction to Garrett and Anderson's jealousy formed a wedge between them. But it was the lie Anderson told that cracked their bond, setting Olivia adrift.

It had been two weeks since the freeze-out, as Billie had jokingly called it.

Two weeks since Anderson had said a kind word. They'd become polite roommates—simply informing the other of their where-abouts. Before Anderson had left to meet his agent in the city, he politely provided details regarding his screenplay. It was a semi-autobiographical spoof of his life. White guy from an affluent family forgoes his wealth to become a comedian. He moves in with his poorer relatives and eventually becomes a better person.

"Of course, I didn't come from a rich family," Anderson quickly rushed on to explain when Olivia asked which parts were true.

"But I've learned and grown through comedy. You've got to listen and observe to be a good comedian. But what makes you better than all the rest is when you expose the parts that make us sad, flip it, and turn it to triumph."

Something soft fluttered inside of Olivia's stomach. She could practically taste his passion for comedy. It quickened the cadence of his words and strengthened his tone when he described his goal to convey hope and self-discovery. He later asked Olivia if this would be something she'd watch and she replied, "Of course, because it's yours."

He smiled, the curve of his lips an inch lower than usual. It occurred to Olivia that it wasn't the answer he wanted to hear.

Olivia understood she missed the mark and there was a gap between her statement and his expectation, but they weren't at a point where they understood each other's silences. As Dr. LaGrange had nicely stated, "If he can write a screenplay, he can communicate his feelings."

In their last session, Dr. LaGrange had pointed out that Olivia tended to preemptively defend Anderson while putting down her own communications style. Olivia knew it had mostly been because of defending Anderson from her godsisters earlier in their relationship, and recently the guilt she'd felt for her attraction to Garrett.

Soon the object of her infatuation, along with her guilt, would move away. Just yesterday, she spotted a *For Sale* sign near the end of the yard.

Olivia felt equal parts elated and deflated.

Garrett was gorgeous, but inconvenient. She didn't need his secret smiles, his waves, his adorable little girl skipping along and yelling "Hey, pretty lady!" to Olivia every time she stepped outside on the deck to watch the water.

Nor did she need Anderson breathing down her neck, watching and waiting for her to screw up. Never, in her twenty-eight years, had she done anything brash. She was determined not to break her record.

A knock on the door broke into her reverie. Whitney stood on the other side in her usual armor of oversized designer glasses, linen pants, and a gorgeous teal shirt that crisscrossed in the front and back.

"Hey, Whitney."

"Hey. If you're busy, I don't have to come in."

"No, no, that's fine." Olivia stepped back to let her in. She offered her unexpected guest juice, tea, coffee or water. It was too early for wine and Olivia had work to do. Whitney declined it all and sat on the sofa.

"I see your boy is moving."

"Anderson? No, he's just in New York with his agent."

"I'm talking about Garrett. Did you see that For Sale sign in his yard?"

"Yes," Olivia nodded. "I spoke to him, and he assured me he would try to sell it to a family who—"

"Please. He needs to stay here and let little Zora grow up with friends and family. She'll especially need us without a mother figure in her life."

"Maybe, but that's really his decision. I'm sure he's carefully considered his options."

Whitney shrugged. "We're losing this community. Back in 2009 guess what the demographics were for SANS?"

Olivia shrugged. "Seventy percent Black, thirty percent white."

"Wrong. We were a hundred percent Black." She emphasized the B in Black as if she were giving a phonetics lesson. "Now we make up only sixty-five percent."

"Twelve years? That's alarming."

"It is! Now we've got ASK and other greedy-ass people who can't afford the other towns trying to encroach on our property. I'm no longer interested in letting them feel comfortable when they're out here stealing our piece of the pie. We've got to fight back."

"But how?" Olivia shook her head. It wasn't as if they could harass their neighbors to sell. Neither Olivia nor Whitney could look into their pocketbooks.

"I'm thinking through some options. But I think the first steps are education." The way she nodded, Olivia had a feeling her realtor friend had no actual plan. "We're dealing with your generation, mostly. The elders understand legacy and if they sell, they're more mindful of who they sell to," Whitney pointed out bluntly. "What would make the difference to you?"

Olivia considered her words. She truly wasn't the target demographic. Ama and Omar had changed the trajectory of her life, down to the neighborhood and schools she attended from elementary to grad school.

"It's hard to say. I've lived a different life."

"Ah, don't tell me you're a trust-fund kid?"

"No." Olivia shook her head. "I just lived a very charmed life."

"Charmed is fine, but it's still your generation. You aren't a little old lady, so tell me, what are the best channels or avenues to reach out? Is social media the best way, email, video, hell, a brochure?"

Olivia thought about how she wooed some of her younger clients, who were still at least a decade older. Everyone knew you fished where the fish were. Her clientele swam anywhere from uber-exclusive clubs to schools and sorority networks. However, the common denominator was that everyone, be they wealthy or not, enjoyed being wined and dined.

"What about a garden party? We could block off the neighborhood and station tables along the street. Perhaps we can have it catered, but we can ask neighbors about their favorite foods? Something nostalgic they cooked with their family here in SANS."

"Oh, Olivia. You are on fire, girl."

Olivia smiled. "We can include videos and pictures of then and now. Let's tell the story and history through our own experiences. Once they understand the importance, I think that will at least address the issues of selling to ASK. But having access to money, well, that's a different story."

Whitney snapped her fingers. "Then I'll invite people with money as well. I have a list of potential buyers I can hit up. So, are you in?"

"To plan? Sure."

"Planning and securing those interviews. While we're filming, we should ask why they plan to sell."

"That's a superb idea. If you think they're open to it, a survey to track sentiment could prove extremely impactful."

"Whatever you say, Ms. Jones." Whitney smiled, clutching her purse. "I'll reach out to Mr. Whittingham next. He's a master at getting folks to volunteer for things they don't want to do. Addy and Kara are in, I'm sure. I think we should shoot for Labor Day weekend. That can be our kickoff event before everything else rolls out. We need everyone alert and sober, so it's best to do it at the start of the weekend."

"That'll give us about two months to plan. I think we can do it, besides the Fourth of July fundraiser."

"Thanks, girl." Whitney stood. "I'll be going now. I feel much better after speaking to you."

"I'm glad."

Whitney's hand lingered on the doorknob.

"Olivia?"

"Yes?"

"I'm so glad you're here. We need people like you."

"Oh, I'm not doing much." She waved off her neighbor. No, her friend. She warmed at the thought.

"You're a problem solver. You're smart and kind, though you like to pretend to be an ice queen."

Do I? Olivia sighed. She never once pretended to be an ice queen, she just wasn't overly warm. Between Cindy and Ama, she'd gotten it honestly.

"I'll be in touch soon. Thanks." Whitney tossed a smile over her shoulders before she left.

Olivia's smile dropped. She wasn't sure how she had gotten herself involved in everyone's agenda when she couldn't figure out her own life.

CHAPTER 11

BUSY BEE

June 2021

As Olivia stretched for her morning jog, she heard a chirpy voice whisper, "Pretty Lady. Hey!"

She heard a voice near Garrett's yard but didn't see a body.

"I right here!" The lid from an olive green container lifted, revealing Zora.

Olivia crouched beside her. "What's going on? Where's your father?"

"Shhh. He'll hear you. We're playing hide-and-seek."

Olivia nodded, looking around for Garrett. She was fairly certain he did not want his daughter hiding outside.

"Zora!" Garrett's panicked voice boomed.

Zora giggled behind her hand but remained hidden. Olivia popped up from her position.

"Come back!" Zora hissed.

"Don't worry. I'm just saying hello, so he doesn't find you."

Olivia hurried toward Garrett, who paced the yard. "Hey." She rushed to him. "It's okay. She's over there, hiding from you in the storage box."

"I told her to never go outside and—"

Olivia shushed him. "I told Zora I wouldn't give away her hiding place. Just walk with me and you'll find her." She reached for his hands and squeezed, though it looked like he needed a hug. "You can reprimand her after you *find* her."

He sighed. "I want to do it now."

"If you do that, I lose the cool neighbor points. Then she won't trust me."

He nodded. "Oh, Zora! Come out, come out wherever you are!"

A snicker echoed from the box.

Garrett let out an exhale, shaking his head. "Hope you aren't outside. That's not allowed."

"I in the house. The yard's the house," Zora answered teasingly, though she remained hidden.

Olivia bit her lip, attempting to hide her smile. Zora was too smart, too cute, and probably too much trouble.

"I said stay inside." Garrett kept his voice light. "Which means no more hide-and-seek if you don't listen."

Zora lifted the lid and popped out. "Here I am!"

Olivia gasped, pretending to be surprised while clutching her chest. She winked at Zora, who burst out into a fit of giggles.

"Zora." Garrett strode to his daughter. "You're supposed to stay *inside* the house."

Zora dropped her head. "I sorry. Granny Ruth always found me."

Her lips trembled. Before she could full on cry, Olivia jumped in. "Why don't we all go for a walk?"

"A walk?" both daughter and father asked with incredulity.

"Yes. Let's clear our heads with the morning air."

Zora stretched her little hand in the air and waved it around. "It's not too hot and not too cold. Good for the head." She said with the sageness of an elder.

"Exactly. When I get sad or mad, I walk. After I walk, I feel much better."

"But you like to run," Garrett argued.

Olivia walked ahead of him and then turned around. "I can slow down for good company."

The trio walked down the beach. Olivia had planned to jog to Bea's place but went in the opposite direction. Zora skipped ahead, yelling her intentions to find a seashell.

"Besides working and jogging, what are you up to?" Garrett asked.

"I'm sleuthing."

"What does sleuthing entail?"

"Looking for my father's family." Olivia told him about how the Jones family summered for a few months every year until . . . until she wasn't sure. She'd have to ask Mr. Whittingham.

"Have you heard of the Jones family?" she asked in a hope-filled voice.

"No," he said and shook his head. "But that doesn't mean we can't figure it out."

"We?"

"I love a good mystery. And as an attorney, I'm naturally gifted at research and interviews. That is, if you want my help. I know you have your *fiancé*." The way he said "fiancé" sounded raw, dirty, unwelcomed.

Her fiancé was currently in New York with his agent. He knew about her intentions to find her father yet had offered no help. She shrugged away the disappointment.

"Okay, I could use your skills. Where should we start?"

"Mr. Whittingham for sure, since he said he knew your father. I'd ask for his mother's maiden name."

"Ah," Olivia snapped her finger. "I've been asking about the Jones, but maybe it's another family name if the connection is through the matriarchal line."

"Exactly. We'll document all the names he knows, make a family tree of sorts. We can ask some elders around town. Then we can go to the library and search for newspapers."

"Hmmm." Olivia nodded. "You are good at this."

"I'm a pretty resourceful guy." When he winked, Olivia looked away.

Zora returned and walked in the middle, grabbing both Olivia's and Garrett's hand.

Zora looked around and then leaned closer to Olivia. "You can hold my hand, right?" she asked in a small voice.

Guilt swarmed her stomach like a group of angry bees. "Yes. Of course."

Garrett cleared his throat. He sounded like an angry papa bear.

Olivia scrambled to change the subject. "How's the s-a-l-e going?" Olivia asked, spelling out the word.

"What's a Sally?" Zora asked.

"A person we know," Garrett quickly answered.

"She's doing okay," he said to Olivia. "Taking her time."

"I imagine Sally wants to be done by the end of summer."

"Yes. We, I mean, she needs to get ready for school."

"Oh, like me?" Zora asked, looking up at her father.

"Exactly."

"Well, tell her to think about what I said. It's important for her to find the right . . . person."

"Oh, I think she has."

The news of him leaving sank like a rock in her stomach. She stopped walking. "She did?"

Garrett and Zora stopped, his eyes grew serious. "Yes," he confirmed. "She found the perfect person. Smart, beautiful, but the person is preoccupied with someone else."

His words surrounded her, sucking the cool, clear air out of her lungs. Surely, he didn't mean her. "Then I guess Sally didn't find the right person if they're taken."

"Depends on your point of view."

She didn't want to ask, but she did. "And what's yours?"

"Feelings are free. Love should be given, not possessed."

"I . . . don't know what to say to that. To say to you."

"Don't say anything." He turned to his daughter. "Zora, is your head clear?"

"Yep!"

"Then we should go." He tugged her hand. "Let's let the pretty lady get her morning jog in."

"Okay," she said in a put-out voice, but she didn't move. "Will you come over and play with me?"

"Absolutely," Olivia promised. "Not hide-and-seek, though. I'm not good at that game."

Zora shook her head. Her half dozen plaits swung with the movement.

"I'll see you soon." Olivia waved at father and daughter and then resumed her morning routine.

During Olivia's morning jog, she diverted from her typical route and jogged toward the far side of the beach, near Bea's beachfront. She wondered if Bea's garden was as magical as the image she held in her memory. Everything from Bea's herbs to her flowers were a sensory feast. Not only that, but there was something about the woman that seemed familiar. Not in a comfortable way, but Bea felt important—like a crucial ingredient to an enigmatic recipe.

Olivia slowed when she reached the convent, taking in the green oasis in the front yard. The "green" was a combination of grass and edible herbs with sprinkles of yellow and pinks and purples, some flowers, mostly herbs used for healing. A stone walkway bisected the green, forming an arch from one end of the yard to the other.

Bea had set her storefront at the center of the walkway.

It was no less stunning than when she first laid eyes on it. But this time, Bea stood out front of the teal pop-up booth with rows of colorful jars and bottles lining the wall behind her. A few customers waited. The line of customers didn't surprise Olivia. Bea's hair products had worked wonders on Olivia's tresses, so much that the next time she returned to New York, she would bring a few bottles for her hairdresser, Travis, to sample.

When Olivia waved, Bea looked down.

She'd wait her turn.

Olivia walked along the stone walk, stopping to take in the wraparound porch. A trio of teal blue pots, the same color as her booth, sat under the bay windows. The seating options were simple with just one white wicker rocking chair and a small side table placed near a pendant light fixture mounted on the house. Olivia felt a prickling sensation along the back of her neck. She turned, finding Bea's light eyes staring at her. When Olivia pointed to the porch, Bea mouthed the word "Yes," and returned her attention to the customer standing in front of her.

Olivia climbed the four steps that looked like the recipient of a new paint job and unlike some of the houses in SANS, the sturdy steps didn't groan from age. She sat in the cushioned rocker, gliding back and forth, taking in the refreshingly charming porch with renovated railings featuring a series of diamonds and ovals that didn't block but simply enhanced the ocean view.

Nearby were a tangle of herbs in an earth-fired clay plot. Olivia took a deep breath and leaned back. She hadn't realized she drifted into a light sleep until Bea's voice broke into her white noise from the sea.

"Hey." Bea propped against the railing.

Olivia was startled. Heat, partly from the sun, mostly from embarrassment, warmed her cheeks when she took in Bea, who looked like the grumpy Mama bear who found Goldilocks in her bed.

"What are you doing here, New Girl?"

"It's Olivia. Olivia Jones."

"I know who you are," she responded. "What brings you to my side of the beach? Are you here to pay for the products?"

Olivia wanted to dig a hole in the ground and jump in. "I'm so sorry, but I forgot the cash. I . . . I wanted to ask hair questions."

"Do you not have a stylist? Because they would be the best advice for hair care."

"My stylist, Travis, is back in New York."

"You should try Dita. She's good, I hear. She uses my products for her clients."

"I'll make a note of that," Olivia promised.

Nautical knots of doubt twisted and tied in her stomach. She obviously wasn't welcome, and she wasn't sure what drove her to the apothecary's storefront. It was so unlike herself to seek someone out, but lately Olivia gravitated toward this woman who conveyed certainty. Olivia knew deep down, Bea had carefully crafted her own path and strutted it. Olivia remembered the feeling—she'd lived it. And now she desperately wanted that feeling to return.

"Well, I'm packing up now, so . . ."

"Can I help?" Olivia quickly offered.

"I, umm, yeah. Sure," she said the last word with conviction.

Olivia and Bea packed up her products and folded the table and tablecloths in silence.

"So, Mr. Whittingham tells me that your home used to be a convent?"

Bea nodded. "Yes. It was a home for young wayward girls, as they used to say. Girls who'd become pregnant without a husband."

"What made you buy this property?"

Bea stopped her folding. "You're a little nosy, aren't you, New Girl?"

"Just curious. I love the history of this area and you've made this place . . . breathtaking. I'm instantly happy when I'm here."

"Me, too." She said in a voice strong with pride. "Mother Eileen sold it to me. She worked here for fifty years."

"How did you convince her?"

A smile spread across her face. It wasn't big or bold, but small. "It didn't take much. As time moved on, as people became more progressive, there wasn't a need to steal away in the night to have a child in secret. Anyway, she persuaded the Church to sell it to someone who'd respect the history but make it their own."

"I imagine it wasn't a happy place."

Bea crossed her arms, seeming to stare at her home, but the far-away look in her eyes seemed to stare beyond the convent, miles of memories away. "When I bought the property, I could feel the melancholy and sadness. For the babies the girls gave away. For the mothers, each flower I've planted represents their fears. I wanted to turn their pain into beauty so if someone ever stumbles back to trace where they came from, I want them to realize their mamas did the best they could, that they found a magical place where they could give birth. A beautiful memory, even if they're too young to remember."

"That's . . . really wonderful." Olivia swallowed around the growing lump in her throat. "I'm sure the mothers or fathers will appreciate it, too, should they ever return."

Bea nodded. "Exactly. No sadness, no regrets for their decisions. Hopefully, they see if places can change, then people can change. You just have to give people the space and time to transform."

"And if you don't get space or time?"

Bea blinked twice, her attention firmly on Olivia. "Then you take it."

Olivia didn't know how to respond. She'd never been able to just *take*. Everything required time and order. Even her meteoric rise through her firm took time in terms of education, strategic placements and wins for clients. Wining and dining not only her clientele but her bosses to convey competence.

Bea had made it sound easy as drinking water and breathing air.

But if Olivia took what she wanted, a delicious night in the sheets with Garrett, she would hurt Anderson. Suddenly, Olivia couldn't wait to leave Bea's magical oasis.

Olivia offered her thanks and jogged back home. The sun, usually warm and generous, shone like a spotlight on her back. She couldn't outrun the rays. She couldn't outrun her thoughts. Typically, she flew across the sand, but today it slowed her pace. The dirt kicked up by her speed slid inside her socks. Though the sand was soft, it felt like a million pebbles covered her feet.

When she returned to an empty house, Bea's advice haunted her. But her voice wasn't the loudest in her head. It was her own voice that whispered what exactly she wanted. *Who* she wanted.

Garrett.

She stuffed his name, his voice, his image to the dark recess of her mind.

"No." But that voice deep, deep inside of her whispered another answer. "Yes."

With Anderson gone for a few days, she'd gotten together again with Addy, Kara, and Whitney for dinner and drinks at Whitney's home.

"New Girl." She heard a soft voice behind her.

Olivia spun on her heels and found Bea standing behind her. She had on an outfit similar to the one she wore last time. Combat boots, an off-white tank top, cargo shorts, and her light brown curly hair covered with a yellow-and-turquoise scarf. Yet even so, she looked as if she'd stepped off a runway in Milan. "Oh. Hey, you," she said with starch in her voice.

Bea's advice still weighed heavily on her mind. Perhaps this woman wasn't the key to figuring out her life. Her advice had caused some sleepless nights.

"Just a *hey*?"

"What do you mean?"

"A few days ago, you popped by unannounced. Now you're giving me the cold shoulder."

"I'm . . ." Olivia shook her head. "I apologize for my rudeness in both respects to your home and now. You'd like your money, yes?"

Olivia opened her purse. For the past few days, she'd been nervously walking around with Bea's money. Just in case.

"I didn't stop you for money, but yes, I'll take it now." Bea took the money Olivia offered and stuffed it in a storage pocket in her worn black backpack.

"Where are you off to?"

"I'm guessing, that like you, on the way to Whitney's."

"For dinner?" Speculation laced her voice. For the few months she'd been here, Bea never attended a social event.

"No, Whitney wants to talk to me about my donations for the pop-up. I'm bringing by some things for her to look over."

"Oh, nice. Your hair care line, I presume?" Olivia resumed walking and Bea followed.

"No. My world-famous honey."

"Your honey?"

"Yes. I sell it at the grocery store, too, so don't get any ideas." She wagged her finger.

Olivia refrained from rolling her eyes. Bea made her feel like a stalker. "How long have you been making honey?"

"I don't. The bees do."

"Okay, how long have you been taking care of bees who make the honey?"

"Around the same time I became an apothecary. Once I started, um, traveling, different methods fascinated me. I didn't have a lot of money to spend. I certainly didn't have health insurance, so I was on my own. From there, I discovered I liked beekeeping and being an apothecary."

"Oh, wow. Where have you been?"

Bea shot her a sharp look, but still she replied. "All over. I've forgotten more places than I've been to."

"Ah, you're a nomad." *Maybe she had to lose herself, to find herself.*

"I prefer the term 'wanderlust.' And not any longer. I've settled in this community . . . for now."

"Ah, so you plan to stay in the old convent."

Bea stuffed her hand in her pockets. "Listen, New Girl."

"Olivia," she corrected.

"I know who you are."

"Yet I know nothing about you." Olivia tried to dilute her harsh tone, but spectacularly failed.

"Why do you need to know?" Bea stopped walking. "Why are you so damn curious about me?"

"I don't need to know. I just . . ."

"You just what?" Bea's voice turned granite.

Olivia knew she'd struck a nerve. She didn't know how or why.

"I admire people who know who they are and what they want. And I'd like to understand their process and how they've achieved their success."

"It's called life experiences."

"I know but—"

"You're an analyst, right?"

Olivia found it woefully ironic that, again, Bea indeed knew much more about Olivia than she did of the cantankerous neighbor.

"Yes."

"You gather data, study things."

"That's a high-level version, but yes, a part of my job is to study patterns."

"I know this is an occupational hazard, but you can't do that to people."

"Do what?"

"Analyze them within an inch of their lives. Not everyone is an open book like Mr. Whittingham and Whitney. Not everyone likes to talk about themselves."

Olivia completely understood Bea's stance. "Okay, I won't . . . won't ask you anything else."

She increased her speed, hoping to leave Bea in the dust. The woman kept pace with her, staring at her while Olivia held her head and power-walked in silence.

"I don't think you're a bad person," Bea offered a paper-thin olive branch.

"Why, thank you," Olivia replied breathlessly in her attempted escape from Bea, and embarrassment.

"I just think you're lost."

Olivia stumbled, stopped, turning to stare at the woman. "I am not lost." She wasn't. She was well on her path to discovery. She had a therapist, a fiancé, and a new home to prove it.

Bea laughed, still keeping pace, still a thorn in Olivia's psyche.

"I know lost when I see it. I hope you find what you need, New Girl. Just know that it won't be through me. Otherwise, you'll be disappointed," Bea said, her voice as blue as her eyes.

And with that parting statement, Bea left Olivia in the dust.

CHAPTER 12

THE ORIGIN OF BEES

One of Bea's first memories at the convent was of a sad man hanging from a wooden cross. A thorny crown covered his head, which drooped to his shoulder. Blood trickled from the temples down to his brown beard. Even in his sleep, the man looked sad.

Every morning, Mother Eileen washed and starched a white cloth, and lovingly draped it around the sad man's waist.

She knew the man on the cross was important because Mother Eileen, as well as the other sisters, clasped their hands together and prayed silently, or sometimes out loud, in front of the audience of children.

Anytime the kids did anything wrong, like slide across the polished wood floors, the sisters tsked, accompanied with soft-served warnings about Jesus' disappointment.

The image, still clear in her mind, hung like a framed photo within the curves of her memory banks. It only took her forty-odd years to understand why she could recall the image so vividly. He was the first person she disappointed. Then came the nuns and later her adoptive parents.

The night before she left the convent, Mother Eileen took her to the altar one last time. She whispered, "Don't forget to pray." She pointed at sad Jesus. "He's always watching, and he wants you to do your best."

The words followed her across the country to California, into the home of her adoptive parents. For six years she used Mother Eileen's words as a mantra.

Her mother, Kathy, smiled at Bea's reflection in the mirror. "Arms straight down your side."

"Yes, ma'am." Her strong, confident voice didn't match her eleven-year-old body. She followed her mother's instruction, making sure her pleated navy skirt fell well below her fingers and her socks, determined to slouch, hit mid-calf.

"Make sure you don't wrinkle your shirt."

Bea didn't see how she could wrinkle the supremely starched white oxford shirt. Still, she nodded.

"Aren't you happy? Smile, sweet girl." Her mother had a soft, pleasant voice that rarely went past a low volume. She didn't have to. With her towering height, beautiful face and figure, people leaned in closer because they *wanted* to hear her.

Her mom's voice always put her at ease. Especially when, at five years old, the nuns packed her bags and told her to go home with the beautiful strangers who looked like her. It was her mother's low voice that said, "We're your family, Sweet Girl. I promise we're nice and we'll treat you well."

But the morning she dressed for the first day of school at Saint Celia, an all-girl's private school, she knew that even wearing the same thing wouldn't help her fit in.

"Are you afraid to make friends again?"

Bea nodded. "Yes. Girls, they don't . . . don't like me."

"They're just jealous." Her voice went snappish.

Bea wasn't so sure of that. They didn't know what to do with her or how to categorize her. She wasn't white. The thick mop of sandy brown curls gave that away. Not that Bea wanted to keep her heritage a secret. But it was the blue eyes that confounded everyone. Her family, though fair-skinned, didn't have the same color eyes. Some girls even spread a rumor that her mother had an affair with a white man. When Bea told them the truth of her adoption, and that she did not know who her biological parents were, the bullying intensified.

"Don't worry about them," her mother said, attempting to soothe her fears.

Sure. Bea snorted, but she didn't roll her eyes. If her mother didn't want her to worry about girls, then why send her to an all-girl school?

"The girls at this school are much more respectful and refined. Trust me." Her mother winked, seeming to read her mind.

She suspected her mother, a former beauty queen, was horrified her daughter struggled with girl friendships.

Her father didn't like that the boys started sniffing around, which is probably why they forced her to attend the private Catholic school.

"You're smart and beautiful. You'll fit right in," her mother assured her.

Her mother wasn't right, but she wasn't entirely wrong.

After a few months in school without Bea making friends, she overheard her parents. Her mother wondered if Bea had fears of attachment, due to her biological mother's abandonment.

Her mother's remark confused her, made her sad, left her cold. It was also the tone she used. It wasn't soft, but held a tired, heavy weight.

Bea desperately didn't want to disappoint her parents. She figured out a way to crack the social code and faked her friendships.

She had one real friend named Ria. Together they adopted the quiet, shy girl personalities. Not so strong that they threatened queen bees, but popular enough to not be outcasts. Anytime she was invited to a party, Bea pretended that either her parents were strict or that she had plans with Ria, who would sometimes come over and watch television. Her parents soon figured out that she didn't act like herself in school and expressed disappointment that she didn't feel comfortable with showing her authentic self.

Bea had tried to be what they needed, but she failed again. It was then she realized that she would only ever disappoint not only the man she used to pray to on the cross, but those she loved.

But she'd tried hard to not be herself. To be normal, have meaningful friendships like her siblings and parents and find things she excelled in. Through lots of trial and error, Bea found two things she loved: swimming and art. Both were solitary pursuits.

Though she had always been thin, in the water her body felt weightless, yet strong. Whatever she needed, the water provided. When life felt too heavy, floating made her light as a feather. When she felt chaotic or depressed or lost, she found peace in propelling her body through the rippling waves.

Her parents encouraged her to compete, and at the tender age of twelve, she crushed every local record. Her coach even hinted at training for the Olympics.

But that required a stage and practice and people and crowds. She could imagine homespun stories of the little orphan who found a home and triumphed despite her circumstances.

Pressure to perform perfection was something she felt as soon as she stepped across her adoptive family's threshold. Three years into competition, she backed away from training, and her father, who'd eagerly embraced the dream to parent an Olympian, begrudgingly supported her decision.

Without the Olympic talk, she enjoyed swimming again and with her newly gained time she shifted her focus on art.

Bea loved her creative mind, loved the crazy stories she spun about characters she wished she could befriend. Her parents had invested thousands of dollars on canvases, art supplies, and classes, ignoring Bea's protests. A canvas was meant for an audience, but the blue-lined sheets from a notebook were just for her.

At eighteen years old, she forfeited her various art and swimming scholarships and committed to the path of discovery. She'd worn the right clothes, had the right education, attended all the right extra-curricular activities, but she couldn't shake the feeling that everything was temporary, and that Bea was simply the benefactor of pure dumb luck.

Even more dark thoughts led her to believe that her parents only loved her because she fit in to the aesthetics of a fair-skinned affluent Black family.

That epiphany hadn't come easy. It took years of ill-fitting friendship groups, of wearing masks that didn't mesh with her personality. She'd tried, she really had tried to be the dutiful daughter, the darling sister, the perfect scholar. It had all worked out until it hadn't.

Because if she were truly as spectacular as her parents, Kathy and Johnathan, had boldly proclaimed, then why hadn't her mother stuck around?

So, like her biological mother, she left her family. After graduating high school, she roamed thousands of miles away, clear across the globe. She had a beautiful face and body, and she used it to her advantage to grace the runways in Milan and modeled everything from clothes to jewelry. Her face was even splashed across international glossies.

She dined in Parisian elegance, ate thousand-dollar meals like venison layered with thin slices of savory black truffles. Partied with foreign diplomats who whispered promises of fortune for a night or two or three in their arms.

It was through her modeling when she first came across drugs at age eighteen. She was one of many beautiful girls who modeled for an upscale agency in Paris. Bea had always been naturally skinny. She'd maintained her weight as a swimmer, but even that wasn't enough. Being so skinny, you could see her bones—the "unofficial" requirement to model back then. It didn't seem like such a big deal to shoot up. The benefits when she first started had outweighed the bad. But then she neglected her family, her job, her health.

Nearly a year later, Bea finally contacted her family. She apologized for her actions, acknowledged the hurt she caused, but firmly stated that she liked her new life. Through her travel, she found like-minded souls who finally gave voice to define what she'd felt her entire life—wanderlust.

Through her travels, Bea had found a mother figure. She wasn't soft-spoken as her mother, Kathy, but Althea was just as beautiful.

She gave her purpose and saved Bea when she'd become rundown and exhausted from life. A time when drugs ravaged her body, her energy, and sometimes her morals.

Althea, her landlord, who hailed from Jamaica and immigrated to the UK, where Bea lived, educated her on the benefits of herbal medicines.

"Since you're determined to destroy your body, drink this." Althea put the cup directly under Bea's nose.

Bea groaned, her weak body shivering beneath a thin sheet.

"Silly child," Althea hissed. "Drink, now. Before I pour it down your throat." Her affronted tone added even more cadence to her accent.

She'd assumed the old woman had given her coffee and nearly spat out the concoction. It had been milk thistle, which she later learned aided in liver function.

"Don't . . . feel good," Bea croaked from her parched throat. The illness was entirely self-inflicted. During those years, she'd been exposed to a lot of drugs and alcohol, leaving her dehydrated and sometimes delirious.

But soon the milk thistle had done wonders to her body. Excited about a new discovery, she ran in a pair of pajamas and a flannel shirt, knocking on Althea's door at the crack of dawn.

Althea opened the door and asked, "What's going on?"

Out of breath, Bea asked, "What else can herbs do?"

Althea slammed the door in her face and told her not to come until the rooster crowed three times.

She counted the crows and returned. Alethea smiled. She loved Bea's curiosity and was eager to pass on her generational knowledge to her young tenant.

After multiple threats of being kicked out of Althea's home, Bea stopped partying and using drugs, opting to walk the gardens instead of runways with her matronly landlord.

But what had changed her life was when Althea taught her about beekeeping.

Althea had told her about leaving her family and honeybees behind in Jamaica. When the woman recounted her story, she'd seemed more upset about leaving her bees to her ex-husband rather than her family. Bea knew there was more to the story, but she never asked. She figured if Althea wanted to share, then she would.

Bea preferred she didn't. Because if Althea shared, that meant Bea would have to tell her about the family she abandoned to backpack and then model across Europe. She would have to confess that her family wasted tens of thousands of dollars on her education and art and swim classes.

Oh, yes. Althea, who scrimped and scraped, clawed herself out of poverty, created her own business, and moved alone to a foreign country and thrived as a landlord, beekeeper, and apothecary, would never understand.

Althea didn't suffer fools. She didn't like waste, but truly abhorred it in human form, which is why she often tossed Bea out of bed, dousing her with water when she wouldn't immediately respond to her gentle nudges to wake up.

If she knew Bea's actual story and experiences, she would buy her a ticket back to California and force her to stay. But eventually Althea kicked her out. She had no choice when Bea found herself back in the tight grips of heroin.

Tears swam in Althea's brown eyes when she demanded Bea leave. The day she left, Althea didn't say goodbye, but she left her a basket loaded with all the tinctures and tonics on her doorstep. The same things she gave Bea last year when she discovered her addictions.

Bea opened the door, collapsed to the ground, gathered her knees to her chest and allowed herself to cry. She felt tiny and tired and alone. The hot tears streaming down her face did nothing to warm her cold body. This wasn't the reason she left her family. Heroin wasn't the adventure she sought, yet she'd allowed it in. Bea dabbed at her tears with a monogrammed cloth—another thing Althea had gifted Bea—and left the place she called home.

And then years later, she thrived.

Years later, she learned to forgive herself for disappointing Althea. By the time she'd gotten herself together to mail a written apology, it was too late. Bea's fingers shook when the postcard returned. She was too afraid to confirm if Althea was still angry or dead.

In her heart, she knew the answer.

Althea's lessons lived on, and there were so many fascinating things she'd passed on. First, Bea never expected bees to live in a hive that looked like an old office cabinet. Embedded inside were wood frames with food grain plastic inserts and bee's wax.

There were so many fun facts that made Bea fall in love with bees. When Althea told her queen bees laid upwards of two thousand eggs per day for a period in the spring, she hadn't a clue that it still wasn't enough to save bees from near extinction.

Bees were essential to human life. In Bea's eyes, they were little superheroes, the way they pollinate food so that humans, plants, and animals could survive.

Through Althea and her bees, Bea warmed at the thought of being essential to someone.

If she were essential, her biological mother wouldn't have abandoned her. If she were essential, her family would have sought to understand her, visit her, and maybe even attempt to drag her home.

Bea found that person who made her feel essential, her Black Superman. The timing, however, wasn't the best.

After she returned home to California to live with her parents, they immediately noticed something was wrong and sent her to rehab.

Thankfully, it worked. She'd always be grateful to her parents' gift—the gift of loving her despite her faults, the gift they gave her in connecting back to the things she loved. Long mornings in solitude where she swam in their indoor pool. The rest of the day included art under the soothing sounds of pan flutes and chimes.

It was months later Bea had attended Comic Con. Months later before she fell in love with Mike at first sight in a cramped room at the San Diego Convention Center. With his thick black glasses and trim, fit body, he looked as if he'd stepped out of the inked comic book pages. Later Bea joked he looked like a Black Clark Kent, or rather Calvin Ellis, Superman, from the alternate universe.

Bea knew two things when she met him. One: he was her soulmate. She knew it because he wore a T-shirt of Bumblebee, a Black fictional superhero from Teen Titans. And he genuinely geeked out when he saw her drawings—because of her talent, not because she was beautiful. The second thing Bea knew was that one day she would break his heart.

However, she didn't realize she would actually break two hearts.

Bea figured after years of traveling the world, she could settle, and live a normal life. After the convention, they were with each other day and night. Mike delayed his trip back home for a week but couldn't do more since he owned and manned his comic bookstore in Queens.

After Mike left, there'd been a giant-sized hole in her heart. After only six weeks of knowing him, she followed him to New York City for a visit and never returned home to California.

For two years, they were deliriously happy. Bea had found a home and a routine that hadn't stifled her. She helped Mike during the day at the store and had a part-time job at an herb store in Queens, and occasionally modeled. She set up a beehive on the roof of their apartment building. At night, she drew her own Afro-Latina bee superhero, Abeja.

Her superhero was a combination of Captain Planet, who rid the world of mutant pollutants, and Wonder Woman. Abeja had amazing eyesight and, with two wings, flew a hundred miles per hour. Best of all, if she needed to sting her opponent, she didn't die, but was severely weakened.

One night, after they made love, Bea grabbed her sketchpad, wondering out loud if her character was too boring. "You've got to make her have a fatal weakness and a fatal flaw," Mike advised. "If you can make them clash, even better."

If Bea were a superhero, her weakness would be drugs. It was the rush, the warmth, the euphoric energy that kept her hooked. It was better than expensive food, good sex, and it made her feel warm. Warmer than she'd ever felt with anyone before Mike.

But later she couldn't deny the cons. The word "*slow*" came to mind when she recalled that dark time in her life. Slow to move, slow to work, slow to react.

The six months in rehab she'd done right before she met Mike hadn't been enough. And now she could admit, it was too soon to commit herself to someone. She was in no position to promise someone forever when she barely kept the promises she made to herself. But she truly thought that love could overcome her addiction.

Then she'd gotten pregnant. Mike had been over the moon. Bea rode the wave of his enthusiasm, though the thought of being responsible for someone so tiny and defenseless scared her senseless.

But what could she do? The baby growing inside of her, swelling inside her stomach would soon come. Her family had been ecstatic. They thought a baby would anchor her into one place.

No one could abandon a baby.

Except her mother.

Except Bea.

As soon as the baby had been born, Bea couldn't sleep. It was due in part to the crying baby, but even when her baby girl was quiet, she couldn't rest.

She didn't feel that bond with her baby. The baby was cute, and Bea felt guilty and frustrated that she couldn't show her love. When she held her baby, she didn't feel warm, she felt invaded. For weeks, she tried breastfeeding, but the baby seemed intent on rejecting everything about Bea.

It was a few months post baby when she went back to the thing that made her feel warm all over.

Mike knew. He didn't push her away. When she woke up cold, he held her. His arms were warm, his words warmer, but nothing compared to the weightless feeling, the highs where the drugs took her. Her baby's cries couldn't reach her there.

Mike gently guided her into rehab, even made her agree to see a therapist. Nothing seemed to stick. Those days, she sat on the roof and sat in silence with the bees.

"I've got an idea," Mike said to her, while gently rocking their baby on their rooftop.

"What is it?" Bea asked, staring at her hive.

"Don't be mad, but I found someone I think you should meet."

Her adoptive parents had paid enough money to persuade someone to unseal her adoption papers so they could discover if her parents had any history of mental or physical illnesses or addictions themselves. They wanted to help Bea. And when she met her biological mother, whom Mike had painstakingly tracked down, that's when she finally felt a spark of life again. Suddenly, all the pieces snapped into place.

Because her mother, Ama, was a force of nature.

Bea discovered Ama was a wanderer, a rich one who wore four-inch heels, pearls, elegant dresses, and owned fabulous purses. Ama skipped across states and countries with inimitable style, and hadn't allowed anyone, or anything, to stop her rise.

If she would've stopped for a baby, Ama never would have been the success she was on Wall Street, nor married Omar, the love of her life.

Bea wanted to impress the impeccably dressed woman. She wanted to emulate her. But she never could. Not on their single income with a small baby in a smaller apartment in Queens.

She loved Mike, and before the baby, she loved her life. But now everything felt foggy. She couldn't find the motivation to get up and feed herself, much less her husband and baby. She just wasn't herself. It wasn't Mike's fault. Or Ama's fault.

Or the baby, Billie's fault.

A few months later, Bea left her family again. But this time it was harder. As she packed her things and ran like a coward into the night, she shook harder than she had in the throes of going sober. But she'd done it. She'd changed her name from Edie to Bea, shed her identity like snakeskin, and wandered back to the other side of the globe. In her heart she knew it was the best decision for not only her, but for Mike and Billie as well. If she'd stayed, she would've ruined them.

Bea thought she had time until the inevitable confrontation with Billie, her biological daughter.

Billie who was also Ama's granddaughter.

The web was tangled enough, but Ama, or maybe it was Mike, had taken it upon themselves to make Ama a mother figure to Billie—something she never offered to her own daughter.

She thought she'd be an old woman, not in her late forties, living alone like a nun for a few decades in her magical garden before she met the daughter she abandoned.

But then like an hourglass turned over, the sands of time began slipping rapidly away. Omar had come to her six years ago, with pictures of a college-aged Billie (and her godsisters), warning her that he planned to gift Tremont House to Olivia and that Ama and Billie were likely to visit sooner or later.

And then four months ago Olivia—instantly recognizable from the photos—had come to her garden.

Even though Olivia hadn't discovered her identity yet, she likely would. Sag Harbor was a small, close-knit community, and secrets had a way of coming to light. But she couldn't make herself leave the only place that had truly felt like home.

Soon, her mother and her daughter would likely arrive.

And Bea knew when the time came, it would be hell on earth.

CHAPTER 13

A WOMAN'S INTUITION

June 2021

After her morning jog, Olivia found Mr. Whittingham waiting for her near the dock on the beach. They'd made a date to play chess in her backyard.

"Hello, neighbor!" he waved at her as she slowed to stretch. "Is now still a good time?"

Olivia smiled. He was half an hour early, cutting into her shower time. "If you could give me a few minutes to grab something to drink and to change, that would be great. Would you like anything?"

"I'll have water, please."

"Of course."

After handing him a glass of cold water, Olivia ran upstairs for a quick wash. When she stepped into the dark bedroom, Anderson turned on the bedside lamp. He pushed himself up, resting against the headboard.

"What's the rush?" His sleeping eyes turned sharp as he took in her naked body. He'd returned just last night after meetings with his agent and a show in Brooklyn.

"I'm playing chess Mr. Whittingham out back. He's a bit early, but I don't want to keep him waiting."

Anderson nodded. "Ah. Tell Mr. W. I said hello."

"You can tell him yourself, you know." Olivia shrugged a simple striped cotton short-sleeved shirt over her head.

"If he's here when I get up, I'll say hello."

"Really?" she asked, while sliding a pair of linen pants over her hips.

Anderson shrugged. "I just get the feeling that he doesn't like me. Well, not me. He just doesn't like us together."

She knew that wasn't what Mr. Whittingham was thinking. The last time Mr. Whittingham stopped by Anderson hadn't bothered to say hello. Elders, especially in the Black community, expected respect. It was beyond the optics of being rude, but to not give that due respect when the world so often overlooked Black people.

Olivia didn't have the time to explain cultural nuances to Anderson.

"Mr. Whittingham is nice. He would like it if you said hello at least, but it's your choice." Olivia returned downstairs and was back outside in fifteen minutes.

"I'm sorry I took so long."

Mr. Whittingham shook his head. "I just checked my watch. Looks like I was early. You know, I was so excited about our game that when the sun rose, I just hopped out of bed." Olivia laughed when Mr. Whittingham bounced in his seat. His antics reminded her of the scene with Grandpa Jo from *Charlie and the Chocolate Factory*, when he rolled out of bed after Charlie won the golden ticket.

Olivia looked at the concrete chessboard. During her time upstairs, Mr. Whittingham must have placed the pieces on the board. He sat on the white side, his back facing the beach. Olivia settled opposite him, in front of the black pieces.

"Care to make a wager?" His voice went serious, but still held its color.

"Sure thing." Olivia smiled. She couldn't think of what he'd want to bet.

"If I win, you'll take another piece of advice." He quickly glanced at the house behind Olivia.

"And if I win?" She had a feeling his advice had something to do with Anderson, something she did not want to hear.

"I'll tell you more stories about your father."

"Deal." Olivia, now as serious as ever, waved her hand toward him. She had so many questions. "Your move, I suppose."

"I didn't sit here to make the first move, by the way. I wanted to make sure a beautiful woman had the best view."

Olivia wrestled with a smile. "Don't soften me up, now."

They grew quiet, concentrating as the other made their moves. She loved chess and often played with Omar for hours. Ama would often shoo them away from the board, forcing Olivia to spend time with her godsisters.

For the first time in a while, Olivia seemed to be on the losing end with less material, but hope remained. She had more quality pieces, including her queen. She could end the game in four moves, though she didn't relish it. She enjoyed this quiet, beautiful morning with her favorite neighbor.

"You're pulling my leg, aren't you, young lady?"

Olivia feigned innocence. "Oh, no. I'm all in."

Mr. Whittingham laughed. "You know, I haven't lost to anyone since Carole died." He waved toward the board. "Come now, let's end it."

When Olivia exclaimed checkmate a few minutes later her neighbor laughed again. "God loves a humble servant. Thank you for humbling me so early in the morning."

"Your wager gave me proper motivation." Olivia clapped her hands. "Now I'll have my winnings, please, sir. Can you tell me what my father liked?"

"How about I tell you about his dislikes?"

Excitement nearly pushed her out of her seat. "Please."

"He hated swimming. Ironic, seeing as the family visited here every other summer. His mother's sister previously owned property here and so they alternated visiting the other over the summers. Your grandparents have beachfront property, too."

"W-where?"

He cleared his throat, shaking his head and shrugging his shoulders. "Not in SANS, but I'm sure I've got it written somewhere."

"And my other relatives? I suppose my great aunt or uncle?"

"Ah, the Bakers. They sold a while ago and moved to Amherst, New Hampshire. But they usually visit over Labor Day."

"I'd love to get their full names?"

"Jeff and Sandra Baker. Sandra, your aunt, was your grandfather's sister."

Garrett had been right about the maiden name. Olivia committed the names to memory to look up later.

"Do you plan to reach out?" Mr. Whittingham asked in a careful voice.

"Yes. Eventually. I need to get some things in order first."

As if she could get Cindy "in order" and on board. Despite her mother's heated response, she wanted her blessing in connecting with her family. Not to mention the fact that her mother's words about the family's hatred had tempered her enthusiasm.

"Hmm. Well, let me know. Maybe I can introduce you to them if they visit this year. They didn't last year because of the pandemic. I think Jeff's got to be careful with his asthma."

"That would be nice, thanks."

"Anyway," he continued. "He hated swimming with a passion. That's why he pretended to be sick when I first met him. He liked quiet and solitude."

"Except when it came to the ladies?" She recalled his previous comment.

He chuckled. "Well, yes. He was a good kid, just a scamp in that regard."

Olivia couldn't stop the frown from turning her mouth upside down. She wanted to keep the perfect image of her father, who adored her mother, in her head.

"Did he break a lot of hearts?" Olivia didn't like the thought of her father being a heartbreaker. Not when men had broken her heart so many times over the years.

"He slowed down when he graduated from high school. He liked this young lady from back home. Mooned over her all summer. Wouldn't so much as look at another girl."

"That must have been my mother," Olivia muttered under her breath, but apparently not low enough because he nodded.

"I think so. Cindy, right?"

"Yes . . . great memory."

"The key is hydration, a healthy diet, and sleep. Hey, since you won so soundly, I've got another prize for you."

He pulled a picture from inside the small pocket of his yellow polo shirt.

"A picture I took of your father. You can have it."

Olivia's hands shook as she reached for the rare picture of her father.

He sat on a deck. The picture captured his side profile. She assumed he was twenty-one at the very least because of the beer in hand. He stared at the sea as if water held the key to life. His forehead crinkled, and his lips flatlined.

"Why does he look so sad?"

"He was upset with his brother."

"Why?"

"They bickered a lot, you see. As they grew older, they grew apart. After you were born, they completely lost touch. It hurt your father because, at one point, they were best friends. He loved his brother very much."

"Why did they argue?"

"I wasn't as close to CJ's brother, but from what I could observe, they were just different. His brother had that big-man-on-campus-persona. He liked swimming and fishing, big on the outdoors. Your father loved books and was a huge cinephile. But their parents squished them together in everything . . . well everything that his brother liked. CJ chafed against that. I think sometimes he argued with his brother just so his parents would let them separate."

Olivia sighed. "I hate to see my father so sad. In the pictures my mom has, he seemed like a cheerful man."

"I think it's important to understand all facets of a person, don't you agree?"

But before she could agree, Mr. Whittingham stood. "I'm off to my walk now. You have a good day, young lady."

"Thank you for the picture," she called to his back.

A heavy feeling cloaked the morning air.

Something about that entire exchange didn't sit well with Olivia. For one, how could he remember her mother's name but not the place where her father was born? Mr. Whittingham was the historian of SANS, the purported unofficial mayor, who possessed a treasure trove of knowledge and an iron-clad memory.

Olivia felt as if Mr. Whittingham was leading her blindfolded down a dark path, turning on lights every so often to show what *he* wanted to reveal.

Maybe there was a good reason her mother had asked her years ago not to go rooting around in the past.

When Olivia returned to the house, she propped the photo near the framed picture of her father and her . . . uncle. Chuck, or Charles, is what Mr. Whittingham had called him.

"He's hiding something." She voiced her suspicions out loud. For now, she would follow his lead. And she hoped that whatever she found at the end of the path wouldn't hurt her as much as Omar's revelations.

She sent a message to Garrett.

OLIVIA: I've got my aunt and uncle's names. You were right—a different family name known as the Bakers. Sandra and Jeff. Does that ring a bell?

GARRETT: No, but . . . looks like we can schedule a trip to the library. How about Friday around lunch?

Anderson would be leaving on Friday for a gig. It would be perfect timing.

OLIVIA: Yes! I would love that. Thank you!!!!

GARRETT: It's a date. See you then.

"It's not a date," she muttered while her heart fluttered.

"You think it's something, too, right?" Olivia whispered as if she and Dr. LaGrange weren't alone in her office.

"You are an incredibly intuitive person. If your gut is telling you something isn't all that it seems, it's likely the case."

"You believe in intuition?" Olivia asked in a scandalized voice. She didn't mean to judge, but that didn't seem like practical advice from a psychiatrist.

"Yes. It's a muscle to be worked. I suspect you use your intuition for your clients."

"Absolutely not. I analyze trends, review data, then advise my client on how to invest."

"But the data doesn't say Olivia you must do X to get Y or Z."

"We have tools that practically give us the answers."

Dr. LaGrange rotated her neck, stopping when her chin touched her shoulder. After a few sessions with the doctor, Olivia knew this was her way of collecting her thoughts before she pulled something from her psychological warfare toolbox of gentle reprimands, unrelenting stares, and uncomfortable silences.

After a combination of silence and stares, Dr. LaGrange finally broke the quiet. "You form a decision based on figures, trends, and your *experience*, correct?"

"I suppose, but I can't just rely on intuition." Olivia waved a hand as if she were swatting a bug. Intuition was a lower form of gambling.

"I never advise to *only* use your intuition. It's a gut check, not a gut reliance. But don't overlook it. Lean into it. That's why I've asked you to journal."

"Really? How am I supposed to check on my intuition through journal entries?"

"You can review what you wrote, how you've felt in big and small moments. And you can verify the results of anything you assumed or guessed about yourself and others. Your words stand as a historical account. When I review my entries, I've always found that I could always spot trouble early on, but I didn't understand the why until it came to fruition. Now if something doesn't feel right here"— she pointed to her stomach—"or here and here"—she pointed to her head and heart—"I don't stick around to find out why. I simply stop and pivot until my internal radar settles and feels good."

Olivia nodded. Just this morning, she had the same thoughts about Mr. Whittingham's hidden agenda. As for Anderson, she felt something was . . . off. She couldn't put her finger on it, and she certainly had no intention of pivoting away from their relationship based on something as passing as a feeling.

"Let's loop back to Anderson," Dr. LaGrange suggested.

"Certainly." Olivia shifted in her seat, attempting to get comfortable for the lightning round of questions.

"You've had some anxiety regarding his ability to provide. Now that it has been alleviated, how do you feel?"

Olivia shrugged. "Being in entertainment still isn't solid. What happens if the project falls through? And will the option money be enough for him to survive until they film the show?"

"Have you asked him about this?"

Olivia shook her head. "He's continuing to deliver food. Apparently, he doesn't get a big payout all at once and he doesn't want to blow through the money."

Dr. LaGrange simply stared at Olivia.

"Why aren't you saying anything?" Olivia cut into the silence. The woman cost way too much money to just sit there like a log.

"I'm waiting for you to answer my question from . . ."—she looked down at her slim gold watch—"forty-five minutes ago. Do you *want* to marry Anderson?"

Olivia shrugged. "I don't know." She shook her head. "Does I don't know mean no?"

"What do you think?"

"I asked my question first."

Dr. LaGrange gave Olivia a patient smile. "What do you love about Anderson?"

"He . . . makes me smile. He's funny and nice, truly he is. He doesn't judge, he doesn't stare at other women, and he makes me feel beautiful."

"He sounds like a great friend."

"Please, Dr. LaGrange, I'm just not sure. And then there's my attraction to Garrett. I feel confused and guilty. Sometimes I feel like if it wasn't for my godfather's letter, I wouldn't feel so indecisive."

"What about his letter?"

"He told me I deserved this knight in shining armor, but does he really exist?"

Dr. LaGrange sipped water. "I think it depends on how you define it. It can mean security and financial freedom for one person, loyalty and fidelity, or what feels like a soulmate connection."

"Is that a fair expectation?" Olivia muttered more to herself.

"What's fair is to understand your needs and desires and be upfront with potential partners. Otherwise you're lying to yourself and others. Then it's a colossal waste of everyone's time."

"I just don't understand. When I met Anderson, it seemed as if my godfather delivered him on a platter. Like he wanted him for me."

Dr. LaGrange blinked her eyes a few times, as if she couldn't believe what just came out of my mouth.

"What is it?"

"You argue with me about intuition, but you believe your deceased godfather conspired to connect you with Anderson from beyond the grave?"

"I know it's silly but—"

"It's not silly at all, Olivia," Dr. LaGrange said, raising her hand. "I simply wanted to point out the hypocrisy."

Olivia snorted, looking down at her manicured bone-colored nails. "Are you allowed to call your clients hypocritical?"

"I didn't call you a hypocrite. I find you to be incredibly sincere." Dr. LaGrange smiled. "Now back to your question about your godfather's intentions . . . let's assume he connected you with Anderson, but not for the reason you're thinking."

Olivia dropped the attitude and focus on Dr. LaGrange. "What's your theory, doctor?"

"Every relationship—whether friendship, work-related, or romantic—teaches you something. Perhaps Anderson is here to teach you a lesson in love. So far, you know things you like and don't like in living with someone else outside of your mother. You know you want someone well-matched in terms of career."

"But that just seems . . . it seems superficial to feel that way," Olivia argued.

"During our first session, do you remember what I told you about how trauma from your childhood could affect the decisions that you make today?"

Olivia nodded. "Yes."

"You said you loved Anderson because he thinks you are beautiful. Your mother never affirmed your beauty. Perhaps you're with Anderson because he makes you feel the warmth you never received from your parent."

"Oh." Olivia exhaled. She blinked a few times. She recalled the adage that daughters married men like their fathers. But was there anything about daughters and a mother's love?

"Instead of deeming yourself superficial, unpack what affects your self-esteem."

"I . . . I have high self-esteem."

"In certain aspects, absolutely," Dr. LaGrange said with a nod. "Do you have a mirror?"

Olivia nodded, searching for a small compact in her purse. When she found it, she leaned over to hand it to the doctor.

Dr. LaGrange shook her head. "Open it."

Olivia followed her instructions.

"Now look in the mirror, and say 'I love you, Olivia.'"

"I . . ." Olivia laughed. "This is silly. I'll say it when I'm alone."

"No, say it now. I'll step outside if you'd like."

Olivia stared at her face. Her almond-shaped eyes looked at her like a deer in headlights.

She snapped the compact shut.

"It's okay. Practice at home."

Olivia shook her head. "No wonder I can't say I love Anderson.

But I think I do. I really enjoy him. I like his humor, his kindness, his passion. He's an entirely wonderful man. I just don't like that . . . I have a feeling he's hiding something from me."

"Then maybe Anderson is the one for you. If he's the right one, he can wait until you figure out things for yourself."

Olivia's heart spiraled down to the pit of her stomach. "What does it mean when I can't make it work with a good guy?"

"Human, Olivia. It makes you human."

☼

After her session with the doctor, a ding sounded from her phone on the way to her car. She reached over to her purse and found a message from Garrett, waiting for her.

GARRETT: Something came up from work and I need to go back home for the weekend. Can't make it to the library this Friday. Will reschedule.

Olivia sighed, shaking her head. She wasn't sure if she was more disappointed that she wouldn't see him or that she'd have to wait a little longer to figure out her family.

OLIVIA: No worries. I've got their names and I'll go by myself. Thanks for offering.
GARRETT: No, please. I want to help. Let's reschedule, okay? Next Friday?
OLIVIA: No, not a good time. I'll check my calendar.

Olivia pivoted from home and went to the library. With the help of a librarian, she found one article about the Bakers and Jones.

Her fingers shook as she clicked to zoom in on the picture and caption.

From left to right: Daniel Jones, Christine Jones, Sandra Baker, and Jeff Baker toast champagne at the Sag Harbor Gala to raise money for local AME church.

Olivia's focus lingered on her grandparents. Though the picture was black-and-white, she could clearly see the family resemblance in her grandmother. She had the same shaped eyes, nose, her facial structure flawless.

Her grandfather, Daniel, was bald and looked dashing in a tuxedo with a bowtie.

Olivia printed a copy of the article and photo. When she picked up the warm, freshly inked paper, she held it close to her heart. A satisfied smile stretched across her face

"I'll find you soon," she promised.

"They're nothing but a den of vipers." Her mother's voice sounded like a bad omen in her head.

But how could she trust her mother's opinion? How did she know she wasn't lying about her family?

She would have to ask in person where Cindy couldn't hang up the phone and hide. Her mother had plans with friends for the Fourth of July. But maybe she would come for Labor Day weekend.

Olivia nodded, loving her plan. She wouldn't let her mother hide from the past anymore. It was time to move on and meet her father's family.

CHAPTER 14

SOMETHING WORTH
FIGHTING FOR

June 2021

Early on a Tuesday morning, Olivia received her first pink slip. That is what the neighborhood called the tacky flyers that ASK, the redevelopment company, stuffed in their mailboxes. She hadn't been surprised by the intrusion, based on how often her neighbors talked about the aggressive campaign. If anything, it was interesting that this was the first time she'd received a slip. But then again, Anderson checked the mail with an obsession. Olivia assumed he'd been waiting for some sort of special designation or a check.

Olivia snapped a picture of the slip and sent a text to Whitney, who then replied with a red expletive emoji.

But it wasn't until Wednesday morning that Whitney called and excitedly *informed* Olivia that they would interview a few families who'd planned to sell to ASK. Olivia logged off early from work to accommodate the appointments.

"Hi, Whitney," Olivia greeted as she slid into the passenger seat. The cool air from the AC cut into the brazen summer heat.

"Hey, lady. Thanks for joining me last minute."

"How could I say no?" Olivia said with a smile. "But next time, please give me a few days' notice."

"I'm sorry, girl. That flyer incensed me into action. I just started calling people right away. Fortunately, today worked for everyone. Anyway, thank you again. I'm sorry to inconvenience you."

Olivia buckled her seat belt and then waved her off. "I told you I would help where I can."

"I know we have a great neighborhood, but sometimes I forget how wonderful this neighborhood and people can be."

Olivia smiled at her friend, though Whitney concentrated on cruising down the street before she took off on Hillside Drive.

She easily bopped to an oldies soul station playing from the radio, songs she'd heard often during her childhood. Cindy loved the ballads and, not that her mother would admit it, she also loved the dance songs from the nineties.

"Who are we meeting today?"

"The Jackson family first. They've been here for four generations, so it's a shock to discover they plan to move."

"Excellent. Do you have a base of questions to ask them?"

Whitney shrugged. "I plan to wing it, but mostly I want to listen. The purpose is to understand their motivation so we can convince them otherwise or maybe craft our message around those who intend to sell."

They soon parked and stepped out of the car. Unlike her and Whitney's neighborhood, their lawn wasn't as precisely manicured. It looked nice enough. Mowed lawn and manicured bushes saved them from getting fined by the HOA, but the yard had an ombre hued ranging from cabbage-colored crabgrass to lush pea green fronds.

The old trees dotting the front yard stood alone, without mulch or rocks to cover some patches near the base.

The Jacksons weren't a couple, as Olivia had assumed. The siblings Tamika and Tyrell were just over thirty years old. Tamika's husband and son walked the beach for the duration of the interview. The brother, Tyrell, was still single, though by the grin that spread across his face when he greeted Olivia, along with the lingering stares, he seemed ready to change his single status.

Olivia tucked her hair around her left ear, hoping the flash of her engagement ring would cool his ardor. He looked a little disappointed, seeming to nod to himself. He shifted his attention to Whitney.

Whitney and Olivia exchanged pleasantries after they settled across from the brother and sister at the kitchen table.

"Thank you both for agreeing to meet with us. Unlike ASK I won't hide my intentions," Whitney said, somehow keeping an even tone. "I'd love to understand what ASK promised you to convince you to sell to them?"

Tamika shifted in her chair. "It started with flyers, like everyone around the neighborhood received. And like everyone else, Ty and I ignored them. We used to," she tossed a look at her brother. "We made a wall of flyers at one point. But then I lost my job. I work in HR in the airline industry. Thankfully, my husband works in tech, but we live in Connecticut primarily so we can't continue paying our half of the rising property taxes. And Ty . . ."

"I quit my job." He waved his hand at Whitney when she frowned. "Don't give me that look. I'm a nurse, and I'm burned out."

"Fair enough," Whitney said, raising her hands in defense. "What will you do now?"

Tyrell shrugged. "I don't know. But the thought of returning to the hospital makes me nauseated."

His sister leaned over and gave him a hug. He squeezed back, and that little squeeze made Olivia's heart warm. "Tamika told me to go back to Sag Harbor to recharge, and don't get me wrong, it's been good for me. She and her husband, Rob, let me stay for months by myself before they visited for the summer."

"When I came down with my family and saw that wall of flyers we created, it was like a sign for us to sell and give us a cushion to live our lives comfortably." Tamika darted her attention toward her brother. "I can't make Ty go back to that war zone. I can't control the job market, and Lord knows I've tried to find a job."

"It's a matter of money," Olivia finally interjected.

"Absolutely," Tameka nodded. "We want a good deal, and we want easy because, trust us, it wasn't easy for us to come to this decision."

"And ASK is easy?" Whitney dropped the fight in her voice, transforming to calm and supportive.

Olivia gave her a mental high five. The Jacksons didn't need admonishment. They weren't sellouts, they were simply drowning in a turbulent, pandemic sea without the means of a safety net.

"Yes, they take care of everything. They have this relocation package that includes free moving services within five hundred miles and junk removal service. They even hooked us up with the Goodwill for donations."

Whitney stared at the table, her eyes misting. "Why didn't you tell me or anyone what was going on? We take care of our own. I promised your mama . . ." she sighed. "We take care of our own."

"Yes, but you can't pay our bills," Tyrell said, his tone as sad as Whitney's.

"I know, but it's like . . . we're losing the neighborhood to these sharks. We can't just sell to the highest bidder. You know they're just going to tear down your home and build a hideous mansion."

"If they want to make it a mansion or vacation home, then that's their choice." Tyrell's voice went hard.

"C'mon, now. It was just sixty years ago when they wouldn't sell to someone like you or me. Your home," Whitney pointed to the floor. "This beachfront property was one of a few places where we could refill our well. Where the trauma of segregation and racism and the exhaustion from fighting for equality could cease for just a little while," Whitney's voice sounded as tired as the ancestors who'd found just a little peace in this slice of heaven.

"This is more than some vacation home. This isn't just the Hamptons," Whitney whispered, with simmering anxiety in her voice. "This is more."

Olivia leaned forward, interjecting to head off tension. "Did you grow up in this home?"

Tamika, who'd become teary-eyed during Whitney's speech, nodded while she dashed away tears.

"We lived with our mom and Big Mama—that's our grandmother. Mom and Big Mama lived here until five years ago, when our grandma died. Then our mom got married and left for Florida. She gave the house to us."

"She passed on a legacy. I know it hasn't been easy to maintain everything," Olivia looked at them both, sincerity ringing in her voice. She turned toward Tyrell. His macadamia-like exterior made it extremely hard to crack, but Olivia was up for the challenge. "And my goodness, I'm sure it was absolutely soul-crushing to go into the hospital day in and day out."

Tyrell nodded. "I know it sounds crazy for me to quit my career because it's such a specific skill set. I haven't figured out my next steps, but I know I shouldn't return to the floor. My mind and heart isn't in it, and I don't want to hurt a patient through negligence from burnout."

"Maybe you don't return to the floor and shift to administration?"

"Admin?"

"Mhmm. I have a girlfriend, Charidee, who transitioned from the floor. She makes sure the hospital and staff operate within the correct medical guidelines."

"Oh, yeah. We train on safety and procedures." He looked just past Olivia's shoulders, as if lost in thought. "That sounds . . . good.

I enjoy training people. The nurses and doctors always come to me for help."

"If you're interested in learning more, I'd be happy to connect the two of you."

He smiled. "Yeah. I'd appreciate it."

"And Tamika, I'd love for you to send me your résumé. My company is slowly but surely rehiring staff again. I'm not sure what the plans are on the HR side, but I'm happy to ask. And I also have a soror who's the VP of HR for a tech startup. They're booming right now in terms of business. Of course, none of the options are in the travel industry, but—"

"I'll take any leads, thank you."

Olivia reached into her blush-colored Tory Burch tote and pulled out her business card. "Shoot me emails and I'll get you to the right people."

Whitney sighed. "And hey, if you need to sell, we can help you out. Come to me, not . . . *them*."

The siblings offered their sincere gratitude.

Olivia pulled out her phone. "Now that we've got ASK out of the way, let's end it on a high note. We would love to record your favorite memories of growing up in Sag."

Olivia and Whitney wrapped up with the Jacksons after about an hour. Once Whitney returned to the car, she sighed.

"You're great at this."

"Great at what?"

"Helping people. I'm not going to lie. I wanted to tell them off, but sometimes I forget that not everyone here is rolling in dough."

Olivia nodded, fully agreeing with Whitney's reminder. After speaking to the Jacksons, she was incredibly grateful to Ama and Omar for setting her up for success.

Whitney interrupted her thoughts with a joke. "Are you sure your last name isn't Pope?"

"What do you mean?"

"Olivia Pope from *Scandal*. You just rolled into their house and was like, 'It's handled.'"

Olivia smoothed absolutely no wrinkles from her shirt as she took in Whitney's high praise. "You had the good idea about interviewing them. I just think that if they have solutions or at least see a light at the end of the tunnel, they may reconsider selling their homes."

Whitney smiled. "Maybe. If they change their minds, I'll figure out a way to get them out of the claws of ASK. All right, on to the Smiths, then we'll wrap up with Garrett."

Olivia's stomach dipped at the mention of his name. She'd successfully avoided Garrett for a week, very hard to do with a next-door neighbor with a sociable child who squealed every time she saw Olivia.

The meeting with the Smiths wasn't as productive. It wasn't that they weren't open to talking, but they were too far gone in the selling process. The ink was dry, and they were on the way out of the neighborhood.

Olivia would have preferred the interview had gone longer than twenty minutes. She needed way more time to anchor her defenses for Garrett. Thankfully, Whitney would be there to diffuse any chemistry bubbling between them.

At least, she'd hope.

"Last interview of the day. Are you ready?"

"Of course," Olivia took on the tone of competent financier. When they arrived, Garrett and Zora were sitting on the porch. From the looks of it, Zora held Garrett's rapt attention. Olivia let out another small breath. Between Whitney, her extrovert neighbor, and a precocious five-year-old, Olivia felt she should be in relatively safe hands and firmly distanced from her hormones.

"Whitney, Olivia." Garrett acknowledged both, but his eyes lingered on Olivia.

He was a vision in coral, the same shade as her purse. He wore a simple collared shirt, khaki cargo shorts, and leather sandals. And the same steel and sapphire watch he'd worn when they were at the ice cream parlor.

Garrett covered his watch and winked when Olivia's gaze lingered on the timepiece.

"Hi." Olivia tugged on her purse straps like a nervous schoolgirl. She cleared her throat, put aside her lust-filled thoughts, and gathered her professionalism. "Thank you for allowing us to talk to you about selling the house."

"Yes, of course." He welcomed them in, directing Zora to go upstairs. He offered wine. Whitney accepted, but Olivia did not. It wouldn't be wise for her to be anything but sober around Garrett.

Whitney, who found her rhythm after the Smiths, immediately launched into the purpose of the interview and what they'd hope to accomplish.

"Anything to add, Olivia?" Whitney tried to engage her in conversation.

"No. You've covered it all," her tone stiff and lively as cardboard.

Whitney tossed her a what-the-hell look and continued. "What made you decide to sell independently, and without my help, instead of going through ASK?"

"You know I'm a real estate attorney, so I plan to do most of the heavy lifting myself. I just needed someone to take pictures and post online."

Whitney harrumphed. So much for a gentle touch with Garrett.

"Now, don't be that way." He took on a tone Olivia imagined he used with Zora.

"Whatever. You're selling," Whitney snapped. "Why?"

He'd told her the same thing he told Olivia. Though he had enough money today, it wasn't so much that he felt he'd leave a safety egg should he pass away.

"I could and should sell my mother's quilts, but it's hard to part with them. I know it sounds crazy, but she put her heart and soul into the blankets. Whereas the house is just a house, not a home."

"You don't really believe that, do you?" Whitney essentially repeated what she said to the Jacksons about the history and legacy of SANS.

"I understand the historic significance, but people make homes. This house"—he waved a hand—"doesn't feel the same without Mom. There's no warmth. It doesn't smell like lemons and home cooking. And without her, it's too quiet. No gospel music in the mornings. No Motown hits at night."

Weeks after his death, Olivia visited Omar and Ama's apartment in the city. Without the smell of Omar's cigars and oak scent from whiskeys and cologne, the apartment felt like a mausoleum.

A cold numbness encased her body, but watching Ama, so tiny and hurt on the couch, she swallowed her sorrow.

She'd tried anyway, but her throat was too tight with pain.

Immediately, Olivia sprung into action, sourcing the ingredients for a hearty soup while her godmother curled up like a child on their velvet cream couch that wasn't made for sleeping. After weeks of weeping, Ama cried herself out until all that remained were dry whimpers and lifeless stares. But finally after a few long months, Ama came back to life.

With time and intention, Ama eventually came back to herself. She visited her goddaughters, traveled, dined with friends, and visited old peers, carving a new life without Omar.

And that's what Garrett and Zora must learn to do. "Make new memories," Olivia said, finally jumping into the conversation.

"You and Zora talking on the porch when we pulled up . . . that's a beautiful memory. At least, it looked beautiful from my stand-point. Strolls along the beach, her holding her daddy's hand to go to the ice cream parlor—that's a memory, too. The fundraiser you'll be hosting—"

"With help from the two of you, right?" Garrett looked panicked.

"Right." Whitney and Olivia confirmed.

"You have a community of people who look like your little girl," Whitney said. "A girl who can look up to the Pretty Lady who looks like her and eventually she'll understand that Olivia has beauty and brains. She'll have her aunty Addy, who can make her laugh, and her auntie Kara, who can teach her art. She'll have Mr. Whitting-ham to learn the history so that she doesn't sound as crazy as her daddy when he forgets his legacy." She winked at him, Olivia as-sumed to soften the blow.

"She will know love, not only from her father, but from us," Oli-via added. "You aren't alone, Garrett. I see it in your eyes that you think you are, but you have us."

He dropped his head. His hands gripped his knees so hard, his knuckles nearly jutted out of the sockets.

Olivia closed the distance and kneeled by his chair. She stroked his hands and gathered them between her own, silently offering him her strength and understanding and energy.

He didn't look up, but she could feel his struggle, the bounce of his leg, the strain from his shaking body.

Whitney leaned in for a hug from Garrett. When she finished, she lightly patted his shoulder. "We will always have your back, right, Olivia?"

He lifted his head up slowly, his wet eyes locked on hers. She tried to ignore the white-hot heat between them. The need in his eyes that called to her heart, her soul, in a way no one had ever done.

She licked her lips, attempting to quell her hormones. The action had done nothing for her but appeared to spark something in Garrett. His sadness disappeared and, in its place, hunger. His eyes settled on her lips. He looked at her like she was an ice cream cone dipped in chocolate.

She wanted him to lick and suck and devour.

Whitney cleared her throat. Olivia snatched her hands away.

"Hello, here for Garrett as neighbors, right?" Whitney reminded Olivia of her promise.

"Y-yes. Of course. If you or Zora need anything, I'm only a few steps away."

Garrett shook his head. "Sorry. Look at me, a grown man crying."

"Crying is healthy," Whitney cooed. "Charles does it a lot."

"A lot?"

"He's a big ol' softie. He even cries sometimes for sappy movies." Whitney smiled. She looked at Olivia. "Why don't we head out? Olivia here can record you later."

"Me, record? You know I'm not the best and I . . . I . . ."

When Whitney squinted her eyes and Garrett seemed to look at her in humor, she fumbled out a confirmation.

"See you soon." Olivia rushed outside, marching across her spongy lawn.

Whitney was hot on her heels. "Olivia, sweetie." Whitney tapped her shoulder.

Olivia turned around. "Yes?"

"You know Garrett likes you, right?"

"I . . . like him and his daughter, too. They'll make great neighbors should they decide to stay."

Whitney offered a kind, patient smile. "I think you know what I mean."

Olivia shook her head.

"He's a wonderful man and you know he's been through a lot. Please . . . please know what you want."

"I'm with Anderson. Garrett knows that." Olivia's voice went cold. She was very much at the peak of tiredness, defending the validity of her engagement.

"Okay." Whitney tilted her head, narrowed her eyes. Her body seemed at odds with her verbal agreement. "Well, if that's the case, then Garrett is responsible for his feelings."

"He is." Olivia's tone was aloof.

"Don't worry . . . I'm not the type to put the onus on women. I've got your back, too, girl. I'm sorry if it didn't come off that way."

Olivia smiled, breaking their tension. She believed Whitney. She wasn't one to mince words.

"I'll see you in a few days for the fundraiser planning." Whitney walked to her car.

"I'm looking forward to it." Olivia waved at her friend and then closed the door.

Olivia berated herself after she closed the door. She shouldn't have touched Garrett. She felt too much, exposed too much, in front of Whitney.

Outside of the Fourth of July fundraiser, and the interview, oh and the Labor Day kickoff event, she'd try to avoid Garrett. In fact, she had a trip planned to East Hampton to meet up with her friend-slash-hairstylist Travis for the weekend.

She would take the reprieve, spend time with her fiancé. She would piece herself together and she would erase all thoughts of Garrett and ice cream.

CHAPTER 15

CLOSING THE DISTANCE

June 2021

Everyone was gathered in the living room of Whitney's home. Instead of the two long plush sofas sitting on either side of the room, a chaise near the bay window, and a table in the middle, the space was optimized to accommodate many guests. The acrylic glass table with a curved wooden base stood flush against the wall. Various wines housed in sterling silver buckets filled with ice were place on the side table. Olivia assumed Addy, the local food and wine dilettante, had catered the appetizers and desserts.

Olivia poured herself a glass of Pinot Grigio, then waved at Whitney, who stood at the front of the room, near a TV mounted on the wall. The slide presentation displayed on the large screen was titled "Pop-Up Art Gallery Fundraiser," and served as a delicate reminder that it wasn't a social hour.

"Starting in three minutes," Whitney mouthed.

Olivia nodded, then took a small black slate plate and added blueberry goat cheese spread across a flaky bread, pimento croquettes, and prosciutto-wrapped figs. Looking around the room of just over a dozen people, Olivia realized she recognized most of her neighbors by face and name. This was all thanks to Mr. Whittingham, who walked her up and down the beach to introduce her to the neighbors.

After Olivia settled on the edge of a white chaise near the hallway, Whitney greeted her guests.

"Thank you to our volunteers." She looked around the room, making eye contact with everyone. "And special thanks to Garrett for allowing us to host the Art Gallery fundraiser on his beautiful lawn. Mrs. Brooks kept a beautiful yard, didn't she?"

Everyone murmured their agreement, including Olivia. Unlike the all-white pebble garden in her yard, Mrs. Brooks' lush green yard was treated or, rather, dyed more times than a graying septuagenarian. The startling bright green complimented the purple and blue hydrangea bushes that lined the porch.

"Mrs. Brooks loved supporting the SANS Kids Day Camps and volunteered just about every summer. And what better way to acknowledge Mrs. Brooks' legacy than to name it the first annual Ruth Brooks Summer Enrichment Fundraiser?"

Whitney smiled as everyone clapped. Olivia's attention drifted to Garrett. His throat bobbed. It looked as if he tried to swallow his sorrow.

Olivia knew the waves of grief well. Grief didn't ring the doorbell or knock, asking for an invitation to come in and bring on the pain. No, it rushed in, tossing the body, crushing the spirit wave after wave until you've collapsed.

Squeezing her hands, she dug nails into her palms, a quick fix to repress distressing memories of Omar. If she allowed the memories to come forth, she would drown.

But Garrett, with his wide eyes and labored chest heaves, looked like he needed a lifeline.

She exhaled in instinct—but also to breathe out whatever foolhardy thing that drove her desire to reach out and comfort Garrett.

Though she couldn't bring herself to look away, she would not touch him. Instead, she pushed through her discomfort and con-

veyed her understanding, through eye contact; hopefully, he inter-
preted the meaningful looks as understanding his pain.

Garrett's brown eyes bore into hers with pure need. And like jet
fuel, it propelled her need to touch.

Garrett leaned back against his chair, arms crossed around his
body—not in defense, but as if his arms were the only thing that
could hold him together.

Olivia cleared her throat and looked away, focusing on the
hostess.

Whitney clicked a small remote in her hand and took her guests
through the presentation, which included highlights on a variety of
artists like Kara, crafters, and quilters, including Mrs. Brooks, and
even honey from Bea.

"Now we'll need assignments for volunteers. I've taken a stab at
matching volunteers based on professional experience and interest."

As much as Olivia wanted to support the fundraiser and despite
how much she admired Whitney's organization skills, her friend
couldn't hold Olivia's attention.

While Whitney's voice droned on, Olivia and Garrett's eyes
found each other again.

The sea of chairs and people faded into an opaque cloud.

Garrett regarded her seriously—like a puzzle with thousands of
pieces that he could never put together but would happily die trying
to complete.

"Olivia." Whitney's voice snapped her back into reality. "Can you
manage the cash and in-kind donations?"

"Yes?"

Whitney smothered her smile. Addy and Kara did not. Addy even
elbowed Kara, leaned in and whispered something that made Kara
snort with laughter. Olivia imagined it was something the friends
did often. She, however, did not enjoy being the source material for
their jokes.

"I . . . of course. I would be happy to do it."

"That's not the only thing she'd love to do," Addy joked.

"Hush, Addy." Whitney rolled her eyes.

Whitney continued assigning tasks to the volunteers and then split them into smaller committees. As soon as the meeting concluded, Olivia, still embarrassed by her behavior, rushed outside like her sandals were on fire.

"Olivia." She heard Garrett calling after her.

Olivia hurried out of the house, though his voice nearly compelled her to stop, turn around, and . . . and do nothing. Waving a hand in the air, she swatted at her thoughts.

"This is madness." Olivia could only imagine the spectacle she'd made—power-walking through her whispered chastisement.

"Olivia." Garrett closed the distance, no surprise given his height and stride. She could feel his heat on her back. She slowed her pace and tossed a look over her shoulder. If he wanted, he could reach out and grab her arm. There weren't any neighbors around, but she still wished he wouldn't do anything to cause more whispers and stares.

"Please, Olivia. I just want to check on you." The sincerity ringing in his tone slowed her pace.

"Oh, I'm fine, Garrett. How about you?" she blustered through her greeting. She continued walking, hoping he'd fall back.

He did not.

"Are you okay?"

"I'm fine."

"You don't seem fine." He called to her back. "It's been a while since I've been in a relationship, but anytime a woman says they're fine, they usually aren't."

"Here's the thing." Olivia stopped and spun around. "We aren't in a relationship. We aren't anything to each other. We're practically strangers."

"We aren't strangers. We're neighbors," he smiled.

"Fine," Olivia amended. "We are neighbors . . . who don't know each other."

"We're neighbors who are attracted to each other." Garrett's eyes gleamed, daring her to pretend.

Her heart pounded furiously. She didn't like his words, his eyes, especially his tone. It was *too* comfortable, as if they'd known each other for years instead of days.

And this made her very uncomfortable.

Shaking her head, she backpedaled away, attempting to create enough distance from Garrett and his assertion. But as she took two steps back, he took one giant step forward, eating away at the gap.

Garrett looked at her as if he already knew the dips and grooves of her body.

"Wait. I'm sorry. I shouldn't have said the truth out loud."

"No, you shouldn't have." She rounded the corner to her home. "Goodbye, Garrett." Olivia ran inside her house and shut the door. She clutched her chest, her heart overtaxed.

"Wine." She pushed off the door. "I need wine." Opening her refrigerator, she pulled out a chilled bottle.

"He thinks he can just . . . say whatever he wants?" she growled while pouring well over six ounces. Olivia gulped and prepared the second of many pours. "I have a fiancé."

An absent fiancé making people laugh somewhere in Brooklyn, but one all the same.

She grabbed the rest of the bottle, and a beach blanket. Then she padded past the bench patio set that extended halfway past the deck. She shrugged off her heels at the edge where the backyard ended, and the beach began, and nearly tumbled down the pathway.

But she made it.

The moon was full, tugging the waves in to crash even harder against the shoreline.

She flapped open her Wekapo nylon blanket and laid it across the sand. It wasn't soft, but it was functional. Tonight, she didn't need luxury. She wanted peace.

A noise behind her startled Olivia.

She sighed, looking up, her hopes for peace dashed. "Oh, it's you."

"Yeah, it's me."

He handed her a small square-shaped package.

"What is it?"

"Chocolate. I told Zora that I made you mad and that I needed to apologize. She told me to give this to you. She said chocolate makes everything better."

"Where is she now?"

"With a babysitter. They're watching a movie upstairs. Zora gave me advice and then shooed me away."

Olivia took the chocolate. If it wasn't for his baby girl, she would've tossed it into the ocean.

"I'm sorry I've made you uncomfortable."

"I'm engaged, you know."

Garrett's attention zeroed on her ring finger. "I'm aware."

She followed his gaze. The ring felt hot and tight, as if it wanted to fuse itself into her skin. Punishment, perhaps for her feelings. How she wished . . . how she wished she'd met Garrett before Anderson. How she wished she had the space, without the heaviness of guilt, to explore her attraction.

"I'm mad." She hadn't meant to say that part out loud.

"At me?" Garrett sat beside her, a little too close, given her confession.

"At both of us." Olivia finally gave Garrett her full attention. "I'm mad at you because . . . because the attraction isn't one-sided. I feel it, too, and I'm ashamed of my feelings."

"Because of your guy."

Olivia nodded. "Marriage should be sacred."

"You aren't married."

"That's my intention."

"Can I be totally honest with you?"

Olivia looked up from her ring and nodded.

"Life is too short to do things you don't want to do."

"I . . . I'm sorry about your mother, but that shouldn't excuse you or me from doing . . ." she tossed up her hands, "whatever to people."

"Both can be true. If you're having cold feet or second guessing yourself, then maybe you should take a step back and reevaluate."

"I barely know you. I'm not going to risk my relationship on a fling."

"I don't do flings. My energetic little girl depends on me. I have a job that's built on relationships and reputation in a small-knit community. And honestly, it's been damn hard to look at a woman since I lost Dana. But when I look at you . . ."

"When you look at me?" Olivia leaned in with bated breath.

"When Dana died, it felt like time stopped. But when I first saw you, time didn't stand still. It sped up. And it made me realize all the things I've been missing. It made me face the fact that I've been coasting along, not really immersing myself in anything. Doing just enough where people wouldn't worry. Enough that people didn't suspect that I wasn't happy."

Olivia sat still, giving no immediate reaction, but on the inside her chest, her neck, her face—*everything* burned.

"All of that from one look?" She pushed the light question through her tight throat.

He chuckled before answering. "What I'm saying is . . . you make me feel. You move me. You make me forget my next breath. But it's beyond how you look. Can you guess the first thing I saw when I stepped inside of my mother's home?"

Olivia shook her head.

"I found your note on the counter. Mr. Whittingham put the soup in the refrigerator. It was the first meal I had in my mother's home after she died. Since I heard the news of my mom's passing, I'd been in a daze. I couldn't stomach anything and no matter what I did, I couldn't fight this feeling of ice-cold dread." He patted his chest. "Nothing, not even Zora, could make it go away. But then I warmed up your soup. I ate it."

Olivia's eyes blurred. She could feel the tears pushing through.

He licked his lips and swallowed again, like he had at Whitney's. Olivia knew it wasn't pain, but something else that overwhelmed him. "I felt so warm, Olivia," he whispered, soft, desperate, like a prayer. "Down to my bones. Zora even smiled when she scooped up the soup, and let me tell you, that little girl is just as devastated as me. She loved her gammy. She doesn't remember her mom, but she misses having a mom. Tasting your soup, seeing my daughter smile . . . it was like the sun peering through a cloudy sky. You made me feel like we could get through this."

Olivia shuddered. When she made the soup, she never knew Mrs. Brooks wouldn't get the chance to eat it. But she was glad to be of use. To make him feel good.

"I'm glad you and Zora enjoyed the soup."

"It was more than a meal." He gave her a bright smile. "After that, I desperately wanted to meet the woman who my mother teased me about during our last phone call. I asked Mr. Whittingham, and he told me about you: the smart, beautiful lady that runs like the wind."

"Oh."

"Yes, oh." This time he had laughter in his eyes. "Maybe for *you* it's just a physical attraction. But for me, it's more." His expression transformed from playful to serious as fast as lightning. "I like you, Olivia. I'm sorry about Anderson. I'm not that guy who targets women in relationships. And if you were married, I wouldn't even go there. But you're not. To be honest, it's hard for me to even care about him when I see you."

"You shouldn't say that to me." She reached out to cup his face. Her heart ka-thumped at his confession. "I don't know . . . I don't know how I feel . . . I . . ."

"That's okay. Just give me time to convince you. Give me a chance to make you feel what I feel every time I see you."

Olivia leaned forward and kissed him softly. She reveled in the softness of his lips, the warm, tentative breath that eventually let loose an exhale. Most importantly she basked in the decadence of their first kiss. Her heart sped faster; the heat of his kiss zipped energy to her mouth down to her toes.

Olivia leaned away—she didn't want to but the need to breathe trumped her desires. She licked her tongue, tasting chocolate. The man really liked sweets.

The curtain of desire shattered. She remembered now she was on the beach, in public, for all to witness. "I, um, we shouldn't have—"

Garrett kissed her back fully, no hesitation.

This time, Olivia successfully pulled away. She gripped her wine bottle and grabbed the chocolate. "I should really go now."

"I can walk you home."

"N-no, thank you." Adrenaline pumped throughout her body. She felt giddy, guilty—a tainted runner's high. She shook her head as if to shake some sense into herself. "I can get there just fine." Olivia cleared her throat. "Hey."

"Yes?"

"I think . . . maybe we should keep things friendly. I won't pretend that I don't know you in social settings, but we should limit our alone time, don't you think?"

A little smile curved on his lips.

"Why are you smiling?"

"Because you don't know just how small this community is. I'll always respect your decision. But if you change your mind, just knock on my door."

"Okay." She would never knock on his door. Not for *that*.

Garrett continued sitting on the beach, staring at her as she ran—yes, ran—away.

CHAPTER 16

INDEPENDENCE DAY

July 2021

The morning of the Fourth of July celebration, Olivia had woken up early, jogged, and then, at the edge of dawn, began organizing the artist's stations with the help of Addy and Whitney. It was Olivia's first neighborhood event, and she was determined to ensure its success, despite her inappropriate kiss with her neighbor.

The sun's rays shone brightly, highlighting Mrs. Brooks' famous yard, a picturesque place to host the Pop-up Art Fundraiser.

Garrett stepped outside and jogged over to the volunteer squad on his lawn.

"Good morning, ladies."

Whitney narrowed her eyes and sucked her teeth.

"At some point, you have to forgive me." Garrett slung his arm over Whitney's shoulder. "Why are you so upset?"

She shrugged from his embrace. The word "upset" was a mild description of Whitney's reaction when she'd heard of Garrett's plan to sell. He'd even gone outside of Whitney's real estate company to put the house on the market. When she found out the news, she'd called Olivia, giving her an earful, damn near blaming Olivia for Garrett's decision . . . as if *she* could convince her neighbor to keep his home.

When Whitney arrived that morning, she'd angrily yanked up the For Sale sign and tossed it on his porch.

"Go away, Garrett." Whitney didn't look up. She just worked like the devil, putting together booths like her life depended on it.

"I can't go away. It's my yard," he replied in a teasing voice.

"For now." Whitney shouted over her shoulder.

Addy jogged over to greet Garrett, and likely to diffuse the tension. "Good morning, friend." She leaned in closer for a hug. "Thanks again for hosting the fundraiser."

He nodded, surveying the yard. His attention snagged on Olivia.

She ignored him, only letting out her bated breath when the heat of his gaze seemed to move back to Addy.

"Mom would've loved this."

"Yes. She was such a good woman. Did I tell you I started taking up quilting a few years ago?"

"Yeah, Mom told me."

"Anyway, the other day I wanted someone's opinion about my pattern. I picked up the phone and . . . well, you know."

"I do," he lowered his voice. "Mom taught me a thing or two about quilting. You need an expert eye? Call me. I'll come over."

"Seriously?"

Olivia sneaked another peek. This time Addy caught her staring and winked. She leaned closer, grabbing his hand.

Irritation twisted around Olivia's body. Not because of the flirtation. She'd heard it directly from Addy's mouth that she and Garrett were childhood friends, and beyond that, their body language, well up to that point, had been purely platonic.

The anger simmered inside Olivia's stomach because Addy, full cup of gossip and three-fourths childishness, clearly wanted to get a rise out of Olivia. If she weren't a neighbor, Olivia would ignore her existence entirely.

"Yeahhhh, girl, I'm that good." The way he emphasized "Yeah" made Addy chuckle. Olivia wanted to laugh as well, but that would break her code of self-imposed silence.

"Your boy is multitalented."

"I didn't know having a big head equaled talent."

"At least I don't have an egghead."

She reached for her head, stopping midway when Garrett chuckled.

"I do not!"

The way the two friends bickered, made Olivia cherish the re-lationship with her godsisters even more. Once things settled a bit—i.e., Garrett returned to New Jersey, and Anderson felt more secure—Olivia would invite her godmother and sisters to her home.

"It'll be fun." She whispered to herself as she arranged framed art.

"What will be fun?"

Olivia yelped and turned to face Garrett.

"I was thinking of inviting my godsisters for a visit."

"Really?" Garrett smiled. "I would love to meet them."

Olivia nodded. "Maybe."

Oh, no you won't.

She could only imagine the looks she'd received from Billie and Perry. No way would she find herself in the same situation as Perry had been in last year with her fling. The good news was that Perry now had Baby Libby, and she'd grown even closer to her husband since their near divorce.

Olivia walked away, surveying the yard, and gasped at its mag-nificence.

Many of the in-kind donations had been garden art from local artists. There were twisted, wired flowers that reminded her of the floral majesty in Bea's yard. Colorful stake glasses stood like daisies in the grass. Addy had taken special care to hang and smooth out wrinkles from Mrs. Brooks' quilts, only one of which was on sale.

When Olivia placed labels and placards with descriptions of each quilt, she noticed tears in Addy's eyes. Olivia had read the description, and she had to admit, Addy had done a good job telling the story. One that stood out was Garrett's birth blanket. It didn't just include ducks and frogs and baby blue colors, it was a story of love and hope. In one frame, there was a pregnant woman with a complicated knot inside of her stomach, instead of a baby. If she guessed correctly, the pregnancy hadn't come easily to Mr. and Mrs. Brooks. When Garrett was born, it truly was a gift from God.

Next, Olivia strategically placed a host of tiny tables and booths on the lawn. Whitney even created a diagram, ensuring logistic success in the spacing of tables and art throughout the yard.

On center stage, in the middle of Mrs. Brooks' yard, stood a white tent that included most of the featured artists' works. Whitney put the finishing touches on Kara's green-and-pink six-by-six canopy. Her booth included both originals and prints of her work.

"I'm going to change," Olivia yelled over to Whitney. "I'll return when it starts." When her friend gave her the okay sign, she hustled back home, ready to shower and get Anderson up and ready. It would be the first time they attended a neighborhood event together.

Nervousness wormed inside of her stomach. There were so many things that could go wrong—from Garrett's reaction to Addy's snarky innuendos.

She also worried Mr. Whittingham would give more unsolicited advice, but in front of Anderson this time.

Yet everyone in the neighborhood was nice. Even Addy seemed hospitable when the mood struck her.

We'll be okay, she promised herself. Determination firmed her spine. The fundraiser would go off without a hitch and honor a woman she'd only just met.

And if not . . . well, she would continue to hold her head up high.

Olivia stepped into the house and found Anderson sitting near the kitchen island, typing away on his laptop when she crossed the threshold.

"Hey!" Olivia smiled. "You're up early."

"Yep. I've got some notes from a consultant the studio hired." He smiled like he'd just won a million bucks before grabbing his water bottle.

"I would love to read your screenplay when you're ready."

Anderson hesitated. The water bottle lingered near his mouth before he took a sip. "Sure. I just want to shape a few things up before I share."

Disappointment weighed her down as she made her way to the refrigerator to grab the bowl of fruit. It was obvious Anderson did not want her to read his screenplay, but she couldn't figure out why.

Olivia nibbled her lips. Dr. LaGrange encouraged open communication.

I'll just ask. She took a deep breath, exhaled. "Anderson, I've got a question."

Anderson, who'd resumed working, stopped when she called his name.

"Uh, oh."

"What does that mean?"

"You've got that inflection in your tone."

"Inflection?" She scrunched her nose.

"You know the thing that women, especially sisters, do when they're about to go off."

"Ummm, excuse you." Olivia crossed her arms and stared him down. She did not give one damn how he perceived her.

"Sorry, baby. Just an observation. Please, ask away."

Olivia huffed. "Why won't you let me read your work? Are you worried that I won't like it?"

"No." Anderson turned fully to face her. "I just . . . there are a lot of things in this screenplay that I'm still processing. It's like I've got my entire world on display and I'm afraid to show it to you."

"Yet you plan to have it on the big screen. So what's the big deal?"

"It's just a limited series."

"A series that thousands upon thousands of people will stream." Olivia shrugged. "Why can't you show me?"

"Just give me some time. I want it to be perfect. There's still a lot of slashing that's happening and—"

"It's fine." She waved him off. "I'm taking a shower. Can you be ready in about an hour?" She asked, glancing at her watch.

"Of course." He nodded, his expression serious.

"Great."

"Olivia?" Anderson called for her just as she hit the stairs.

"Yes?"

"I'm sorry I've been absent lately. But starting today, I'm plugged in. I'm all yours."

Olivia nodded, but she didn't smile. She refused to pretend that his reluctance to trust her hadn't hurt.

After a hot shower, Olivia felt much more relaxed. Ama had taught her to project a positive attitude if she wanted things to go well. And today, she desperately wanted things to go her way. That would include her new friends fawning over Anderson, Garrett keeping his distance, and the fundraiser making tons of money.

Anderson looked dapper in his mint green polo shirt, salmon shorts, and loafers. He swept his hair back and looked just a breath away from East Hampton Fresh.

They stepped outside, Olivia with her tortoiseshell Moscot Original sunglasses and Anderson with brown-hued aviators. Though Olivia wasn't vain by nature, she was secretly pleased that they'd made a striking pair.

Addy waved and whistled as they descended their steps. Garrett stared at them with a puppy dog expression stamped across his face.

Olivia adjusted her sunglasses, grateful for the buffer. "Hi, everyone."

A crowd gathered around them. Olivia supposed it was because they hadn't formally met Anderson, just curt waves in passing on the rare occasions they were out together.

"This is my fiancé, Anderson." Olivia looped her arm around his.

"Nice to meet you all." Anderson gave them all a winning smile.

"Oh, it's the delivery man in the flesh," Addy cracked.

Olivia's arm tightened around his. "He actually just sold his screenplay."

Anderson nodded and went on about his deal, even pulling out his phone to show the article in the *Deadline Hollywood*.

"I hear you're pretty funny, too," Addy pressed. "When's your next stand-up?"

"It's later this month. I'll be at a small club in town. You're all invited, of course."

"Oh, I'll definitely be there," Addy promised. Her eyes gleamed in a way that told Olivia Anderson would entertain her one way or the other.

Whitney raised a hand. "Charles and I are in, too. We can make a night of it. Maybe do dinner before your show?"

Anderson shook his head. "You ladies can eat, but I have to get into the zone. But, hey, let's grab a drink afterward. That's how I hooked Olivia." He winked at Olivia.

"Oh, tea," Addy said and slapped his arm. "Tell us the story of how you hooked miss ma'am over here?"

"In my Uber," he answered Addy.

"Ohhhh," the group gasped. They didn't seem to make fun but were genuinely interested in their love story.

While Anderson merrily chatted away about their first meeting, Olivia's attention darted around the group. Addy looked bemused and laughed often at Anderson's sprinkled-in jokes. Whitney looked intrigued and asked detailed questions about Anderson's screenplay. Kara, who stood close to her husband, Rich, nodded along, gasping and *aww*-ing at appropriate moments.

Garrett stood away from the crowd. His attention focused on Zora, who skipped along the lawn, hopping over lawn decorations.

Anderson squeezed her hand, bringing her attention back to him. "Olivia, babe?"

"Yes? What's that?"

"They're asking about the wedding date?"

Olivia shrugged. "Still working through the details. The venues are having less flexibility on cancellations and—"

"Cancellation? Why would you cancel your wedding? We've got the vaccination now," Addy asked, clasping the necklace resting on her collarbone. "You should look at Habberidge Hills, they're not far from here and . . ."

Olivia jumped in, cutting her off when she saw Anderson's skin was flushed. "I'm speaking of flexibility in pushing back dates if there's another variant. I have a girlfriend who's been trying to get married for the past year and a half. Now the venues are telling her she must host it by this fall or else her deposit is forfeited."

"Oh, right." Addy shook her head.

Olivia grabbed Anderson's hand, shooting Addy the death glare. "Let's look around, shall we?"

When they walked away, she heard Kara noisily exhale. "Addy, really?"

"What did I do?"

"You really should think before you speak."

Olivia decidedly ignored the duo and guided them toward the opposite end of the lawn. "Look, I'm so sorry. That's the woman who snapped a picture of you. She's a mess."

Anderson nodded. "I knew what you meant. Hey, we should find some art for the house, yeah?"

"I suppose so," Olivia agreed, though she wasn't convinced she could find statement pieces among the pop up. Still, it didn't hurt to try.

For the next half hour, Anderson and Olivia carefully walked across the lawn together. The mixed crowd milled about. It wasn't incredibly diverse—mostly Black but a few white patrons had found their way into their SANS oasis. Though it wasn't hard to find, it was three or four miles from Main Street, with trees as tall as giants.

Like oil and water, anytime someone of a different race would stand too close, the other would slide away. But there was only so much space on the lawn. Olivia looked around nervously, wondering what others thought of their union as they walked hand in hand, slicing through the thick wave of segregation.

"Oh, there's Bea." Olivia waved. A crowd stood by her table. "Do you mind if we stop for a visit?" she asked Anderson.

He nodded. "I need to check on something, but you go ahead. I'll be back."

Olivia stood third in line behind an older white couple for ten minutes. The conversation between the couple had been benign as they stood waiting their turn. Olivia caught snippets of family, work, and shopping. The conversation lulled for a bit, but then the man kicked it back into gear.

"This is a really pleasant area, huh?" the man said to the woman. From their matching white shirts and blue jean shorts, and the lightweight sweater wrapped around their shoulders, Olivia assumed they were siblings or a couple.

"It is. I didn't know they hosted so many events here. It's quaint." The woman clapped her hands.

Olivia noticed the wedding band.

"Quaint?" The man chuckled. "It's a gold mine. They're doing a lot of renovations for some of the urban areas. David bought property in Azurest for a steal."

"Really?" the woman lowered her voice, but she couldn't quite hide the greed.

"It's been in a family for generations, but the guy needed a pay-out. Bet he's not the only one," the man tried to whisper the last part, but the arrogance of his voice carried.

"Maybe we can buy some investment properties here? I bet you it'll be the next East Hampton in a few years with a little redevelopment."

Olivia cleared her throat loudly, her anger mounting. Whitney's assessment had been spot-on. People collected SANS property like baseball cards.

The startled couple glanced behind them. The man looked at Olivia, raised a so-what eyebrow, and stuffed his petite hands into his pocket. The woman had the grace to blush.

Blessedly, they shushed the conversation and rushed to the table to purchase Bea's honey.

Bea smiled broadly at the couple, though her eyes sparked like blue flames sprouting from a stove's eye. Olivia took a step back for fortification. The couple who boldly stepped forward had no such instinct.

Bea wagged a finger. "No honey for you."

"W-what? What do you mean? We waited in line." The middle-aged man blustered.

"This is my neighborhood. We don't want your redevelopments, and we don't have an 'urban area' that needs redevelopment. It's called historic. Now, move along," she waved at the couple.

They didn't argue with her, but they stomped off, making a lot of noise.

Olivia smiled when she stepped up to Bea's table. "Am I good enough to buy your honey?"

"Of course, you are, neighbor." Bea's eyes sparked with mischief.

"I'm glad you said that. I was . . . at a loss. I should've said something."

Bea shook her head. "I'm feeling feisty today." She leaned in and whispered, "Believe it or not, I've overheard several conversations like that today." She leaned back. "But when you cleared your throat . . . well, that motivated me to say something, too. Why should they feel welcome here when they want nothing to do with the neighborhood? They just want to buy our stuff, be it product, art, or land."

Bea abruptly changed the subject as she pointed to her bee products. "The honey is harvested without disturbing bees," she informed Olivia. Though placards with descriptions had been placed along the table, Bea skipped through her types of honey mixed with sage and acacia and eucalyptus.

"How do you harvest without disturbing the bees?"

"You use a fume board to move bees out of a honey box," Bea said and patiently explained the rest of the process.

"That's so fascinating."

Bea gave her a shy smile. "It's a lot of fun. But most importantly we have to protect the bees because the bees protect us."

Olivia nodded. She was slightly familiar with the argument, seeing as her godsister Billie was an environmentalist and marine biologist.

After the conversation, Bea handed her the products. She refused to give Olivia a bag because of the proximity of her home. Olivia agreed and rushed back to her home to put up her purchases. On her way to the yard, she spotted Anderson in a heated argument near their porch with another man.

"Frank wants you back home."

Anderson slapped the back of his hand against his palm. "No. Hell, no. You and the rest of them are a bunch of assholes. Leave me out of it."

"Anderson?" Olivia stood at the bottom of the porch.

"Olivia." He hurried over to her.

"Who is he?" she leaned in and whispered.

"Allow me to introduce myself." The man with chestnut brown hair walked easily down the stairs. He had blue eyes like Anderson's but his were startling intense. "I'm Bradford. Anderson's cousin."

Olivia shot Anderson a look before greeting his kin with a smile. "Nice to meet you." While Olivia offered her right hand, he glanced down to her left and pulled both hands toward him.

"Oh?" Bradford turned his attention to Anderson. Olivia couldn't quite make out his expression, but the look was . . . wry. Unimpressed. As if he found Olivia lacking.

She snatched her hands back.

"I see congratulations are in order." Bradford stepped back. "You are absolutely stunning." He tossed another look at his cousin. "And this stunning woman deserves a better ring. You could easily—"

"You need to leave, Brad. You're done and so am I."

Bradford nodded and walked off, unhurried and unworried.

Which worried Olivia.

"I'll be seeing you, Anderson."

He winked at Olivia and in seconds he disappeared into the crowd.

"No more lies, Anderson," Olivia said in a shaky voice. "Tell me now . . . who is that man and what does he want?"

CHAPTER 17

WHO IS THIS MAN?

July 2021

"We're talking. Now." Olivia rushed past the door and into the house without looking back at Anderson.

The thought of hearing another excuse soured her stomach. Sure, Bradford had introduced himself as Anderson's cousin, but when he held her hands, it made her skin crawl. And there was something else, something predatory, that lingered in Bradford's eyes.

Olivia wanted all the details so she could prepare herself should she ever lay eyes on him again.

Once she entered her home, she washed her hands and then placed the honey into the pantry. Anderson moved silently about the house. Olivia gave him a few minutes to volunteer information. When he hadn't, she launched into her investigation.

"You have a cousin who lives here?"

"I had no idea he would be here." He leaned against the island counter.

"But you knew he lived here."

"He's not in Sag Harbor. Probably commutes."

Olivia settled on the sofa in the living room. "You don't seem to be close."

Anderson laughed. "That's putting it lightly."

Olivia remembered him calling his family a bunch of assholes.

But it didn't match up with all the wonderful things he said about his mother who'd passed years ago.

Though he never spoke of his father. Why was that?

And why hadn't Olivia realized that before?

Well, today she had the time.

"You seemed to get along with your mother."

"She was the most beautiful and most wonderful person in the world. But my dad . . . he's an asshole. A racist asshole."

Olivia gripped her knees. She'd been right about her instincts toward Bradford or whoever he was. "Is your father the Frank that Bradford mentioned?"

Anderson nodded.

"And they want you back into their racist fold?"

"Bingo. It took a lot for me to pull myself out. For years, I stood silent while they screwed people over. I couldn't do much as a kid, and my mom shielded me from his side of the family as much as possible. They divorced when I went to middle school."

A light went off as he shared his past. "That's why you didn't want me to read your screenplay?"

Anderson looked down at the ground. "That's why they pay you the big bucks."

Olivia stood and squeezed his hand. "Thank you for protecting me from your family. I appreciate it, I do. But I'd much prefer that I'm prepared in these situations. No more secrets, okay?"

Not that anyone could prepare for racists, but Olivia staunchly believed in curating one's environment. If anyone showed a modicum of racism, she carefully cut them out of her life unless they worked together. In those instances, it was work only and limited social interactions during corporate gatherings.

"Olivia, I—"

"You can't account for your family. Trust me, I know that. Let's get back out there."

"Are you okay?"

"I'm fine. Let's not give your cousin another second of our time."

Anderson rushed across the room and kissed her. "You really are sweet."

Olivia laughed. "Say that a little louder for my neighbors."

"You've got it." They walked outside, smiling at each other.

Anderson made good on his promise and yelled, "Olivia's the sweetest woman in the world!"

A few people glanced their way, but mostly, people strolled along. Outside of her neighbors, she imagined most guests were from the city and nothing much could ruffle a native New Yorker's feathers. Olivia hid her chuckle behind her hand.

The confrontation on the steps had been unexpected, but she was glad to know more about Anderson. Maybe now he would share his work.

The fundraiser continued without a hitch. However, Olivia noticed Whitney frowning intensely near Kara's tent.

"She doesn't look happy," Anderson commented. "I wonder if she met my cousin."

Olivia laughed as they walked toward Whitney, Kara, her husband Rich, Addy, Garrett, and Mr. Whittingham.

"All okay?" Olivia asked.

"No. Hell, no," Whitney snapped.

"Some white guy told Kara her paintings are racist AF." Whitney used air quotes when saying "AF."

Kara looked like she was about to cry. Addy and Kara's husband, Rich, flanked her on either side. Addy gave her friend a side hug, while Rich held her hand in solidarity.

"I know it's not true, but I just feel . . . violated. He just trampled over our safe space."

Olivia nodded her agreement. That's exactly how she felt about the older couple in line. The SANS neighborhood held magic.

Mr. Whittingham grunted while he scanned the crowd. "Sometimes I wonder if these kids understand their history. We've been here since the 1800s. We came here for work in the whaling business, but we made our own homes, cut the wood of our homes and our churches. This place is precious and we've got to hold on tight."

He shot Garrett with a direct stare. Garrett didn't look away, but rather thoughtful at Mr. Whittingham's quiet challenge.

"You're right." Kara agreed with a shaky voice. "I don't think they get it. Mom and Dad made sure I understood my history. This place," she pointed down to the land beneath her feet, "is special. There wasn't 'Stormy Weather' for Lena Horne when she came here."

"Preach," Addy said with jazz hands.

"Ruby Dee and Ossie Davis and Harry Belafonte rested their heads at the Whittingham's residence." Kara's voice grew as powerful as a Baptist preacher. "*The* Langston Hughes performed speeches on our beaches. So, who is this man to tell us, tell *me*, that I'm racist when his very presence is offensive to our ancestors?" She snorted. "Huh?" her attention drifted toward the homes.

"What is it?" Rich asked.

"Looks like I figured out my next project."

Olivia smiled. "Sign me up for a copy." Kara's words empowered and encouraged Olivia to roll up her sleeves and fight.

"Stand in line," Addy said with a smile. "My girl is amazing."

"I feel like they're scoping us out, checking for weaknesses," Whitney crossed her arms, bringing the mood back to somber. "One of them had the audacity to ask Garrett about his house being up for sale."

"I thought you hid the For Sale sign?" Olivia asked.

"I did. But I can't stop them from looking it up on the internet. Mr. Sellout over here has his property all over Zillow."

"Hey, now." Garrett raised a hand. "I'm sorry about this, but I told you why I can't."

"You can keep it, I know you can," Addy argued. "You just don't want to be bombarded by the memories. But you'll make new ones. You heard Mr. Whittingham. Please reconsider."

"Yes. Don't leave poor Olivia to deal with a racist neighbor," Whitney added.

Garrett stared at Olivia, smiling at her for the first time since the fundraiser started. Well, to be fair, Olivia had avoided him at all costs.

"No, I wouldn't want to leave Olivia in bad hands."

"I'll protect her." Anderson pulled Olivia closer, moving the attention to them. "If the buyer ends up being white, hopefully they're cool like me." Anderson surveyed the group.

"Well, we just met you, so the jury is still out." Addy looked him up and down.

"We aren't all bad, trust me. I'll prove you wrong."

Addy, even Mr. Whittingham, gave Olivia a look, as if to say, get your man.

Olivia grew annoyed, mostly at Anderson. Did they not just get bombarded by his racist cousin?

"Kidding, kidding," Anderson attempted to diffuse the situation. "Besides, Olivia here can take care of herself. You should see her in action when she's talking to her one of her coworkers, Chad, Chase . . . who is it again?"

"Chase. My boss."

"Right. My woman can hold her own against anyone."

"She shouldn't have to deal with it to begin with, at home or at work," Garrett replied. "She shouldn't have to protect herself. If you're going to marry a Black woman, you need to understand she's going to deal with microaggressions at work, and trust me, that shit is tiring."

"What does that matter? She's beautiful," Anderson said.

"Obviously so," Garrett said in a hard voice. "But that doesn't stop people, be it Black or white, from passing her over for someone white or lighter."

Anderson tried to close the distance between them, but Olivia stepped between them in the middle. She placed a hand on Anderson's pounding chest.

Her cheeks blazed with embarrassment. She didn't want to have this conversation in a crowd. "Let's go," she whispered to her fiancé.

Anderson shook his head, his attention on Garrett, who towered over them. "Look, I'm aware colorism and racism exists but she got a promotion six months ago. My girl is majorly talented."

Olivia felt like an accordion squeezed by Garrett and stretched by Anderson. While she appreciated Garrett imparting a teachable moment, now wasn't the appropriate place. For this subject she needed copious wine, a therapist, and her closest girlfriends.

He didn't get it. She still bore scars from her childhood; she wasn't ready to share that with Anderson—with anyone who didn't know her well.

Just recently it seemed in vogue to unpack colorism, but back when she was twelve years old, Olivia instinctively knew she was treated differently, but at the time no one would really listen. And if they did, they chalked it up to jealousy or insecurity. She couldn't articulate it back then, but growing up she remembered R&B and rap songs that exalted light-skinned women. Even in movies, many of the main heroines in Black films were light- or brown-skinned, not black, especially in romances.

They were always the prize.

Olivia knew there were much deeper reasons behind colorism but many times over the years she'd felt crazy—like she was shouting her feelings into the void. She wished she had the void now, instead of center stage at a lawn fundraiser.

"Do you know how much harder she had to work than her counterparts?" Garrett defended. "Don't tell me you don't realize that—"

"Enough, Garrett." She shot him a thanks-a-lot look. "It's fine."

It wasn't fine. Her neighbors looked at Olivia like they felt sorry for her, and worse, she felt sorry for herself. When she first met Anderson, he seemed to understand the goings-on in the Black community. And what he didn't understand, he usually took the time to educate himself on. But there were times when he wanted to talk about a police shooting, when he wanted to pick apart every detail in a high-visibility case.

And sometimes, she wanted peace. She needed time to go inward, reflect, heal from the communal trauma each death regurgitated.

Anderson threw his hands in the air, as if warding off the group. "I'm heading back."

Olivia sighed. "I'll catch you all later. Whitney, call me for cleanup, okay?"

"Of course. If you need more time, don't stress. Mr. Whittingham and I can recruit some help, right?"

Mr. Whittingham nodded, his eyes soft and understanding as he looked at Olivia. "Of course. Take care of yourself in there."

Olivia turned to leave, but before she could walk away, Kara called for her. She lowered her voice to a whisper. "I don't mean to be disrespectful, but that not all white folks thing is . . ." she stopped speaking, as if struggling to find the right words.

"Not cool," Addy said as she sidled up beside them.

Kara pointed to her friend. "Yes. That's it."

"Kara!" Olivia admonished her new friend.

Kara gave her a quick hug. "Sorry, don't hate me but . . . I'm sure this is something you guys can work out."

Olivia accepted the hug, purely because of exhaustion. This day had turned out to be spectacularly horrible.

Kara released her from the hug. "I'll see you later. Have a good evening."

Olivia gave them a strained smile. "You too."

At the entrance to her home, she paused. She wasn't ready for the conversation with Anderson, but she would have it.

She didn't have to wander far to find him. He sat at the breakfast table, elbows on the table, chin resting on his fists.

Olivia paused near the door before heading his way. "Hey." She sat across from him.

"What happened back there?" Olivia gentled her voice.

"I feel like our neighbors are making me out to be the enemy. And it pisses me off, because people like Bradford and my father are the ones that divide us. Not me."

Olivia nodded. When Anderson first asked her to marry him, she knew they would eventually have to have this conversation about race in America. It wasn't enough to acknowledge differences, but to consider the emotional labor it would take to converse and educate on things a Black partner would already know.

"This isn't about good or bad. I know you're a good guy, and soon our neighbors will, too. But the *not all white people* thing? We know that and it was entirely unnecessary to say it."

"Why not? I wanted them to know that I'm not like that."

His defensive tone, the way he leaned back, crossing his arms like a defensive toddler, reminded Olivia of a phrase Ama often said in a situation when one of the godsisters protested a little too much.

"A hit dog will holler."

Olivia had a feeling that phrasing wouldn't go over well, so instead she opted to say, "Then you *show* them through actions, not meaningless words. What you don't do is diminish our feelings, especially in a moment of frustration."

"Why do I have to prove anything to them, anyway? This is just a summer home. We'll be back in New York soon. We'll be among our people."

"These are my people, too."

She adored Mr. Whittingham's dapper style, along with his advice and wisdom. She respected Whitney's commitment to protecting the history and legacy of the community. She loved Kara's passionate and open nature, the very opposite to her own. While the jury was still out for Addy, she was authentically and unapologetically herself, an aspect that Olivia deeply admired.

And Garrett . . . she just plain liked him. He was a wonderful dad, thoughtful and kind. She couldn't explain just how, but she knew he had a good soul.

"Can we set a wedding date, Olivia?" Anderson asked again as if he knew her thoughts lingered on Garrett.

"I still haven't spoken to Ama."

"*We* are getting married. Not Ama. Us. So, what will it be?"

"I think . . . I think we should slow down."

"Slow down?" Anderson let out a frustrated sigh.

"It's not that I don't want to marry you," Olivia quickly reassured him. "But we haven't known each other for long. We just jumped into the engagement quickly. Then the shutdown pushed us together in close quarters. We've had maybe a half a dozen dates. I mean, I just met someone from your family today." She stopped her barrage and paused. "What do you think?"

"I know what I want. But you don't know what you want," he coldly replied. Hands on the table, he pushed himself up, then walked upstairs.

She didn't follow him because he was right: Olivia Jones did not know what she wanted.

Before she could dwell on her failings, a text dinged from her phone.

When she saw Addy's name, she nearly ignored it. She didn't need another kick when she was already below sea level.

Hey! Mr. Whittingham asked me to text you. Once you're done with
your guy, party on the beach at sunset. I suppose he can come, too. ☺

She'd forgotten about the party Mr. Whittingham was hosting.
She offered to help but after she told him about serving on the
Fourth of July committee and the Labor Day events, he declined,
stating there were plenty of neighbors who could pitch in.

Olivia glanced upstairs at the picture Anderson had purchased,
small squares in various colors including turquoise, deep blue, and
slate gray, some of which intersected and overlapped each other.
The cool and crisp art had been a pleasant surprise, and she really
adored it. Though he wasn't sure of their neighbors, she recognized
his effort to make this place a home.

Olivia did not quit.

She fixed things.

She could fix them, too.

Another ding from her phone, this time from Kara. She didn't
hesitate to open the message.

Remember to wear white for the beach party! And bring Anderson. We
promise we won't bite.

Olivia went upstairs. Anderson sat propped up in bed. The glow
from his laptop illuminated his face.

"I'm sorry if my words and actions hurt you. But I would love it
if . . . if you could join me down at the beach. There's a party—"

"A party? Really, Olivia?"

"Yes. I want us to get past this . . . awkwardness with the neighbors."

"It's not awkwardness. They're determined not to like me. I
should've known it would be this way."

"What are you talking about?" Olivia scrunched her nose.

"There's even a beware sign at the top of the neighborhood."

"A beware sign?" Olivia frowned. "What are you talking about?"

"The blue sign that says this neighborhood is an African-American Community."

Olivia inhaled, looking at the ceiling for strength, a clue as to how to navigate this land mine.

"You heard Kara and Whitney and Mr. Whittingham out there. This neighborhood is important. And right now, yes, it's under attack for gentrification. The people who are throwing money at our neighbors aren't looking to join a community. They're looking for their next Airbnb investment or just a beach house. That doesn't mean that we aren't welcoming."

"We?" Anderson scoffed. "Since when did you become *we*?"

"Since Omar purchased this home. Since I became friends with my neighbors. Since I decided to protect this place." The volume of her voice grew with each assertion.

Redevelopment companies like ASK tossed out millions of dollars—life-changing money for anyone whether they needed it or not.

Anderson nodded. "Look, I get it. And I'm sorry, but I'm passing on the beach party."

Olivia clasped her hands together. "I'd really like for you to come. If only for a few minutes."

"I'm on deadline," he replied, his voice as thin as his excuse.

"You can't avoid our neighbors forever."

Anderson folded his arms and gave her a look as if to convey "just watch me."

Something raw crept up her throat. While she understood why Anderson felt sore about the beach party, she had no plans to be the middleman between her neighbors and her fiancé. Did he make a thoughtless comment? Absolutely. But people weren't the sum of their mistakes. Olivia knew she couldn't and wouldn't force him into a stressful situation.

However, that wouldn't stop her from fellowship with her neighbors.

"I wish you a productive working session." As soon as she wished him luck, loud music pumped through the speakers. Olivia smiled to soften the irony.

Ignoring her sullen fiancé, Olivia changed into a white linen jumpsuit. She pulled her hair into a high-top bun and put on thin pearl drop earrings and a thick pearl bracelet that covered the entirety of her wrist.

At half past eight, the party was in full swing. She felt a bit silly bringing a bottle of wine from the local winery when there was a full bar, covered with florescent lights.

"When did this happen?" Olivia whispered to herself. She'd been so focused on the front yard she hadn't noticed the party setup on the beach. About a hundred feet from the bar stood a DJ booth. A crowd of dancers rocked near the speakers. A beautiful couple stood in the middle of the dance floor, the woman had wrapped her legs around the man's waist. The man thrust his pelvis, the woman bounced her body, they were passionately in sync with each other, not the music.

"All right, Dirty Dancing." One of her neighbors yelled at the amorous couple. They danced harder and the man thrust so hard the woman fell off his body and toppled onto the sand. Olivia covered her mouth but then stopped when the woman popped up like a daisy, laughed and danced again.

"She's here!" Kara announced. She grabbed Olivia's wrist and dragged her to their smaller group in a quieter area near the shoreline.

"When did you get here?" Kara yelled over the music.

"Just now." Olivia lifted her wine bottle. "Where should I put this?"

Kara threw her head back and laughed. "Right in my cup, neighbor." She lifted a stout blue cup. "Addy has a bottle opener. Wait right here."

Olivia scanned the crowd, her attention snagged on Rich, Kara's husband, and Addy rocking back and forth, while whispering to each other. Kara walked toward them. Addy said something to make Kara laugh, though Kara punched Rich's shoulder.

Addy pulled the bottle opener from her clutch and the trio walked toward her.

Addy reached out her hand wordlessly for the bottle and then popped the top. She slipped the stopper into her purse, and then graciously poured a cup for Olivia, Kara, and Rich.

"Thank you." Kara raised her glass. She scanned the beach—there had to be near a hundred people crowding the area.

"This is the entire neighborhood?"

"Yes," Addy answered and then took a sip of the wine. "Sag Harbor Hills, Azurest, and Ninevah neighbors all come together. Plus, family and friends. Occasionally some interlopers will come in from the yachts." She pointed at the floating fleet of yachts. "You can spot them quickly."

"Ah. The wardrobe, I suppose."

"Wardrobe and the way they wonder around, like a deer stuck in headlights," Kara added. "Like, ahhhh! Who are these prosperous Black people? How did they get the money to buy this property!" She waved her hands and screamed like an actress in a horror movie.

Olivia shook her head laughing. "No way."

"Way," Addy slurred.

"Oh. Looks like your guy is here." Addy pointed behind her.

Olivia smiled as she turned around. "Oh, he must've changed his . . ."

Her words dropped and rolled with the tide. It wasn't Anderson, but Garrett with a fitted white V-neck shirt that showcased the smooth panes of his chest. White linen pants had been rolled just above his ankles.

Olivia didn't have a chance to shoot Addy a murderous glare, she was too occupied by Garrett.

"Oh, hello." Olivia smoothed her hair for some reason. When she realized her preening, she dropped her hand and clutched her cup.

"Olivia." Her name poured out of his mouth like honey.

"He doesn't say our names like that, does he, Kara?" Addy not-so-softly said to her best friend.

"Nope," Kara said wistfully.

"Yeah, he better not," Rich joked, but there was a little edge to his voice.

Garrett raised his hand. "You don't have to worry about me, man. You've got your hands full as it is."

Kara punched Garrett in the arm, much like she'd done to Rich a few minutes ago.

"Yeah, he does," Addy snorted into her plastic wine cup.

"Hush, Addy." Kara for once stopped joking with her friend. They looked at each other for a few seconds but it was Addy who dropped the stare game, looking away. Silk Sonic's "Leave the Door Open" blared from the speakers, breaking the tension.

Kara twirled in place. "Let's dance." She grabbed Olivia's hand and dragged them away from the group. Kara jumped into the center of a dance circle and lifted her white tulle skirt. Her feet kicked up the sand as she danced what seemed to be her annoyance away.

Olivia joined her, hoping that she, too, could dance the blues away. She felt eyes on her—she knew who they belonged to, but she refused to look his way. She danced for herself, anyway.

If Garrett just happened to be turned on by the way she shimmied her shoulders, or the slow whine of her hips, that was on him. After dancing for a few songs, someone tapped her shoulder.

"You look thirsty." Garrett handed her a cup.

"What is it?"

"You like gin and tonic, right?"

"H-how did you know?" She'd never drank much around Garrett, and if anything, she always drank wine.

"Addy told me." She looked at her neighbor, who still hung near the shoreline chatting with Rich.

"Thank you." She smiled at him, drinking the cocktail a little too quickly. She stopped dancing and merely rocked back and forth while the DJ switched it to old-school dancehall music.

"Having fun?" Garrett asked.

"A blast." Olivia told the truth. Many people had come by, shaking her hand, and in some cases introduced themselves. It was genuine. It wasn't a who are you, where are you from and what do you do, but rather, looking people directly in the eyes and welcoming them to the neighborhood.

"How about we go for a walk?" Olivia offered, surprising herself.

"That's okay with you?"

"It is."

Garrett placed a hand on her back, guiding them away from the crowded area.

His hand seared the small of her back, his calloused fingertips dragged along her smooth bared skin. Olivia's mouth flooded with moisture. This man was a living, breathing tall drink of water and she felt like she'd trekked the desert for forty days and forty nights.

It wasn't love, that would be ridiculous. But she felt something for him.

"I've got to get back soon. The sitter arrived a few minutes ago, but I don't want to be too far away." He checked his phone and seemed to relax when there were no missed calls.

"Thanks for helping today. My mom would've loved it."

"I'm surprised that was the first time that happened. Your mother's lawn is simply gorgeous."

Summer on Sag Harbor   211

"Best in the neighborhood. I used to mow it every week growing up, but now she's got—had a guy take over."

"I need his info. My landscaper had an emergency with one of their kids and he'll be gone for a few months."

"I've got you." Garrett said it in a way that meant more than lawncare.

"Did Zora have a good time?"

"Oh, yeah. She wants to stay here longer. She says she doesn't want Grandma's house to go away."

"She realizes you're selling."

"Yep. As soon as I hired a photographer, she followed her around asking questions before I could head her off."

Olivia laughed. "Oh, I bet she was not pleased."

"No." Garrett's voice held humor. "She was here a bit earlier for the beach party. She was looking for you but . . ."

"I was home."

"With Anderson."

"Yes."

"I'm sure I caused some tension between you two, but it bothers the hell out of me, Olivia. Not that you're with someone but will he truly have your back? Like with the dark-skinned comment." He shook his head. "My baby girl is already going through it. It started at daycare."

Olivia wanted to pretend like she was surprised, but she wasn't. Kids noticed differences as soon as parents pointed them out.

"She came home crying because her best friend, Kaitlyn, asked her why was she so dark and that she should run away from the sun."

Olivia huffed. "Wow. That's . . . an oldie but goodie." She remembered her own experiences growing up. At first it started as genuine questions but then devolved into insults.

"What did you say?"

"I told her she looked like her mother and her mother was a gorgeous Black queen. Every morning, when we brush our teeth, I get her to look in the mirror and say 'good morning, Black princess. I love you.' I affirm her beauty and her worth. And after a year I noticed a difference. She only wants Black dolls who look like her. She likes books that have characters who look like her. I tested it once, but she wouldn't even look at the book. I may have overcorrected," he said with a laugh.

Olivia laughed along with him. "You're a great dad. To be honest, I'm still dealing with the wreckage of low self-esteem. My mom . . . she never affirmed my beauty. She always found me to be lacking."

"You know you're gorgeous, right?" Garrett asked slowly.

"I do . . . truly, I get it. But sometimes I find myself adding an 'if only' or 'I'd look better if I wore this shade of color, or I need to avoid a light pink or red shade of lipstick because it doesn't look good on me.'"

Thinking on it, Olivia often fought past whispered insults in her head. "Keep up the good work with your daughter. If I had your voice in my head, telling me I was beautiful while growing up, well . . . I think I'd be a different person."

"I could tell you every day now. But you wouldn't like that, would you?"

Olivia shook her head. Oh, she wanted it. She just didn't want to want his compliments . . . or him. It wasn't part of the plan.

Garrett didn't say anything for a long while. "I've been thinking about what you said earlier. About us not being alone together. I'm sorry I've made you uncomfortable. I'm going to respect your relationship with Anderson. If he's what you want then who I am to question?"

Olivia stopped walking. She stared at him, but she couldn't make out his expression in the darkness. Though, she didn't need to see him when she clearly heard the sincerity in his voice.

"I'd like for us to be friends," Olivia offered.

Garrett still didn't speak, his silence startled her heart. "If you don't want me—"

"I'll take you anyway I can have you, Olivia. Friends it is." He cleared his throat. "Say, have you been to the Caribbean and Craft festival?"

"No." She shook her head. "Can't say that I have."

"I'll take you there. As friends, of course. Anderson can come, too."

"When is it?"

"Sometime in mid-August. Like the thirteenth or fourteenth."

"He'll likely be back in New York."

"He's got more meetings." She'd guessed.

"Okay." His voice picked up in energy. "Let's head back. I need to get home to Zora."

They passed the beach party and walked near their homes. Olivia tripped on the uneven sand, but Garrett stopped her fall. Pulling her close to his side, one arm wrapped around her waist, the other held her hand.

"Olivia?" Garrett whispered before he walked up the path to his home.

"Yes?"

"Goodnight, Beautiful Black Queen."

Olivia exhaled, her heart whomping against her chest. After her conversation with Garrett, she felt energized. Instead of going home, she returned to the beach party and danced with her neighbors under the moonlight.

Around midnight, the party concluded. Olivia returned home to her backyard, washed her feet with the water hose in her yard, and softly crept back inside. By the time she went to bed, her heart pounded a complicated beat. She knew she played a dangerous game.

Yet it didn't feel like one. It was real, not cheap, nothing salacious.

Instead of moving closer to Anderson she rolled away, placing a hand over her heart. She didn't know what was right or wrong, up or down.

Maybe in time she would understand her complicated feelings. The saying goes that time heals wounds, but time also allowed for discovery. And for once, Olivia wasn't afraid to discover herself.

CHAPTER 18

THE HAMPTONS

July 2021

Never in all her years had Olivia been grateful for a party save for today. Travis, her dear friend and hairdresser, had rented a lush mansion in East Hampton. Olivia hadn't returned since the party with her old coworkers. After a poor experience, between the gossiping and copious drinks, she promised herself to never convene with coworkers outside of work.

Though she never thought to dismiss East Hampton entirely, there were far too many interesting locales to travel to.

When Travis came calling, she came running. For the past decade, he'd permed and pressed her hair into perfection. He even warned her years ago to move away from relaxers, or what he called "creamy crack," because eventually her hair would thin from the chemicals.

She wanted his reaction to her new 'do, or rather, her transitioning hair. Though she followed Bea's advice to check out Dita, the woman's schedule had been booked to the gills, and she wouldn't be able to see her until next week. For now, Olivia had viewed a million YouTube tutorials, and made hair concoctions from mixing bananas, oil, and yogurt and using Bea's products. Somehow, her hair had survived, and even thrived under her inexpert care. At the moment, she styled her tendrils into small strawlike twists that hung just above her shoulders.

Traffic was busy for her and Anderson's drive from Sag Harbor Hills to East Hampton. Although it was less than ten miles away, it felt like hundreds of miles. From the crawl-like flow of traffic to the distinct look of the homes. From what Olivia could glean through the seven-foot landscaped shrubbery, the homes transitioned from white, or bark-brown shingle style homes in Sag Harbor, to massive structures ranging from new white farm homes set on several acres of land to a mishmash of shingles and bricks with austere gray roofs.

East Hampton residents firmly straddled between colonial seaside and opulence. Some had done it extremely well, while others had built mansions with an identity crisis.

And then there was Travis' rental home, which suffered from no such identity crisis. It was pure opulence—modern architecture with thick glass panes that let in natural light.

Anderson reached over the console and grabbed her hand. "It'll be nice to have a change in scenery, yeah?"

"Yes," Olivia agreed.

Anderson and Olivia were the first to arrive. Travis stood on the balcony and waved his arms in the air, directing them to the pebbled driveway that led to the garage. One side of the double garage opened. Anderson took it as a sign to park the car. By the time they'd parked and pulled out luggage, Travis was standing in the driveway.

Olivia accompanied her friend while they walked toward the front door. He'd gathered his curly hair and pulled it into a low ponytail, but she knew once the party was in full swing it would hang loose. His ensemble included a short-sleeve turquoise shirt, with a few unsnapped buttons, baring his shiny brown and smooth chest. He wore dark blue shorts that sat just above his knees and low-top laced sneakers. The gold woven Saint Laurent logo stood out against his white shoes. It was the perfect summer Hampton look but Travis had remixed it to add more personality.

"Welcome, friends." Travis opened his arms and hesitated. "Are you taking hugs?"

Olivia nodded, suddenly emotional. The friends' embrace was tight and long. After letting go, Olivia stepped back into Anderson's waiting arms.

"Travis, this is my fiancé, Anderson." Olivia squeezed his side with her arm.

"Great to meet you," Anderson said as he offered his hand.

Travis smiled and shook his hand. "Glad to finally meet you. Come in." Travis grabbed Olivia's bag. "You two love birds will be upstairs, next to moi." When he pointed both hands toward himself, she noticed his royal blue painted nails.

"Cute."

"I know." Travis winked. "I'm going to send these WASPS running to the hills." When he showed them to the room, Anderson went inside to store their luggage.

Travis grabbed her hand before she could follow him inside.

"What is it?"

Something caught his attention, and it took a few seconds for her to realize that his eyes were aimed at her hair. "Your hair is looking . . ."

"I know. I'm trying something new." Olivia picked at her hair. "I'll twist it out once we get settled."

"No, it's looking good. May I?" Travis reached for her hair and Olivia nodded.

"It's soft. Really soft." He twirled her hair. "No split ends. Hair is thick and healthy. I'm impressed."

"Why thank you."

"What products are you using?"

"Have you heard of Abeja?"

Travis shook his head. "Can't say that I have."

"I'll show you."

"Do that. And I'll do the twist out. I miss playing in your hair." He gave her a big dramatic frown.

"You mean you miss *me*, right?" Olivia winked.

"Sure, sure. You, too. Meet me in the bathroom. I'll get set up."

Olivia grabbed her products from the leather Fendi bag Omar had gifted her years ago.

His last gift.

No, that wasn't right. His last gift had been the house and community. He'd given her SANS, the greatest gift of all.

She bent over to grab the bottles wrapped in a recycled bag within the Fendi bag.

"What are you up to?" Anderson asked.

"Travis is going to do my hair."

"Oh."

She turned around to face Anderson. "What do you mean, oh?" She turned to face him.

"I mean . . . I thought your hair was already done."

Olivia shook her head. "No, it's a new style I'm trying now. You twist it and when you untwist it, you get these corkscrew curls."

Anderson fingered her hair. "Hmmm." He leaned over, inhaling. "You smell sweet."

"I am sweet."

"I know."

She turned around, wrapping her arms around his waist and gave him a deep kiss.

He smiled when she pulled away. Passion deepened the blue hue in his eyes. "I miss this."

"Me too." Olivia knew exactly what he meant. She missed easy.

Lazy kisses, passionate lovemaking. Maybe this weekend they could press the reset button. Away from neighbors, new friends, work.

Garrett.

"I'll see you soon. You can go explore, make a drink, or take a nap."

"A nap sounds good before everyone arrives."

He pulled his gold three-quarter-sleeved shirt over his head. "Don't want to wrinkle my shirt."

"Is that new?"

Anderson shook his head. "Had to break this out of the vault."

"It's very nice."

He looked embarrassed by the praise.

"Have fun." Olivia gave him another kiss, this time featherlight.

"I'll miss you," he immediately returned. He had a love-sick puppy look on his face, hamming it up so hard it made Olivia laugh.

"I'll miss you, too." She gave him another kiss and then slipped into Travis' room.

"Okay, so here are the products." She handed it to her old friend. He turned it over and squeezed a dime-sized drop into his hands. After rubbing the product in her hair, he unraveled her strands.

"Oh, I love the glow, the smell. This is good stuff." Travis murmured to himself.

"Like magic, right?"

"Nothing is magic, honey, but this is close. A sis created this?"

"Not entirely sure of her ethnicity, but I'm fairly sure she's mixed with Black."

"I must meet her."

"I'll ask, but she doesn't do people." Olivia recounted the few times they bumped into each other, and the times where she jogged to her apothecary.

"You were a woman on a mission. I've never seen you like that outside of your work."

"Yeah, well, these days I'm over it."

"Over what? Work?"

Olivia nodded.

"Can't believe Ms. Jones will be part of the Great Resignation."

"It's just not the same. I make people and companies who already have an obscene amount of money, more money. Meanwhile, some folks are struggling to keep their heads above water."

Olivia thought about the residents in SANS who had no choice but to sell to companies like ASK. Upwards to three million dollars was life-changing money and developers knew just how to hit stubborn owners—build around them until the rise in taxes forced them into a decision.

"I'm smart and creative. I'm sure I can figure out how to work around them," Olivia muttered to herself.

"What's that, babe?"

"Nothing." It wasn't nothing. It was something. The wheels in her mind whirled. What if they could fight fire with fire? Money with money? It was a little unorthodox, but maybe they could figure out a way to buy investment property for those who couldn't afford not to sell? Or create a way to help them pay property taxes.

"So, who did you invite for the week?"

"A few of my fave clients. My boys Brian, Tim, Ced, and Harper," he rattled off his close friends. "And some friends are inviting friends. Tim is dating some guy in your neck of the woods. Do you know an Eric Perry?"

The name sounded familiar, and she told him as much.

"Well, yes. He's coming and asked if a few folks from your neighborhood could come. I don't really know them, but he swears they're good people."

"Who?" Olivia's heart pounded. The only neighbor she was in the mood to see right now was Kara and Whitney. This wouldn't be Mr. Whittingham's scene.

"Not sure. I'll have to pull up my phone. One of the guys is a retired ballplayer."

"Ballplayer?" Olivia snickered. "Which sport?"

"It has a ball."

"Most sports do."

"Meh." Travis shrugged. "I'll check once I'm finished with your gorgeous hair."

"Is it Charles Parks?"

He snapped his fingers. "That's his name. And his wife."

Olivia let out a deep exhale. "Okay, they aren't so bad."

"Right. It'll be all good, babe. Trust me."

She trusted Travis with many things: her hair, a to-die-for key lime pie, and a secret—despite the stereotype that his profession were gossips. If asked to keep a secret, Travis could and would keep her confidence.

Last, she trusted Travis to have the best intentions.

Which is why she did not immediately leave when her boss, Chase Lackey, showed up the next day during brunch, already drunk.

Looking at the small affluent crowd, a few who were clients of Array Capital, it should not have surprised her that Chase would arrive. He and his wife, Marcel, loved the Hamptons and summered here every year.

But why here, and why now?

Travis and his actual guest, Harper, who was also Chase's client, immediately escorted him upstairs after his driver gently dumped him on Travis' doorstep.

Olivia pushed her strawberry-guava mimosa aside and massaged her temple.

"What's wrong?" Anderson whispered.

"You know the man who stumbled in here?"

Anderson shook his head. "Didn't get a good look."

"That's my boss."

Anderson winced. "Bummer, but we can still have a good time. Let's just ignore him."

Chase Lackey wasn't an easy man to ignore. The best Olivia could hope for was that he slept for most of the day and his wife, Marcel, would come to collect him.

Olivia nodded, sipping her mimosa. "You're right. He probably won't be here for long."

Mentally shoving at the gray cloud lingering near her head, she went on with the day. The grounds were gorgeous and included a cobbled pathway that led to an older cottage with a yellow door. The cottage was surrounded by green foliage and a mixture of flowers, and included a beautiful meadow and, near the edges, a cluster of low-bush blueberries. A small, wired bench stood to the side of the small home.

"Bea would love it here."

"Feels like one of those fairy-tale homes." He looked at Olivia, a look of challenge and determination. "Should we go inside?"

Olivia shook her head. "No. Not until we know what Travis' rental includes. Someone could live here, maybe a groundskeeper."

"Then we'll ask." Anderson rapped his fingers against the door and shouted hello.

While he waited for an answer, Olivia shot Travis a quick text.

OLIVIA: Is the cottage near the house part of the rental?
TRAVIS: Yes! Lockbox near one of those bushes. 1111 is the code. Have fun. ☺

Olivia searched for a lockbox and found it among the blue flowers. When she pressed the code, the top popped open, revealing a small key.

Turning around, she tapped Anderson's back. "I've got a key. Move aside."

"How did you . . . ?"

"I texted Travis while you yelled like a loon." She inserted the key, twisting the lock to open.

Anderson's shoulders shook when he laughed. "Again . . . that's why they pay you the big bucks."

"Indeed." She opened the door, revealing a quaint studio-style cottage. The old-world bones of the house clashed with the new, including a stainless-steel oven, microwave, and Bluetooth speakers. A wide-screen television sat on a refurbished TV stand. The owners painted the walls a fresh spring yellow.

A queen-sized bed, flush against the back wall, took up precious space in the small cabin. The bedding was black, with a mountain of yellow, pink, and black accent pillows.

"This is not what I expected." Olivia frowned a bit. She wanted the enchanting cottage to feel like a world away. She wanted to forget about Chase, forget about her mounting disdain for her job and the people she served.

"It has a bed." Anderson wrapped his arms around her waist. "It'll take us years to move all the pillows, but I'll make it worth your while." He kissed her neck, on the spot that made her knees shake.

Olivia turned, then wrapped her arms around his neck. She kissed his chest, his neck, leading up to his lips.

"I'll take that as a yes."

"Definitely," Olivia whispered against his lips.

"I'll shovel the pillows. You get naked."

Olivia giggled as she slipped off her pants. By the time she started unsnapping the pearl buttons on her shirt, Anderson had made a pillow mound on the floor and shrugged off his shirt and shorts.

Anderson helped her work her buttons and lifted her onto the bed. "I'm glad we got away."

"Me too. Though . . ." she walked her fingers up his bare chest. "We have a bed at home."

"Home?" Anderson snorted. "That's not my home."

"Oh . . . okay." Olivia tried to get them back in the groove by sucking his lips.

"I mean, you don't think it's home, do you?" he asked.

Olivia's head hit the lone pillow on the bed. "Anderson, are you really discussing this right now?" Olivia lifted her eyebrows.

"Yeah, sorry. Dumb. Seriously dumb."

Olivia squeezed her eyes shut and let the warmth of his hands guide her away from her irritation and back into ecstasy.

Anderson ripped open a foil packet, rolled it onto himself and rocked inside of her.

Olivia winced from the friction. She wasn't fully aroused, not after the sarcastic comment about her home.

"You okay? I thought . . . well, I thought you wanted it." He slid out. "We can stop."

Olivia shook her head. She needed this. It'd been so long since they had been together. Her Sag Harbor home had seemed to create a rift between them. And it *was* her *home*.

"No. Kiss me." She gripped his neck, lowering his lips to hers.

"It's about what I said earlier?"

Olivia nodded. "It threw me off, is all."

Anderson gathered her close. "I'm sorry," he whispered against her neck. His words rang with sincerity. Olivia tried, she really tried to recapture the flyaway feeling of passion that burned just minutes ago.

"Let's just . . . lie here for a few minutes," Anderson suggested.

Olivia sighed and finally gave into the cooling off.

"Next time, I swear on my honor I won't say anything so stupid before sex."

"But you meant it . . . right?" Olivia held her breath. "You aren't happy in Sag Harbor."

Anderson exhaled, the hair of his chest brushed against her bare back. "It has nothing to do with you and everything to do with me. I've been laser focused on this screenplay. Then it actually happened, I sold the freaking story of my dreams. And now, for the first time in a very long time, I have a clear vision of what I want to do and who I want to be. I really want to go for this."

"You should." Olivia turned around to face him. "I'll support you all the way. I'm so excited and proud of you."

Anderson's eyes didn't go bright like she expected, but darkened. "I'll be traveling a lot from New York to California."

Olivia nodded. It wasn't impossible for them to make it work. Ama and Omar had their Central Park apartment and their beloved home in Oak Bluffs. They were in sync in everything they had done. There were many times when Ama traveled the country without Omar. The same for her godfather. They had something special, so real anyone could see the tether between them. No matter where they were, even in varied time zones, they always told each other good morning and goodnight.

Olivia told Anderson as much, but he still didn't seem convinced.

"Do you want to move to LA?" she asked.

"I don't know . . . maybe? It's a practical place to live for my career."

"Oh." Something cold shifted along the edges of Olivia's heart.

"Would you be open to moving?" he asked.

No. She didn't voice her opinion, and merely shrugged.

"It just depends." Her voice cracked. Her heart did, too. She'd imagined they'd live in New York City and summer in Sag Harbor, maybe eventually move for good once they retired.

Do comedians/actors ever retire?

Olivia licked her lips. "If you're traveling constantly, wouldn't it be nice for me to stay in a safe neighborhood with people who'll look out for me? Like Mr. Whittingham and Whitney?"

"What about Addy?" Anderson joked.

Olivia let out a groan. "I'm not entirely sure if Addy and I are compatible when it comes to friendship."

"Ah, she's not so bad. Just a busybody."

Olivia looked at Anderson as if he'd gotten a personality transplant. "Not so bad? She took a picture of you delivering groceries to her sick grandmother."

"Trust me, I know her type. She's bored, but I don't think she's all that bad. Deep down, she's probably got a heart of gold."

More like fool's gold, Olivia thought unkindly.

"She's certainly an immovable staple in this community," Olivia conceded. She wasn't one to dwell on gossip. Nevertheless, Olivia wondered if she was the one with the problem. Addy had been the first to welcome her into the neighborhood, inviting her to girl's night. She just had no filter. She was too free with words, without thinking about how it landed with others.

Olivia had her fill with harsh words from Cindy. She wouldn't willingly put herself in that situation with an acquaintance.

"Should we get back?" Olivia suggested.

Anderson shook his head. "Let's stay here for a while. I like the quiet."

They fell into a light and comfortable sleep only to awaken suddenly to music blaring from outside. Daylight had passed and transitioned into night.

"I guess the party is starting," Anderson said in a voice clogged with sleep.

"Once it starts, it rarely stops," Olivia said in a foreboding voice. If her memory served correctly from the last time she came with her coworkers, it was a brunch party at noon, naps around four or five, and then party from nine until dawn. Some stragglers like Olivia who didn't binge drink and were chock full of energy squeezed in networking with potential leads, people who were ready to expand their portfolio. Years later, wine made her sleepy and she couldn't do over two glasses at a time.

She stretched her arms and exhaled, preparing for the onslaught of wine and words.

"Let's go back. Travis is probably worried." She checked her phone that she'd placed on the nightstand beside the bed. As expected, she found Travis' text messages waiting for her.

TRAVIS: Where are you???? Your people are here. Told them you were shacked up with lover boy.

Olivia smiled, shaking her head.

OLIVIA: Don't be brusque. We simply fell asleep in this adorable cottage. Tell Whitney and Charles we'll be there soon.

Olivia watched as Anderson dressed. His abs flexed as he buttoned his shirt. He had the right body for Hollywood and soon he would dazzle the world with his rock-hard body and award-winning smile.

She frowned at the thought. And what would they think of her? She could practically imagine the comments.

Not skinny enough. Too dark. Not good enough.

No. *You, Olivia Jones, are a gorgeous Black queen.* She repeated the mantra in her head until her mood lifted.

"Not that I'm complaining, but why are you still naked?"

Olivia smiled, covering up her low thoughts. "Our neighbors are here."

"Whitney and Charles, right?"

"According to Travis." Olivia stood to change. "Don't worry, we'll stick close to each other."

"Yeah, of course. And they aren't staying the entire weekend, right?"

She shook my head. "Charles and Whitney like to lay their heads in their own beds."

Anderson linked his hands with Olivia. They walked side by side down the path. At first glance, Olivia noticed twenty or more guests milling about the front lawn, and even more inside.

"Oh . . ." Anderson let his voice trail off. "I thought this was an intimate setting. Like a dinner party?"

"Oh, no. Travis knows everyone, and he likes to party." Olivia squeezed his hand. "Sunday is the dinner party, so after tonight, he'll prune the crowd away. It'll just be less than a dozen, I imagine."

"You do this thing often?"

Olivia shook her head. "Oh, no. I prefer quiet and more intimate settings. But Travis rents a property in the Hamptons every year. He used to show me pictures."

Two years ago, an up-and-coming singer, Nya, stopped by and partied with Travis. After a wild night, she posted #Oneof-ThoseNights. Travis talked about it so often, Olivia was surprised he hadn't hung and bronzed the Instagram post.

"Olivia!" She heard a voice she didn't want to hear, at least for forty-eight hours. Just across the lawn Addy waved her hand in the air, surrounded by familiar faces including Whitney, Charles, Kara, and Rich and . . .

Olivia's stomach plummeted to the turf green lawn. Garrett. He seemed just as shocked when he noticed the pair.

"I thought it was just Whitney?" Anderson hissed with heat.

"Me too," Olivia whispered with a smile. "But they're here. Let's say hello and then we can move away if you'd like."

"Oh, yeah. I'd like that a lot." He bit out.

CHAPTER 19

LOVE LANGUAGE

July 2021

Olivia maintained her smile while they walked toward their neighbors. "Hi, neighbors!" Olivia borrowed Mr. Whittingham's friendly greeting.

Whitney, Kara, and even Addy dove in for their hugs. Anderson shook Charles' and Rich's hands.

Garrett took noticeable steps away from the group. A crinkled w-shape sat in between his eyes.

"Do you know the host?" Olivia asked the group. The strain of maintaining her friendly smile fatigued the muscles around her mouth.

Charles nodded. "I don't know Travis well, but one of his friends, Ced, is my former PT."

"Ah, that explains it." Olivia nodded.

Anderson diffused the awkward air. "I'm glad you're here. I was thinking I missed the memo with the dress code."

"What dress code?" Addy asked.

"You know, a white shirt, sweater tied around the neck, shorts, loafers, entitlement."

"I know that's right." Addy lifted her hand for a high five.

Whitney, who stood close to Olivia, whispered. "Charles' friend said to bring anyone. We mentioned it to Kara and Rich, who mentioned it to Addy and Garrett. We didn't realize when you said you were going out of town to visit a friend . . ."

Olivia shook her head. "No worries."

"Garrett certainly didn't realize it either," Whitney rolled over Olivia's apology. "We really had to convince him to come with us. He hired a sitter and everything."

Olivia turned completely to face Whitney, placing a hand on her friend's shoulder. "We're all adults. Nothing is wrong with fellow-shipping together."

Whitney's shoulders drooped.

It was then Olivia truly knew that Whitney and the others had not conspired to sabotage their weekend. She would just have to convince her fiancé, who didn't have the camaraderie with her neighbors just yet.

"I'm getting a drink," Olivia announced to the group.

"Right behind you, babe. You can't leave your official pourer." Anderson grabbed her hand, and they walked up the slight hill into the impressive home. Laughter and clinking and conversation filled the house. Travis stood in the center of the living room next to the television, with a cup in hand and an old Fourth of July hat on his head. He swung his free hand in the air, conducting his drunken partygoers into a song.

"Olivia!" He shot a hand in the air and waved. "Come 'ere."

"I'll get you that drink," Anderson leaned down and whispered. "Looks like we need to catch up."

"If they don't have rosé, I'll have a—"

"Gin and tonic," Anderson said with a chuckle. "You're easy."

She remembered Anderson laughing at discovering her boring preference. It was practically the drink of choice in the finance industry outside of sipping bourbon or whiskey.

She walked to her friend, who leaned in to hug her. "Did you see your friends?"

"Yes. All five of them," Olivia said with a little heat in her voice. She refused to be stressed, and she was practically a pro at avoidance.

"My, my, if it isn't Ms. Olivia Jones."

She turned her attention toward the stairway near the entryway. Chase, her boss, leaned on the railing and slid down the steps.

I guess Marcel didn't scrape him off the floor just yet.

"What are you doing here?" Chase asked.

"Travis is my friend." She looked at said friend, who she'd now call Mr. Six Degrees of separation.

Travis raised his hand and whispered behind his hand. "Who is he?"

"My boss," she hissed.

"Ohhhh. I don't know this man."

"Yet he's here," Olivia's voice held a reprimand.

Despite his stupor, Chase still looked like a financial exec dressed casual on the weekend—dark slacks, starched and nearly wrinkle-free light blue shirt, and the infamous loafers Anderson had mentioned.

"How's your summer?" her boss slurred.

"So far, so good." Olivia crossed her arms.

"It's weird to have you around, well . . . online. 'Livia here—"

"Olivia," she calmly corrected.

"Yeah . . . she takes the entire summer off to go frolic with the Amelia Vaux Tanner. She's the—"

"I know who she is," Travis cut in, a frown etched on his face. He also knew through Olivia's moaning who Chase was to her—the gaslighting, client-stealing boss.

"Who invited you to my shindig?" Travis smiled.

"Oh, it was Harper. He's a client of mine."

"Interesting," Travis said in a voice that belied the opposite. Chase swayed, too far gone to care.

"How's Marcel?" Olivia asked of his wife.

"Oh. Yeah. Not good. Or maybe she is good without me. Getting a divorce." He yelled the last word loudly.

"I'm sorry to hear that." Olivia tried to muster sympathy but couldn't quite hit the right tone. Chase wasn't an easy man to work with, so she could only imagine him as a husband. Actually, she didn't have to stretch her imagination too far. There were times when Marcel chided him for his off-color remarks. Or the time when he forgot her birthday and instead of taking accountability, he yelled at his secretary, who called out sick the day before.

Good for Marcel. Olivia could only hope she found someone worthy of her time.

Anderson arrived at her side, offering her wine.

"Thank you." She took a greedy gulp. She needed the liquid encouragement.

"Hey . . . do I know you?" Chase pointed toward Anderson.

Her fiancé finally noticed her boss and greeted him with a frown. Olivia smiled at his good instincts.

"You don't." Olivia shook her head. "This is my fiancé, Anderson."

"Anderson . . . Anderson . . ." Chase snapped his fingers. "Andy, maybe?"

"No. Just Anderson," his voice stoic.

Chase snapped his fingers again. "I know you. I'd know that pretty boy mug from anywhere. You went to school—"

"Out east," Anderson hastily cut in.

Olivia and Travis both swiveled their attention fully onto Anderson. Her fiancé shifted from one foot to the other, lowering his head as if to physically duck and dodge the question.

"Out east where?" Olivia lowered her voice. She didn't want to argue in front of her boss for so many reasons, but this could not wait.

"Princeton," Chase quickly replied.

"W-what?" Everything inside of Olivia shook—her voice, her

legs, her faith in this man she'd planned to marry. When they discussed his education, he said he'd just graduated from high school and dropped out of some unassuming college on the East Coast.

She stared at Anderson. Misery swam in his eyes.

"Oh, Olivia," Chase's voice flipped from slurred to smooth. "You didn't know you bagged a Princeton—"

"Enough, Chase," Anderson growled at his former classmate.

"You've got to be kidding me." Olivia rushed from the crowd. She knew nothing of her fiancé, and every day it became clearer. Slipping outside through the sliding back door, she milled around several sets of Adirondack chairs and bistro tables, down the back path to the magical cottage.

Just an hour ago, things were so simple. She heard Anderson's heavy footsteps behind her, but she refused to look back. When they arrived at the cottage, he finally spoke.

"Olivia, I'm sorry." Anderson's voice whipped fury inside of her.

Olivia spun to face him. She squeezed her fists, wanting to give into the urge to hammer them against his chest. "I don't . . ." she choked on the words. "I don't understand you. I don't know you." She shook her head.

"I know there's no excuse." Anderson shrugged his shoulders, looking down.

"Why would you lie?" Olivia leaned against the door. "You made it seem like you never finished college, let alone an Ivy League."

"I attended Princeton. So what?"

Olivia chuckled, but without humor. "Yeah, I know that *now* because Frat Boy Chase, of all people, told on you."

"I don't like to talk about my past."

"Well, I do. I've showed you every part of me, especially the messy parts. Yet you can't even tell me what's on your résumé?"

"I dropped out."

"Why?"

A quick lift of his shoulders told Olivia everything she needed to know. He would never willingly tell the truth.

"Did something happen in college? Something traumatic or—"

"It was life changing." He dropped his head, looking down at his shoes. "But it wasn't . . ." He glanced to the side, as if debating about telling Olivia the truth. His attention drifted to her with pursed lips. A steely look shuttered his face. "It's not something I want to talk about."

"Do you honestly want to marry me?"

His expression opened like the sun breaking through stormy clouds. "I do. I really do."

"Then tell me who you are," Olivia's voice pitched high with tension. "Tell me where you came from? I won't shy away from the ugly. But I can't not know you. I . . . I won't marry a stranger."

"I'm not a stranger. I'm still the guy who loves you. The man who cuts fruit for your morning smoothie. The man who dropped to his knees and asked for your hand in marriage. And the *only* man who'll make love to you for the rest of your life."

"I'm not asking you for a . . . a deep dive into your past all at once. But you have *got* to give me something."

"You have me right now. That's something." Anderson's voice grew agitated. "Who cares how I grew up?"

"I care. Your childhood shapes you and if you aren't careful, some of the bad parts can follow you into adulthood."

"I'm not like that. I don't need some head doc digging into my past and making me examine every feeling." He locked eyes on Olivia, his expression as ugly as his words.

Despite the perfect temperature outside, the muscles in her stomach hurt with cold tension. "You mean like me?"

"Look. There's nothing wrong with therapy, but it isn't my thing. My therapy is getting onstage, and—"

"Making people laugh. Cracking a joke to hide your pain. You say you're being real, but you aren't. Your material is about everyone else but *you*." Olivia crossed her arms. "Is that truly therapeutic?"

Anderson rocked back as if she'd lobbed a boulder at him.

"I need some time to think." Olivia pointed to the door. "I'm going inside."

Anderson rammed his fingers through his hair. "I don't like this. There's too many people we don't know here. Anything can happen."

"I have the key." She pulled them out of her pocket. "I'll lock the door so that *no one* disturbs me."

"I'm not in the party mood either. I'll . . . be upstairs in our room. Call or text me when you figure things out."

"No, you call or text me when you're ready to face your past." On that parting shot, she inserted the key into the door and slammed it shut in Anderson's face.

She moved to the window, peaking out the blinds to make sure he'd left. After staring at the door for a full minute, he cursed and walked back to the house.

Olivia threw herself on the bed, staring at the ceiling. "Omar? If you're up there, I could use some help. Did you really want Anderson for me?"

If so, how could Omar want someone who couldn't be honest? He had to know she couldn't bear dishonesty. Not after what he'd done to her and her father.

"What is he hiding?"

He'd gotten downright ugly with her when she prodded. Every cell in her body told her to run, abort mission. But she couldn't help but wonder what if . . . what if something so awful happened that he couldn't bring himself to share?

What if she turned him away when he needed her the most?

She recalled the way his eyes went cold. The loose smile that she loved had tightened into twin stern lines. He'd drawn his shoulders up, as if gearing up for war. But a war of what? Of words? Of truth?

She looked down at her phone, scrolled her favorites. Her fingers lingered over her godmother's number.

Ama.

She'd know what to do and who to discreetly tap for information. And if the news were something too dark, or too big to bear, Ama would come.

Her hands shook as she typed the text.

I need help. Can you investigate Anderson's background?

Before she convinced herself otherwise, she sent the text. She wasn't sure of the current location of Ama and Carter, but she knew Ama would not respond via text. Her godmother would pick up the phone and call to ask why Olivia needed this information.

Just in case, Olivia quickly followed up.

If you're up, I can't talk now. But I'll call you. I'll tell you everything.

Which coincidently wasn't much—she knew nothing about her fiancé.

Olivia sighed, deflating from the swell of anger. She had a plan, and planning made her feel marginally better.

"Shhh." Someone jiggled on the door. "Guess it's locked." She heard a woman's voice—Addy's voice.

"Damn. Guess we'll have to wait."

Her heart lurched when she recognized the voice.

She didn't want to confirm who it was. She had enough drama and pain to last a lifetime. Olivia dropped to the floor, her knees scraped against the woven rug. She pushed off her knees and crab-walked to the window to take a clarifying peek.

"I . . ." Addy hesitated, a weird look crossing her face. "Guess so."

The man's back was in front of the window, his turned away but Olivia recognized the horizontal stripes. When she first noticed it, she thought it looked cute—like Rich had coordinated with his wife. She swallowed, making room for the rise of emotion.

Addy grabbed his hand, and they walked away, but she glanced back, her eyes narrowed. Olivia gasped and stumbled away from the window. There was no way she could see Olivia. Nevertheless, her heart pounded.

Mentally, she reviewed the facts. Addy and Rich hadn't kissed, hadn't said anything that showed they were cheating, but it was in the body language. The holding hands—totally unacceptable no matter the friendship or history. That they walked into the dark, intent on getting inside a secluded cabin.

"Should I tell her?" The drink she'd speedily sipped sloshed in her stomach. She'd done it before—broken the news of infidelity. Last time it'd been to her godsister Perry when Olivia noticed her husband's inappropriate comments and a video on some woman's Instagram.

Again, it had all been in the body language. All in the eyes. And yes, Perry hadn't appreciated how she delivered the news, but eventually her godsister accepted it as fact. Now she had a daughter—they were better for it, though sometimes Olivia wondered if Perry secretly hated her for tossing her husband's infidelity into her face. To be fair, Olivia hadn't tossed so much as Perry treated the news like a detonating bomb.

She'd judged their situation too harshly. She hadn't listened with kindness or understanding. And after kissing Garrett, dear Lord, did she ever understand the lure of temptation.

Olivia stood, then moved to the chair near the bed. Tapping her lips, her mind whirled through the plausible scenarios.

The scenario of telling Kara because it was obvious Addy and Rich had something going on—to what end and how often remained to be seen.

Kara didn't need to know right now. Not with alcohol and strangers afoot. Not in a foreign space where she couldn't get away without a car. No, she deserved peace. She wouldn't break the news in Kara's home, but she wouldn't tell her at a favorite haunt. Olivia thought she could invite her for a walk near the water. The ocean could have a therapeutic effect.

She closed her eyes, took another moment of deep breaths before a knock interrupted her thoughts.

Olivia stood, wondering if on the other side she would find another amorous couple or Anderson.

Her breath caught when she opened the door.

"Olivia." She heard the one voice she ached to hear all night.

She widened the door when she recognized the voice. "Garrett?"

He stepped out of the shadows. "Sorry. I didn't mean to scare you."

"You didn't." Not in the way he thought. His presence made her happy.

She stepped outside the cottage and leaned against the door. "Are you looking for me?"

"No." He shook his head. "I was looking for Addy. I saw her storm this way, muttering your name, so I figured something was wrong."

"Oh." Disappointment spun up in her stomach like a cyclone.

Garrett laughed. "Would you rather I look for you?"

"How well do you know Addy?" Olivia decided not to answer his question.

"Very well. We all grew up together."

"You, Addy, Kara, and Rich?"

"Yeah. Kara and Rich were childhood sweethearts. Addy and I were kinda like the third and fourth wheels."

Olivia snorted. Maybe she loved Rich all this time. Maybe she grew tired of being the lone wheel in their messy trio.

"Did you two ever . . ."

"No." He shook his head. "Never. We even went on double dates a few times with other people. She's like a sister to me."

"You don't . . . do you ever wonder if . . ."

"If what?"

Olivia snapped her mouth shut. Kara didn't deserve speculation or gossip. She needed to go to the source first.

"Nothing. Are you having a good time?"

"No," he laughed at the admission. "Not at all."

She opened the door. Her heartbeat sped at the question. "Do you want to come in?"

He raised an eyebrow and followed her inside.

"What?"

"I thought you didn't want to be alone with me."

"I don't think it's wise."

Garrett moved toward the door. "Then I'll go."

Olivia grabbed his wrist. "No, stay."

"All right." He grew quiet for a bit. He chose a single chair near the desk.

Olivia sat on the bed, her eyes on her neighbor. "I'm mad at Anderson." She surprised herself with the confession.

"Why?"

"He's not been forthcoming about his past. He and my boss attended Princeton and when we met, he made it seem like he was this working-class guy, shuffling to get by."

"And that doesn't make you happy."

"No." Olivia shook her head. "I mean, good for him for getting into an elite school but screw him for lying to me."

Garrett didn't respond. He stared on, as if he knew she needed to let out more steam.

"I've . . . had many people lie to me all throughout my life. I'm even going to therapy because of what happened, and I don't want to enter a marriage based on secrets."

"Then don't enter it."

Olivia laughed. "Simple as that?"

"Yes. It's that simple." He rubbed his hands across his jeans.

"But then he does nice things. Like . . . like last week, I told him that I needed new shoes because I couldn't find the ones I wanted in town, and you know what?"

"What?"

"He bought my new shoes. Right size, right fit. The brand I love. He even got my favorite color."

Garrett chuckled.

"Why are you laughing?"

"Did he say he got them for you?"

Olivia shook her head. "No." She recalled her sending a picture of the shoes via text. He replied "nice."

"They're from me, Olivia."

"You . . . you what?"

"Zora spotted your shoes when we walked along the beach. I guess they tumbled down. Anyway, she wanted to bring them to you. Instead, we walked them further into your backyard. I noted the brand, the style, the size, and purchased a pair in your favorite color."

"How did you know I liked that shade of pink?" It was more of a blush color. She hadn't even realized it was her favorite, but she had more shoes and purses and blouses in that color.

Something else popped into her head. "You bought the chess pieces, too?"

Garrett shrugged. "Noticed those, too. They've seen better days.

And now that you and Mr. Whittingham play more frequently, I figured you could use a new set."

Olivia shook her head. She figured Mr. Whittingham bought it for her. She knew for sure Anderson hadn't. She planned to say thanks when they played again next week.

"I'm not trying to buy you or anything." He looked away. It was hard to see the truth, but Olivia could hear it. She could even feel it—warm and nonjudgmental.

"I see gifts are your love language," Olivia teased.

He turned to face her, staring her deep in her eyes. "No, Olivia. I'm more of an action guy."

"Action?"

"Yes. And I'd like to take you to dinner."

"As friends? As neighbors?"

"How you want to define it is up to you." Garrett folded his hands together.

"Where would we go on this neighborly outing?" There was a tremor in Olivia's voice. Despite her anger toward Anderson, she felt wrong to meet him alone.

"There's an Italian restaurant not too far from us. Great atmosphere and the food is good."

"I love Italian."

"I know." He replied simply.

"And how is it you know?"

"I can't reveal my sources. So, is that a yes?"

Olivia let out a breath, tilted her head back, and released it toward the sky.

"We can research your family before. We haven't made our trip to the library just yet."

Olivia lowered her head, nibbling her lip before the answer yes could leap forth.

"Oh, did I mention that I'm staying?" Garrett sweetened the deal.

Olivia jerked her attention to face him. "You are?"

He nodded. "Yes, and year-round. Besides, Zora is happy, the happiest she's been in a long time. Somehow in my adulthood, I forgot about how special this place is. Lately I've been driving some places I used to go as a kid. I had a great childhood."

Olivia nodded. "There's a lot to love about our place."

"Our place." Garrett nodded. "There's no other community like it. A part of me wants to shout it to the rooftops, but another part of me wants to keep this place sacred."

"Well, it's too late for that. The outsiders are determined to put us on the map. And not in a good way."

"Okay then, Whitney Jr."

Olivia smiled. She tilted her head, staring at the beautiful man in front of her. "Yes, I've been indoctrinated, but she's right. SANS is living history and it would be a damn shame to let it go without a fight." Olivia hadn't realized how desperately she needed a safe space from work. But seeing Chase stumble about and wreck her good time, causing a rift between her and Anderson, she knew she needed a place to rest outside of her beloved New York City.

"I think that's the issue. For me, I forgot how special it was. If it weren't for you, Whitney, and Addy it would've been so easy to get the best offer from ASK."

Olivia flinched at the mention of Addy.

"That's why we're doing an event for Labor Day weekend. We want to remind people why we love this neighborhood and how we must protect it."

"Oh, yeah. You need to tape my recording, right?"

"I'd forgotten about that," Olivia lied. She only thought about it three times a day.

"Then we'll make a day of it. Library, video, and afterward dinner. I can show you some special places to visit for bonus material."

"Fine." Olivia nodded.

"Fine as in, yes?" His voice pitched to that of an excited kid.

"As in yes. But only because we're filming and researching my family."

"Of course. This is a business and neighborly dinner." He stood and then offered his hand for a shake.

"Deal?"

"Deal." Olivia took his hand and shook it.

He pumped her hand up and down, but then he didn't let go. He looked at her in silence, his warm hand enveloping hers. Olivia's heart skipped like a scratched record.

She didn't want to let him go. She pulled him down to the bed.

"Olivia," he growled.

He warned.

She didn't want a warning. She wanted a taste.

She leaned in, cupped his face, kissed him.

The warmth of his tongue explored, plundered. He took over, shoving away her shirt.

"Are you sure? Are you very sure?"

Olivia's hands shook on his face. His eyes cleared, grabbed hers, entwining his long, beautiful fingers with her own.

So warm and beautiful and perfect. Their skin tones nearly matched, glistened, and glowed under the soft lighting.

"Your hands are so soft. So beautiful." When she kissed the back of his hand, she realized he'd move their hands from his cheek.

"I like you. A lot." He stood from the bed, walking toward the door, whispering his confession. "But I—"

"I like you, too." She cut him off before he could cool the moment. She stood and closed the distance.

His chest rose up and down.

She placed her hand over his beating heart.

His brown eyes drilled into her, as if assessing her soul. It felt like hours, staring, not breathing. The very molecules in the air stopped.

Until it didn't.

Garrett must have seen what he wanted in Olivia's eyes. He unsnapped her bra, pulling it off in seconds.

Olivia struggled with his shirt, mainly his tie. He had too many buttons, at least a million, not to mention that damned Windsor knot.

After wasting precious seconds, he took over. He grabbed his tie from Olivia, unwound it, and then wrapped it around his hand.

Olivia stripped down to her panties. Garrett paused at the last button, before shrugging off his shirt with his eyes riveted on her body.

His powerful hands reached out, kneading her breasts, carefully avoiding her nipples, like he knew it would skyrocket her too quickly to pleasure. The bright light in the room showed his entire glory. Ripped abs, with hair sprinkled across his flat stomach and broad chest. She imagined running her nails through the coarse hair, reveling in the texture, the juxtaposition to his smooth skin.

Her attention traveled from his torso to his face. The intensity in his eyes stole her breath. She couldn't breathe, but she could move. And she did. Slow and seductive, she slid his boxer briefs from his trim waist, over his muscled ass, down to his feet. She lowered herself to her knees and looked up.

Garrett's chest heaved, as if he'd been running a lifelong marathon. His eyes weren't glazed over, but sharp, clear. He knew what he wanted—Olivia.

As if she held the key to his next breath.

She reached out, wrapped her hand around his thick, warm dick, stroking him in slow and firm tugs. From his low groan, she knew he loved it. On all fours, she leaned closer and slowly inched him inside her mouth.

Large and hard and beautiful.

She hallowed her mouth, giving way for his size, swallowing, and sucking, using her mouth and hands. He tasted sweet, with just a hint of salt. So delicious she wanted to indulge in his taste all night.

"Olivia." Breathless, desperately, as if he didn't know what was up or down, right or left. Right or wrong.

Wrong.

Everything about the moment. Her tongue on his cock should feel wrong.

She couldn't muster guilt or propriety at the moment.

Everything felt absolutely right.

Blood rushed to his engorged head. Tie still in hand, he gripped it like a lifeline.

Her stomach spasmed at the colossal weight of her desire, clashing with the sweet ache of her center.

She needed this, needed him. All of him. Out of her mouth and inside of her.

So wet . . . so damn wet.

She slid her fingers between her folds, giving herself much needed release.

"No. Let me," Garrett pleaded. "Been dreaming about this. About you."

He stepped back, lifted her into his powerful arms, and walked them back against the wall. Rearing back like a powerful bull, he thrust inside of Olivia, past the groove of muscles.

Her back slammed against the wall so hard, she swore there'd be a streak of yellow paint down her back. His nails dug into her back, the pain adding to her pleasure. He rocked inside of her, thorough and thoughtful and hard.

Insistent. As insistent as the message in his eyes.

I want you. Be with me.

She closed her eyes, blocking out his silent plea, letting the wave of her orgasm consume. She wanted to melt into him, feel the pleasure that she gave him, share the ecstasy that he gave to her.

He pulled back and rocked inside her again. A framed picture dropped to the floor and cracked against the hardwood.

His groans filled her ears. The sweetest thing. The sweetest symphony.

Her name poured from his lips to her ears, setting off another orgasm.

He walked them to the bed. Olivia thought that he must be exhausted but nothing on his face showed it. He dropped Olivia on the bed. His dick still stiff.

Olivia's eyes went wide.

He's not done.

He'd gathered her wrists and tied them above her head.

She tugged at the silk tie, rubbing against her wrist. "Garrett?" Her heart thunked against her chest.

"I want you tied to me. Not just this." He tugged at his tie. "But with me."

"Garrett." She closed her eyes and answered breathlessly.

She couldn't process what he really meant.

His warm fingers trailed from the valley of her breasts to the valley in her core. "But I'll settle for this. For tonight . . . for now." He tongued her nipples, bringing renewed energy and pleasure.

He moved inside her again. She sucked in a deep breath. She loved the feeling of being tied to him, taken over by him—in more ways than one.

Never the damsel for long, she rolled her hips, meeting his powerful blows, driving him deeper inside. But it didn't slow him down. He was ruthless, relentless.

His large, cool hands stroked her breasts again. The dual pleasure was more than Olivia could take. A large tsunami built inside of her . . . again. Both of them yelling their release, they stared at each other as the frenzied storm they built crested then quieted to peaceful bliss.

He quickly untied the binding.

Oh, no. What have I done?

Olivia ran her fingers through her tresses and pushed herself up from the bed.

"No," Garret said, his voice unrepentant. "That was beautiful. You were magnificent." He pulled her closer.

"This is wrong. Anderson is—"

"Not. Here."

He wrapped her tighter in his arms. They laid silent and content for just a few more moments.

Garrett kissed her temples and dressed quickly.

"I have to go. We're leaving soon."

"Okay," she whispered. "Be safe."

"Have a wonderful night, beautiful Black queen."

"You . . . too."

He snorted.

"Not the queen part, but you know . . . beautiful Black king."

He turned away, laughing. "I'll take it." He opened the door and stepped outside.

He did take something—his strength, his warm presence. His scent.

Funny, she missed him already. She wasn't sure if it was anger or disappointment, but she didn't miss Anderson at all.

CHAPTER 20

A NEW LIFE

July 2021

Olivia had a very important date with an important man in her backyard.

"Hey, neighbor!" Mr. Whittingham waved his hand high in the air.

Olivia smiled, warmed by the greeting. She didn't think she could get enough of Mr. Whittingham's wide, knowing smile.

"Same sides?"

He nodded. "Always. I see you've got a new set. It feels smooth." He stroked the queen piece between his fingers.

Olivia didn't tell him about it being a gift from Garrett. Or the sex in the magical cottage three days ago.

She wasn't ready for that knowing smile to shift into a satisfied grin. Though Mr. Whittingham never said as much, she had a feeling he would welcome her involvement with Garrett, whom he treated like a son.

Olivia knew that stuffing down her emotions wasn't healthy, and she had all intentions of exploring those feelings in an expensive therapy session later that day with Dr. LaGrange.

And then later she would have wine and chocolate.

"Have you heard any news about my great aunt and uncle coming for Labor Day?"

Mr. Whittingham nodded. "Unfortunately, they won't make it out this year. They still want to be careful. But they do plan to come a few weeks later. If you're okay with it, I can share your phone number and email address with Jessica. Jessica is friends with your aunt and uncle. She's still in touch with the Bakers."

"I would love that! Could you ask Jessica if she can pass along their information, too? With their permission, of course."

"I'd be delighted to ask." After moving his chess piece, he asked, "Did I ever tell you about the time your father won the talent show when he was thirteen years old?"

Olivia leaned forward, moving her piece with barely contained energy. "What was his talent?"

"Singing."

"Really?" Olivia looked up, trying to recall if her mother mentioned that about her father. Olivia frowned when she realized Cindy hadn't mentioned his talent.

"Yes. He was like a little Michael Jackson and Tevin Campbell all in one."

"What song did he sing?"

"He was ambitious, but he loved 'Purple Rain' by Prince."

"Did he play the guitar?" The guitar solo was the most iconic part of the song.

"No." Mr. Whittingham laughed so hard, he wheezed. "He tried." Mr. Whittingham sputtered out words Olivia couldn't understand.

She smiled, waiting for him to get his bearings.

He lifted a finger, sucked in air before starting again. "He tried to recruit some kids to join his band, but no one knew how to play the guitar except one person."

"Who?" Olivia had guessed her uncle, his brother, and she knew from Mr. Whittingham's stories that her father wouldn't want to do something with his twin.

Mr. Whittingham pointed his thumb at his chest.

"Noooo." This time, Olivia laughed right along with him.

"Afraid so, my dear. He rejected me at first. You see, he wanted someone younger."

"Mhmm."

"More fun," he added.

"You are soooo much fun, Mr. Whittingham."

"That I am." He nodded. "Well, he found out real quick that he didn't have much choice. It was partner with me or perform 'Beat It' with his brother. He didn't want to share the stage with him."

Olivia rolled her eyes. The more she found out about her dad, the more she found him to be contrary.

"To be fair, your uncle couldn't sing. And he was a bit of a ham, too. Whereas your dad wanted to take this seriously."

"Okay, so did he let you join his band?"

"Yes. I played it, best I could, and we won $100."

Olivia whistled low. "That's quite a prize for a thirteen-year-old boy."

"He insisted on splitting the money. I said no, of course, but he was adamant. He said a deal was a deal and there was no way he could do Prince without a guitar. He bugged me so much about it, I had to take it. Though I gave it back to him on his birthday and then some. Bought him a microphone stand and a speaker. I think your grandparents didn't like that much, but they let him have it."

He paused for a minute, tapped his chin before he made his next move. "Can you sing, Olivia?"

"Not at all. Well . . ." she thought about it. "I'm not terrible, but I don't enjoy singing."

"Hmm. Good to know."

Olivia moved her pawn. "Sounds like my father was talented and fair."

"You've got it." He wagged his finger. "Oh, sometimes he didn't make the right decision at first, like when he rejected my offer to play guitar." He winked at Olivia. "But he eventually came around to it and did the right thing. I think that's something important to know about your father. He never made the same mistake twice. He learned that early on."

"Your turn." She waved toward the chessboard.

"Oh, yes," Mr. Whittingham nodded. "Want to know something else?"

"Yes, please." She absolutely treasured story time with Mr. Whittingham, regardless of the topic.

"Checkmate." He clapped his hands and let out a loud whoop.

"I thought the Lord loved a humble servant?" she asked, referring to what he said when he lost to her the first time.

"He also said, let us rejoice today and be glad. And today, Olivia, I am glad."

☀

Olivia briskly walked through Dr. LaGrange's office. They had much to discuss, no time for pleasantries. In her hands, she clutched the frilly pink notebook Dr. LaGrange had given her as a challenge to journal her feelings.

"Did you know my favorite color is pink?" Olivia sat on the couch across from her therapist. "Is that why you gave this to me?"

Dr. LaGrange smiled. "Why do you keep asking about the journal? I didn't select the color as a psychological exercise."

Olivia's shoulders slumped forward. "It's just that . . . Garrett said he'd realized my favorite color is pink, or rather, a specific shade of pink called blush."

"I'm familiar with the color," Dr. LaGrange offered an amused smile.

"He's bought me gifts. Thoughtful gifts . . . a new pair of running shoes. They're highly rated, and he purchased them in my favorite color. Then . . . then he replaced the chess pieces for my board outside."

Dr. LaGrange leaned back, her head tilted from its usual left position to the right. It was her *think before she spoke* pose.

Olivia opened her mouth, held a breath, waiting for the judgment.

"That all seems very nice, but how does it make you feel?"

Olivia snapped her mouth shut, thinking about the doctor's question. Scenes from their night in East Hampton flashed in her mind. She rubbed at her collarbone, tracing the trail of his tongue.

That night in his arms, along with the gifts, made her feel cherished, noticed—which also made her feel terrible because Anderson wasn't neglectful.

He hadn't deserved what she did. She was a cheater. No better than Damon and Perry and fucking Nate, the neighbor who had an entire fiancée.

I'm just like him. She gasped aloud.

An ironic full circle. Tears welled in her eyes when she remembered the misery he'd caused. The doubts, the worthlessness.

"I . . ." Olivia licked her lips. "I'm a cheater."

"What's that?" Dr. LaGrange leaned in as if to hear better.

"Garrett and I had sex. Hot sex. Sweaty sex," Olivia blurted. "I licked the man like an ice cream cone, and I still want more." She whispered to Dr. LaGrange in a father-I-have-sinned voice.

Dr. LaGrange adjusted her glasses, looked at her notepad, and then back at Olivia.

"Why did you have sex with Garrett?"

Olivia recounted what happened at the party.

"You cheated because Anderson hurt you?"

"Yes and . . . because I wanted to. And yes, I was so damn angry with Anderson. I just didn't think."

"Hmmm." Dr. LaGrange tilted her head. "You *did* think, which drove your actions."

"No, I didn't." Olivia shook her head, fueled by denial.

"What problems do you have with Anderson?" she challenged in that gentle yet firm way that Olivia both admired and hated. The prevalent issue standing between Olivia and Anderson was that he withheld important truths. The chasm between them wasn't fixed, but it grew with every lie-laced minute that passed between them. And now she added more fuel to the lies.

"I like the gifts," Olivia finally answered after some time. "It's things I need and things that I like. It's not even about the money spent. I like that Garrett is thoughtful."

"Does Anderson know about the gifts?" the doctor asked in a slow and cautious cadence.

"Absolutely not. Until I talked to Garrett, I thought the shoes came from Anderson. He's the one I talked to about my need for a new pair. Not to mention that he lives with me."

"You mean you live together?"

"That's what I said."

"You said *he* lives with *me*." Dr. LaGrange smiled. "Like a roommate who contributes to your mortgage."

Olivia crossed her arms. "I feel like you're leading me to the water when you should just get to the point."

To anyone else, Olivia likely sounded rude. But after close to a dozen sessions, Olivia and Dr. LaGrange maintained a direct communication style. It worked for their personalities, though there were times when Dr. LaGrange refused to give an answer, forcing Olivia to "sit" with her feelings.

"I would tell you the same thing." Dr. LaGrange waved a hand. "Get to the point . . . with Anderson."

Olivia groaned internally "Well, damn."

"What is it?"

"I should break off the engagement." Her voice trembled. She felt like a monster, but it couldn't be helped. She couldn't erase what had to be done.

And she didn't want to.

"Why?"

"Because I'm not my best self with him. And I don't think I make him better and I . . . I don't love him." Thinking back on their conversations about his occupation, where to live, the comedy gigs, she realized that she'd made him second-guess himself.

Dr. LaGrange flashed a smile. Her eyes brightened, and it looked as if she wanted to give Olivia a round of applause, or maybe a cookie.

Olivia sighed. "And now I have to go home and break up with him."

Dr. LaGrange shook her head. "Indeed. It's not something you can outsource."

Olivia laughed despite her mounting headache.

"I can do this, right?"

"Of course."

"I *should* do this, right?"

"You should honor your feelings and if you don't love him, set him free. It's the kindest thing you can do. And you are kind."

"No, I'm not." Olivia shook her head. "I had sex with our neighbor. I'm a cheater, bottom line."

"Stop with the labels." Dr. LaGrange raised a hand in the air. "They're uncreative and it never leaves room for complexity. You had an unkind moment, but you are kind. Break off the engagement. Perhaps have someone nearby in case things get sticky. I would advise to leave your home."

"He won't hurt me."

"Perhaps not, but let's be safe, yes? Besides that, you'll give him space to process, pack, and leave."

Olivia nodded her agreement.

Dr. LaGrange jotted notes on her pad. "Besides Anderson, is there anything else you want to discuss? How is your job coming along?"

"Speaking of being more decisive, I think I want to leave my job."

"Really?"

"Yes. I'm seeing things more clearly. We must organize if we're going to fight against giants like ASK. We need to educate ourselves on the taxes and cost-of-living projections. If our residents can't afford it, we can't make them feel guilty about selling. But we can be strategic on selling to people who care about community. We can create a queue of potential buyers."

"I think that's a wonderful idea."

"Really? You don't think I'm being an impulsive millennial?"

Dr. LaGrange shook her head. "I would never associate impulsive with you, Olivia. I find you to be incredibly thoughtful and fair."

"Except for breaking up with Anderson." Olivia paired the self-deprecation with a laugh.

When Dr. LaGrange didn't laugh with her, Olivia moved on. "I can afford the career move, too. I'm planning a meeting with my financial advisor who also consults about business. I want to make this official, or maybe partner with Whitney. That is if she wants to strike up a partnership."

"You won't know until you've asked."

Olivia nodded. "I'll ask." She let out an airy laugh.

"What is it?" Dr. LaGrange asked.

"I just can't believe that I, Olivia Jones, will participate in the Great Resignation." She shook her head.

"Don't think of it as a trend."

"But isn't it? We're a bunch of burned-out people refusing to work."

"I'd like to think of it as burned-out people refusing to settle for less. People who know their worth and aren't afraid to bet on themselves. And there is absolutely nothing wrong with that. Think about it. Let's step through the path if you quit your job, shall we?"

"Yes, but let's go through the bad scenario first."

Dr. LaGrange smiled into her fist as if she were catching a cough. "All right. Close your eyes."

Olivia followed her command.

"You've just quit your job and now you're an entrepreneur. It's been a rough year. You haven't hit any of the goals you set. Residents are selling to the highest bidder and ASK is developing in areas considered historic. With all that has happened, you will end the company."

Olivia's heart squeezed. She couldn't imagine failure because it wouldn't be something that she could dust herself off and try again. They were fighting for legacy—for the soul of this community.

Adrenaline rushed her veins like jet fuel. She couldn't let companies like ASK win. Not in her neighborhood. She balled her fists.

"How does this make you feel?" Dr. LaGrange's calm voice pierced through her frantic thoughts.

Olivia opened her eyes. "It's hard for me to imagine failure. I'm not one to give up so easily."

"And that's perfectly fine. But if you fail, will you lose your business acumen?"

"No."

"Would you be able to get another job in your field? Are there any barriers that would stop you from reentering the workforce?"

Olivia shook her head again.

"So win or fail, you still have the soft and technical skills that you'll likely use for your company. Bonus, you'll gain skills in entrepreneurship. Big picture: you'll still have *you*."

"I guess, but am I—"

"You *are* good enough." Dr. LaGrange flattened Olivia's protest.

"I know that," Olivia lied.

"Olivia, I'm not one to give business advice, that's not my forte.

But from what you've outlined, I think you'll have all the information you need to figure out your next steps. I know you'll thoroughly consider every plausible scenario before you take the leap."

Olivia positively beamed at her compliment. Glancing at her watch, she noted the time and realized she had a minute to spare. "Before we end, I want to give you something." She slid the journal to the doctor.

Dr. LaGrange stared at the notebook. "For me?" Dr. LaGrange gifted her with a rare grin.

Olivia clasped her hands together. She didn't know what to do with them after clutching the journal for so long. "I'll need that back next week."

Dr. LaGrange. "No, you can have it."

"What? Really? I thought you wanted to read it."

"No. I wanted to gain your trust and I want you to trust yourself. You've done that." She handed the notebook back to Olivia. "Well done."

"Hey! Was this a test?"

Dr. LaGrange laughed. "No, it's not a test. The notebook is yours. I'm proud of you."

Olivia stood, ready to leave.

"I'm proud of me, too." Her heart thumped, shooting sparks of joy throughout her body. A satisfied smile spread across her face. "I'll see you next week."

Olivia smiled all the way down the steps to her car. Some days, therapy felt like an expensive way to pick at old wounds. But when she compared her life to before—before the pandemic, before Omar's crushing revelation, before she realized everything in her life had fallen perfectly into place to fix what had been broken in her father's death—she realized discovering herself and what made her happy was the best way to live.

Now she had to find the courage to take what she wanted.

Olivia glanced at her watch for the thousandth time while waiting for Anderson to return home. Seated on the table was his favorite wine—a red cabernet from Napa Reserve. She was on glass number two by the time he arrived.

"Anderson!" She jumped from the couch so quickly wine sloshed on her pants.

"Hey. Where's the fire?" he said in that low voice of his. The voice that had and still turned her on. *Focus.*

"I've been thinking and . . . and we should talk." She returned to her seat and patted the cushion beside her.

"Okay. Is it about the other night with Chase?" His fear was apparent in his hoarse voice. In his eyes.

Olivia sniffed. "Yeah," she whispered just as softly. "I don't think I can marry you."

"Babe." He lowered his head, his calloused hands gripped his knees. "You're breaking my heart."

"You've got a lot going on and there's just so many secrets between us."

He raised his head, his eyes leveled on her. "I know if I could just get more time. I can get there, I swear. But don't give up on us. Don't give up on me." He grabbed her hand. Pulled her closer.

"Just give me more time."

"How much?" she hated herself for asking.

"A few weeks . . . maybe?" The uncertainty in his voice made her surer about her decision.

"I'm telling you I want to end our relationship and you still can't open up?" Olivia shook her head.

Anderson raised his hands in the air. "How about this? I leave.

Stay in our apartment in New York. I've still got that gig coming up at the Comedy Club down the street. We can talk then."

"Anderson, I—"

"Just take a break. A small break. Maybe if I'm gone, you'll miss me?" The hope in his voice pierced her heart.

Olivia tried hard for her attention not to drift left toward Garrett's house. She shook her head instead. "I don't know."

"All I'm asking for is a few weeks before you make a decision that alters the rest of our lives," he pleaded, his eyes wet.

"O . . . okay."

"Yeah?" he asked, relief clear in his voice.

Olivia's voice was so tight it pained her to speak. She nodded instead.

"You won't regret this. I'll work on myself. Tell you everything." He stood. "Do you mind if I stay the night? I'm a little beat."

"The guest room."

"Thank you, Olivia. Thank you for giving me a shot."

Olivia averted her gaze. If he only knew. He wouldn't be giving her gratitude—he'd curse the ground she walked on.

He walked up the stairs, slowly. She didn't move a muscle, and simply stared at him as he walked away. She silently cursed herself for being a coward.

Two weeks. She promised herself. Then she'd break it off for good.

CHAPTER 21

A LOT LIKE GUILT

August 2021

Olivia pulled into the parking lot of an Italian restaurant, her hand gripping the steering wheel. After parking the car, she pried her fingers off the wheel and pulled out her makeup, dabbing away at the moisture that formed across her forehead and cheeks during the short twenty-minute drive.

"It's not a date. Just a . . . business meeting between neighbors." After texting back and forth, they decided to do video and dinner for the evening and a trip to the library the following week.

"And no sex." Olivia chastised herself through her reflection. She needed to sort her life before adding more drama. But the woman staring back at her—with flushed cheeks, red lips, and expertly applied eyeshadow—told a different story.

She smoothed her hands down her little black dress and stepped outside. Glancing at her watch, she noted the time at seven twenty-five, just five minutes before their reservation. Olivia could use one more twirl in front of the mirror to check if the deep-V that dipped in both the front and the back still looked good on her. Instead, she opted to look at her red Manolo Blahniks and do a quick ankle check.

"You look beautiful." A deep voice that should have been illegal answered her question.

"Oh, hi, Garrett." She smiled at him. When she left the house, she'd noticed his car parked in the driveway.

"I took an Uber." He seemed to answer her question. "Not Anderson's, of course."

Olivia clutched her purse and stomach when she heard her soon-to-be-ex–fiancé's name.

"He's not here."

"Ah. He's got a gig?"

Olivia shook her head. "We're taking a break."

"Because of . . . of me?" he asked with undisguised hope in his voice.

Olivia shook her head. "No. Because of me."

"Think of me as your filming crew." She reminded him coolly of the purpose of this meeting—he was part of the nostalgia video campaign for the SANS neighborhood event.

"Shall we?" He grabbed her hand and led the way into Il Capuccino.

Her heart exploded behind her chest.

They walked up to the front of the restaurant. "Brooks, party of two," he confirmed with the tall host who immediately guided them into the dining room.

Maybe it was her imagination, but all eyes seemed glued on them as they walked to the small table near a wide window with a beautiful and romantic view. When the host tried to seat her, Olivia cleared her throat.

"Could we sit toward the back, over there?" She pointed to an empty table.

He glanced at Garrett as to confirm. Olivia skewered the host with a look.

"Whatever the lady wants," Garrett replied in an even cadence.

When the host turned his attention back to Olivia, she skewered him with a you-really-tried-it look.

"O-of course, madam."

Garrett laughed once they settled into their seats. "The poor guy is probably checking his body for exit wounds."

"Well, he shouldn't have looked at you as if you answered for us."

"No," Garrett shook his head. "He shouldn't. It's just that I asked for the best seat in the restaurant when I called for reservations."

"Oh." Olivia's breath caught. "I must have ruined the experience for you."

"No," Garrett said as he opened his menu, without looking down. "I forgot that sitting across from you is the best view."

"Garrett." She shook her head, pulled on the flimsy paper menu as a divider.

He grabbed her hands, lowering them both to the table. "Olivia, it's just dinner. You don't need to hide from anyone. Everything we did that night was beautiful and nothing to be ashamed of." His voice was deep and smooth and melodic. It reminded her of a love song. No, it was more like one of those songs from the old days that sounded a lot like love, but was fully baked in lust. The, I can do you better than your man, song.

Garrett smiled, slow and dangerous.

He was a damn menace.

An intriguing and handsome menace.

The server came before she could reply to his dangerous proposal.

Her throat muscles, tight with tension, loosened when the server asked for appetizer and drink orders. "I'll have the Rockefeller oysters, please. What do you recommend for a white wine?"

Dinner had not only been delicious, but it was also her first fine dining experience in Sag Harbor. She had a delicious Tagliolini dish while Garrett opted for Branzino.

After dinner, she suggested a walk. Per Garrett's instructions, she'd brought shoes for walking. He wanted to show her his favorite childhood haunts. They drove to the first location and she was surprised when Garrett directed her to the A.M.E. church.

"Can I film you here?" Olivia confirmed.

Garrett nodded. She pulled out her tripod and centered her iPhone on the stand. Because it was dark outside, she set up simple lights, including a light ring stand.

"Introduce yourself, how long you've been a resident and why this place is significant to you."

"I'm Garrett Brooks. I'm one of the full-time residents here, growing up with my mother and father, Ruth and John Brooks. I moved away when I went to Harvard."

Olivia bit back a surprised exhale and nodded for him to continue.

"Now, with my mom's passing, I'm back and I'm here to stay. The building behind me is the St. David A.M.E. church. It was built by the hands of Black and Native Americans in the 1800s. Now it's a Baptist church. We had services, of course, but I remember fish fries to celebrate graduates and a cooling off on hot summer days with popsicle parties. Anytime I walk up these three steps, I feel a sense of peace and . . . and pride."

"Why is that?"

"I'm proud because of its history. This was a safe space for people. A safe place for Black folks to rejuvenate their spirits, but also to have social gatherings. This church is even rumored to have been a location for the Underground Railroad. I'm not sure, but I wouldn't be surprised. It was a place to escape for our Native American brothers and sisters, too. Think about it . . . they'd been run off their own damn land. They could congregate with us because we were all displaced kindred spirits. So," he looked at the church, his back now facing the camera, "when I think about our neighborhood, it reminds me of this church. A safe place teeming with history. A place that deserves to be protected."

He looked back at the camera. "And . . . that's why I'm stay-ing." Olivia stopped filming, her hands shook as she stopped the recording.

"That was, um, superb. No need for more takes. We can go home—"

He shook his head. "We aren't done yet. I've got to take you to my favorite spot on the beach."

After they walked back to Olivia's parked car, they drove to Ha-vens Beach. Olivia wished they would have come earlier to watch the sun set. Like most residents, Olivia stored blankets and folded chairs in the trunk. Garrett guided them to his favorite spot.

Once they settled on Olivia's large, waterproof beach blanket, they stared at the docked sailboats. The air was sticky, and despite Olivia's efforts, she couldn't dust the sand away from her body.

"This is nice."

"It is. I forgot all about this. We had a small graduating class, but the weekend after school ended, we came to this beach as teenagers. Sandwiches, wine coolers, beer." Garrett chuckled. "Doing things we had no business doing."

Olivia didn't know much about that. Cindy knew her where-abouts at all times during the school year because her schedule had been so structured. And during summers on the Bluffs, Ama had eyes and ears everywhere—even for the ever-elusive Billie, who slipped out at night.

Garrett scooted closer. "You've got some sand on your face." He leaned closer to brush it off her cheeks.

The pads of his thumbs seared her skin, pushing her tempera-tures into the hundreds. She could use water, cold water, not just for her throat but for her entire body.

He didn't move away. He leaned closer, a warm breath on her neck.

Not good. Not good at all.

Her lips quivered; her heart quivered. She lifted her head, instinctively seeking to be closer to this incredibly warm man.

"Olivia Jones." He squeezed his eyes shut. "You are dangerous."

She felt dangerous. She wanted to be dangerous. Which is why, perhaps, she leaned closer to him. Her lips were not even an inch away from his.

With one hand she pushed closer, bracing herself, with the other she cupped his face.

She was exhausted, so exhausted from running away from her feelings.

"Kiss me, Garrett." Olivia knew what she'd said, yet it felt like it wasn't her own voice—like the devil on her shoulder that popped up since the day she met Garrett.

He didn't hesitate. His warm mouth melded with hers, the salt of the air danced on his lips, his tongue. She licked his firm lips, encouraging him to take over, to conquer.

His hands wrapped around her waist, tightening with tension, with passion, while his lips explored.

It was the best kiss of her life.

Better than chocolate and Brie cheese and rosé.

Better than kissing Anderson.

Her body temperature instantly cooled.

She broke their kiss.

"Oh, God. Oh, God. I'm sorry." She stood from the blanket, her chest heaving from her labored breaths. She shook her hands.

"We shouldn't have—"

Garrett raised a hand. His beautiful brown eyes turned to stone. "Let's not spoil the night with regrets." He stood, waited for her to pat away the sand and flick her blanket.

They walked back to her car. Her mind was blank all the way to the house. As soon as Olivia turned off the engine, Garrett opened the door and marched across their yards. Garrett stood with the keys to his front door. He didn't glance her way. No goodbye, no thank you.

Just an angry silence.

Tears blurred her vision. He didn't want to hear her regrets, but she had them. She disappointed herself, her fiancé, and Garrett.

She knew she'd made a mess of things. But somehow, even after their passion-filled night, she'd vowed to think things through.

She wanted to make the right decision.

As if he could hear her thoughts, Garrett spun around and returned to her car.

"Olivia." Garrett stood outside her car. She rolled down the window while simultaneously wiping her eyes.

She sniffed before she replied. "Yes."

"I'm sorry I walked away from you. But we're good. No hard feelings between us, okay?"

Relief untangled the quadrupled knots in her stomach. "I'm sorry. Anderson and I are on a break, but I told him I'd give our relationship some thought and last time we were together I . . . I didn't think. I like you and I'm sorry I've given you mixed signals."

"I like you, too. You haven't given me mixed signals. I just hate the thought that you regret what we did. It didn't feel like regret to me. It felt like so much more."

Olivia nodded. Even with Dr. LaGrange's encouraging words, she felt lower than dirt over what she'd done to Anderson.

"From now on, I won't have any expectations. I'll—"

"You should have expectations and I don't want you to lower them. I just need time for myself. Okay?"

"Okay. I'll be around." He patted the hood of her car and walked away.

"Garrett?"

He spun around.

"Tonight was the best."

His bright smile eclipsed her guilt. She liked his smile. She liked it a lot.

☼

Olivia sighed when she received an email from Chase about this "exciting new idea" to recruit Black clients. She clicked on the meeting link, arranged her face to neutral, and prepared for this magnificent idea that would ultimately land entirely on her plate.

"Ms. Jones, how are you?"

Though she didn't say anything, she simply widened her eyes, conveying surprise. It seemed as if Chase wanted to reestablish an air of authority despite her witnessing him vomit the entirety of his intestines.

"Chase." She replied with an air of pseudo-sympathy. "How are you these days?" She could see her image on the screen. She nearly smirked when she nailed the effect.

Her boss had ruined her weekend, though Perry and Billie agreed that his slip about Anderson's lies had been a godsend.

Chase cleared his throat. "I'm good, I'm great, really. The reason I scheduled this meeting is that management hired a DEI—that's diversity, equity, and inclusion—consulting firm to evaluate our company."

"Oh, really?" Olivia feigned ignorance. It had been her idea to hire a firm after management tapped her for the umpteenth time on ways to recruit diverse talent and clientele. But after years of "great ideas" that never moved to execution, she grew tired of the diversity Olympics game her company played—they said all the right words but never could stick the landing.

The last time they'd asked for her opinion was a few months ago, which happened among a slew of social injustice protests. She'd gently reprimanded them about never going forth with her ideas and suggested they hire a firm to consult. She'd gone over Chase's head, just as she had many times over the years when she clocked that he didn't mind presenting an idea as his own or taking a client from Olivia because she was too *junior*. Chase's boss, Andrew, a VP at the firm, realized the brains behind the operation and hinted at fast tracking her into senior management.

That promise should have happened earlier in the year, but Olivia hadn't followed up to move things along—she understood why now. It was time for her to carve her own path.

"So," Olivia said, squaring her shoulders. "What did the firm come up with?"

"For recruiting, they suggest we partner with the Black and women MBA programs. We can start recruiting directly from diverse associations and universities."

"Great idea." She refrained from rolling her eyes. She'd made that recommendation five years ago. "What else?"

"I've been tasked with heading up a campaign to increase our Black clientele. The firm evaluated our marketing methods, and they brought it to our attention that we aren't presenting an accurate representation of the country's demographic in our advertising."

"Agreed."

"And, well, we want to make a splash. We're hiring an agency to develop new creatives and we also want to launch a campaign that touches all forms of media, as well as a grassroots campaign."

"That actually . . . sounds superb, Chase."

"We'd like you to sit on the committee for final approval of the agency. We want to make sure it's minority-owned, but of course, we'll have our marketing department spearhead managing the agency."

"To confirm you'd like me to review the RFPs and presentations?"

"Exactly. Our marketing department will pre-vet so you can be involved in the final selection process."

Olivia offered him a genuine smile. "I would be . . . yes! I'm happy to do it." They majorly surprised her in their thoughtful involvement of her time. In the past, he would have tasked her to research and give it to the marketing team.

"Oh, and there was one more thing. I wanted to run the idea by you first before I pitch it to senior leadership. But it occurred to me you are hyper connected within the Sag Harbor community." He let out a long sigh. "Actually. Wait. I'd like to apologize about last week." He didn't look away and stared straight into the camera.

"It's fine. I know divorce can be a lot."

"It is. I've been with Marcel since college. I took her for granted and now I'm realizing that I've taken many people for granted. Like you."

Olivia couldn't stop her mouth from dropping open. "M-me?"

"Marcel told me all the time I treated my team like my personal assistants instead of competent financial experts. Time and again you have gone above and beyond. You know, I was jealous when you skipped over me and secured Andrew as your mentor, but I'm glad you did. He's the one who's been fighting for your promotions. I'm sorry for that and I won't do that again. I'm going to . . . attempt to look for opportunities to increase your exposure. I have this idea, if you don't mind listening?"

Olivia, with her mouth still wide open, shook her head. "S-sure. Go ahead."

"It occurred to me there's a strong and healthy community in Sag Harbor. Hearkening back to what you've said before, we should be more intentional in courting diverse clients. I wonder if we can use our same model . . . a warm lead, dinner or maybe a social-distanced rooftop event, and we can mix in some of our current roster of diverse clients as well."

Olivia had hosted events many times over. Each time, she attempted to make the list as diverse as possible. Though it seemed like this event would be hyper-focused. But now her network included her neighborhood. An uneasy feeling spread in her chest. Just when she considered life outside of the firm, now they wanted to pull her deeper into their corporate web.

She sighed, wishing this would've happened five years ago.

Chase nodded. "I'd like you to consider leading it up again. I know it's a lot of work and I would give you all the resources and staff you need. We would love some recommendations and maybe a chance for you to host the kickoff event."

"It's a good idea, Chase, but I'd like to think about it."

His eyes flashed with alarm. "Oh, um, of course. I'll be here if you have questions."

"I'll reach out soon. Thank you for the opportunity."

He nodded just before she said goodbye.

She clicked off the meeting and pushed away from her desk. It was mid-afternoon, too soon to log out of work, but she needed to stretch her legs. Instead, she removed her laptop from the docking station and moved her office outside on her beautiful deck.

She tilted her head toward the sky, soaking in the vitamin D. Her phone buzzed again, and she sighed. Chase's request had surprised her, and she wasn't sure if she wanted her first hosting event, sponsored by her employer, to squeeze money out of her neighbors.

She glanced at the phone screen and winced when Ama's name flashed across the screen.

So much for rest.

"Hello, Ama."

"Hello, cher. Have you been avoiding me?" Ama's voice wasn't critical, but Olivia felt like the insecure fourteen-year-old who'd disappointed her godmother.

"No." Olivia shook her head. "Of course not. I've been busy with work and life and . . . I'm sorry. I shouldn't have texted you in the middle of the night."

"Don't apologize for asking for help. You are so strong and independent and capable. But sometimes I miss you asking for my advice."

"You do?"

"Yes. We work in the same industry and so I understand the things you've experienced." She harrumphed. "Doesn't matter if it's the seventies or now, white men still don't like it when a Black woman is in the same room with them, making decisions."

Olivia cleared her throat. "Well, I could actually use your advice right about now."

"For Anderson?"

Olivia glanced over her shoulder, her neighbors were the biggest threat of eavesdropping. Once she confirmed all was clear, she responded to Ama's question. "Yes, him and my job."

"Well, go ahead, cher. Tell me about Anderson first. That's why you contacted me."

Olivia recounted everything—the secrecy, the screenplay, even her mixed feelings about Garrett.

"Of course, cher. I'll do this for you if that's what you still want."

"What would you do?"

"I only do background checks on my enemies or a potential business partner. So, you've got to ask yourself why."

"I know he's lying, and I want the truth."

"There are multiple ways to skin a cat, cher. If you keep allowing him to retreat, then he'll keep it up. You granted him a break instead of cutting things off. He may think he can get away with keeping his secrets."

"I gave him an ultimatum. A few weeks. I think he has motivation to tell me the truth."

"But all of it? Or just the bare minimum, and that, cher, is the first clue."

"A clue to what?"

"Compatibility."

"I thought you liked him for me."

Ama had even hinted in the past that Omar put him on her path just for Olivia.

"I liked it when he made you happy, but now he is not. My loyalties never change. I am team Olivia Jones."

Olivia warmed at Ama's support. She missed this. She missed her godmother.

"So . . . would you like for me to proceed?"

Olivia shook her head. "No. I'll get him to talk."

"Now, remember this—if he does not talk, then you must walk," Ama pronounced. "You are too smart to sit around and wait for breadcrumbs." Ama huffed. "Enough about Mr. Anderson. Tell me about your job."

Olivia wanted to laugh at Ama getting worked up, but she knew her words were true. He would talk or she would walk—it was as simple and heartbreaking as that.

Olivia cleared her throat, readying herself to drop another bombshell on Ama. She was more nervous to talk about a career change than about Anderson.

"I . . . I want to quit. I'm not being impulsive or anything, but I want to step into a new direction." Olivia's words collided together like a car wreck on I-78.

Olivia spent the next thirty minutes telling Ama about SANS and ASK and her neighbors who had fallen prey to the redevelopment company.

"Oh, your community sounds simply wonderful, and I must meet this Whitney."

"She's a little . . . rough around the edges, but you'll love her."

"I like rough. I grew up with rough. But in Louisiana, we mix up sugar with our spice to make it seem nice. But we're all the same," she said airily.

"I suppose so." Olivia looked around the beach again, confirming no neighbors were afoot.

"Looks like you're finding your purpose," Ama whispered, her voice pure honey. "I'm so pleased for you."

"I always thought I lived my life with purpose, but these days, it's been apparently clear that it isn't true."

"I read an article the other day. They're calling it a quarter-life crisis." Ama laughed. "You feel trapped and dull, right?"

"Right," Olivia confirmed. "Did you ever feel that way?"

"Yes, but I experienced this much earlier in my life. I had to make some tough decisions. Decisions a lot of women back then would've thrown stones at me for doing. But I did it my way and I have no regrets. After that, I didn't feel so much as trapped. I didn't know my purpose yet, but I knew I was meant for greater, and I just had to create enough space in my life to accommodate for greatness. Every goal I set, I accomplished. And after I checked it off my list, I created new goals. To me, that's how you fill your life with purpose. You always have goals, and you surround yourself with the best people. And if this new venture makes you feel like life is worth living, then you have my blessing. Not that you need it."

Olivia stared out at the sea, her haven. A haven shared by many before her, and she hoped she could leave this slice to her children one day. "That's what Omar gave me," Olivia whispered. "Community. Legacy."

"That he did." Ama's voice was rich in love.

"But I had Oak Bluffs, I . . . I could've had it if you would have given me the house."

"Oh, baby. I've hurt you so much. I can't tell you how sorry I am."

"But why Billie?" she whispered. "Why not me?"

"You know when I told you about the decisions I've made in the past?"

"Yes."

"Well, cher, decisions aren't stagnant. They have a ripple effect that can go on for decades. Now I'm not sure Billie told you just yet, but I got pregnant early. Too early. And I gave that baby up for adoption. And years later that baby had Billie."

"I . . . yes, Billie told us about what happened." Though her god-sister had been very matter of fact in the retelling, Olivia could hear the suppressed pain in her voice.

"I think it's only fair to give Billie a home when I'd taken it away from her mother. And then her mother took away her home from Billie. I want Billie to have a place, her own place to call home. To raise her babies with Dulce. I don't want her to run away like me and Edie. Can you understand that?"

"I do." However, her statement made it clear that Ama had always known her choice. So why did she make it seem like Olivia had a shot at her home?

Olivia shook her head, shook away her accusatory thoughts. She was done rattling Ama about Oak Bluffs.

"I appreciate your advice. I have a meeting. I should go now."

"All right, but don't be a stranger."

"I won't."

"I'm glad we talked. We're back in New York, now."

"Really?"

"Yes. And I'd like for us to schedule a visit. I can come there, or you can come see me. Figure things out with Anderson first, then let me know. I'll be here for a spell."

"Why did you come back?"

"Because I knew you needed me. Besides, it's too darn sunny in Lake Como. I missed my city."

Olivia laughed. Lake Como was perfection, and she was sure Ama had a blast shopping and sunning. "Bye, Ama. I love you."

Neither she nor Ama were very expressive, but she'd realize that life was too short to hide feelings.

"I . . . I love you, too, cher. So very much. Please take care of yourself."

"I will. See you soon." Olivia ended the call, heart bursting with love for Ama, for her community, and for herself.

After her call with Ama, Olivia realized the distance to courage wasn't as far as she'd thought.

CHAPTER 22

IN IT FOR THE BEES

August 2021

Olivia took on the challenge from her boss and hosted the Black Wealth Is Black Love event in late August, before the Labor Day events.

When she asked for Mr. Whittingham and Whitney's help, they quickly stepped in to identify the neighbors who would benefit from financial planning and investments from her company, Array Capital.

The caterers she'd hired swept into her home, setting up a food-warming station for the heavy hors d'oeuvres on her kitchen island.

"Would you like to try samples of each dish, ma'am?" the banquet manager asked Olivia.

"Yes, please."

The older woman pulled out a small, thick white plate and arranged several selections to sample.

Olivia moaned when the explosion of flavors—a medium-rare beef tenderloin rolled in crushed peppers, drizzled with a creamy horseradish, all atop a buttery-light toast—hit her taste buds. She sampled the other dishes, including a delicious sun-ripened tomato dip mixed with whipped Greek yogurt and flavorful feta cheese. Other appetizers included mushroom puff pastries, lamb chop lollipops, and sweet dessert bites, like sugary sweet banana beignets and tangy lemon parfaits.

The company had brought in workers to help Olivia rearrange the living room and dining room furniture, adding tallboy tables and chairs edged along the living room and sofas near the television.

Like Whitney, she connected an HDMI cable for the presentation on the flatscreen television.

The doorbell rang five minutes before the official start time. Knowing her neighbors, it was likely Mr. Whittingham, the perpetual early arriver. Whitney had joked that they should tell Mr. Whittingham an altered time for at least half past the start time.

Olivia walked toward the door, grinning with excitement at seeing her neighbor.

She would never lie to him about the start time because she enjoyed their quiet moments.

Second, she understood Mr. Whittingham's obsession with punctuality because it'd been important to Omar.

For her godfather, it was one of the few things he could control back in a time when he desperately wanted the respect of his colleagues.

"Back then, white folks wanted any sort of reason to discount you. If you're not on time, you're lazy. If you don't dress well, you're poor and uncultured. Sometimes it's a mind game, a battle of wills for them to conclude that I was just as experienced at my job as the rest of them."

Ama, who'd been in the room when Omar had given his opinion, huffed.

"Please. You think it makes a difference if we're on time or not? They'll go quiet when you make them money . . . simple as that. I don't need their respect." She'd focused her eyes on Olivia. *"You don't either, cher."*

Omar gave a slight nod, the thing he did often when Ama opposed his opinion. *"Well, I said back then is how I felt. Now it's just a habit. Still, I think you should respect anyone's time, no matter who they are."*

"I suppose." Ama shrugged and focused her on Olivia. *"But cher, I'd rather you be the type of person people wait for."*

When Olivia opened the door, she dropped her smile. "Addy. I didn't realize you would be here."

"It's a party about Black love and Black wealth, right?"

"Yes."

"I'm Black. My friends love me and I'm wealthy." She raised a wine bottle. "I brought wine from my personal collection. I know you like rosé so I . . ." she lowered the bottle. "I saw you at the cottage."

"Addy," Olivia sighed.

"Yes?"

"Are you attempting bribery to dissuade me from speaking to Kara?"

"Yes," she answered without shame. She stepped past Olivia and entered her home.

"How much is it worth?"

"What?" Addy spun around.

"Your wine?" *And your friendship with Kara.*

"Oh, it's reasonably priced, but it tastes simply divine. You know, you shouldn't be swayed by price as it doesn't denote whether the wine tastes good."

"How much?"

"Fifty?" She responded as if asking a question.

"Hmm." Olivia crossed her arms. "Still not enough to change my mind."

"Fine. I'll just refrain from mentioning to your fiancé, Anderson, that you not only had a date with Garrett but the two of you were in that same little cottage until midnight."

Out of habit, Olivia glanced upstairs, though Anderson wasn't home. He'd been renting an Airbnb until she decided their status.

"It wasn't a date. I filmed him for our Labor Day event."

"And the cottage? Let me guess, you two were just talking, right?"

Her skin boiled. Olivia was known for her ice-cold persona. No matter the insult, she would never sink to their level. On rare occasions, the only people who could get under her skin were her godsisters. However, today she dropped the civility. It was somewhere deep below the earth's core.

"You aren't one to take on accountability, are you, Addy? You just throw it right back instead of owning who you are and what you've done." She knew her type—the pretty and fun girl who skipped along while she caused destruction. Addy didn't seem at all remorseful about her actions. At least Olivia put some distance between her and Anderson.

"What about your accountability? Here you are flirting with a single man who's just healing in the romance department. You're leading him on, yet you pretend to be a Girl Scout." She shoved the wine toward Olivia. "So take this peace offering and stop pretending like your shit doesn't stink."

Olivia's mouth dropped. In all this time she'd been thinking about her guilt, and Anderson's feelings, she'd forgotten about Garrett's. Somehow, she'd lumped him in the cheating category too and subconsciously labeled him as a cheater.

But he was a good guy, a great father.

The look in his eyes after the beach flashed in her mind. "Addy, you're right about Garrett."

"I know."

"But Kara's your friend. Your best friend. Imagine how she'll feel when—"

The doorbell rang before Olivia could finish her sentence. Kara and Rich opened the door before she could let them in.

"Oh hey, Addy. I thought I heard your voice." Kara glanced between the two women. "Everything okay?"

"Of course!" Addy hooked Kara's elbow. "Olivia was just giving me a hard time about my wine! I had to defend my honor as a sommelier, of course."

"Yes. Of course." Kara nodded. Rich, who stood off to the side, stared at Olivia. It wasn't harsh, but thoughtful. Like he couldn't quite figure out her angle. If Addy had told him what occurred the night of the Hampton party, and Olivia guessed she had, he should be more nervous.

They really have no respect for Kara.

The remaining neighbors showed up and to her surprise Bea, whom she'd invited, showed up with Mr. Whittingham in tow.

Bea immediately sought her out to apologize. "Sorry about my appearance. Mr. Whittingham and I spent a little too much time at the apiary."

"Oh, you were with your bees?"

Mr. Whittingham nodded. "It's a magical experience. Hey, we should invite her to come next time, right?"

Bea glared at Mr. Whittingham, who gave her an encouraging nod before politeness forced Bea's acquiescence. "Um, yes. We can plan for some time next week if you want to come."

"I would love to," Olivia quickly replied before Bea rescinded the invite.

The meeting started late and despite the rockiness between her and Addy, the event had been a resounding success. The queue of Black wealthy patrons had been filled, and better, it would truly be beneficial to her neighbors.

Whitney and her husband, Charles, already had a firm to manage their massive wealth, but they were open to jumping ship, as their firm hadn't attended to their recent needs.

Whitney hung back after the meeting at Olivia's request.

"I want to be honest," Olivia began. "I'm thinking of quitting my job. Don't get me wrong, they'll serve your needs, but I won't be your manager."

"Oh . . . kay. Then why did you host this event for your company?" Whitney asked in a gentle voice.

"I suppose I'd like to go out with a bang. Make it easier for the Black women in the company who follow in my footsteps." Olivia shrugged. "To be clear, I'm not quitting because I hate my job, it's more because I want to explore entrepreneurial pursuits."

Whitney raised her wineglass. "Hmmm. Do tell."

Olivia took a deep breath, ready to give her practiced speech. "I want to create a company that can combat corporations like ASK through education, financial literacy programs, and cultural events. I'll start here in SANS and maybe expand to other neighborhoods. But I truly feel if we're proactive and figure out the formula to success, we could avoid the destruction of historically Black neighborhoods and cities."

Whitney's eyes grew wide.

Olivia held her breath. "So . . . what do you think? It sounds vague now, but I really feel—"

"You, Olivia Jones, are brilliant. And I would love to work with you." Her voice was rich with admiration.

"Really?" Olivia grinned.

"Yes! Of course. I've been wracking my brain about how we can fight. Outside of stuffing their tailpipes with bananas, I've got nothing."

Olivia laughed. "Where did you get that idea from?"

Whitney chuckled low. "I don't know. Some cartoon I watched with my niece. Seemed like a decent idea at the time."

"Well, I promise we'll come up with a better plan . . . together."

"So does that mean we're partners?" Whitney's voice filled with hope.

"I would love that, but let's do a few events together and see how we gel. If it works—"

"It'll work," Whitney confirmed.

"Fine. Once we have a few events under our belts, let's draw up some paperwork."

"Fantastic." Whitney grinned. "I'm looking forward to working with you in an official capacity, soon-to-be partner."

"Well, maybe."

"Definitely," she countered. "Let's go, Baby Love," she shouted to Charles. "Talk to you later . . . partner."

After Whitney left, Olivia journaled about her day. She was all smiles.

"What's your goal with bees?" Olivia asked Bea.

Bea, who wore a long-sleeve shirt, hadn't put on the hat and veil just yet. She inspected Olivia's outfit and gave her a thick, sting-proof beekeeping jacket.

"Give me a minute, will you, New Girl? I want to make sure the bees don't sting you."

"Do you think they'll attack?" Her heart pounded against her chest. Up to this point, beekeeping seemed fun and mysterious. Now she questioned her sanity.

"They're friendly, but I always err on the side of caution. Especially when I introduce them to new people."

"Do they know many people?" Olivia couldn't imagine Bea giving tours to SANS residents.

"Just you and Mr. Whittingham. I'm sure they'll miss him today." She said it in a serious voice, so Olivia took it to mean the bees liked him, which seemed odd.

"I was all about the honey at first," Bea answered in a quiet voice.

"I learned how to bee keep from an apothecary. So, for me, it started with practicality. But then I fell in love . . ."

"With a person?"

Bea let out a bark of a laugh. "No, no. That ship has sailed, crashed, and burned. By me, of course," she muttered the last part to herself.

"I'm in it for the bees now. They deserve a strong sustainable habitat. Now don't get me wrong, I get things out of the relationship, too. Honey, hand salves, something Mr. Whittingham loves. Lip balms. And they help make my garden thrive."

She gave Olivia the hat and veil. "Are you ready?"

"Yes!"

"Put on that hat and we'll be ready to go. Today I'm going to check for swarming."

Bea guided Olivia deeper into the back of her property. It took five minutes to arrive at the apiary. Four small boxes that reminded Olivia of bird boxes stood three feet apart from each other. Bea had painted the boxes white, as well as her signature aquamarine blue and yellow.

A simple folding table stood just beyond the beehives. She motioned Olivia to follow her and picked up what looked to be a torch and lit the insides of a silver cannister.

"This is a smoker. I'm going to add it to the hive." She picked up a bar to pry the top open.

Then she sprayed smoke into the hive. After the smoke, Bea picked up a fuming board and hung it on the side railings. For long seconds, she didn't speak, examining it.

Olivia was too afraid to speak, especially when she noticed what looked to be thousands of bees clinging to either side of the board. Bea motioned to Olivia to move closer. "You see how the frame looks? Filled to the gills." Her voice was rich with satisfaction. "Just gorgeous."

Olivia nodded. She wouldn't call it gorgeous. The cluster of buzzing bees sent a chaotic combination of frightening yet fascinating energy through her body. Being among thousands of tiny things that had the power to heal and harm made her feel like she was walking a thin tightrope between the Empire State Building and Central Park Tower.

Bea floated over to the next box. "Hello, my lovelies. You are looking just gorgeous today." She brought the next frame for Olivia to inspect, though she didn't know what to look for.

"We want to make sure the queen isn't here."

Olivia nodded again.

"You can speak, you know." Olivia heard the humor in Bea's voice.

"Umm, how does the queen look?"

"See how all these lovelies are fuzzy and moving around? It's like they can't keep still?"

"Yes."

"The queen has a shiny back. She's very queenly and doesn't move around as much." She pointed toward the middle. "She's usually in the center while the worker bees feed her and take care of her waste."

She thought of Ama, the way people moved around her, while she stood. Her comment came to mind. *"I'd rather people want to wait on me."*

Ama had big Queen Bee energy and Olivia knew she wanted to be Queen. For so long, she thought of herself as a worker bee, making everything better for everyone around her. Her job, Anderson, Cindy, even Omar and Ama.

But she never felt like she was the center of someone else's world. For Omar, it had been Ama, as it should have been.

For Perry, it was her husband, Damon; and for Billie, her wife, Dulce.

But Anderson couldn't bring himself to do that one thing. And the entire time Olivia had orbited around him, busying herself to make him more comfortable. Creating excuse after excuse for their broken relationship. And when she couldn't take it any longer, instead of making a clean break, she cheated. It had been three weeks and he still hadn't talked about his past. Oh, he'd text her several times a week. A joke, a meme, an *I miss you* message, but never the truth. Yesterday he asked about her coming to see him perform in Sag. She would go and maybe after the show, they both could share their truths. Regardless, she couldn't live in limbo any longer.

"No more," she vowed to herself.

"What? I have one more to check. If you're bored, then—"

"No, no. I'm thinking out loud. About something else." Apparently, the life of bees made the perfect allegory to her life.

After surveying the swarm, Bea led them back to her home, motioning Olivia to take off the jacket, hat, and veil.

When Bea took off a layer of clothes, stripping down to her tank and jeans, Olivia noticed a familiar-looking charm.

"That's nice." Olivia pointed at the bee charm that rested at Bea's collarbone.

Bea looked down, twisting the yellow bee charm between her thumb and finger. "T-thanks."

"Where did you get it from?"

"Why do you ask? Are you suddenly into bees now?" Her voice waved like the ocean.

"No. I have one just like it. So do my godsisters. My godmother gave us the necklaces when we were little. It's just . . . unique that's all."

Unique didn't cover it. It'd been custom made by one of Ama's favorite jewelers.

"I don't recall where I bought it. Probably from a thrift shop." She shrugged. "Look, I think we're done for the day."

"If I offended you, my apologies."

Olivia asked a simple question about a necklace, but it felt like more. With her strained relationship with Anderson, she knew how to spot lies.

The way Bea carried herself, as if the boogeyman could jump out at any moment, led her to believe she suffered from abuse, or perhaps she was on the run.

"If you're in trouble, I can help. Or . . . keep a secret if you need to keep a low profile."

Bea laughed. "Oh, New Girl. I'm no one's victim, but thank you." She bit her lip, staring at Olivia.

"You aren't on the run?"

Bea looked at the floor, staring at her steel-toed boots. Then she lifted her head and stared at Olivia. "Does being on the run from yourself count?"

"I believe my therapist, Dr. LaGrange, would say yes."

"Hmm. I could use one of those," Bea muttered.

"I highly recommend her. A mutual friend recommended her to me."

"Kara . . . I know. She's practically shoved the woman's card down my throat. But I have Mr. Whittingham to talk to."

"He's a good person to speak to. I always learn something," Olivia agreed.

Bea nodded. "When I first moved here, he knocked on the door. I ignored it, but he found me one day with my bees. He was delighted that SANS had a beekeeper and made me promise I would teach him. He came every week, and he's just as good as me now. Then, over time, he just sort of wormed his way into my life. He's like family, but he's *not* family, you know?"

Olivia understood that very well. And that was her original mission. But somewhere along the way finding her father's people continued to get pushed down her priority list. She'd been avoiding the library meeting with Garrett after their dinner, and she had yet to hear back from Mr. Whittingham about sharing her aunt and uncle's information.

"Where is your family? Are they . . . gone?" Olivia whispered.

Bea shook her head. "Despite my abandoning them, they are just fine. But I think . . . I think it's time for me to try to reach out again." Bea licked her lips. "If you were my family, would you forgive me after a very long time?"

Olivia crossed her arms and leaned against the table. "My father died when I was a child. My mom . . . she wasn't emotionally available. Now I realize she was in mourning. She didn't have the tools to heal, I know that now, but I still feel abandoned."

"Have you forgiven her?"

Olivia shrugged. "I'd like to talk to her and, yes, I want to forgive her. But she has to own how she raised me and realize she rarely showed me love."

Bea's eyes softened. She leaned over and gripped the worktable. "I hope they can forgive me. I hope it's not too late."

"How long has it been?"

"Too long. Decades."

"Why are you reaching out now?"

She twisted the chain of her necklace. "Because the universe demands it and my time has run out. Because I've healed, and I've found a home."

"Do you regret leaving?"

Bea shook her head. "I think it was the best thing I could do for them. I just wish that I would have been more gentle, less selfish. I needed to be free to find myself. I just wish I hadn't dragged others in my descension."

Hearing Bea's pain, Olivia realized something. Whereas Bea

acknowledged her mistakes, Cindy would not. Her mother would not apologize. Maybe she didn't even recognize the trauma she'd caused.

"Thank you for this conversation," she said to Bea. "I think I need to do something important."

Bea she nodded and wished her good luck.

Olivia didn't wait until she returned home. She pressed the contact under the name Cindy, instead of mother.

"Hey. I would love for you to visit Sag Harbor."

"I don't want to cause any fuss. I'm not sure how big the house is but three can be a crowd."

"Anderson is no longer living in my home. I have room."

Seconds stretched on to a minute. It was as if they were playing the quiet game.

"So, will you come?" Olivia prodded.

"Yes. Of course. I wouldn't mind getting out of this house."

"Is the school still letting you work from home?"

"Oh, yes. You know we don't play here."

"Excellent. Are you available on Labor Day weekend?"

"Hmm, no. I don't want to be around a crowd."

"What about the following weekend? September is still the summer."

"Yes. I can do that." Her mother hesitated. "Is . . . everything okay? What's the rush?"

"No rush, but I'd like to see you."

"Okay, then."

The phone went silent. Foolishly, Olivia waited to hear the sentiment returned. Instead of letting her disappointment bloom, she continued. "I'll text you my address, along with some instructions, in case you get lost."

"I'm sure I'll be fine. It'll be good to finally go to the place Chris called his second home."

She wanted to see Cindy's face and hear her voice, observe her reaction when she saw the pictures of her father, Chris, hanging in her home.

Best of all, she wanted her mother to heal so that she could tell stories of her late father. Through Mr. Whittingham, she'd learned about her father from adolescence to early adulthood. From her mother, she wanted to understand the man, the husband, the father.

"I'll see you soon. I can't wait."

"Sure, me too. Bye now."

CHAPTER 23

IS THIS LOVE?

August 2021

Anderson had a week until his time was up. He'd begged and pleaded with Olivia to change her mind and had said the state of their relationship affected his ability to perform stand-up.

Olivia had been sorely tempted to do a ceasefire but Ama's fiery phrase, talk or walk, had looped in her mind like a mantra. Despite their hardships, Olivia didn't want the relationship to end, but she knew she had to stick to her ultimatum.

ANDERSON: Are you still coming to my gig tonight?
OLIVIA: Yes. Whitney and Charles, Kara and Rich will attend too.
ANDERSON: Awesome, see you then. Maybe we can talk after?
OLIVIA: That would be great. You can come over.

Tonight, something will change.

She was frightened. Over the past few weeks, she'd missed Anderson's presence. She hoped something would happen tonight to give her the right answer for the future of their relationship.

Olivia blew out a breath and turned on the television to watch the news. The station covered a local protest of an event facility who discriminated against gay couples. A swarm of citizens surrounded the building with signs and coordinated chants.

The camera swept across the grounds and Olivia immediately recognized the cursive script and sign: Habberidge Hills. It was the facility Addy had mentioned when she'd been so nosy about their marriage plans.

A woman in her thirties with a cute pixie cut filled the screen. The camera panned away from the three other anchors seated at a desk in the studio and zoomed in on the anchorwoman's face. "Habberidge Hills temporarily closed their doors just two days ago after accusations of discrimination for same-sex marriage. A couple discovered they had had their wedding reception canceled without notice. Initially, Delia Jacobs, one of the brides, attended meetings with their planner. When her partner, Grace Stevens, attended the final meeting, the couple discovered the owner's *feelings* about their marriage during a heated exchange, after which the owner canceled their reservation just days before the event. Jennifer Collins is at the location where citizens are protesting." She spoke to her colleague, now on a split screen.

"Yes, Camelia, the crowd is energized, organized, and angry. They've prided themselves on being an inclusive community and many were surprised by Habberidge Hills' apparent contempt for same-sex marriage." She waved her slim hand toward a woman who looked to be in her early forties. "I'm with Delia now." The field anchor turned to face her and offered the microphone. "Can you tell us what happened during the meetings with Habberidge Hills?"

"I've been dreaming of my wedding day since I was a little girl, and I've been marrying my Barbies off since ten years old. I'm the planner in the relationship, Grace, not so much, so I attended most of the meetings and planned our wedding day. A week before our wedding, Grace arrived to review the run of show before the guests arrived. We planned to have a small, non-traditional ceremony, but we wanted to make sure everything was in order. The staff had been incredible, but it was the owner, John Habberidge," she shouted his name with fire, "who was incredibly rude to us. He said that's not what his late wife would have wanted for the facility. After we left, Grace was in tears. We no longer wanted to get married there, but we had no choice, you know?"

Delia sniffed tears.

"Oh no," Olivia whispered. She could no longer eat her breakfast. "I won't be getting married there." Not that there was going to be a wedding now anyway.

The interview continued. "Anyway, I told my best friend, Taylor, who planned to marry his fiancée here next year. They immediately canceled. Our community came together, and we discovered many other stories like ours, and not just discrimination against same-sex couples. We're sorry for the staff, but John has to go."

"And how would you go about doing that?" the reporter asked. "Many people come from outside of your town to get married here."

Olivia could see why. The grounds were simply beautiful with a pond surrounded by flowers. The facility itself looked to be like a cathedral, with white marbled floors.

"We don't care! He can sell to someone else." She shrugged. "If he doesn't, well, he's going to be in for a rude awakening. We won't let racists, sexists, and homophobic people destroy our community." She turned to face the crowd and shouted, "Isn't that right?"

"Yes!" they shouted, and a new chant began. "Love is Love!"

Another woman blew a kiss from the crowd and Delia pretended to catch it and place it in her pocket.

"And there you have it. As you can see," the field reporter waved toward the crowd. "When a community comes together, you can move mountains. I have no doubt their voices will be heard, and change will come."

"Thank you, Jennifer. We will certainly keep everyone posted. Next up, a young girl stops a kidnapper in his tracks."

Olivia turned down the volume, but her mind was racing.

"Amazing." Energy coursed through her body. She could see it now. She just needed to get the whole community in agreement.

She grabbed her phone from the table and stepped outside. The vitamin D instantly lifted her spirits, though she didn't need much. The newscast had given her ideas on how to organize the community, or rather, the gaps that existed.

"Whitney, how are you?" Olivia sang over the phone.

"Pissed."

"Oh, oh. What happened?"

"Those assholes at ASK just filed a request. Get this, they want to build a beach tower."

"Where?"

"Near Bea's home," she hissed. "It's not like we're on a big public beach. I've got a feeling they want to create something for commercial use. Like one of those beach shack restaurants." She lowered her voice and whispered, as if saying it out loud would make it true.

"Oh, no." Olivia shook her head.

"It's fine. We'll deal." Whitney exhaled. "Anyway, I'm looking forward to tonight. Would you like to ride with me and Charles?"

"Yes, thanks." Olivia hadn't thought of logistics. "But listen, I saw a story today on the news and I got a little idea."

"Oh?"

"Yes. Have you heard of Habberidge Hills? It's a wedding venue not too far from here."

"Yes. One of my girlfriend's nieces plans to get married there."

Olivia winced. "She may need to find an alternative. They're in hot water for discrimination against same-sex couples."

"Oh, nooo. Ayana really had her heart set on that place."

Olivia went silent, waiting for her friend to process.

"Okay, tell me about your brilliant idea. And then I need to call my friend."

"The community is basically driving them out. Granted, it's a local business and nowhere near the size of ASK, but the citizens were livid and organized. They called on the news crew and I'm guessing they'll be pariahs soon."

"So . . . we should do the same thing?"

"Exactly."

Whitney didn't say a word. Olivia pressed the receiver closer to her ear.

"But how?" Whitney finally broke the silence, her voice cautious. "Girl, you know they don't care about us. Hell, I can't tell you how many untold David and Goliath stories there are, especially in Black communities."

"We've already got video footage of residences sharing memories. First let's hit them in the feels. Let's invite media, not just the local papers, but a magazine or the *New York Times*. We can make it provocative and call it the last Black neighborhoods in the Hamptons, or something like that."

"I . . . guess we could try."

"We should try. Listen, I have a friend who works for a magazine in a big market. I can get their feedback on the pitch and see what works."

"Okay, sure, if you think we have a shot."

"We can't tell ourselves no just yet, Whitney. I know ASK is getting aggressive, but we've got to keep going."

"You're right, it's just that I saw another blue-and-white For Sale sign. Pretty soon we're going to get pushed out and lose what makes us unique. A tale as old as time but it's like . . ." Whitney blew into the phone, rattling Olivia's AirPods.

"It's like I see us twenty years from now. And we won't be wading in the water looking for crabs. We won't do our Labor Day Races, or art pop-ups. It'll just be another bland neighborhood."

"I know. But we can fight. We can win. I know you've been doing this for a while, and I know you're tired. But we need you. We've got to show ASK and our neighbors that it's more than money. We give this place meaning and culture and flavor. And to lose us and to give away our history is to lose a piece of ourselves and those who came before us."

"So, how do we fight?"

"We fight with money and power. Let's shore up our influence in local politics. Let's do a . . . like an investment club but for real estate in Sag Harbor. We can pool money to buy out our neighbors who need to sell. Then we carefully select people who'll contribute to the neighborhood."

"Olivia, that's a brilliant idea. Let's talk about it on the way to the venue."

"Sounds good. Now go call your friend."

"I will, see you later."

Just as she ended the call, Olivia heard an adorable voice call out to her. "Hey, Pretty Lady!"

She found Zora with a bucket in her hand. Olivia scanned the beach for her father but couldn't spot Garrett.

"Where's your—"

"Zora!"

"Here, Daddy."

"Zora, you can't run off like that." Garrett pulled a deep breath. He looked at Olivia and smiled. "Thanks for finding my little pumpkin."

"I'm not a pumpkin! I'm a little girl."

"And so you are." Olivia smiled down at her. "What are you up to, little girl?"

"We're building a sandcastle. You want to play?" Zora batted her adorable large brown eyes, rimmed in the longest lashes she'd ever seen. She glanced at Garrett, who batted his equally long eyelashes and shrugged.

Olivia couldn't say no. She bent over and offered her hand. "I need a shovel."

"Okay!" Zora gave her a mini pink shovel, then she took off running.

"Where are you going?"

"To me and Daddy's favorite spot!"

Before she could protest, Garrett grabbed Olivia's hand and dragged her down the beach. "We've got to keep up."

"Have you seen me run?" Olivia smiled. "You don't have to drag me along. I can pull my weight." She picked up the speed and only slowed when Zora seemed to find their magical spot.

"Oh, I've seen you," he agreed. "I'm just holding your hand because I want to." He winked at her.

Face burning, Olivia turned away to hide her smile. She pulled her hand away when she noticed Zora giggling at the two of them.

The trio settled on the sand. Thankfully Olivia was wearing a shirt and yoga pants that she didn't mind getting dirty.

For an hour they sat in silence, building the sandcastle under Zora's bossy instructions.

"Pretty Lady—"

"Ms. Pretty Lady," Garrett corrected his daughter.

"Oh, yes. Ms. Pretty Lady, can you build a moat? It needs to be thissss big." She traced a circle in the air.

"Got it."

"Daddy, you're the bucket patter."

"As usual."

"I'm the best at packing sand." Zora looked at Olivia while shoveling sand into three buckets. "Daddy says so, and he doesn't lie. Not ever."

Olivia looked at Garrett. "Not ever?"

"I learned early in life that it leads to nowhere. Mom and Dad had a way of knowing everything."

"The price you pay for living in a close-knit neighborhood."

"Exactly." He paused and looked toward the water. "Guess that's not such a bad thing for Zora. I could get the neighbors to keep tabs on her. Make sure some little"—he looked at his daughter—"knucklehead isn't getting her into trouble."

"This little angel?" Olivia smiled at Zora, who blinked innocently and smiled with a smear of sand on her face.

"Never."

"That's right, Daddy. I'm an angel," she sang.

They bantered on, Olivia immensely enjoyed their company and laughed and smiled so hard her stomach and cheeks ached.

"You know, I would be happy to look after Zora, too. If you ever need a day or night out, give me a shout."

Garrett nodded. "She does like you. A lot. She talks about you all the time."

"I like her, too," Olivia admitted. She could see herself giving Zora great advice, shopping trips in the city—just like Ama had done with her, Perry, and Billie.

"Does she have a godmother?"

Garrett nodded. "She does, but Marilyn fell off after Dana died."

"Well, if you're open to it, I would love to be Zora's. I know it's weird but—"

"It's perfect. You'll be to her how Ama is to you, right?"

"Exactly, right. That is, if Zora is up for it."

"I think that's a good thing." Garrett nodded. "Thank you for offering."

"Thank you for accepting." Olivia smiled while digging her moat.

"Hey, Zora. How would you feel if Olivia became your god-mother?" Garrett asked his daughter.

Zora gasped, her little hands covered her mouth. "Like a fairy? Do you fly and have glitter?"

"Oh, no." Olivia shook her head. "Like real life. We can go shopping, play games, talk, and I can talk to you about important things when you get older."

"Like boyfriends?"

"Hey, now! No boyfriends until you're eighteen."

"Okay, Daddy." When she rolled her eyes, Olivia burst into laughter.

"We can talk about anything you want. So what do you say?"

"I say, yay!" Zora smoothed her castle. "Can you do another moat for this one?" she pointed to her newly minted sandcastle.

"Sure thing."

Garrett mouthed "That was easy," making Olivia laugh again.

"Hey!" Kara waved from a few feet away. "Oh, that looks so pretty." She kneeled, observing the castle.

"It is." Zora nodded. "Me, Daddy, and my godmommy did it all together. Like a big happy family."

Kara's eyes grew wide. She slowly looked at Olivia and pursed her lips.

Olivia shot to her feet. "Well, I've got to get going." She dusted the sand from her pants. "See you soon, Little Angel."

"Okay. Can we play tomorrow?"

"No baby," her father quickly answered. "Another time."

"Yes, we can definitely play another time, maybe this weekend," Olivia promised. She moved her attention toward Kara. "Do you have a second to talk?"

Kara dropped her smile but nodded. "Sure, if you want to."

Olivia didn't want to, but it was the right thing to do. She was sure of it.

Kara chose the direction, toward Olivia's house.

"Kara, I . . ." Olivia licked her lips. "I don't know how to say this. I . . . I don't want to say this, but I think there is something going on between Addy and Rich."

Kara stumbled. "Oh, yeah?" Her voice was cool, her gait steady and smooth. "Why do you think that?"

"The night we partied in the Hamptons. I saw them holding hands in the dark. They came to the cottage near the wooded area, away from the main house. Addy . . . knows that I know. She's asked me to back off, but I—"

"Maybe you should do that." The sarcasm in her voice was clear.

It startled Olivia so much, she stumbled over her feet and words. "D-do what?"

"Step off." Kara's tone transitioned from lake-calm to hardened steel.

Why was it that every time a woman tried to warn their friend of infidelity, they were the ones who got their head bit off?

Olivia swallowed the anger rising in her throat. She'd given her the facts and if Kara wanted to pretend otherwise, there was nothing she could do about it.

"Okay, I'll step off. I'm sorry if I offended you." Olivia's apology was as thin as her patience. "See you tonight, if you're up to it."

Kara stuffed her hands into the pockets of her denim shorts. She tilted her head to the sky and let out an awful groan.

"Wait." Kara raised her hand. "Just . . . just wait." She looked around and then waved at the sand and plopped down. "Take a seat next to me. I'll only say this once."

"O . . . okay."

"I love Rich. Rich loves me. But somewhere along the way, we just lost that . . . spark."

"Spark?"

"We just don't do it for each other. Well, it's streaky. Some days he looks good to me, and I think, hey I married an attractive guy. But most times I don't feel any physical attraction." She shrugged and let her shoulders droop. "But he's my best friend in the entire world. When I get a commission or great reviews, he's the first person I call. I care about his opinion, and I want the best in life for him and for us. So . . . our marriage is more of a partnership. Addy and Rich are enjoying each other, and they can. They don't rub it in my face. They don't make out on our couch. They *are usually* discreet, and believe you me, I will talk to them about this."

"But what about you? What about your needs?"

"Right now, I want to create art. I want to travel when the rest of the world opens back up. I've occasionally had lovers, but very brief and discreet. They know the score and they know I'll never leave my husband. Nor will Rich leave me. It took us a long time to get to a good place, thanks to Dr. LaGrange. We're honestly thrilled right now."

"Well, then . . . what about Addy?"

"Addy understands more than anyone how our marriage functions. She has no intentions of getting married. She's like a bee who likes to skip around and pollinate different flowers."

Olivia winced. She didn't think Bea would appreciate the comparison.

"All of that is to say our marriage is a partnership. And we won't do anything to fuck that up. But you know about that, right?"

Olivia shook her head. "I don't."

"You do." Kara bumped her shoulders. "You're so busy trying to solve everyone else's problems . . . the neighborhood, making sure Mr. Whittingham isn't lonely . . . me. You aren't focused on your own issues."

"What issues?"

"Do you really want to marry Anderson? Or do you feel like he's your only choice? Because honey . . . the way Garrett, hell, the way Zora looks at you, you've got options."

"I . . . I . . ." her mouth opened and shut like a marionette with a drunk puppet master.

"I'm off!" Kara hopped to her feet while Olivia looked dumb-founded. "No more talks about me, Addy, and Rich, okay?"

"Thanks for explaining everything." Olivia called to her back. "I'm sorry I was rash."

Kara spun around, walking backwards. "Don't apologize to me. Apologize to poor Addy. No wonder that girl's had a stick up her behind for the past few weeks."

"Tell her if she comes tonight, that I'll make it up to her some-how."

Kara waved and turned back around.

Olivia sighed. The world was so much more complicated than she imagined.

CHAPTER 24

THE MAN IN BLACK

August 2021

"How's everyone doing?" A thin man with gray-streaked hair paced the stage. "I'm Miguel, your emcee for tonight."

A few people hooted. Olivia clapped.

"We've got a great lineup tonight. Starting up Tony Dev, Jenny Nweke, and lastly Anderson Edwards." He let the crowd clap before he continued.

"While the acts are up, we ask that you stay in your seats. Keep it masked unless you're eating or drinking. We don't need any of you laughing *on* the talent." His tone was light, but his eyes told the crowd he meant business.

"I mean it." He pointed at the crowd. "I will Lysol your ass and then kick you out." He bounced on his feet and lifted his leg into a pathetic kick, much like a toddler on his first day of taekwondo. The crowd roared with laughter and even Olivia chuckled at his antics.

"Just kidding. Look at me." He waved a hand down his body. "I'll get Big Don to kick you out." He pointed to the bouncer at the door. "My skinny ass ain't carrying *any* of you. I can't even carry my wife." He looked around, as if checking his surroundings, and then put the mic closer to his mouth. "I'm the little spoon in the relationship." He whispered into the mic.

Olivia coughed up her drink while Whitney smacked the table and laughed.

"I love that shit. Listen, I'm not an alpha dude. I'm not." He shook his head. "I'm cool with that. My wife grew up with three brothers and they *hate me*. Seriously, they do. Her older brother asked her what she saw in me. Granted, it was a valid question after the incident." He stopped pacing and shrugged. "See, what happened was that a raccoon tried to end me. Have you ever seen a jacked raccoon? Had to be at least five feet. Claws ten inches, at least." He clawed at the air. "He tried to get me, but I ducked and dodged, rolled into the corner. I *may* have screamed," he chuckled into the mic.

"So yeah, my brother-in-law asked my wife in front of me. Kinda in front of me. I'm in the corner, remember? Recovering from my near-death experience. When my brother-in-law asked what she saw in me, she answered. 'Oh, he makes me laugh.'" He mimicked a high-pitched voice.

"Anyway, at some point, I got my confidence back and I was like, yeah . . . she likes my mouth." He raised his eyebrows like the Rock.

The crowd thundered with applause, and the comedian paused for effect.

"Made my wife laugh. Her *hermanos*? Not so much. Anyway." He slapped his thigh. "Let's get our first comedian onto the stage. Get out here, Tony."

Whitney leaned in and chuckled. "Oh my God, if the host is that funny, I bet Anderson is a hoot."

Olivia nodded. "He really is." She scanned the room. The venue was small—a bar packed in the corner, a dozen bistro tables packed in the middle, and along either side were two sofas that were deemed the VIP section toward the back of the room. Olivia, Whitney, and Charles sat in the section. Kara, Rich, and Addy bowed out, not to Olivia's surprise as she'd expertly inserted her foot firmly into her mouth.

Quite a few patrons who recognized Charles greeted him with hearty waves or flapped their wings, something he and his fans did back when he played professional basketball. Though Olivia rarely watched sports, she knew his nickname was the Eagle, because he sailed in the air with dunks or blocks.

After an hour, the first and second acts had finished. The first had a squeaky voice that added to his humor. The second one talked about her childhood as a second-generation African growing up in the States. Olivia liked her overall, but Whitney loved her and immediately stalked her on social media.

"She might be good to hire for an event for the neighborhood."

Olivia nearly suggested hiring Anderson, but she held back. Depending on what he shared, tonight could be their last interaction.

"Excuse me, ma'am. But the guy at the front says he knows you and Anderson." The security Big Don whispered in her ear.

Olivia stood and looked past his broad shoulders, but she couldn't see the person. "I can't see them. Did they leave a name?"

He shook his head. "No. But they both claim they're friends."

Whitney grabbed Olivia's wrist. "It's probably Rich and Kara. They said they would try to make it."

"Oh, yes." Olivia nodded. "Send them over. Thanks for asking."

"Next onto the stage: Anderson Edwards."

Olivia clapped along with the crowd.

Anderson waved from the stage, a mic already in hand. "I just passed Jenny and asked her about the energy out here, you know, to get a beat. And she says," he chuckled before he shared with the crowd. He tutted and mimicked her accent. "Just like a white man.

"I was like What do you mean? Then I thought, sure we do a lot of shit. Sailed across the ocean blue with diseases and muskets. But today . . . today I haven't done anything just yet," Anderson sighed. "Then I asked her for advice, and she says . . . Don't be ashy."

He paused and he got a few laughs from the crowd. Olivia forced herself to laugh. She didn't love that he mimicked Jenny's accent.

"I . . . what?" his voice went high. He threw his arms in the air. "I'm incredibly confused right now. I'm about to marry a Black woman, so I know what ashy means, but not . . . in that context."

Whitney bumped her knees against Olivia. When Olivia looked up, Whitney widened her eyes and mouthed, "Married?"

Olivia shrugged her shoulders, though her frustration mounted.

The chuckles from the crowd gained momentum, seeming to infuse Anderson with energy. He slapped the side of his head. "No. I'm not saying that she's ashy. I'm saying I know what it means. We started living together once the shutdowns happened. She took one look at my Suave lotion, and gasped." Anderson clutches his chest. "She's like, what is this?

"And I said, Oh, it's lotion. It says it's revitalizing on the bottle. That's how you know it's good. A day later I can't find my lotion. I find her shea butter and there's a Post-it on the top with a message. 'Use me.'"

Olivia fidgeted in her chair; the breath she held burned the inside of her throat. She didn't enjoy being a part of his routine, but it wasn't so bad.

"Before we go anywhere, she's like 'ash check!' and I'm checking her back, her ankles. She does not play about moisturizing."

The crowd laughed.

Olivia twisted and twirled the pear-shaped diamond necklace like a smoker with a day-old nicotine patch. The laughter of the crowd sluiced over her as if she were immersed in sea water.

Whitney leaned over and bumped her shoulder.

"It's fine. I'm fine," she replied automatically.

Anderson continued his routine. "Next day I use it and I'm shiny as shit, man. Seriously, I know it wasn't just me, because on one of my food deliveries, this little girl ran outside to grab the food and stopped dead in her tracks, covered her eyes with her arm and wailed."

Anderson pretended to be the little girl and squealed. The audience found it hilarious. Olivia did not.

"I'm not lying to you. Genuine, heart-wrenching tears. Her dad comes out and, dude, he's pissed. He's like what did you do to my daught—ahhh!" Anderson dashes across the stage. "Now he's screaming. My eyes, my eyes! At this point the dog comes out, barking. He's ready to bite a plug out of my ass. But then he sees me and just howls like Scooby-Doo. He's like *arrruuuuhhhh*.

"So, I put the food on the doorstep and slowly back away. I'm back in my car and it hits me. I'm a freaking superhero." He slid across the stage. "I'm Shiny Man," he said in a voice that sounded like one of those eighties superhero movies. "I can glide at the speed of a bullet, blind you with my shine. You can't catch me because I'm too greasy. I'm getting away.

"But I realize I had to use this power responsibly. I couldn't just walk around overly moisturized, scaring the citizens of Sag Harbor." He bounced on his feet.

"Anyway, I went back to Suave. I'll let Black people have it. The power was too great." He shook his head as if sad.

Olivia stole a glance at Whitney, who had a strained look on her face. She need not say a word, because Olivia felt it all—the humiliation of being called out as a Black woman to be used as the butt of a joke about cultural self-care. The joke seemed light on the surface but boiled with cruelty.

He didn't understand that ash could signify being poor, or lack of caring. It even caused anxiety.

"I'm sorry," Olivia whispered to her friend. She was sorry in more ways than one.

"Hey," a voice whispered from behind her. Before she could turn, she witnessed Whitney's face transform from secondhand embarrassment to annoyance.

Olivia swerved her attention and gasped when she recognized Anderson's cousin, Bradford. Beside him was another man. From the startling blue eyes, he looked to also be in the family. The guy offered a weak wave and shrugged, as if to apologize for whatever was to come. Standing just behind him was an older man who, without permission, sat on the couch beside Olivia.

"What are you doing here?" Olivia directed her venom at Bradford.

"You know him?" Whitney's voice grew louder. Some patrons turned to stare at them.

"It's Anderson's cousin." *Racist cousin.* And by the looks of the older man strongly resembled Anderson, she'd guessed his father.

"Anderson's cousin works for ASK?" It wasn't Whitney who asked, but Charles who'd leaned forward and nodded toward their black polos.

Olivia's heart plummeted to the floor. There it was. Stitched in bold white capitalized letters just above their pockets: ASK.

Olivia couldn't see Anderson. She could only focus on the damning ASK logo. Clutching the edge of the splintered wood table, she forced herself to stand, head swimming, heart dreadfully full.

The particles in the air ceased to move, she rubbed at her neck, finding it difficult to breathe. "I n-need air."

Someone grabbed her hand and guided her outside. The sun had set since she first stepped into the darkened club. She walked nearly half a block before losing steam.

"Breathe." Whitney rubbed her back. "Breathe, Olivia."

"H-he lied to me," Olivia's voice cracked. "They all lie."

"Who?"

"Men. My godfather, the guy I dated who had a fiancée. Now

Anderson. Doesn't matter the age or race, they all lie." Olivia's voice trembled.

"Let's get you out of here," Whitney gently advised. "We have a guest room. You can stay at our place."

"Absolutely not." Olivia her raw whisper scraped her throat. She paced back and forth like a wind-up toy.

"What did you say?" Whitney leaned in closer.

"No," her voice grew stronger, louder. "It's my home. He can go with his cousin. They can camp out at that monstrous ASK building."

"Excuse me." The other guy who'd walked in with Bradford and Anderson's dad approached them as if they were startled, doe-eyed deer.

Charles stepped in front of Olivia and Whitney. Whitney stepped in front of Olivia, entwining their hands together. Olivia squeezed her hand, taking in her warmth. She hadn't realized how cold her hands had gotten.

"Hey man, don't come any closer," Charles warned.

"I . . . I won't." The man had a strong Boston accent. "I'm just checking on Anderson's lady."

"Not his lady for long," Olivia snapped.

"It's not what you think. Anderson cut off the family a long time ago. He's not involved, but Frank—"

"Who?" Whitney asked.

"His dad. Frank wants to reconnect. When he found out that Anderson had a performance tonight, he wanted to see him. He wanted to understand why he left our family business behind."

Olivia snorted, and attempted to walk in front of Whitney, though her overprotective neighbor tugged her back.

"Anderson is welcome to do what he pleases," Olivia spoke from behind Whitney's back. "He's been doing that for the past eighteen months."

"Again, it isn't like that. Frank's not doing so well, and he wants to mend fences. He's not trying to ruin what you two have or anything. He's just a man who wants to make up to his son and—"

"He's just a guy who's gobbling up property without a care in the world," Whitney interrupted. "Stop making him seem like he's anything but a greedy old man."

"Olivia!" Anderson jogged closer to them. "Olivia." He let out an exhausted breath when he caught up. "Shaun, what are you doing here, man?" he addressed Mr. Peacemaker.

"Just trying to settle things down. I'm sorry I didn't warn you about Frank."

"It's fine. Just . . . can you get those knuckleheads out of here?" Anderson sounded five decades older.

"You got it." Shaun nodded. "I'll call you later."

Anderson didn't answer. His attention fixed on Olivia. The man walked away.

Anderson cupped his neck. "Can we talk?"

"Yes," Olivia immediately agreed. "Let's go."

"Wait." Whitney shook her head. "Are you sure you're okay?"

"I'm fine." Olivia lowered her voice and whispered, "I've got to handle this tonight."

"Call me after . . . or else I'm coming over with the cavalry."

She didn't doubt Whitney would form a cavalcade of Mercedes, Range Rovers, and Porsches in front of her home, which is why she promised to call.

Whitney and Charles stared at them as Olivia and Anderson walked to his car.

Olivia strapped herself in. When Anderson turned on the car, the radio blasted alternative rock.

With shaking fingers, Anderson lowered the volume.

"Listen, Olivia. I'm not a perfect person. I can be self-centered and . . . and stupid. But I swear I'll put everything on the line tonight. If you decide to walk away afterward, well . . . I understand. Truly."

"All right." Olivia blanked her thoughts. It felt as if she'd zipped through the stages of grief. At first, she couldn't believe her eyes when she recognized the ASK logo. Realizing Anderson's familial connection to the neighborhood's enemy skipped her right over to anger.

She wanted to lie to herself, to pretend that they could get past this, but she didn't see how they could.

Not to mention, while his neighbors worried about keeping their properties and protecting their legacy, Anderson had stood like a wolf among them.

I led the wolf to their doorsteps.

Something ugly twisted her insides, an unbearable pain that neither antacids nor apologies could heal.

Minutes later, they arrived at her home.

"Wine?" Anderson offered.

Olivia shook her head. She'd had a terrible cocktail at the comedy club. Besides, she didn't want anything to relax her mood.

She sat on the recliner and crossed her legs. Anderson made himself a whiskey neat and sat on the love seat across from her. He took a deep sip of his drink, closed his eyes on the gulp.

"I need you to talk."

Anderson shook his head. "I don't know where to start."

"At the beginning. I want it all—your past, what made you feel comfortable *lying* to me all this time." Olivia's tone turned beetroot bitter. "Pretending as if you were poor when you can afford this entire block."

Anderson swallowed. "My mom and dad got divorced when I was twelve years old. We lived in Boston. Nice neighborhood. Schools, I had it all. My father . . . wasn't an easy man. He's a megalomaniac, and nothing was ever good enough. He acquired a business and then moved on to his next target. He got himself a looker of a wife, a good son. He cheated . . . a lot, and it got to the point where Mom couldn't pretend anymore, not when the kid who lived two streets over had the same eyes, same hair, and same last name as my dad. He embarrassed her, treated me like an asset, so my mom packed us up and we moved."

When they first met, Anderson claimed his mother and father were both dead. But it seemed they were both alive. The lies were intricate and deep and gross.

She decided not to call him out in the moment, but she sure could use the wine.

"Your mother moved you to Queens?" Olivia asked.

"You got it. Mom was a beauty queen, but she didn't have money. She stayed with my dad for so long because she thought it was best for me. But when she saw I went from a happy-go-lucky kid to an extremely anxious child, she knew she had to gather the courage. She knew it was far better scratching it out on her own than struggling to be this picture-perfect family." Anderson paused for a second, lifted the glass to his lips and sipped.

"My aunt recommended a decent divorce attorney. Mom didn't get alimony, but she got child support. He pushed back on that, too, and we got pennies compared to what he could afford. But Dad had the connections, and he wanted to teach Mom a lesson. So I worked hard, got a partial scholarship to Princeton and a job to cover the rest, made my mom happy."

Anderson looked straight ahead, as if he were watching his past like a movie. "Second semester freshman year, my dad contacts me out of the blue. Says he's proud and he wants to help me." Anderson laughed. "Figured out later that he found out I was on scholarship, and he didn't like the fact that I worked. Not with his last name.

People would think he was a deadbeat. But college kicked my ass, and it was hard working and going to school. I couldn't keep up and . . . shit. Ashamed to say, I took his help."

"He's your father. It's the least he could do," Olivia replied.

"Yeah, well, that money came with strings. First, it started off with visiting him and 'his side of the family' once a month. Then he tried to get me into the fold of the business. I admit I liked the idea of having a job lined up for me after college. Those rich assholes at school, like your boss Chase, always bragged about how mommy and daddy had a sweet gig lined up for them. So I wanted to see the other side of things again." Anderson took another sip of his drink.

"I interned with him the summer before my sophomore year. Learned he was a serial entrepreneur, venture capitalist by trade with the blood of a corporate raider. The way he ran his business and steamrolled companies made me sick to my stomach. Not to mention the family is vicious."

Olivia felt the noxiousness on her skin the first time she met Bradford. She rubbed at her elbows, holding herself tight, bracing herself to listen to more of Anderson's toxic tale.

"Bradford was the golden boy. The one dad had selected to take over since he had a bastard son he'd yet to officially claim and then me, who was out of his life. But when I came in, Bradford got jealous. Sabotaged me left and right. He's a dumbass, but he's charming. So he was great at creating a sense of comfort for their targets before my dad, the king cobra, struck down the business. They had this whole sick game they would play with companies they planned to take over."

Olivia's stomach soured. She could only imagine how many employees they'd fired. "What made you walk away?"

"My mom. She was sick, beat cancer once, but it came back. I told her I'd reconnected with Dad, but I didn't tell her how involved

I'd become with his business. I knew it would break her heart, and she would question if she made the right decision for us back then. But she noticed my panic attacks. She noticed how much I popped antacids. She asked me straight out what was wrong with me, and I finally told her. And God, Olivia, she looked so sick. Not from the chemo and radiation, but soul sick. Like she was ashamed she would soon leave this world and her only son would become cruel." Anderson shook his head. "She said as much."

Olivia could no longer remain detached. She leaned forward, wiping tears from her face. She didn't know if it was Anderson's pain or being triggered by the talk of death but her body involuntary vibrated with grief.

"She said I was foolish, but I argued with her. I told her with Dad's money, I could cut down on the piling medical bills. And then she said . . ." He took a shuddering breath. "She said if he's so good, then why did he slam the door in her face when she asked him for help the first time she had cancer? She had to stop working, and she asked for alimony. He'd known then, right after she left, about her cancer diagnosis. Still, he said no."

A tear rolled down his cheek. "That part, I didn't know. Mom had kept how sick she was to herself. I knew . . . I knew about the cancer, but she said it was the kind you could fix if you caught it early. So I believed her.

"I confronted Dad, in front of golden boy Bradford and the rest of the clan. Asked him why he left Mom hanging when he could easily afford it. And you know what he said?"

Olivia shook her head.

"Your mom is a user. She used me, she left me and tried to use me again. Your mom beat cancer once, she'll do it again.

"I . . . remember feeling hot all over. Just like a volcano was inside of my stomach, and lava sloshed around, and I punched him so hard he bled like water from a faucet. Then I renounced him, his family, and told them all to go to hell. I changed my last name to my mother's maiden name. Then I dropped out my junior year, second semester."

"Do you regret it?" Olivia asked.

"No. Mom died that same year, but I got to spend a lot of time with her. After she died, I was so angry. Someone advised me to go to a grief counseling meeting. I got the address mixed up and ended up at an improv meeting. I got on stage and *improvised* an argument I wanted to have with my dad. It was all the things I wanted to say to him when Mom died. It wasn't all sad. When I finished, I found a bunch of eyes on me. Some filled with laughter, with tears, but I made them feel and it made me feel."

Olivia wanted to reach out, to soothe and ease his pain but she couldn't quite unclench her fists. There were more truths to be uncovered. "What about ASK? Did you recognize them when you saw the sign?"

Anderson nodded. "Yes. But I promise you, Olivia, that I'll do everything in my power to help you fight them. I know the enemy inside out. I can help. I want to help."

"You don't even like it here," she argued.

"That's not true. I just didn't like the fact that I could be outed by my family at any moment."

"But you said—"

"Let me help, Olivia."

"Even if we aren't together?" she whispered.

Anderson's body jerked as if Olivia's words pierced his heart. "E-even then." Anderson nodded, tears brightening his eyes.

"I can understand how this would be hard to share. It's hard for even me to unpack, but you even claimed your father died when you met me."

"He was dead to me."

"As much as you'd like to pretend, he is indeed alive and wrecking people's livelihoods. I'm sorry, but I just . . . I can't continue with this relationship."

"Is there anything I can do to make it right?"

Olivia shook her head.

"I'll pack my things. I'll . . . I'd like to stick close. Help."

"I can't tell you where to go, but it can't be here."

"I'm sorry, Olivia. I'm sorry I dragged you into my mess. I tried hard to cut ties with my family but . . . Frank is not a man who easily walks away."

"I don't need space because of your family. Because of *you*, I need space. I gave you multiple opportunities to come clean. And with everything that I've been through, I only needed the truth."

"What about love?" Anderson asked.

"What about it?"

"I gave you love. You needed that, too."

"That's not—"

"Don't." He raised his hand. "You needed me. Don't tell me otherwise. When we met, you were still grieving your godfather, your father, and then the house in Oak Bluffs. You didn't have love, and I gave it freely."

"I had love, Anderson." And no, she may not have had the love of her mother or from a man, but she had her godsisters, and her godmother, Ama.

"And now I finally love myself." A warm feeling rushed her body. She was an entirely decent person. She cared about her community, offered a helping hand, and mostly, got along well with others.

I like myself, too.

Over the years, Olivia hadn't given much thought to whether she enjoyed her own company, but her jogs along the beach had been meditative. It was as if all the garbage that littered her neural pathways cleared. She just needed time to discover herself.

Her attention drifted to Anderson—his wet eyes, drooped shoulders, a man defeated.

"I've got more stuff upstairs. Can I come by later?"

"Of course. I'll be around."

He reached for her hand, and she squeezed his. They stared at each other. Memories of Anderson holding her close, whispering sweet promises in her ears in the early hours of the morning.

Back then, even during the pandemic, she'd felt hopeful.

Cherished.

Only now she realized she hadn't felt that since Omar died. And ever since, she'd been blindly jumping from hookups to relationships, seeking that familiar feeling that no one—not even Anderson—could replicate.

And how could he? Omar gave her confidence and comfort when what she really needed was to love and complete herself.

"I'm sorry, Anderson. Our relationship ending isn't on you. It's on me, too. You gave me love, but I didn't love myself. And as a result, I said things I shouldn't have said. I did things I shouldn't have done. For that, I'm sorry." Tears pushed through, burning her eyes, clogging her throat.

He let out a shuddering breath. And, in that moment, Olivia knew those were the words he needed to hear. She hoped their relationship wouldn't haunt his future.

"Goodbye, Olivia." He kissed her forehead. It was a goodbye to Anderson.

But as for herself, it was a resounding hello—to the discovery of herself and the new life she'd created.

CHAPTER 25

LABOR DAY WEEKEND

September 2021

If another person looked at her as if she should swan dive into the waters of the bay, she would toss the white folding chair she had in hand into the sea.

Apparently, news traveled fast about Olivia and Anderson's argument at the comedy show. Olivia assumed Whitney had told Kara who told Addy who told . . . everyone.

Addy had immediately forgiven her, showing up with a bottle of red wine with store-bought pita chips and hummus.

Olivia hugged the busybody woman. Admittedly, she'd been so off base about Addy. Her rather brash neighbor had a good heart.

Speaking of said neighbor, she beelined toward Olivia, looking her over with the precision of a drill sergeant.

"I'm fine," Olivia said as she waved Addy off before she could check in for the trillionth time.

"Don't get all snappy," Addy snapped. "Do you have everything you need for the *'Don't Sell Your Legacy'* meeting?"

Olivia laughed. "That's not the name of the meeting."

"What is it then?"

"'SANS Legacy: A Look Back in Time.' And it's not a meeting, it's more like an informational party."

"Of course, it will be. That's why I selected the caterer. We need actual food this time."

Olivia just barely avoided rolling her eyes at the slight. Whitney had explained her faux pas in not including Addy, the neighborhood foodie, for her opinion in catering selections. When Olivia selected a completely new caterer for her "Black Love Is Black Wealth" event, Addy wasn't pleased.

"I'm so sorry I didn't run my caterer by you," Olivia offered a half apology, mostly sarcasm. "Though, if you recall, we weren't friends and you weren't invited."

"Oh, yes. You were trying to out me."

Olivia shushed her. They weren't alone on the beach, but everyone was busy setting up for the event.

"No one's listening. No one's even close. Now repeat after me: People are . . ."

"Complicated."

Addy nodded. "And you should really keep your nose . . ."

"Out of other people's business. Unless you're Addy."

"Hey, that last part is unspoken." Addy crossed her arms, pretending to be offended.

"Speaking of business, have you spoken to your dreamy next-door neighbor since you gave Anderson the official boot?"

"It's only been two weeks."

"And?"

"And I'm . . . sad." Even with therapy, Olivia struggled to emote to friends new and old. She took a deep breath. "He lied to me, but he was a good guy. And it's unfortunate because, for a time, I saw myself building a future with him. And now I'm alone again."

"You don't have to be." Addy winked. Before Olivia could protest, Addy added, "But I get it. Give yourself time to process. I'm very sure Garrett will stick around."

"Yeah. Anderson, too." He didn't come by or call but he did text daily to check in.

"What do you mean? He's not living with you."

Olivia shook his head. "He's still at an Airbnb. He wants to stick close—"

"For Uber deliveries?"

"Addy." Olivia's voice held a warning.

"Sorry. I won't make any more jokes about your ex-fiancé."

Someone caught Addy's attention. "Hey, Mr. Whittingham. Hey, Garrett!" she waved.

Olivia's gut clenched as the two men walked down the path.

"Doesn't he look nice?" Addy whispered.

"Mr. Whittingham has a great sense of style."

"You know who I'm referring to."

Garrett wore a patterned white-and-gray shorts ensemble. The zippered V-neck shirt exposed part of his smooth pecs.

"Look at those hoochie daddy shorts," Addy teased Garrett when they arrived at their location.

Garrett looked down. "I specifically asked the girl at the boutique for longer shorts, but she said they don't make them long anymore. Whatever that means."

Addy snorted. "Yes, and good riddance to long shorts. They looked awful."

Olivia smiled. If Travis were here, he'd kindly let them know to thank the gay community for hoochie daddy shorts. He wasn't a fan when heteros acted as if they invented the style.

"Do you need a hand?" Garrett directed his question to Olivia.

"Sure, she does," Addy answered. "See those stacks of chairs?" she pointed a few feet away. "You can help us set up the rows in front of the big screen."

Mr. Whittingham whistled. "That's a big screen."

"My company sponsored the AV," Olivia informed them.

"That was really nice of them," Mr. Whittingham said. "So what are they getting out of it?" he raised an eyebrow.

"A company logo on the program. And I will ever so slyly thank our sponsor and plug them before the event kicks off."

"That's not a bad deal," Mr. Whittingham said, nodding. "We've got to set up another date for our game. How about next Sunday?"

Olivia shook her head. "Sorry, but my mother plans to visit next weekend."

"Oh?" Mr. Whittingham crossed his arms. "I'm sure you're looking forward to that."

She looked forward to it as much as a dentist appointment—it would not be entirely pleasant, but it was entirely necessary. "We've got a lot to discuss."

Mr. Whittingham winked. "Well, I'll help with the chairs. Addy, can you show me the way?"

"Oh, sure, Mr. Whittingham," she responded brightly. She tucked her arm around his, smiling up at him.

"They could be less obvious," Olivia said and turned to face Garrett. She waved toward the shoreline. "I could use a walk. How about you?"

Garrett tilted his head, smiling at Olivia as if seeing her for the first time.

"What?"

"It's just the first time you've proactively acknowledged their attempts at matchmaking. And the first time you've invited me to do something."

Olivia shrugged. "I'm tired of pretending. Not saying they are right to do it, but I've decided to face things head on."

"And I'm a thing to face?" He bit his lips, not seductively to inspire lust, but a habit he often did when something or someone intrigued him.

He'd done it often with her, and like always, it jump-started her hormones.

"No, you're a warm-blooded man who is an exceptional father. A great son, and . . ."

"And?"

"A good neighbor," Olivia finished.

"I could be better than good, if you'd let me."

"Oh, you're good enough."

"Thinking that's not the case."

"Why not?"

"Oh, because you never reached out after our date."

Olivia nodded. "Ah, yes. I'm sorry. I was all mixed up about Anderson."

"You're still with him? I thought you broke up after . . . everything."

"No. We're done for good this time." Olivia slowed down, her eyes on the water as if her courage lived inside the waves. "I like you." Olivia stopped walking and swallowed the premature affirmations threatening to shoot out of her mouth. "I like you a lot," she repeated. "Not in a forbidden way, but in a way that's entirely freeing. And . . ." she took a deep breath. "That's all I have. And I know it's not fair to you, but that's honestly how I feel. So, I'd like to take a step back." She stepped back as Garrett took a step forward.

"What are you doing?"

"Helping you think." Garrett had something in his eyes, something that robbed Olivia of her senses.

He reached for Olivia's dangling earrings. "You usually wear studded diamonds or pearls."

"I'm trying something new." Perry sent them to her. She had a penchant for finding the most stunning jewelry that straddled the line of Olivia's style yet stretched beyond her conservative nature.

"They're beautiful." He stepped closer. "You're beautiful," he declared, wrapping an arm around her waist.

When Olivia scanned the area, he gently twisted her chin and attention back to him.

"I don't care who sees, and you shouldn't either."

"But they'll think—"

"They already know we like each other. They can keep talking." He lowered his mouth, sucking on her bottom lip. The sand gathered around her feet like cement.

She couldn't move. She didn't want to move. Her breath rushed out as if she'd sprinted down the beach. His aroma was no longer at a teasing distance, but ever present, the scent of cool waters.

He would stick to her skin like he stuck in her memories. His lips touched hers, light at first. Then he sucked, drawing her deep, deep, deeper into his honeyed web.

Olivia patted his chest and backed away. Her heart, overworked and stressed, ka-thumped against her chest. "I, um. I'm off. S-see you tonight, neighbor."

"Sounds good, *neighbor.* But how about you put me to work?"

"No," she shook her head vehemently. "You're too much of a distraction."

"A distraction?"

"I mean, we're already covered."

Olivia wasn't completely on the other side of facing things head on. Not when Garrett flipped her senses on its back. "You just be ready for tonight. We'll depend on you and your story to convince the others to keep their homes."

"You've got it. See you soon, Olivia."

"Bye." Olivia jogged away and then walked when she carved enough distance between them.

She touched her lips. Their first kiss had been incredibly long and passionate. But right after, she felt a strong pang of guilt. She'd been incredibly disappointed in her lack of resolve.

But the man melted her resolve like ice on a hot day in New Orleans.

Thirty minutes past sunset, the residents began trickling in.

Bea, her favorite loner, sat in the back despite Mr. Whittingham waving her to the saved seat near the front. Mr. Whittingham firmly pointed in her direction and then down to the chair beside him. Bea shook her head and slid further down into her seat.

The woman crossed her arms and feet. She had a perfectly blank face. She was the human embodiment of a *Do Not Disturb* sign. Olivia hid her laugh behind her hand, but not before Bea's sea-blue eyes narrowed on her, which made Olivia laugh harder. She could see the smile the woman had failed to smother.

Yes, she was just like the bees she admired—she could sting but was mostly harmless. And under that do-not-disturb aura, she had a giving heart. Whitney told her she was the highest donor for the fundraiser, not to mention how she generously taught Mr. Whittingham the secret of the bees.

Music played from the speakers, buffet stations with gloved attendants stood just beyond the chairs. Residents filled their plates and cups before settling in the chairs.

Olivia took the stage after most residents had finished up their meal.

"Welcome everyone! We are so pleased you joined us for the official kickoff for Labor Day weekend. We're here today to celebrate you and the history of our neighborhood. Before we begin our festivities, we'd like to thank our sponsor Array Capital who donated the funds to rent this lovely screen and projector. So, without further ado, let's begin the program!"

Olivia switched on the video, which started off with Mr. Whittingham walking toward Whitney's couch. He wore a navy-blue blazer, khaki pants, and a striped shirt. Off-camera Whitney's voice could be heard.

"Can you introduce yourself?"

Mr. Whittingham flashed a smile. "My name is Joel Whittingham III. I've been coming to Sag Harbor for seventy-five years and I live in Sag Harbor Hills. I was eleven years old when we first came for our summer vacation. My father picked out the land, purchased it, and built our summer home."

"Wait a minute. Your father just picked the land and built a home? That must have been hard to do, especially back then."

"In a matter of speaking, yes. My father and mother were both special and ambitious people. My mother, Mary Whittingham, was a top scholar and in 1902 was one of the first one thousand African Americans in the United States to graduate college. My aunt was the first Black female naval officer, and Eleanor Roosevelt supported her. So yes, it was hard, but no, for people like my family, it wasn't even on the register of impossible."

"Wow."

"Yes," Mr. Whittingham said and smiled. "But I digress. I summered here as a little boy."

"There weren't a lot of homes back then. Just trees and woods, but you could feel the specialness of the community. And when more people built their homes—some for the summer, some for year-round—it became quite clear that there is no place like SANS. Around the second year here, I met my dear friend, Colin Powell. As soon as the sun rose, we took off. We fished and swam and rode bikes. We were so . . . free here. Don't get me wrong, I loved my home in Brooklyn where my family lived most of the year. Took us hours to get here. There weren't any Jitneys or four-lane highways then."

"Oh, that's right."

"We made a day out of it. We packed our lunch, and it felt like a field trip. But as soon as we entered the village"—Mr. Whittingham stroked his cheek—"it felt like the weight of the world melted away."

"Even as a child, you felt that weight?" Whitney asked.

"Of course. I was a young Black boy in the forties. Just imagine going from the concrete jungle to a place on the water. It felt like magic, seeing the moonlight reflected on rippling waves. You could hear crickets and scampering deer. Not the bustling horns from outside my window in the city. My mother and father would sometimes roll out a towel; we'd lie on our backs and trace the stars."

"If you lie down in the middle of Brooklyn, you're liable to get run over."

Mr. Whittingham laughed. "That's right, Whitney. Lots of good things about the city, but it's busy. It was nice, even as a kid, to have quiet. It was special to form relationships with people who looked like you while experiencing a different world."

"Mr. Whittingham, you've seen a lot of esteemed visitors in Sag Harbor, like Langston Hughes, Lena Horne, and the Clintons. Why do you think they liked it here?"

"Well, Mr. Hughes knew my father. They were roommates in college."

"Really?" Whitney feigned a gasp, as if she had no idea. Olivia smothered a laugh. Whitney knew everything.

But Olivia scanned the crowd, their heads tilted back, eyes on the screen. They were enraptured. She wondered if they'd ever stopped to listen to Mr. Whittingham's stories. Or maybe in some cases, they'd forgotten them.

"Yes," Mr. Whittingham said. "He introduced my mother and father to each other in college. And fun fact, he wrote a poem about my mother—she was quite beautiful."

"So they were close friends?"

"Very. He came to visit. They sat on our porch writing and reciting poetry. I think he wanted to refill his well, just like everyone else. But the unique thing about Sag Harbor is that he could truly rest among people who looked like him. You've been in tense situations before, right?"

"Yes. Several."

"Right, your body can't relax. There's this knot in your throat, in your back, the tension just locks your body, jumbles your insides."

"Mhmm."

"Sometimes you don't know how tense you are until you relax. Until you have fun. At Sag Harbor, he, and I imagine the other celebrities who frequent here, could be unguarded, so to speak, because our community is like family. Your body *feels* that strain, carries it. And we have got to let that go, if only for a little while."

Mr. Whittingham's words poured over the crowd.

That's it. That's why she loved Sag Harbor. She not only could be herself, but she'd *found* herself. Tears welled in her eyes. Omar had given her so much more than a house. He'd given her peace and unconditional love. She didn't recognize it before because she didn't love herself.

"Now you live here year-round."

"Since 2004."

"A lot has changed," Whitney set up the bait.

"We were a one hundred percent African-American community a few years ago. But slow and steady, we lost our neighbors. We're losing our legacy and losing ourselves. Don't get me wrong, I understand why people are leaving. I understand it's hard to keep up with the property taxes alone. But I think of SANS like a pot of stew warming on a stove. We take some out, but we replace what we took out of the pot. We need to keep the fire going, keep the ingredients fresh and flavorful. We add back the things that made us wonderful. Otherwise, we'll go cold and bland."

"You're saying we've lost our seasoning?" Whitney asked, humor lacing her tone.

There was a murmur from the crowd. Some laughed, others looked contemplative or uncomfortable.

Olivia smiled. That's just why they created the video series. They wanted the residents to feel.

"Oh yes. We are a community of substance and history. We must protect our heritage with pride, and we do that by being thoughtful about the growth and development of our community."

"How do we do that? What are tangible things we can do today?" Whitney quickly asked. Olivia looked at the screen waiting for the answer she already knew.

"We do that by not selling to just the highest bidder. We sell to people who want to add to our community, people who want a legacy for their children or people who need refuge. We vote— locally—not just on a national level. We get leaders who can help us do things like register our neighborhood as a historic landmark, which we've done, and someone who can help us manage the taxes. We need leaders, young leaders like some people here today, who can funnel their intelligence and energy into helping us fight redevelopments that would take away the soul of our village."

Whitney sighed. "It sounds simple, but it's really not simple."

"No. But it worked for the civil rights era. We were organized. We were strategic and unrelenting. Young folks will just have to put a little skin in the game to protect what's ours." His brown eyes bore into the camera. Olivia hadn't been there when they filmed, but Whitney had been absolutely correct in playing his video as a kick-off.

Whitney ended the interview and after the video stopped, the residents stood and gave Mr. Whittingham a standing ovation. Olivia waved Mr. Whittingham to the front, and he said a few words of encouragement. Throughout the event, they played a few more videos from longtime residents including Garrett while people fellowshipped with each other.

Whitney and Olivia didn't include a hard sell, other than a directive to sign up for the community newsletter. The editor had agreed to give them a dedicated section about redevelopment and houses selling within the SANS neighborhood. Olivia had also created a website that included the neighborhood's history and how everyone could be involved.

Garrett found Olivia folding chairs after the event. He grabbed one from her hand and stacked it on the neat pile near her backyard.

"That was an exceptional event," Garrett complimented.

"I think so, too." She looked around at a few neighbors who stood and chatted near the stage.

"Do you have plans tomorrow night?" Garrett asked.

"Not really. Just excited about the Labor Day Races tomorrow."

Garrett laughed. "I don't think you're any more excited than Zora. She plans to go to sleep early so she can be well-rested for the race."

Olivia laughed. "I'll be rooting for her."

"She'll like that. Would you like to get dinner? My sitter is looking to make more money to spend for the weekend."

"I . . . sure. I would like that. Are there any reservations?"

"Probably not, actually. Why don't we have dinner at your place? I could cook," he suggested.

"Can you cook?"

"It's passable."

"I'm in the mood for crabs. Why don't you take me crabbing?"

"W-what?"

"You've been talking about your childhood and crabbing and . . . I've never been. I'll cook."

Garrett laughed. "You've got a deal. I can probably swing it for to-morrow, though Zora will be with us if I can convince her to come."

Olivia smiled. Perfect. She'd love time with her goddaughter. Be-sides that, with Zora around it would keep things safe.

"I know why you're smiling, but we're still on for dinner. Zora is just going to be there for the crabs."

"But it wouldn't be fair for her to do all that work without enjoy-ing the fruit of her labors."

"After she watched *The Little Mermaid*, she refused to eat crabs and lobsters."

"Yes, I can see how that is traumatic. We can cancel and—"

"No. I'll take you crabbing. Now that I'm thinking on it, I'll see if Mr. Whittingham will watch her."

Olivia could only imagine Mr. Whittingham's sly smile if Garrett told him who he planned to take crabbing.

"Okay, I'll be here." Olivia jerked her thumb toward the house. "Just text me if you can't make it. If not, we can make plans for another time."

"Oh, I'll be in touch. "Don't make any other plans for tomorrow night."

After about an hour, Garrett confirmed details.

Me and you tomorrow at 8 AM before the Labor Day Races. I'll be on the beach with the nets and equipment. ☺

Olivia readied for bed, hopeful and excited about crabbing with Garrett. The guilt associated with her wanting to spend time with him no longer weighed her down.

But she still felt something for Anderson. He wasn't something to be easily erased, and their time together had meant something to her.

CHAPTER 26

A NIGHT TO REMEMBER

September 2021

Olivia changed three times and was nearly late for crabbing. She had no idea what to wear—a swimsuit, a shirt, shorts, or pants?

She finally googled and found that she needed a sun hat, sunglasses, and quick drying shirts and waders. She had all but the latter, but luckily Whitney let Olivia borrow her hot pink waterproof boots and overalls.

When Olivia walked outside, she found Garrett standing on the sandy beach with his back facing her.

"Garrett."

He turned around at her voice and smiled at her, his white teeth gleaming in the sun.

A gentle smile curved his lips. "You'll need to walk with me to the marsh. We'll be walking in the water, too. We may even find some mussels."

They walked a half mile away from their homes, chatting about Zora and the fun Labor Day weekend events until they reached soft damp land with shoots of knee-high grass.

Pockets of grass surrounded the water. Olivia stopped when she couldn't tell the depth. "Is it deep?"

"Not too deep."

She surveyed her hot pink overalls and boots, hoping they were indeed water-resistant. Wading in the marsh wasn't exactly romantic, but she'd been the one to suggest their outing.

"You can't back out now." Garrett seemed to have read her mind.

"What if I just look at you?" Olivia took a step back. "I'm a visual learner."

Garrett laughed and shook his head. "I've got you. I promise." His simple words pulled at her heartstrings like the moon pulled the tide. He grabbed her hand, sealing her fate, and leaving her with no other option but to trust and follow him into the unknown.

Once they were waist-deep in the water, he stopped guiding them. He didn't let go of her hand.

"See. It's not too far, right?"

Olivia nodded, her mouth bone dry.

"Okay, I'll be right back. Need to grab a few things." Garrett hurried back to the drier land to grab nets and a bag.

In his hand, he held what looked like a wide wired colander.

"Ta-da. This is the world-famous Garrett Brooks trap. Well, it's not my trap. Mom and Dad taught me," his voice went low and somber.

Olivia clapped her hands to snap him out of his funk. "How does all this work? Explain this to me like I'm a five-year-old."

"Like Zora?"

"Exactly."

He grinned. "See this?" He pointed to two small metal objects strapped into the trap. "We're using some weights so the trap doesn't flip when we lower it into the water. He pointed to the bright orange straps. "I've replaced the strings so they don't break."

"Makes sense." Olivia nodded. "What else?"

"Next we've got to bait it." He reached into his small duffel and pulled out a Ziploc bag. "Chicken legs for the bait." He strapped the raw chicken chunks into the trap. "And now we lower it into the water and let the crabs scamper inside."

She surveyed the equipment, which was essentially a chicken and a net. "Oh, this is easy."

"Very. Now you try."

Olivia shook her head. "Oh, I don't want to put the chicken in there." She wiggled her bare hands.

"I've got an extra pair of gloves." He pointed to the duffel. "C'mon. Try something new," he teased.

"Okay, twist my arm, why don't you?"

Under Garrett's gentle guidance, she put the trap together and placed it into the water.

"How long do we wait?"

"Let's check back in ten minutes, but we'll monitor movement. Have you eaten breakfast?"

"No." She'd been too nervous to eat.

He shucked off his gloves, grabbed her hands and walked them back to dry land. He laid out a blanket and gestured to the open space beside him. "I made us smoothies."

"Because you know I like smoothies, right?"

He winked. "Right."

"And who told you that information?"

"I've seen you on the porch drinking a smoothie after a run. It looks super healthy, but mine is a little on the sweet side."

"I like sweet." Olivia grabbed the bottle of bright orange smoothie. "What's in it?"

"Kale, mangos, carrots, honey, and ginger and rounded off with some orange juice and almond milk."

"That sounds really good."

"I've perfected it. Zora likes smoothies, and it's a good way to sneak in fruits and vegetables."

Olivia sipped. "Mmm. This is . . . this is delicious."

Garrett smiled. "How am I doing on this best neighbor thing?"

"Oh, you're in the running for sure."

"Who's my competition?"

"Mr. Whittingham and Whitney."

Garrett grunted. "That's not fair. They don't even live beside you."

"Okay, you're the best right-beside-me neighbor." She rarely talked to her other neighbor, an older Black couple, the Larsons, who were nice, but mostly kept it to a friendly wave as they went in and out of their home.

"I'm honored."

"Where is Zora?"

"With Mr. Whittingham and his son, Slim."

"Oh, that's right. He did mention one of his kids was visiting. I haven't met him just yet."

"He's a good friend. He used to babysit me, so it's surreal that he's now looking after Zora."

They sat across from each other, sitting in silence. He didn't have his easy, warm smile on his face. He looked downright predatory. "I'd like to kiss you, Olivia."

"I, umm. We aren't out far enough. Someone may see us."

He stood and then sat beside her, grabbed a towel and draped it over their heads. "There."

"There, what?"

"Now we're covered."

Olivia giggled at his silliness. "I can't believe you."

"Think of it as an invisibility towel. No one can see us."

As he inched closer, Olivia stopped laughing. This was no longer funny. This was very, very serious.

His lips touched hers, softly at first. Exploring, as if he hadn't tasted her twice before.

Warmth exploded inside of her. She leaned forward, deepening the kiss. Heat shot through each pore in her body.

Garrett broke away from the kiss. "Hmm. There you go again."

"What did I do?"

"Making my world explode."

Olivia laughed against his mouth. She tugged the towel off their heads. "This is ridiculous."

"Let's check those traps." Garrett gave her the line to tug. To her infinite pleasure, there was a trio of crabs in one trap and two in another.

"We'll have a feast!" Olivia clapped. "Do you know how to clean these things?"

"Of course." Garrett snorted. "How about this? I'll cook and clean the crabs. You bring the sides for dinner."

"I can do that." She planned to grill corn on the cob, asparagus, and a mixture of andouille sausage, peppers, and onions.

After their adventure Olivia decided to no longer let Anderson and their relationship linger. He still had some clothes, pictures, and books at her home.

Her hands shook, but she selected the favorites on her phone, a number she would soon delete. She'd geared herself up just to be let down. Her call had been diverted to voicemail.

"Hey. Can you come by this weekend? You still have a few things at the house."

Filled with nervous energy, Olivia cleaned her house, scrambled eggs, all the while checking her phone for a missed call or text.

After checking the time, she sighed when she realized she had another hour until the Labor Day races. Olivia took a long relaxing bath and then showered the remaining suds away. When she returned downstairs to the living room, ready for the races, she found Anderson and his cousin, the "nice" one who'd run after her at the club, in her living room.

"Hey." Anderson waved. He wore a Yankees baseball cap, shorts, and a plain white T-shirt. He had another suitcase filled with pictures, books, and knickknacks from his desk. "I'm here to get the rest of my things."

Olivia pulled her hands behind her back. "Hi."

"This is my cousin, Shaun." He pointed to the man standing awkwardly near the door to Olivia's office, just off the living room.

"I remember Shaun."

"He's helping me pack up. Well, he strong-armed his way over here to help me pack."

Olivia glanced at Shaun before she whispered, "Can we talk?"

"Sure. Let's go out back. Shaun, take my stuff to the car, okay?"

"Of course." Shaun gave Olivia a pained smiled before he lifted a box near the door.

Anderson stuffed his hands in his pockets.

"Can I . . . can I just say something before you break my heart?"

Olivia's throat tightened. She couldn't force out a yes, so she simply nodded.

"I know this won't make much of a difference, but I apologize for my actions. I was so busy hiding my truth, then I got busier following my dreams. Sometime in between, I left you behind. I realize that and I'm sorry. But one thing I never lied about were my feelings for you. The way I feel when I look at you . . ." He shook his head. "I should've been honest. All you wanted was an honest man. And I'm sorry for that."

Honest.

Olivia was the liar. Olivia had cheated in her head and her heart. She squeezed her fists, debating whether to tell him the truth about her and Garrett.

His blue eyes were wet, his head hung in defeat. This would gut him.

Delivering the news would gut her, too. No, she would not tell him about Garrett, but she could offer him some form of honesty.

"I'm not as honest as you think," Olivia let out in a pained whisper. "You alone aren't the reason we didn't work out. I . . . I should've been honest about my trepidation about our relationship. We did things too quickly. We dated for months, got engaged, moved in together. It's like we had our relationship in an air fryer when what I really needed was a slow boil."

"How long did you feel that way?"

"I . . . started having these feelings when we moved in together in the city."

"Before Sag Harbor . . . before . . ."

Olivia nodded. "Before Garrett, yes." She answered his unspoken question.

"Are you two together?"

Olivia shook her head, dashing tears from her eyes. "No."

"Will you?"

"I don't think it would be wise for me to hop into another relationship so quickly."

He nodded. "But you like him?" his voice cracked.

"I do," Olivia answered honestly. "I'm so sorry I hurt you," she apologized, her voice thick with sorrow.

"I still intend to keep my promise."

"What promise?"

"I'm going to fight my family. I'm going to make sure they keep their dirty hands away from this neighborhood. I've already told my dad as much."

"What did he say?"

"Oh, that I won't get my inheritance. He's going to give it all to, and I quote, his other bastard son and my cousin, Bradford."

"Are you sure? We've got a plan to—"

"No. I attack on the inside, you attack from the outside. We'll need a lot of firepower to get my dad to back away."

"Thank you, Anderson. You're a good guy."

"Nah. I'm a fuckup. But I'll do good by you, and by this place you love." He stepped closer to Olivia and stretched out his arms. "One last hug?"

Olivia nodded and stepped into his arms. He kissed the top of her head and held her tight one last time.

The Labor Day races provided the perfect diversion she needed after her conversation with Anderson. The neighbors lined up to rally for the kids. Zora came in second and grinned from ear to ear when she received her silver medal.

Garrett gathered her into a hug and then put her on his shoulders. She pumped her fist in the air, her gap-toothed smile stretched a mile.

"I won second place!" she greeted Olivia.

"I know. I shouted for you on the sidelines."

"Oh. I didn't see you. I was going so fast. Daddy says I'm like The Flash."

"You were a blur."

"You're fast, too. We're both fast."

"We are," Olivia agreed.

Garrett wore a weird look on his face. He stepped back, putting distance between them. "Are we still on for dinner tonight?"

"Of course. Why wouldn't we be?"

"I saw Anderson."

"Yes." She cleared her throat. "He still had some things at the house."

"Oh." He looked away, seeming to be embarrassed by his reaction.

"I'll see you later for dinner, Garrett."

A few hours later, Olivia stood outside on his back porch. Garrett had asked her to meet him outside near the beach.

Her hands were sweaty. She wasn't sure if she was doing the right thing. Like she'd told Anderson, she needed to take things slowly with Garrett.

"Hey." He startled Olivia from her thoughts.

"Thanks for meeting me outside. The sitter canceled and Zora was still keyed up from all the happenings today. If she had seen you, she wouldn't go down easy."

"She's sleeping now?"

"Yes. Finally." He pointed to a small speaker shaped like a bear. "I can hear her, but we can go inside now. If that's okay?"

"I think so."

Garrett raised an eyebrow.

Olivia cleared the frog clogging her throat. "I'm fine. Let's go." She bent over to pick up the pans for her sides and followed Garrett into the house.

"Where should I put these?"

Garrett pointed to the counter. As soon as she placed the platters on the counter, he grabbed her by the waist, spinning her around.

"Now you can put it on me."

Heat surged her body, quickening her motions. Olivia unbuttoned his shirt, not stopping until she revealed the smooth expanse of his chest. He shrugged off his shirt and stood, leading her into his bedroom. The master was on the main floor. Still, he placed his finger on his lips and pointed upstairs, mouthing, "Zora."

Olivia nodded, heart pounding, brain racing at Mach speeds, desperate to figure out if she could survive Garrett.

Before she realized it, they sat on his bed. He stroked her bare shoulders.

"You're having second thoughts."

Olivia nodded.

"Let me guess, your beautiful brain can't see a clean way out of this."

How did he know? Olivia slowly lifted her gaze to clash with his.

"Anderson and I broke up, but I still feel terrible. People have lied to me all my life, and I—"

Garrett shook his head. "Let's just lie here. Talk."

Olivia stiffly fell back onto the bed, her eyes on the ceiling. "What will we talk about?"

"The category is embarrassing childhood stories."

"Umm, okay." Olivia agreed. She had plenty.

"I wanted to be an astronaut."

"Really?"

"Oh, yeah. I watched all the science shows on cable TV. Mom made me this suit for Halloween."

"Oh wow, I bet it looked—"

"Made of quilts."

"Stop it."

"I do not lie. Man, the kids picked on me so bad. They used to call me *Space Fool*. I didn't have the heart to tell her I hated it. But yeah, I decided after that that I wanted to have a career with suits."

"And thus, a real estate attorney was born."

He laughed, and so did Olivia.

"Your turn."

"Well, mine aren't as . . ."

"Pathetic?"

"Hilarious. That's the word I was going to say. Mine are sad."

"You can share sad with me, Olivia."

For the next half hour, Olivia told Garrett about Omar and Ama. About Cindy and Chris.

He exhaled. "That's a lot to deal with. No wonder you're in your head."

Olivia rolled over, her head resting on her fist. "I overthink everything."

Garrett, already facing her, pulled his lips back. A thoughtful look broke across his beautiful face. "That's how it is when you're grieving."

"Grieving?" Dr. LaGrange had mentioned something along those lines, but she dismissed it. "Omar and Chris died so long ago."

"You're grieving what could have been. You're thinking about who you would've been had your father lived or how it would've been if Omar told you the truth sooner. How your mother would be if she didn't lose the love of her life," he whispered the last part.

"I guess I am." Olivia nodded. "You're much cheaper than my therapist."

Garrett laughed. "I've been there. But you know what helps me?"

Olivia noticed he said helps and not helped. He still struggled.

"I believe in something bigger. Mom called it God. I call it universe. There's an order to things. Winter, spring, summer, fall . . . the cycle of nature mirrors life and death. The seasons mirror relationships."

"Right, like some people are in your life for a period of time."

"Correct. We think of it as friendships, but that could be for anything. We're all here to learn something. If you get quiet, you can figure out what the lesson plan is for your season of life."

"Have you figured out what yours is?"

"Love is worth the risk. For the longest time I didn't want to put myself out there to love again. I struggled a lot to love, not only in a romantic sense, but my daughter and my mother. Now, Mom recognized the signs, and she wasn't having that. She told me to get help and snap out of it, and I did. But I held back. Mom's death taught me again that just because I gave fewer hugs or said I love you a fraction less of what I used to, it didn't stop me from loving her. It didn't stop the pain of grief." He looked down, his eyes wet. "So, I'm not holding back any longer."

He stared at Olivia. "Love is worth the pain. From now on . . ." He licked his lips. "I will love fully, without regret, a heart full of hope. Love is what makes life worth living."

Olivia shook with emotion. Leaning over ever so closely, she cupped his cheek and kissed him.

Garrett grabbed her hand, his eyes closed.

"Will you let me show you a moment without regret?"

"Yes," she whispered.

At her confirmation, Garrett gathered Olivia close, kissing her deeply. Everything else melted away.

They undressed each other, slowly. This wasn't abandoned passion, this was thoughtful.

It was the only way Olivia knew how to be.

Garrett grabbed a condom from the nightstand.

"I'm glad you're prepared."

"It's not mine. I won't tell you where I found this." Humor sparked in his eyes but when he took in Olivia's naked body, it transformed to desire.

He trailed kisses along her body. His kisses, his touch, felt electric. He pushed her legs apart and slid in between. Without hesitation he drove inside.

He paused for a moment, his body tense, eyes closed.

"Are you . . . are you okay?" Olivia asked.

"You feel so good," he whispered in her ear, gently rocking inside of her.

She squeezed around him, desperate to feel every inch. He grabbed her back, moving inside of her with control and precision.

He looked down at her, a soft expression on his face, but the tendons of his neck standing out.

"You don't have to hold back with me. I can handle you," Olivia encouraged.

On that, he picked up the pace. Olivia let out a gasp, wrapping her legs around his waist, holding on for the ride of her life.

The tenderness in his kisses, the sincerity of his eyes, planted a seed of hope. The feeling was foreign and overwhelming and a small part of her wanted to soar.

But his thrusts anchored her, he was rooted and planted fully inside of her. The grate of his hands grasping around her waist, the sting of his beard marking her flesh. He stirred her soul, owned her body in the moment. There was no guilt or regret.

He felt right.

He felt like home. Like a steam valve screaming for release, they came together, tremoring in each other's arms.

They didn't speak after, simply stared, soft gazes similar to the ones they gave each other when they first met.

She didn't want to fall asleep, but the sweet satisfaction of love-making had a cost—their energy.

"Wake me up before Zora, okay?"

Garrett kissed her head. "You can stay as long as you like."

Half asleep, she just barely heard him whisper. "You can stay forever."

CHAPTER 27

TWO PEAS IN A POD

September 2021

Olivia stood by the gate as Cindy Jones parked her Honda. She was close enough to hear the audiobook her mother played through her speakers, likely a book selected through her book club.

She grappled with her mass of minced nerves—it'd been that way since Tuesday. First, she cleaned her home from top to bottom, mopping the floors with precision each time sand got tracked into her house. Through several phone conversations, she emoted to Garrett, Mr. Whittingham, and Whitney about her mother. Not in complaint, but overanalyzing activities and restaurants to frequent. Cindy wasn't easy to please. That meant four-stars and above restaurants and experiences. Whitney had gently advised her to drink copious quantities of wine. Her therapist recommended a healthier option, advising her to take off a few days of work in order to center herself.

But Olivia hadn't taken the advice, which showed in her soggy palms and jittery limbs. Another reason she hadn't taken the advice was because she had planned to tender her resignation in late October. She also didn't need more time with her thoughts.

She'd think about Anderson's connection with ASK and sexy thoughts of Garrett. Though they talked at a surface level, they hadn't had sex since the previous weekend. Garrett had been busy transitioning his affairs to Sag Harbor. Olivia and Whitney had gotten together every night to work on their business plan. They wanted everything airtight when they presented to the Investor Supper Club, as they called themselves. One resident had mentioned they were looking to sell. ASK hounded them with promises of millions.

Unfortunately, it was a promise they could keep. So, Olivia and Whitney had worked overtime to think of a win-win solution for the Palmers.

But all the busy work hadn't been enough to quell the impending doom and pounding headache that came with her mother's visits.

"Hello, Mother." Olivia opened the gate.

Cindy, who looked ten years younger, in her late thirties, rather than nearly fifty, looked flawless. She wore navy blue chino pants paired with a three-quarter-length striped shirt. She'd changed her hair, and now had short bangs and a stylish bob that framed her face. Though Olivia wasn't a fan of bangs, the new style suited her mother's angular face, high cheekbones, and pointed chin. If they were close, she'd joke about her new pandemic 'do. Maybe her mother would even compliment Olivia's fresh new curls.

Olivia attempted to grab Cindy's bags, but her mother swatted her hand away—not angrily, Olivia realized her mother never showed her anger. Her words were often cruel, but they weren't spat out in rage. The schoolteacher of twenty years never had to raise her voice to control her classroom. A cold look would do. Cindy was simply an unhappy and dispassionate woman and Olivia struggled to break that cycle.

Olivia watched as her mother, with her head held high, carried her bags toward Olivia's house.

Cindy inspected the house like a seasoned detective, nodding to herself, after walking the distance of her yard.

"Welcome to my home." Olivia opened the door to let her in.

"Your home? You mean you and your fiancé's home?"

"Ah." Detective Jones shot straight to the point already. She probably noticed Anderson's missing car.

"We aren't together anymore."

"Why?" Cindy pursed her lips, but it wasn't a frown. A frown required her to care a fraction more about her daughter's affairs. Pursed lips simply conveyed curiosity.

He lied about his past. We aren't compatible and, oh, yes, I'm having a passionate affair with my neighbor.

Olivia grappled for the right words. There wasn't anything simple she could say to Cindy. If they had the traditional relationship of a mother and daughter, she would've told her already. It was what she planned to do with Ama and her godsisters once her mother left on Sunday.

"We aren't compatible with each other long term." Olivia snipped any lingering misery out of her tone. Cindy would pounce on her weakness and ask questions that led Olivia down a maze leading to an "I told you so" at the center.

"It's a shame." Cindy rolled her bags near the stairwell.

"Is it?" Olivia tilted her head.

"He seemed to care for you. He thinks you're beautiful."

"Well, Mother. I've discovered that someone finding me beautiful isn't enough for me."

Cindy nearly frowned. "Where am I staying?"

"Upstairs. I will carry your bags for you, no arguments." Olivia easily breezed past her mother and grabbed the carry-on and suitcase. "You can follow me to your room if you want."

"That's okay. I'm going to look around."

"Great." Olivia rolled the luggage to the corner of the guest room. She returned downstairs to find her mother staring at her picture of her father, Chris Jones, with his brother.

"H-how . . . ?" Cindy pressed a hand over her chest.

"Mr. Whittingham gave me the picture of dad and my uncle. Do you remember my uncle's name?"

Silence stretched between them. Her mother didn't answer, made no sound as she stared at the photo. Then, in a choked voice, she whispered, "Charles." She picked up the photo, her grip so strong around the frame, Olivia was afraid it would shatter.

She turned to face Olivia, tears welling in her eyes. "His name is Charles." She swallowed and whispered, "Two peas in a pod."

Shock shot through Olivia. It was a rarity to see her mother show any emotion other than disdain. She wanted to close the distance and comfort Cindy, but she stood rooted in place. Cindy wouldn't take kindly to sympathy and hugs.

"Uncle Charles," Olivia whispered. Suddenly, she was desperate to meet her father's best friend and nemesis. "I'm sorry if these pictures are triggering. But it's been . . . really nice to talk to someone about my father. Have you and Mr. Whittingham met? I'd love to introduce you."

"I'm here to visit my daughter," Cindy snapped. She returned the picture to the shelf and neutralized her expression. She really was a beautiful woman with high and sharp cheekbones, skin the color of coffee and cream, and luxurious sandy brown hair that was never out of place.

Cindy cleared her throat. "What's on the agenda?"

"I'm cooking dinner tonight. Tomorrow I would love to take you to the American Hotel for their brunch."

"Have you made reservations?"

"Of course."

"And then?"

"Well," Olivia lifted her shoulders, but stopped herself. Cindy taught her that shrugs lacked confidence. "We can walk the beach." She lowered her shoulders as naturally as possible. "It's quiet and beautiful and then we can go into town and take in the sights."

"Lots of walks."

"Yes. I find that walking and running is a great way to clear the mind."

Olivia had a plan. Though she would much prefer the buffer of the public, she knew she needed quiet moments with her mother to gear up for the confrontation.

And by the looks of Cindy's defensive stance—one arm clasped around middle, her hand twisting the faded chain and locket her late husband had given her—containing a picture of baby Olivia and Chris—she wasn't ready to hear Olivia's truth.

The plan was to roll out her feelings on Saturday evening—not so late that Cindy was too tired to talk, yet not so early that her mother would want to drive back home in the dark. That way, if Cindy wanted to leave early on Sunday as opposed to just after lunch, she was free to do so. In fact, Olivia encouraged it.

"Would you—"

"I'm a little tired from the drive. I'm going to take a nap."

Olivia shook her head. "Okay. I'll cook while you sleep."

Cindy nodded, seeming to be a world away, and walked to her room.

"That went well."

And it would only get worse. "It has to be done," she muttered to herself. Just as she had to expose her wounds in therapy, she'd have to do the same with her mother.

Until then, Olivia diced potatoes. She put on water to boil and stood watching it. The chicken, which she'd planned to bake, marinated in the refrigerator.

Her phone rang. Mr. Whittingham's name flashed across the screen. Her finger hovered over the screen to answer, but she didn't press the green button.

Mr. Whittingham knew about her plans to speak to her mother. She'd been forthcoming about her mother's struggle to show and give love. She told him about the backhanded compliments. The advice she gave about what colors paired well with her dark skin. The fact that she rarely said I love you or gave Olivia hugs, even when she was a child. And knowing her incredibly empathetic neighbor, he wanted to make sure she fared well.

He'd given advice just as good, if not better, than Dr. LaGrange. "Just be patient. Your mother's life changed at an early age, but from what I recall of her, she was very warm and caring."

Olivia joked she must have gone under a personality transplant.

No, she was not faring well, and it'd only been an hour. Olivia went to her office and searched for her pink journal. That way she could get her feelings on paper before the conversation and note her feelings after. Olivia searched her desk and the entirety of her office, but she couldn't find the damn notebook.

She took a deep breath, wondering if she left it at her last appointment. Annoyed at its disappearance, Olivia emailed her doctor to inquire on its whereabouts. Cindy returned downstairs while she finished up her email.

"Are you working?" Her mother asked.

Olivia shook her head. "No. Just sending my therapist an email."

"You go to therapy?" Cindy asked, revulsion in her tone.

Olivia squeezed her eyes shut. She'd never intended to tell her mother outright about her therapy.

"Yes. I've been struggling with my feelings lately and . . . it's been good for me."

"How so?" Cindy crossed her arms.

"It's allowed me to examine my past and the impact that it has on me today."

Cindy harrumphed. "Well, if you want people in your business, giving you opinions, that's up to you."

"I need the help."

"You seem to have it together." She waved around Olivia's house.

"You've got a good job, *had* a good man, though I think you may have rushed into it. You're financially secure—it's the most anyone could ask for in life."

"Yes, but I wasn't happy, Mother." She stood from her chair. "There are things I wanted to understand about—"

The doorbell rang, a chirpy and welcomed distraction. Her phone buzzed as well. Olivia turned her phone on silent while she cooked. She wanted quiet before dealing with Hurricane Cindy.

"Are you expecting someone?" Her mother hissed.

"N-no." She looked down at her phone. The picture of a masked Mr. Whittingham flashed on her phone.

The doorbell rang again, less chirpy, more insistent.

"Sorry. I'll just . . . get that." Olivia unlocked the door and swung it open.

It was Mr. Whittingham, but right behind him was an older handsome man.

With a face who looked much like her own.

"U-uncle Charles?" She looked at Mr. Whittingham, wringing his hand.

She heard a gasp from behind her. She saw her mother, slowly backing away as if she saw a ghost.

"I'm not your uncle, Olivia. I'm your father."

Olivia's mouth went dry. The door swung open, pushed wider by the man who claimed to be her father.

He stepped inside her threshold. "Whoa, now. Take it easy."

It was something about his calm tone, like a freshly paved road without potholes or faded lines, that made Olivia livid.

"What do you mean, whoa? You just told me you're my . . ." a loud sniff thieved Olivia's thunder. She spun around to face Cindy. Tears streamed down her mother's face. ·

"Mother, it's okay. It's fine. We're fine." Olivia guided her mother to the couch.

"I'll get water." Charles hurried to the kitchen and easily found the glasses.

Olivia clasped her mother's cold, shaking hands.

"T-there must be some mistake. Some sick joke," Olivia hissed at Mr. Whittingham.

Her neighbor slowly shook his head.

Olivia's heart pounded so hard it made her head hurt. It couldn't be. All the stories he'd shared, the pictures. Had Chris Jones been her uncle and the surly Charles, her father?

"Mom?" she whispered her question.

"Cindy." Charles kneeled on the other side of her. She finally noticed something outside of his face. He looked like a stylish cowboy with his hat and a red chambray shirt. "It's been a while." This time, emotion poured from his voice. "Take this." He offered her water.

Her mother took it with shaking hands. She gulped down the water.

They all sat in silence.

Olivia's patience grew thin.

"Mom, tell me this isn't true?" She flicked a glance at Charles. "Tell me this man, my . . . Chris' twin is not my father."

She pulled her lips into a tight line. "I'm sorry, Olivia," she replied in a small, shrunken voice. "I'm sorry I lied to you."

Olivia shook her head. "This doesn't make sense." She looked at Mr. Whittingham. "How could you bring him here without me knowing—"

"It's not Mr. Whitt's fault. I've been trying to pay him a visit, but he delayed, making up excuses. Then his son mentioned that my brother's daughter bought a house here. And well, I came to see for myself."

Olivia laughed without humor, teetering near hysteria. "Twenty-eight years later."

"Olivia." Cindy cleared her throat. "It wasn't your father's fault."

"Which one?" she snapped. "Chris Jones or Charles Jones? Did you . . . have a relationship with both of them?"

She wanted to say sex, but not in front of people who were at least twenty years her senior.

"Hey, now." Charles' deep voice boomed in the small room. "It's complicated. I'm sorry that I never got up the courage to push harder to know you. But I'm here now."

"I need you to leave." Olivia stood. She rushed to her door and opened it.

"Please, Olivia," Charles pleaded with her as if he knew her.

She shook her head. "No. I need to speak to my mother. I'll . . . contact you when I'm ready."

She waved toward the exit.

"I'm sorry." Mr. Whittingham, or Mr. Whitt, as Charles called him, stepped outside the door. Charles squeezed her mother's hand, whispering something only they could hear.

He walked to the door but paused right at the entrance. "I know this is a lot, but I've been dreaming of this day for a long time." He reached into his wallet and pulled out a card.

Charles Jones
Mayor, Highland Beach, Maryland

Olivia gasped. Dear God, she was the secret love child of a mayor. A chill ran through her body. She didn't want this; she abhorred scandals.

"Please call me. I'll be here for as long as it takes." His voice was soft, but it still held a promise. He wasn't going anywhere. After all, he was the boy who carved his own path and befriended a man thirty-plus years his senior because he needed someone to take him to the library. He was the boy who performed Prince without playing a stitch of guitar.

He was the boy who made her mother cry.

No, the surly, determined Charles Jones would not leave until she acknowledged his existence.

He tipped his hat and exited.

She turned to face her mother. Cindy dabbed tears with the back of her hand.

"Tell me everything."

CHAPTER 28

CINDY'S CHOICE

June 1993

Cindy pulled her braids into a high ponytail, wrapping a white head-band around the knot of her braid, the same as Janet Jackson had done in the movie with Tupac. She convinced her boyfriend to take her to the movies to see it three times. She liked the main character, who enjoyed reading and writing poetry, just as Cindy enjoyed.

"Stop staring in the mirror. You're going to be late," Cindy's friend Aneesa banged on the bathroom door.

"Coming, coming." When she opened the door, Aneesa gasped.

"What?" Cindy dashed back to the mirror and stared at her reflection. "Do I look okay?"

"Girl, you look good." She snapped her fingers for emphasis. "CJ will choke on his tongue."

Cindy twirled in the mirror, looking for wrinkles or anything out of place. "But do I look like a potential daughter-in-law?"

"Mhmm." Aneesa shrugged. "If I was his momma, I'd lock him inside the house."

"Why?"

"Because of those curves, girl." Aneesa grinned wide, giving Cindy a full view of her bottom row teeth. Her friend rarely smiled widely—she was ashamed of her crooked smile.

Cindy sighed. "Maybe I can put on the flower dress Mama bought me."

"Then you'll look poor."

"I am poor."

"I know that. But Ms. Christine-I'm-betta-than-you-Jones doesn't need to see it, too. You know that woman's bougie."

"So what do I do? I want to make a good first impression." After weeks of wearing him down, Charles promised that after their date at the beach, he would take her home and officially introduce her as his girlfriend. She'd met his parents long ago through his twin, who was her best friend.

"You've got to be you. Besides, she'll probably ask around about you once she finds out you're together. You saw what she did to Chris' last girlfriend, Reece."

Cindy nodded. Chris dated less often than Charles. The girl he'd dated was middle class too, but not nearly as wealthy as the Jones family. Chris had confided that his mother had arranged a meeting with Reece's grandparents, as her mother and father had died years ago. Christine had offered to pay for Reece's first year at Spelman if she agreed to stay away from her precious boy.

The grandmother had eagerly agreed and, much to Chris' dismay, so had Reece. She even offered to meet up in private until after she graduated, but it had been the principle of the matter for Chris. He wanted to be number one. Soon after, Chris enlisted in the military. He'd been in for two years now, but thankfully he was stationed in Fort Bragg, a six-hour drive from their hometown. He often took the weekends to visit with Cindy when he wasn't off to parts unknown.

Her heartbeat tripped just a little. She wondered, more than a few times, about her best friend's true feelings about her relationship with his brother. For years, they were each other's entire world—

which meant the world to a preteen. Two peas in a pod, mama had called them.

But she'd always had eyes for his twin. The quiet one. The mean one.

When he finally stopped kissing other girls and gave her the time of day, she jumped at the opportunity. They started dating the summer before senior year of high school and then for two years. On the surface, Chris had been supportive of their relationship and many times all three hung out at school events or even double dated.

She had Chris' support but now it was time to meet Mama Jones.

She could no longer hide in the shadows, pretending to be just Chris' friend while she dated Charles.

"You can do this, Cindy." Her friend rubbed her shoulder. "You're smart and pretty. Sometimes you're a little mean, but if you put your heart into it, you can win anyone over."

"I am not mean." Cindy smiled at her friend through the mirror's reflection.

Aneesa snorted. "That's why you and Charles get along. You're so grumpy."

Cindy smiled a secret smile. People only called Charles the mean twin because Chris was so dang nice. CJ wasn't mean at all. He just had little patience for stupidity. If anything, he was kinder than Chris because he put action and effort behind his support, whereas Chris was always ready with a kind word and a smile.

The doorbell rang. Her stomach clenched again.

"Who's that? Maybe it's Charles?"

Cindy shrugged. She had plans to meet him.

"Must be him," she muttered under her breath on the way to the door. Thankfully, her mom was at work, otherwise she would've looked at her crazily for having a boy over. It didn't matter if she was nineteen. She lived under Darleen's roof.

Well . . . that rule doesn't mean much now.

When she opened the door, her heart dropped.

"M-Mrs. Jones?"

"Yes." The woman wore a sleeveless white dress, white pearls, white kitten heels. She oozed wealth.

"May I come in?"

"I, um. My mother's not home." She braced her arm around the door. Her sparse apartment did not make for an ideal first impression.

"Oh, I don't need to speak to your mother. I need to speak to you, Pumpkin." She winked and pushed herself through the door.

"I have—"

She waved her off. "I'll be quick and I'll just . . . stand." She said as she surveyed the apartment.

Cindy blushed under the perusal. Though most things were cheaply made, they kept a clean home. The books from community college and poetry were alphabetized and stacked neatly on the shelves. The rugs were almost new, their landlord repainted her living room and the colors clashed. She'd only used the rugs for a month. The walls in the other rooms could use fresh paint, but the walls had been proudly decorated with colorful reprints from famous African American artists. Just beyond her sight in the hallway was the picture of Malcolm X and Martin Luther King Jr. Cindy moved the pictures of the civil rights leaders and Jesus to the hallway.

So yes, there were no originals, and a few walls were off-off white. But she'd argued their apartment was just as clean as the Jones mansion.

"Can I offer you sweet tea?"

"No," she shook her head. "Now listen, I know about your little predicament."

"Predicament?" Cindy looked over her shoulder. She lowered her voice to a whisper. "I don't think—"

"Charles isn't ready to be a father. You, sweetie, aren't ready to be a mother."

"H-how?" she gasped. She hadn't even told Charles. She planned to tell him tonight.

"Oh, honey, I've got eyes and ears, everywhere . . . including at the health clinic."

Cindy mentally kicked herself. The clinic was a county over, but apparently not far enough from Mrs. Jones' reach.

She clasped her hands. "Now let's talk about options."

Cindy shook her head. "I need to speak to Charles first. I know we're young, but I'll be twenty next month and Charles will be done with school next year. I already have my associate degree. I plan to go to a four-year college after the baby to study teaching."

"No, no, no, no, no, sweetie. That's not an option."

Cindy snapped her neck back. "But it is. It's my decision. Excuse me, me and Charles' decision."

"Charles knows you're pregnant."

"He does?" *There's no way.* Charles lacked the patience to pretend otherwise. Did she even know her son?

"I overhead the conversation two weeks ago. You were sick, and he said, 'You should really check yourself out. You've been really sick lately.'" She mimicked her son's low voice.

Cindy's mouth went dry. It was then that Cindy had put two and two together.

"I confronted my son. Asked him what he wanted to do and if I should handle it. So here I am . . . handling it." She pulled out a checkbook. "You want to go to college." She clicked a pen and scribbled on the check. Well, here you are." She ripped the check from the book. "That should cover tuition for two years. You can save up for the rest. Have a nice future." She stared at Cindy. The flimsy check dangled between her red, sharp fingernails. "Without my sons."

"Sons?"

"Chris, too. That boy loves you to distraction, and I can't have my boys distracted over you."

"Because I don't have any money?"

"Because you lack power and pedigree. Charles is going to law school. Then he'll run for mayor and then he's on to the Senate. He absolutely cannot afford a scandal. Do the right thing. Disappear."

Tears gathered in her eyes. Mrs. Jones never even gave her a chance. "Could you leave, please?" Cindy marched to the door and opened it. She didn't look at the matriarch of the Jones family, who still held her head high.

"Here." Christine tossed the check. It fluttered to Cindy's feet.

Cindy shut the door and slid to the floor.

"Oh my God, Cindy." Aneesa ran into the room.

"Y-you heard that."

"Yeah, I heard that uppity bitch. I wanted to slap the taste out of her mouth."

"Doesn't matter what I wear or how smart or pretty I am. People care about power and p-pedigree."

Aneesa looked at her stomach and then returned her attention to Cindy's face. "What 'cha gonna do?"

Cindy wiped her face with the back of her hands. "I'm calling Charles."

"On the house phone?" she shook her head. "Bad idea, girl. Go on your date, confront him about his triflin' mama."

If he even showed. "A-and then?"

"And then we'll see if your baby is going to have a father."

"You think I should keep it?" Cindy rubbed her stomach.

"You can do anything. Don't let that woman roll over you."

☀

Cindy walked to their meetup spot. It was the furthest spot away from prying eyes and aquatic equipment. Though the beach was vast, there was a perfect hiding hole, a dusty shelf that was just out of sight of beach patrol if you sat at the right angle.

Cindy rolled out her beach towel, determined to stay clean. After the encounter with Christine, she felt dirty and unworthy.

At least she hadn't pretended it wasn't his.

They'd conceived a few months ago before Charles left for winter break. They made love at this very spot, hidden from the patrol, waiting for them to make a last sweep before retiring for the night.

This would be the place to share the news. She crossed her legs, waiting.

But he didn't show up at eight o'clock.

Or nine o'clock.

Or ten.

Cindy pushed herself up to stand.

"Hey." Charles stood several feet away.

She jumped at the voice at first, but regaining her senses, she ran into his arms.

He held out his hand as if to ward her away.

"Hey," Cindy said on a sigh. "Your mom got to you."

"Yeah. She told me everything."

"I wanted to be the one to tell you the news. I'm sorry you had to hear it from her."

"I'd rather it had come from her."

"What? Why?"

"You cheating on me."

"I . . ." Cindy shook her head. "No. I would never."

"Are you calling her a liar?"

"Yes," she hissed.

"Really?" He pulled out a picture. It was a picture of her and David. They were outside at a beach party. He tried to kiss her out of the blue, and she pushed him away. But that picture had caught his kiss. The shove she'd given him looked like she grabbed his chest.

The glossy photo trembled in her hand. "He tried to kiss me. I pushed him away."

She handed him the photo. Surprisingly, he took it gently from her hand.

"Thought you would say that, so I confronted David. Beat the shit out of him and he told me you two have been kicking it behind my back."

"That's a lie."

"So why didn't you tell me he tried to kiss you?"

"I . . . I talked it over with Chris, and we both agreed that it was best not to say anything."

"You talked to Chris." His voice went tight and sharp and short. He didn't mind their friendship, but he hated it when Cindy still ran to him first for comfort.

She nodded. "I did."

"Are you dating Chris?"

"No."

"Screwing him?"

"Of c-course not. I love you."

"Then you shouldn't have lied. And you either lied by omission or you've been running after David. I think it's the latter."

Cindy looked up at the moon. It was full and bright. Usually, looking at the sky made her happy, but nothing could make this sadness disappear.

Mrs. Jones had thought of everything. She wouldn't be surprised if she planted David for the photo.

"I go home, I go to work and classes. If I hang out it's with Chris and Aneesa." Cindy's voice sounded ninety instead of nineteen.

"But you—"

"I'm pregnant, Charles."

"Congratulations." His voice was icy.

"You can say it to yourself because it's your baby. *Our* baby."

He shook his head. "Nah. Forget that. You aren't going to get pregnant behind my back and then leave me to pick up the tab."

"We had sex on winter break at this spot." She pointed to the ground. "I'm eight weeks pregnant. Do the math, genius."

"It all seems convenient—"

"Shut up! We conceived this baby here," Cindy yelled. "You told me you loved me. You told me I was yours and then I said that you were mine." Her voice shook. Tears soaked her face. "You made love to me. And I . . . I felt it d-down to my toes. And that night I knew I could never love another man how I love you."

Cindy put two hands over her heart, an attempt to push the fracturing pieces back together. "And I was so happy. So don't . . ." She reached for his hands, but he slapped her hand away.

"Don't do this to us. Tell me you believe me."

"I don't," he growled.

"Talk to Chris. He'll vouch for me about David. He—"

"I don't give a damn about what he has to say. He's just going to cover for you. He always does."

"But he wouldn't lie to you. You're his brother and soon he'll be an uncle."

"He loves you. He's got zero sense when it comes to you. We both know that, so don't even lie."

"S-so, what's next? You're just going to ignore me. You're going to pretend that I don't exist even though I'm pregnant with your child?"

"I want to believe you so bad," his voice shook. He gripped the picture in his hand.

"Then believe me! I'll take a test. Whatever you want to prove I'm telling you the truth."

He looked down, kicked the sand with his feet. "Okay. We'll get a test when the baby is born. But if you're lying to me, Cindy, I won't forgive you."

"I'm not lying."

"Time will tell. Until then, I'll need space."

"You'll have plenty. You're hundreds of miles away at Morehouse."

Charles left without a backward glance, leaving Cindy alone in the dark with a broken heart.

And time? It didn't get a chance to tell the truth. Chris and Charles' father had a heart attack and after that, all hell had broken loose.

Christine, distraught and destructive, sought to eliminate any imperfection. And the sons, equally destroyed by their father's death, let her have the control she so desperately needed and wanted.

Cindy, who'd been five months pregnant, stopped by the house to pay her respects to the family.

She placed white lilies and a polenta casserole on the wood planks and then rang the doorbell. The funeral was two days away. It was early in the morning, and just as she'd hoped, there were no other cars in the driveway.

Charles answered the door. When he saw her, his face softened, but in a flash hardened to anger.

"What are you doing here?"

"I'm here to pay my respects." She bent over to retrieve her food and flowers. "I'm sorry about your father. I know you two were close."

"What is she doing here?" his mother yelled from over his shoulder. "Haven't you done enough?"

"I . . . I haven't. I stayed away like you all asked." She grabbed her stomach. Charles' attention drifted to her belly.

"It's because of you my husband is dead. He's dead!" she shrieked.

"I didn't . . ." she shook her head. What did she mean? She hadn't spoken to the man.

"Your dear Chris never gave him a moment's peace. He accused us of being monsters. He badgered his poor father, at your request—"

"I didn't know."

"He had a heart attack. And now he's dead. So you and that bastard child inside of you can get the hell out of my yard!"

"Enough, mother," Charles growled.

Mrs. Jones stormed towards the house and slammed it shut.

"Charles, I'm so sorry."

"I know." He gentled his voice. "Come walk with me."

They walked a distance from the house.

"Is what your mom saying true? Did Chris and your father argue about me?"

"Yes. It was me, Dad, and Mom. Chris read us the riot act. Told me to get my stuff together or he would take you away from here. I must admit, I lost my cool. We got into a fight and . . . and then Dad dropped dead."

"Oh, God. Oh, God, God, God." Nausea hit Cindy like a storm.

"Look, my mother needs us. I just need you to back off for a few months until she—"

"I'm so sorry about your father, but I've backed way off. I can't control what your mother says . . . you of all people know that. But I need you, too. I won't do this alone."

"Just give me some time."

"How long? Days, weeks? A month?"

"Give me a month."

"Fine. You've got until the seventeenth of next month or I'm . . ."

"You're what?"

"I'm going to do just what your mother wanted. I'm cashing that check and I'm leaving this town. I'll be damned if I let my child suffer. You got it?"

"I've got it."

"Don't disappoint me, Charles." She found the steel in her voice.

He eyed her, respect clearly in his eyes. "Just wait for me. I won't let you down."

☼

September 17, 1993

The rain poured around the bus stop near the back parking lot of the Dollar Store. The bus stop had a hard plastic top but opened at the front, providing little shelter. Cindy had two large garbage bags with all her important belongings and more money in her account than she'd ever had in her life.

She'd need every penny.

Cindy spotted the bus across the street. It was at a stoplight and soon it would arrive at the stop.

Despite her raging hormones, she hadn't cried much in the past week. It was as if something hardened inside of her, forming a lump in her stomach, and each day it grew larger and rounder alongside her baby.

The thing inside of her didn't allow space for feelings like love, but it gave her something tangible, something Cindy knew she would need to survive as a single mother.

A car honked. She wiped tears that were mixed with the rain. She recognized the car, but she didn't move.

Please let it be him. Please let it be him.

He parked the car, flipped on his hazards, and opened the door. A large black umbrella blocked his face. He jogged to the bus stop. Cindy stood belly first, nearly toppling over. She steadied her hand against the plastic wall.

She wanted . . . she needed, to believe he'd come to his senses.

Cindy's gaze dropped to his shoes for clues. They were beat up, muddied. The lump in her stomach expanded.

"C'mon, Pumpkin Pie."

She flinched at the name, gone cold at the greeting. For one, his mother had called her Pumpkin, and she'd only just realized it was in jest.

Second, *Chris* called her Pumpkin. She wasn't too sweet, wasn't too bitter. She was just right.

Her body shivered; her tears no longer blended in the rain. They rolled more slowly down her cheek while the rain raged around them. "He's not coming."

Chris shook his head slowly. Rain dripped from the umbrella. "But I'm here."

"No." Cindy stepped back. "I'm leaving this place. Go back to base. I've got this."

"I'm leaving, too. I'll be stationed in New York. Next year I'm thinking of getting out of the military."

"G-good," she nodded. Chris barely dodged being shipped to the Gulf War and went into some special branch of the Army. Whenever asked about his job or specialty, he went tight-lipped.

"But you're moving?"

"More like I've been told to move," he laughed. "But yes. I'm leaving next week."

"This is insane, Chris. How could you leave without telling me?" She slapped his chest.

He grinned. "I can't tell you all my secrets, Pumpkin."

"I can't just mess up your life—"

"Look, Mom's got Charles by the balls. He's all messed up and blaming himself about Dad's death. But you gave him that ultimatum and he isn't here."

Cindy looked down at her feet, at her off-off white shoes that matched her off-off white walls.

"I'm here, Cindy, and I promise that . . . I'll love you and that little pumpkin pie growing in you for the rest of our lives. And if you think you can return my love one day, then I want more babies with you."

Cindy's head dropped. She cried into her hands.

She cried for her baby.

She cried for her heart.

She cried for Chris.

Why did he have to love her so much?

Why couldn't she love him enough?

But he was here, and Charles was not. She leaned up on her toes, her heart raging at the injustice of it all. "Kiss me."

"What?"

"Kiss me, Chris." She could imagine the picture she made. Hair a soppy mess, eyes rimmed red, her dress two sizes too big because she needed to shop for clothes that would fit her throughout her pregnancy.

He leaned down and kissed her with the passion of a dying man. Like she was a living, breathing princess. He tasted of cinnamon and spice, the gum he so loved.

He felt good and safe and warm.

She broke the kiss. She stared at him, seeing clues to his sincerity. He looked at Cindy as he always had—his expressive eyes never failed to show his love. "Okay, Chris. I'll go with you."

He smiled and picked up her pitiful luggage. "Let's go."

She responded with a nod. She was so cold, she needed to get warm for the baby.

When they got into the car, it occurred to her to ask about his family. About Charles. "What did your family say?"

"Mom says she's cutting me out the will. She'll never speak to me again."

"She'll change her mind. She loves you."

"Mom can't stand to look at me anyway. Besides, I don't need her money. I'm not going to be her perfect son. I'm going to be my own man. I'll be your man."

Cindy smiled. This time it wasn't as stretched but buoyed with hope for the first time in a long while. A flash of red caught her attention, she looked around the parking lot, searching for his car.

It's just my imagination.

"I'll make sure you won't regret it," Chris vowed.

In her heart, she knew Chris would keep his promise. She knew him inside and out.

What she didn't know was that the familiar red Mustang had circled the parking lot minutes after Chris. And the owner, Charles, sat in the car. When he stepped outside ready to claim the woman he loved, she was locked in a passionate kiss, in the arms of his twin brother.

No one would ever know.

CHAPTER 29

THE MAN WITH THE PLAN

September 2021

Cindy clasped her hands on her thigh. Her eyes cleared as if the fog of the past lifted.

Olivia digested what her mother had told her. Chris Jones, for all intents and purposes, had been her father. He'd forsaken his family and his future to be with her mother.

But there was a burning question Olivia had since her mother shared her story a few minutes ago.

"Did you love my . . . did you love Chris?"

He'd gone through so much in his life. Olivia desperately wanted him to have a happy ending.

"It took a little while, but yes. I loved Chris. He loved Nike. Wore Nike shoes, and those Godawful loud windbreakers. I think his mother wouldn't let them wear anything but Polo and Lacoste. But that was his first order of business. So, when he found out you were a girl, he searched far and wide looking for pink Nike shoes."

"Did he find them?"

She laughed. "No. He was so disappointed. So, he . . ." she laughed. "He dyed the shoes, and they looked just awful. Like it got stuck with the colored clothes in the laundry. But he wasn't deterred. He tried three times until he got them right."

She opened her locket and pointed at the tiny picture of Olivia and Chris. "You probably can't tell, but the shoes you have on are pink. I fell in love with him because it occurred to me that he worked so hard to do for others. All he needed was my love. I loved him for so long as a friend that I never allowed myself to think of him as my lover. But my heart mended, and my mind changed. For a while, we were deliriously happy. And I so wanted to give him more children."

"You wanted more children?" Olivia couldn't hide the incredulity in her voice.

Her mother turned her head and blew into the tissue. "Yes. We planned for four."

She couldn't imagine Cindy handling four children. Sure, she would feed them, cloth them, bathe them, but be emotionally available? Olivia shook her head. "I thought you didn't like children."

"What made you think that?" Cindy crumpled the tissue into her fist.

"Oh, I don't know, from the way you treated me."

"What do you mean? I took care of you."

"It's more than . . ." Olivia huffed. She didn't want to argue child-rearing with her mother.

"Anytime I wore something you thought didn't compliment my complexion, you criticized me."

"I . . . I don't remember—"

"Every summer I returned from the Bluffs, you inspected my clothes to make sure I didn't wear a color that made me look too dark."

Cindy looked away, as if recalling the memory. "No, Olivia. I had to make sure that nothing emphasized your figure. I don't know if you recall but men and boys stared at you. I had to protect you. I can understand why you would think that, but I love your skin."

Olivia shook her head. She was sure it was more than wearing age-appropriate clothing. "You sure had a crazy way of showing it. You constantly criticized me."

"It's because you remind me of your . . . of Charles. You're his spitting image in every way. Your temperament, your demeanor, even the way you dress. He loved bright colors. Red, yellow, bright blue." She exhaled loudly. "I think if Chris were still alive it wouldn't have bothered me as much."

Pain spiraled through her chest, cutting up her insides into tiny sheer ribbons. "You hated me because I look like my father. But I look like Chris, too."

"I don't hate you. It's just that you were a constant reminder of him. I just feel so damn guilty about everything." Cindy slouched against the couch like a teenager in the throes of a tantrum. Olivia leaned closer, observing her mom like a rare flower. She wasn't used to her showing emotion.

"I feel like I ruined Chris' life. If we weren't together, he would've left the military and maybe returned home. Then he wouldn't have become a police officer. He would've been safe as a politician, like his mother and father wanted for him. We would've been safe in Highland Beach instead of New York.

"Looking back, I realized I didn't treat you the way you deserved. But my heart," she pointed to her chest.

"I know." Olivia swallowed. "It was broken."

"Shattered to smithereens. I just couldn't see goodness in the world anymore. The first man I ever loved rejected us. His family hated me and the man I came to love more than anything was murdered. Sometimes I feel like everything and everyone I touch is cursed."

"I'm not cursed, Mother."

"You're right. You have it so much more together than I ever did. You're the best of me and Chris and even Charles."

Charles. Her biological father. Mr. Whittingham had been talking about him all along. Funny, he didn't seem so cruel as the story Cindy had shared. But she believed her mother. Olivia was living proof of his choice. Still, she wanted answers, but now from him.

"I'd like to speak to Charles."

"You should. He is your father, and you deserve to get to know him. But please be careful. If his mother, your grandmother, is still alive, she'll sabotage your efforts."

Olivia digested the knowledge. She wished she could look forward to meeting a grandparent. Cindy's mother had died when she was six years old.

"Do you plan to speak to him?" she asked her mother.

"No."

"I'll talk to him when you leave on Sunday."

"That's fine." Cindy rose. "You'll have to excuse me. I'm truly tired."

"Do you want me to take dinner to you?"

Cindy scrunched her face. Olivia had forgotten that she didn't believe in eating anywhere but the kitchen table.

"I don't have an appetite."

"Of course. Maybe we can brunch tomorrow?"

"I think I'll be up for it then." Cindy went upstairs. Olivia poured herself a glass of wine and stared at the pictures of Chris and Charles. Stories from Mr. Whittingham swirled in her head. She needed to clear her mind. She itched for a run. But it was too dark to go outside. She'd run away from her troubles first thing tomorrow morning.

CHAPTER 30

BEA'S BLUES

September 2021

Tip-tip-tip.

Someone knocked on Bea's door.

Bea opened her Ring app and spotted a tall, thin white man through the camera. She did not know this man, but she knew where he came from. She immediately recognized the colonizer uniform—black polo shirt, khaki shorts, bold in design and in behavior, the ASK logo stitched proudly just below the collar.

She wasn't one to waste paper, but every time she opened the mailbox to find a tacky "pink slip" flyer that encouraged homeowners to sell for *out of this world money*, she wanted to rip it to shreds and let it burn.

Bea was above tantrums. She'd learned over the years to use her head, her resources. For years, those resources had been woefully limited. But with her company launching her into a salary bracket that matched her wealthy family, she knew just how to fight money with money.

Whitney had cornered her, convincing Bea of her and Olivia's ideas of forming a secret group to help residents who needed to sell their Sag homes to find the right buyers who wanted to contribute to the community.

Their vision intrigued Bea. Like her superhero, Abeja, she had a mission to save the world from real estate developers who would plow over their homes and replace them with Citarella, Balducci's, and walkable paved paths.

Their residents were leaving. Their culture and community dying. Just like the bees. And the world needed bees, just like the world needed the preservation of thriving Black communities.

And instead of answering through her app or letting the door open, she simply walked deeper inside her house to the screened-in sunroom that overlooked the backyard.

The day was gloomy, partly cloudy, no time for visitors. Bea didn't like the rain. Not for obvious reasons like wet, cold, and darkness, but because the impending storm separated her from the bees. Today would be a day for organizing—labeling her tonics, adding the turquoise blue and white labels on her bee products.

When the knocking stopped, her shoulders relaxed. She checked the camera and saw the stranger's back as he walked down the steps.

"Good riddance," she whispered.

She looked around her sunroom. Glass bottles and recyclable plastics littered the carpet-covered floor. Mr. Whittingham told her she needed to find another location to help her scale up soon.

But scaling up meant more work, more visibility. She couldn't hide in obscurity and, even worse, she'd have less time with her bees.

"And that's why I'm keeping things as is."

She answered her own question. She rather liked the pace and peace of her life.

The labels sat on the long worktable; she picked them up, lined up her bottles, and stickered them.

"Oh. Here you are." The stranger, with blond-brown hair and piercing blue eyes, stood just outside the screen door.

The glass bottle slipped from Bea's hand, crashing on the floor.

"May I come in?"

"Not unless you want another hole in your body," Bea's voice was deadly. She had two guns in her home and a knife stashed under her table, just a stretch away.

Life as a drug-addicted model had also taught her to prepare for violence. The man standing in front of her didn't have much bulk, and three inches on her in height.

She'd have to be quick.

"Oh, I don't mean to cause you harm." A smile curved his thin lips.

"Sure, you don't."

"I'm from ASK." He needlessly pointed to the logo on his polo. "My name is—"

"I don't need to know who you are. You need to leave. I'm *not* selling."

"I know." He took a quick breath, dropped his affable smile. "I know a lot about you, Edie Tanner, age forty-seven, adopted at age six in this very house. It's a nice home." He knocked on the exterior near the door. "It's got some good bones."

"It's not for sale."

"That's okay . . . for now. But if you want to keep your secrets . . . secret, I suggest you let go of this investment business you've got with Olivia."

Olivia! She'd gone and blabbed to Anderson. She heard about his family ties to ASK, the little idiot.

Not to mention Olivia's ties with her godsister, Billie, the child Bea gave away.

Things were changing. Everything was changing. The spotlight, the visibility would come sooner or later. This man would see to it.

She didn't quake with horror, though it shot like adrenaline through her heart.

Wired, buzzed, alarmed. But on the outside she exuded calm like still water. She bent down, stretched, and retrieved her stainless-steel field knife, then held it aloft.

"W-what are you doing?" he held up his hands when he saw her blade.

"I don't know how you came about this information, but that's not who I am. Edie ran away from her problems. Bea . . . stings."

She stepped closer to the door. He tripped over his feet and tumbled to the ground. Boot to the door, she kicked it open, knife steady, missile focused. Her target? His throat.

"Do not think you can threaten me and my livelihood. Get the hell off my property and never return." She leaned over his shaking body, though his eyes teemed with rage.

"Next time, I'll have my gun ready, and I won't miss."

Olivia knew it would rain soon.

She didn't care. It could snow and she'd still run. She needed to funnel the energy and rein in her chaotic thoughts. After a quick stretch, Olivia ran at the speed of light down the beach. She relished the challenging friction of the sand beneath her feet. She inhaled, taking in the salty air. As she expected, rain droplets trickled. She adjusted her hat—an old cap that Anderson had left—and pushed harder.

Her lungs burned, as she thought of her fathers.

Charles and Chris.

Did they run like her on this beach? Compete against each other like they'd done for her mother's heart?

Her heart ached for Chris. Unrequited love for years. While her uncle-father Charles took her mother's heart for granted.

The strip of the beach ended. She stopped in front of Bea's house, bent over, inhaling and exhaling. Salty sweat trickled down her temples to her throat.

"Hey. You!" Bea marched down the steps.

Olivia looked over her shoulder, looking for the person who'd obviously pissed off Bea.

When she found no one, she turned around and pointed to herself and asked, "What's wrong?"

"You. You brought the hound of Satan right to my doorstep."

"Who?" Was she talking about Charles? Did she know him? Or was it maybe Cindy?

"ASK," she hissed. Olivia had thought she told her to ask, but then quickly realized she spoke of the redevelopment company.

"You told them I was an investor in our club."

"No." Olivia shook her head. "I would never speak to them."

"Well then, it was your fiancé."

"Ex-fiancé. And Anderson wouldn't betray us—"

"Yes, he did." She curled her hands into fists. "They looked into my past. They threatened me. I didn't want to be found. Not like this."

"I have no idea what you are talking about."

"Please! Like you don't know." Her voice was low, shaking with fury.

"I don't know."

"Then you need to wake up!" she shouted. "And you need to stay the hell away from me and my business and my life." She slapped her chest. "I've already told Whitney about you. You're on notice." She marched back to her home.

Olivia turned to run to her house. She'd left her phone at home, not wanting her cell to get wet in the rain. She ran as if those hounds of hell Bea spoke of nipped at her heels.

There was no way Anderson betrayed her. He'd been so sincere about supporting their cause. Beyond that, she never told him details about the investment club. She had the details on her computer and in her notebook.

Her journal.

The one that's still missing.

Her heart pounded as hard as her feet against the sand. Surely Anderson didn't take it.

She arrived at her house, immediately dialing Whitney.

Whitney answered after the second ring. "You've got a lot of nerve calling me."

"Listen. I didn't tell Anderson about our plans. Someone must've seen the plans I . . . in my notes. I—"

"There's already been a vote and you're out," she announced, like they were in a sorority.

"I swear I'm not lying to you."

Whitney didn't answer, but she heard shuffling in the back and when she spoke, her voice sounded muffled. "I don't think you're lying. But ever since Anderson came into the neighborhood, there's been nothing but drama. I don't know all about Bea's past, but from what I've gathered, she left her family years ago and doesn't want to be found. Regardless of the circumstances, she deserves her privacy."

"She certainly does, but Anderson has nothing to do with this."

"Girl, you're literally sleeping with the enemy."

"You know we aren't together anymore."

"I'm sorry but we can't have them investigating our people. Maybe if you can get Anderson to back down—"

"He's not involved."

"Who else could've gotten that private information, hmm? Think on it."

Olivia's head swirled. "Maybe someone broke in while I was out."

"Just get whoever to back off. They spooked Bea. Like I said, she deserves peace. She had that before . . ."

"Before me."

"Before Anderson," she corrected.

"I understand. I'll figure this out," Olivia promised.

Her mother came down the steps. A look of concern flitted across her face when she took in Olivia.

"Bye." Olivia clicked off.

She messaged Anderson.

OLIVIA: Where are you? We need to talk. Now.

He messaged her immediately.

ANDERSON: I can come by the house.

Olivia shook her head, though he couldn't see it. She didn't want him at her house. Nor did she want to meet him in public.

OLIVIA: I'll meet you at wherever you're staying.
ANDERSON: Shaun's renting a house here. I'll send you the address.

It was a twenty-minute drive from the neighborhood, and blessedly far enough away from not-so-friendly faces. Not that it mattered. No matter how Olivia viewed it, she was a SANS pariah. Mr. Whittingham, the only neighbor who would likely speak to her, wasn't the one she wanted to talk to.

She pulled into the wooded neighborhood and turned into a curved driveway. When she turned in, she immediately recognized Anderson's blue Prius.

She exhaled. The cousin wasn't home. Which was preferable because they could have an honest conversation without eyes and ears.

She knocked on the door once before Anderson answered with a big smile.

"Olivia." His smile dropped. "Are you crying?"

"Did you . . . have you seen my pink notebook?"

"What?" He opened the door to let her in.

"My notebook?" She stepped into the house.

"No, Olivia. I only took my things. Why would I take a note-book?" He scrunched his face.

"That's where I recorded my personal . . . my feelings. I also used the notebook once for a meeting and there were some key strategies we plan to employ against ASK. I shouldn't have done it, but I did, and now the entire neighborhood hates me. You're the only person who's been in the house. And I just know it's here." She looked around the living room, scanning for clues.

"Wait, slow down. Slow down." Anderson grabbed her forearms.

"You know I wouldn't take anything from you. I would never use your words against you."

Olivia nodded. "I know you wouldn't. But things aren't add-ing up."

Olivia spotted an ASK mug perched on the kitchen counter. She rushed to the kitchen and picked up the mug. "What's this?"

"It's a mug. Not mine, Shaun's."

"Does he work there?"

Anderson opened his mouth and seemed to hold his breath. "Yes, but . . . he's not like the rest of them. He's the good cousin."

Olivia lifted the mug under his nose. "Maybe he's not?" She looked around. "Where is he?"

"At work. Dad called a random meeting."

The Saturday meeting gave her the perfect opportunity to snoop. "May I look around?"

"You're not going to find it here." Anderson shook his head. "But go ahead. Shaun's a good guy. He's actually rooting for us."

"Sure, he is." Olivia muttered under her breath. She wanted to go straight to his room, but she would pretend to search in other rooms first. She pulled out cabinets and opened drawers. It was pin neat and highly organized. She even looked in the bathrooms.

"Anderson?"

"Yes." He didn't stand too far away from her raid.

"Could you look in Shaun's room?" She wasn't entirely rude, but she was at her wit's end.

With her mother, her father, with ASK, even with her neighbors.

"If that's what you want." Anderson's tone belied his disapproval.

"It's what I need. Please." She winced at the desperation in her voice.

Anderson nodded. "Okay. But I plan to talk to him about this."

"Do what you need to do."

He went into Shaun's room for five minutes and returned empty-handed. "Sorry. I looked everywhere. Shaun's a neat freak, so if it's there, I would've found it."

"Okay." Olivia sniffed tears. She would return home and turn over her house again. That would give her something else to focus on. She rubbed her arms. Her body shook with cold, and a tingle tickled her throat.

Am I getting sick?

"I'll go now."

"You don't look so good." Anderson put his hand on her forehead. "You're a little warm. Maybe I should drive you home?"

"No." She backed away, rubbing her arms. "Not a good time for you to be driving around."

"What are they going to do, slash my tires?"

"Of course not!"

"So let me take you home. I'll get Shaun to drive me back—"

"No, thank you. Besides, Cindy is waiting for me."

"Oh. She came."

Olivia nodded. "There's . . . a lot going on right now. Probably why I'm feeling a little rundown. I'll be fine. Just fine."

She rushed out of the house and into the car. Disappointment fueled her speed. She just knew Shaun was involved, but nothing turned up at his house.

Unless he has it at his office.

Olivia shook her head. She couldn't break into the office. Besides, they already had their plan in hand.

Olivia parked and walked into her home.

Cindy sat near the kitchen island, eating a sliced apple.

"Sorry I left. There's a lot going on right now."

"What's going on?" Cindy asked after swallowing.

Olivia shook her head. It would be too much to tell her mother. "Nothing. Do you still want to go to brunch?"

"Yes. I was a bit peckish, so I peeled an apple."

They drove in silence to the American Hotel. Olivia parked in the nearby lot a block away. It wasn't as crowded since Labor Day weekend. Most of the part-time residents and out-of-towners returned to their homes.

Olivia and her mother were immediately seated at a bistro-style table near the bar. Her mother ordered a bellini while Olivia ordered a mimosa. She wished there were a bottomless option, like many of the popular rooftops in New York City.

After Olivia sipped her mimosa, her mother smiled. "Now, I know I've not been the most . . . the best mother to you."

"It's okay. I understand why . . ." Olivia stopped speaking when her mother raised and waved her hand.

"Now hear me out. I'm not your friend and I haven't been the traditional mother to you. But I love you and I care. As such, I would very much like it if you told me what is going on, outside of the news of your father. You don't look so good."

Olivia crossed her arms, ready to defend herself from her mother's words.

Cindy waved her hand again. "I don't mean that in the way I used to say it to you before. I'm not going to tear you down. But you look sick."

Olivia took a breath and then told her everything about the battle with ASK.

"Anderson needs to do more, if you ask me," Cindy replied.

"He searched Shaun's room." Olivia swirled the champagne glass.

"He should make his father stop. By any means—"

"Ladies."

Olivia coughed, nearly choking on her mimosa. She caught the person's reflection in the mirror.

"Oh, hi, Mr. Whittingham. Charles." Olivia nodded at her . . . she didn't know what to call the man. Yes, Charles would have to do for now.

Mr. Whittingham clasped his hands together. "Looks like you have the same idea."

Olivia wanted to smack her head. Mr. Whittingham loved breakfast at the American Hotel. He loved the old-world feel, the dark woods, wallpapered floral walls with pictures of sailboats and landscapes hanging on the wall.

Olivia sighed. "Charles—"

"I know I'm intruding on your life right now. Mr. Whitt told me about your troubles with the developers and your old friend."

"My friend?" she glanced at Cindy, who merely looked the other way while she delicately sipped her beverage.

"Your former fiancé," Mr. Whittingham helpfully supplied.

"Correct." Charles nodded. "It was highly suggested that I give you space. So, I'll do that. But before I go, I'm offering you and . . . you, too, Cindy, a place to stay at my home. I'd love for you to visit. You can stay as long as you'd like. I know a lot of companies are working from home now, and I have plenty of space."

"Your parent's home?"

"No," he shook his head. "I built my own."

On that note, Olivia glanced at his ring finger. There was no flash of gold or silver, not even a faded line.

"And is . . . Christine still around?" Cindy asked with barely held venom in her voice.

"She is. She lives in her own home."

"How far away?"

"Just down the road."

Cindy scoffed. "I won't have my daughter near your mother, do you understand? I'll never—"

"I'll take care of you and Olivia. Just as I intended that day when you drove off in the rain with my brother."

Cindy's face paled. "You . . . you came?"

"You wore a red dress and the star earrings I bought you for your birthday. You had two big black garbage bags, and you walked away in the rain and drove off with my brother." His voice shook.

"W-well, I didn't leave you. You left me physically and emotionally, just as soon as I told you I was pregnant."

"I know. I'm sorry. I . . . there are a lot of things to discuss with you. Now isn't the time." He nodded. "But the offer still stands for the both of you. I'd like to get to know my daughter."

Olivia looked at her mother for confirmation. She turned to face her daughter, her mouth and expression shuttered.

"I'll be in touch," Olivia responded. She refused to speak for her mother now that she knew all that she'd been through.

"I'll leave you ladies to your breakfast," Charles ended the conversation.

Once they left, Cindy waved at the server and lifted her glass. "Two more of these, please." She sighed. "Aye, yi yi, what a day."

"I told you I'd show you a good time."

Cindy barked a laugh and took another sip. "I'm afraid to ask what's next."

"Lobster on the beach."

Cindy nodded. "Sounds like a good plan."

CHAPTER 31

SISTERLY LOVE

September 2021

The little tickle in Olivia's throat transformed into a forest fire. Cindy took more time off work and extended her stay with Olivia.

Olivia had taken a COVID test and, blessedly, it had turned out negative. Still, she called Anderson and Mr. Whittingham, who'd she'd been in recent contact with to let them know she was sick.

Cindy claimed it was love-sickness.

"Not over Anderson, but the life you created. Your dreams have been snatched away without so much as a hello and goodbye. But don't worry. I'll take care of you until you're feeling better. I've got the time."

Olivia's heart warmed at her mother's earnestness. Though she wasn't sure if she and Cindy would last more than a few days, especially after she fully recovered.

It was three o'clock—time for her call with the godsisters. So much happened in the week. She readied herself for the shocked gasps and shouts.

Olivia excused herself from Cindy's watchful eyes and climbed the stairs to her room.

Like clockwork, Perry started the FaceTime.

Olivia answered, then a few seconds later, Billie joined.

"Hey!" Perry waved. Libby sat on her lap and Olivia and Billie ooh'ed and ahh'ed over their perfect niece.

"When is Mommy giving you a little brother or sister?" Olivia asked the toddler.

"Come with Daddy, baby," she heard Perry's husband in the background.

Libby hopped off Perry's lap and ran to her father.

Perry shook her head. "I love my baby to pieces, but she is a daddy's girl."

Olivia smiled. "So, are you going to answer for Libby? When's number two coming?" Olivia knew she wanted a few kids, so she didn't feel bad asking her about it.

Perry gave an inelegant snort. "No time soon."

Her declaration shocked Olivia. "Why not?"

"One of my girlfriends is pregnant and even her husband couldn't be in the delivery room."

Billie scrunched her face. "Oh, well, that sucks."

"Truly it does." Perry nodded. "So yes, until we transition from pandemic to endemic, I'm closing shop."

"Well," Billie smiled awkwardly into the camera. "That may be too late for me."

"What do you mean? What are you saying?" Perry leaned forward, her eyes star bright.

"It means we're pregnant!"

"Oh, my!" Perry clapped her hands. "Congratulations, Billie!"

"Thank you. Oh, I'm the one who's preggers, by the way."

Perry pumped her fist. "Let me see your stomach."

Billie lowered the camera, revealing a still very flat stomach.

"Oh, poo." Perry pouted.

Billie lifted the phone back to her face, laughter dancing in her eyes. "I'm only nine weeks."

Something tickled in Olivia's throat, and it wasn't the cold. "C-congratulations, Billie. I'm so pleased for you."

"Oh yeah, you sound like it." Billie leaned closer to the phone. "You look . . . sick."

"Yeah, she does. I was going to say something, but I didn't want you to snap on me," Perry added.

"Yeah, I'm a little sick. It's not Covid. Sorry, but I am happy for you," she croaked like a frog.

Though she truly loved the news, Olivia still felt a yearning for Billie and Perry's life.

Yes, she was more than aware of Billie and Dulce's struggles for their happily ever after, but they seemed to have it together. Meanwhile, Olivia's life was in limbo.

Tension built in her throat, her stomach, her forehead.

Tiny white and gray dots danced in her vision. She reached for her bottled water and took a large gulp.

"Once you and Anderson get married, you can join the club. Then you can raise your baby in that beautiful home of yours." Billie's voice was incredibly soft and kind.

Olivia hated the sympathy, but she was too weak to argue.

There was no Anderson. She had no community and the father she thought was her father was really her uncle.

Tears seeped from her eyes.

"Olivia!" Perry gasped. "What's going on with you?"

"Yes, tell us. Seriously. Are you and Anderson okay?"

"No." Olivia shook her head. "Anderson's not okay. I'm not okay. We're not okay."

"Tell us what happened," Perry said in a voice that reminded her of Ama—direct but with a dose of goodness.

For the next half hour, Olivia had told them every detail— including therapy, ASK, her affair with Garrett, her breakup with

Anderson, and Cindy's story, which included the discovery of her biological father.

"Holy cramoly. How is your head not exploding?" Billie asked.

"Well, I'm sick, so I think that's my body's way of shutting down."

"What will you do?" Perry asked with the practicality of a seasoned lawyer.

"There's nothing I can do about the neighborhood. My mother thinks I should ask Anderson to get some incriminating evidence on his family, but I don't want to engage him more than necessary. The breakup was tough on him."

"But not on you?" Perry confirmed.

"Not as much as it should." It'd pained her to hurt Anderson, and she missed him—but not as a lover, more as a companion.

"Do you like this Garrett dude?" Billie asked.

"I do. I like him a lot and I adore Zora, his daughter."

"Do not engage." Perry shook her head and crossed her arms to make an *X*.

"Why not? Is it because he has a child?"

"No. You just have too much going on, Olivia Jones. You need to relax, relate, release."

Olivia laughed. She'd forgotten about the summer that they binged on the popular nineties show *A Different World*.

"Maybe I should take Charles up on his offer? Get to know him and let my neighborhood cool off."

"That's not a bad idea," Perry agreed. "Though I don't love the fact that they ganged up on you. It seems bullyish."

A wail from Libby broke into the conversations. "I'm so sorry, but I've got to go. It's feeding time and then off to bed."

"I'm pretty beat myself," Billie said and yawned. "This preggo life is no joke."

"So, am I," Olivia said. "Tired, not pregnant," she clarified with a smile.

"Both of you take it easy, okay?" Perry advised her godsisters. "We're living in hard times as it is. Self-care is necessary."

"We will," Billie and Olivia promised.

"And Olivia?" She narrowed her eyes, while pointing to the screen. "I'll be in touch. Bye now."

She hung up the phone before Olivia could ask what she meant.

Under Cindy's vigilant care of soup and forced rest, Olivia felt better by Wednesday morning. Although it was obvious Olivia was physically better, her mother informed Olivia of her plans to stay through the weekend.

Olivia suspected Charles was the reason for the delayed trip home. She just wasn't sure if what drove her was her desire to protect Olivia or unfinished business with Charles. Perhaps both were true.

Someone rang the doorbell. Olivia padded to the door, finding Garrett on the other side.

He stood in his yard, wearing a fitted black Armani shirt with dark jeans.

"You're looking good," he greeted.

Olivia blushed. "Why thank you."

She motioned toward the flowers in his hands. "Are those for me?"

He nodded. "I wanted to make you soup, but your mother told me she had that covered."

"You spoke to Cindy?" She turned toward her mother, who pretended to watch something on television.

"Yes. I met her while walking on the beach a few days ago. She introduced herself. She seemed to know me." His smile was wide and unguarded.

"I may have mentioned my neighbors." She stepped outside and shut the door for privacy.

She took the flowers from Garrett's hand. "I'm surprised to find you here."

"Why would you?"

"Didn't you hear? Everyone hates me."

There'd been radio silence from everyone, with the exception of Addy. She checked in because she'd heard that Olivia was sick. From her follow-up questions, she could tell Addy wanted a bit more information about what happened with Anderson and ASK. Olivia had responded that she suspected someone had stolen her journal, knowing that Addy would spread the word.

"No one hates you," Garrett said. "They are just on high alert. Whitney thinks we're at war with ASK."

"I agree with Whitney." They stole pertinent information. She couldn't prove it, but she knew it to be true.

"How's Zora?"

"She's loving the new school. She's already friends with the entire classroom and her teacher, Mrs. Sorin, adores her."

"To know her is to love her." Olivia dipped her nose into the white roses and took in the beautiful fragrance.

"I know you're still hosting your mother and Zora will be home soon. But I just wanted to see your face."

Olivia smiled into the roses. "Thank you. These mean a lot."

"I've got a feeling everything will work . . . out." His sentence trailed off when a car pulled up.

She didn't recognize the black town car, but it parked between her and Garrett's house.

"Expecting company?" she asked.

"Absolutely not." He shook his head.

They didn't have to wait for long. A long leg swung out of the car, flashing red at the bottom of her heels.

"Oh, no." Olivia exhaled.

"Who is that?" Garrett whispered.

"Ama Vaux Tanner."

But she wasn't the only one in the car. Perry and Billie both stepped out of the car. Perry in an equally elegant manner as Ama. Billie, on the other hand, jumped out with the same energy as a stripper popping out a birthday cake.

Ama catwalked to her gate, where Olivia and Garrett stood.

She looked at Garrett. "Now, as much as I appreciate a fine-looking man, do you mind returning home? Me and Olivia have much to discuss."

She turned her attention to Olivia, raising her perfectly arched eyebrow.

Olivia knew that look and she wasn't ready for the storm.

"Ama, this is Garrett." She pointed her bouquet toward him. "I've been sick and he just stopped by with flowers."

"How wonderful. A pleasure to meet you, Garrett," Ama nodded, then winked at Olivia.

"Oh, before you leave." Ama lifted a finger. "Call those neighbors of yours. Tell them we've got things to discuss. Tonight. Eight p.m. sharp. Make sure all the people who *think* my dear Olivia betrayed their confidence are present."

Garrett responded with an affable smile. "You've got it." He opened the gate and nodded toward the godsisters.

Billie and Perry whispered among themselves, Perry even giggled.

"Hello, cher." Ama put her hands on the waist of her wide-legged navy blue slacks. She wore a red silk shirt with a stylish bow tied to the side of her neck—it was the perfect outfit to compliment her brilliant and bold personality. "Aren't you going to invite me in?"

Olivia felt like she was in the *Twilight Zone*. Seated in her living room was her mother, her godmother, and godsisters. When they arrived, Olivia quickly went into hostess mode, pouring wine and putting together a simple charcuterie tray with cured meat, goat cheese, and candied nuts.

Ama greeted Cindy like an old friend. They sat on the love sofa, whispering to each other.

Perry paced behind Olivia while she pulled a quick dinner together.

"Are you sure you aren't mad?" Perry asked. "To my defense, it's like Ama already knew what was going on." Perry waved her hand.

Did she now? Olivia kept her thoughts to herself. "No," Olivia whispered back. "I just wish I knew you all were coming."

"It was Ama's idea. She didn't want you to push us off. And let's be real, you would've made an excuse."

"I don't have enough space for everyone and I'm just getting over a cold."

Perry backed away.

"It's not Covid, but I could've made proper arrangements had I known." Olivia kept her voice light.

"Ama's got it covered." Perry shrugged from her safe distance. "And we won't be here for long. In and out."

"What's her plan?"

"I don't know."

"Or you can just come over here and ask me, cher."

Olivia squeezed her eyes shut. She should've known Ama would hear. And yes, Olivia had kept herself busy and away from Ama. She didn't have the energy for another confrontation or bombshell.

"Okay, then," Olivia stopped chopping vegetables. "Please tell me why you're here."

Ama reached into her bag to pull out a laptop and moved to the kitchen table. While the laptop booted, Olivia sat beside her godmother.

"A few weeks ago, you asked me to investigate Anderson."

Billie tsked from her chair, while Perry raised her eyebrows.

Cindy didn't seem the least bit surprised or bothered.

"I did. But I also decided to drop it."

"I did not. I investigated him for myself. Your instincts are rarely wrong, Olivia. My associate turned over files. I told him to go deep and he . . . he did as I asked. He investigated Anderson and his entire family. Anderson's father, Frank, came into his money unusually. He did not grow up in wealth. Frank's father was blue collar. He had the ambition and intelligence, but he lacked the capital. Frank knew he could gain capital by way of a childhood friend who worked for a certain mafia."

Ama pointed her bone white–painted nails at the screen. "You can read the summary here."

Olivia leaned forward and read the investigator's notes. Frank borrowed from organized crime members. He repaid in full, but occasionally they needed Frank's influence to push competition out of the way. That included anything from budding franchises within their *jurisdiction* to politicians. But according to the investigator, he'd fallen out of favor with them. Apparently, they'd asked for something that stretched even Frank's morals to the limit.

"Oh." Olivia clutched her stomach. "Do I really want to go up against this man?"

"Oh, no, sweetie. We don't attack from the front," Ama laughed. "We are the wind, the wind is everywhere, seemingly harmless until it's not. But not something you can pinpoint."

"Whatever does that mean?" Olivia whispered.

Ama cleared her throat. "Frank has received a package that includes his dossier from an anonymous source. He has seventy-two hours to cease the harassment of your neighbors, including one Bea Hampton. He will return your journal and he will no longer develop in SANS."

"Ama!" Tears gathered in her eyes. "Thank you. I . . . I don't know how to repay you!" She leaned over to give her godmother a hug.

Billie and Perry came over to the kitchen, both leaning in for a group hug.

Perry sighed. "Oh, what a relief."

Ama straightened her blouse, which wasn't built for group hugs and neither was her godmother. "Cindy and I were talking about you three. We are so proud of you. All of you are beautiful and accomplished young women. Omar and I were determined that none of you would want for anything. But I'm afraid that we perhaps made you docile."

"D-docile?" Billie sputtered. "Excuse you. I'm a Black queer woman advocating for sustainability."

Ama raised her hand. "You are very accomplished and I know you, as well as your godsisters, fought hard for where you are career-wise. But there's a thing called being streetwise." She quoted with her fingers. "At times one must sharpen their nails," she stretched out her hand, "and claws. We have resources. Learn how to use them sparingly."

"Like paprika."

"Yes, now go upstairs and get ready, cher."

"For what?"

"The next stage is dress to impress. You are an unflappable goddess. And those who doubted you will eat their words."

"I really like the hot pink jumpsuit you have hanging in your closet," Cindy said from the couch. "It'll look gorgeous on you."

"P-pink?" Olivia repeated. She couldn't believe her ears. Cindy always had something sly to say anytime she wore the color.

"Yes. You always looked gorgeous in pink. So wear it. Show them you aren't one to be messed with."

Olivia looked at the clock. It was half past seven. She wasn't convinced Garrett could get her neighbors to gather at her place, but she would still prepare.

She went upstairs, and with Perry's help, styled her hair into waves.

"My goodness, girl. Garrett's going to have a heart attack."

Olivia laughed while staring at her reflection in the mirror. "No. I need him alive. I've got plans for him."

"Long-term plans?"

"Just . . . plans." She didn't know what the future held for her and Garrett, but she liked seeing him. She enjoyed his company and, for now, it would be enough.

The doorbell rang.

"They're here." Billie yelled from downstairs. She couldn't make out what Ama said to Billie, but from the admonishing tone, Olivia was sure Ama told her to lower her voice.

Ama hated yelling in the house.

"Okay. Let me change and I'll be downstairs in a few."

Perry nodded and stood to leave. "I'll pull out the appetizers you prepared for us and pour the wine."

"Hey," Olivia whispered.

Perry turned around. "What is it?"

"Thank you."

Perry smiled. "I didn't do anything."

"You cared. You've always cared about me, but I pushed you away because of my insecurities and because of my secrets. I didn't trust you to bear the load. I'm very sorry and I . . . I love you so much."

Perry rushed to her side again and wrapped Olivia in her arms.

They hugged for a long time. They should have done this a long time ago, but Olivia couldn't see past all the privileges Perry had as a light-skinned Black woman.

Olivia had been so foolish, she knew that now.

"You're a good hugger." Olivia finally pulled back. "I've been missing out all these years."

"Well, now that I know you won't bite me, I'm hugging you all the time. Be prepared."

They smiled at each other. The beautiful warmth of Perry's smile filled her with love.

"I'll let you get ready. Remember, we've always got your back." Perry shut the door behind her.

Olivia swallowed her rising emotion. She wouldn't come downstairs teary-eyed. Ama had been right. As soon as the going got tough, her neighbors turned their backs on her.

Olivia glided downstairs. She looked good. She smelled good. She felt good.

When she spotted Anderson with her pink notebook in hand, she nearly stumbled. Not only that, he stood beside Garrett, chatting away.

The usual players were all present. Whitney and Charles. Kara, Addy, and Rich. Mr. Whittingham sat beside a solemn-looking Cindy.

But no sign of Bea, the one who kicked her in the gut.

"All right, girl. We see you." Addy whistled.

Whitney merely crossed her arms. "Tell us why you gathered us here."

Billie passed around printed pages. Apparently, they'd been busy prepping for this meeting while she primped upstairs.

For long minutes, the room was silent. Olivia's attention turned to Anderson, who read with shaking hands. Olivia moved over to her ex-fiancé.

"I'm sorry you had to learn like this. I . . . I didn't know you would be here. Garrett invited you?"

She felt Garrett's eyes on them, but she needed to speak to Anderson.

Anderson shook his head. "I found the notebook in Shaun's office. You were right. I came over and Ama advised I stay. She pulled me aside and showed me the dossier. It's just . . . embarrassing, you know." His skin flushed red. "I knew my father was a monumental asshole, but it sucks to know how right I am. So here."

Anderson gave her the journal. "I didn't read it." He bent over and kissed her temple. "I'm going to sneak out, before they sharpen their pitchforks. Goodbye, Olivia." The way he said it, she knew he meant for good.

She understood. There were too many bad memories between them. Ones that they could not ignore or navigate.

"Goodbye, Anderson. I'll be rooting for you."

He waved and left.

Ama cleared her voice, signaling Olivia to take center stage.

Olivia stood in the middle of her living room. "Frank has the same information you are holding in your hands. It's been confirmed that ASK will no longer bother our neighborhood."

"No more tacky flyers?" Whitney's voice shook with hope.

"No more," Olivia confirmed.

"No more godawful developments?" Whitney's whisper grew stronger.

"No more." Olivia swiped her hand in the air.

"Girl, you are brilliant," she yelled.

Whitney moved over for a hug, but Billie stepped in her path. "Ah, no. I think everyone in this room owes Olivia an apology."

"You're right," Whitney agreed. The others offered their apologies, one by one.

Olivia graciously accepted.

The door opened behind her. Bea stepped inside. All eyes swung to her. She heard a gasp behind her, but Olivia ignored it.

"Who is she?" Billie asked in a hushed voice.

"Bea." It sounded as if Olivia answered Billie's question, but

Olivia was genuinely surprised to see her neighbor. Bea had been so angry when they last spoke.

"Good news, Bea. Frank's laying off," Addy yelled. "Your secret is safe."

Bea huffed. "No, it's not. Is it, Ama?"

Olivia swung around to find Ama with tears in her eyes.

Ama shook her head. "No, they are not, Edie."

"Edie?" Billie snorted. "I thought her name was Bea. Isn't she the woman who accused you anyway?" Billie walked toward her.

When the two women stood in front of each other, it all clicked.

"Oh, no," Olivia whispered, her heart sinking.

Ama slowly walked to the duo. "Let's step outside. We have much to discuss."

Ama grabbed Billie's hand. Her godsister looked at her, then Perry, as if looking for an intervention.

Olivia shook her head at Perry, who nodded her understanding. Despite the bomb she dropped on Perry two summers ago, her godsister trusted Ama.

Olivia turned to address the remaining crowd. "I hate to do this, but I think everyone should leave now."

Addy leaned in and whispered, "All right, but you've got to spill the tea later."

"Get your tea directly from Bea . . . not me."

"She's like Fort Knox," Addy groaned and stomped away.

Kara reached for Olivia's hand. "Come by my house. I've got some new paintings. Whichever you want is yours."

Olivia tutted. "Do you think you can win me over with your paintings?"

Kara bit her lip. "Of course not, but I'm hoping it's a good start."

"It is." Olivia returned her squeeze. "Go home. It's ok. I'm fine."

Kara directed her attention toward Olivia's home. "Between your mom, godmother, and godsisters, I'd say it's handled."

Olivia smiled. Her life was better than good, it was great.

Still, she was worried about Billie and the stress of the news on her pregnancy.

"I'll come by soon. Goodnight, Kara."

"Night."

Garrett gave her a kiss on her lips. "You're amazing."

"Well, more so Ama but—"

He kissed her, quieting her argument. "You're everyone's hero. You can't go back to the city now."

Olivia's heart sped. No, she would not return to her beloved city. But she would visit, at least for a little while.

After witnessing three generations of hurt women, Olivia knew that life was too short for unspoken regrets. She owed it to herself to get to know Charles. And he'd come for her mother when she left town.

Charles Jones had tried, just not hard enough, and way too late.

But today was a start.

"I'll be seeing you, Garrett. I need to take care of my family."

His gaze scanned her body—not with an appreciative gleam, but apprehension. Like he knew exactly what she'd been thinking.

"I'll be just over there." He pointed to his house. "Talk to me first, okay?"

"About what?"

Garrett shook his head. "I'll be waiting for you." He walked out the door.

CHAPTER 32

A MOTHER'S LOVE

September 2021

Olivia had a beautiful home. It was a damn shame Billie's first view of Olivia's beach came with devastating secrets.

"Billie, cher, I need you to sit." Ama pointed to the bench beneath the picnic table in Olivia's backyard.

"Why?" She ignored Ama's directive and stared at Edie-slash-Bea.

The woman who birthed her. She recognized her now. There was just no question. It was like looking into a mirror, no matter how distorted.

After Ama shared her secret two summers ago, her father, Mike, had shared an old picture of her mother. Back then her hair had been straight, in a cute nineties pixie cut. Now long curly hair hung down her back. She had a tattoo sleeve of bees, flowers, and the sun. They were the same height, taller than the average bear, but Edie was slender in contrast to Billie's athletic build. Funny how someone who only weighed a buck-o-five could crush someone's life.

"We need to talk to you, Edie and I," she pointed to the woman. "We both owe you explanations."

Billie shrugged. "What difference will it make? You dumped her and twenty-one years later, she dumped me. At least I had my father."

Bea didn't flinch under Billie's harsh assessment. She stood there, chin tilted high, her body, a frozen work of art.

It was like staring at a funhouse mirror that aged you ten years.

Bea's blue eyes stared at her. "I'm sure there are questions you've always wanted to ask me . . . so ask."

She didn't want this. She wanted Dulce. She wanted her father.

A large part of her wanted to run away, but she was afraid to run because running was in her genes.

If I run now, maybe I'll never stop?

Billie looked away from her grandmother and mother and stared at the ocean. Maybe she didn't have to run, she could swim. Swim far enough where their demons couldn't pull her down.

"Cher?" Ama grabbed Billie's hands, anchoring her in this moment. "Talk to us."

"Why did you leave? I . . . I understand wanting freedom, but Dad isn't someone who would hold anyone back." Billie stared at Ama, though the question was clearly for the other woman.

"Your father was wonderful."

"He *is* wonderful. He's still alive."

"I'm glad."

"I'm pregnant, you know." Billie touched her stomach. "The line of Vaux Tanner women will continue. My partner, Dulce, and I debated on who should carry. I told her I wanted to do it. Do you know why?"

She looked at both women.

"Because I want to end the cycle. I wanted to show that I could carry a child and stick around. That I would love them no matter how much independence I craved."

"I'm so glad to hear that, Billie," Bea responded with sincerity. "But it simply wasn't that easy for me."

"Then why did you create a family? Why did you give Dad false hope?"

"I was selfish and lost and . . . I should have been there for you. But honest to goodness, I didn't know how to be there for myself. I did so many bad things to myself. I poisoned my body, I drank and smoked and sabotaged any meaningful relationship. And I know in my heart if I hadn't left you and your father, I would've dragged you down with me."

"How brave."

"Billie, enough," Ama scolded. "If you can forgive me, consider forgiving your mother."

"I don't have to do anything. Just like you two didn't do anything about being mothers."

Ama released Billie's hand. She sat on the bench, head bowed, eyes closed.

Tear slipped from Ama's eyes.

Edie, Bea . . . whoever the hell, clasped her middle. She looked up at the sky, staring at the crescent moon.

"It's a good night to swim," she muttered under her breath.

Billie wanted to agree but that would require agreeing with the woman who destroyed her father's life.

"Hey," Olivia said from the door. "Billie, why don't you and I take a walk?" Her godsister grabbed her hand, before she could answer, dragging them away from her backyard, down into the sandy dunes.

Olivia stopped long enough for Billie to take off her shoes before resuming their walk.

"Did you know?" Billie broke the silence.

"No." Olivia shook her head. "It didn't click for me until I saw the two of you together. She'd told me a little about her past. Still, I . . . I didn't guess. I wouldn't pull that on you."

They didn't talk for a few minutes which was fine by Billie. She knew Olivia wanted to give her a break from the drama.

"I thought about her a lot when I was younger. When I saw moms braiding their daughters' hair for swim meets. And sometimes my dad would look so lonely. At night he opened the window and stared out . . . like he expected her to appear out of nowhere. I just . . . hate her, you know? I can't help it. That's the first feeling that came over me. And God knows how I'm going to explain her to Dad. He's going to freak out. Then he'll want to see her. He'll put all his hopes on her when he just needs to move on. Like decades ago. I mean what did he see in her, other than her looks. Seems dull if you ask me."

"Hmm." Olivia stopped walking.

"What is it?"

"She likes bees, just like you."

"She does?"

"She's a beekeeper. And an apothecary."

"That's . . . cool, I guess."

"What do you want to do?" Olivia asked. "I can sneak you away."

"Nah." Billie shook her head. "This is good for now. Walking and talking."

"Then we'll walk and talk."

"You and I are alike. We have some messed-up parents."

"Yes," Olivia agreed. "But something I learned over the weekend. Parents are human. They aren't the smart superheroes we thought they were growing up. They're just sorting through the deck of cards life gave them. Now they're dealing with the consequences of their actions. We haven't gotten to the age where we have deep regrets. We were protected in a way."

"God, I hope I don't screw up my kid. What if they don't like me? They'll love Dulce for sure. She's awesome."

"And so are you. You two balance each other and you will do the same as parents."

Billie let out a shaky breath. "I'm just so scared. Seeing Ama and Edie together, I'm wondering if running away is something in the genes."

"Don't be ridiculous."

"Am I? Ama gave her up for adoption. My mom left me and my father. Statistically speaking, it's not looking good for Dulce."

"Did you abandon your father?"

"No."

"Your godsisters?" Olivia pressed. "Well, other than sneaking out of the house at night?"

Billie shook her head. She was loyal to a fault.

"You gave up an amazing job opportunity to be with your wife. You aren't a runner or a quitter. And Ama and Bea . . . they aren't looking at you with regret. They're looking at you with pride. You've thrived and bloomed where you were planted. If I had to guess, they're thanking God that you broke the cycle."

"I have, haven't I?" Billie stopped walking. Olivia was right. She found peace and freedom being with her wife. She rubbed her stomach, that now had just the slightest pooch that Dulce loved to caress.

"We didn't play rock, paper, scissors to decide who got pregnant," Billie confessed.

"I should hope not," Olivia replied in that sharp way of hers. But instead of bookending her comment with a frown, Olivia wrestled with a smile. Sag Harbor had changed her godsister for the better.

"I was curious how you both decided."

"I begged Dulce to let me carry our child. I want to be tethered to my family. And if . . . if I ever forget myself, I won't forget the personification of love Dulce and I had for each other. I won't ever be easy leaving my wife or child. But if I ever lose myself, I need you to find me." Billie bit her lip, her eyes focused on Olivia. "Promise me."

Ama would let her roam, thinking it's best that she find her way. But Perry and Olivia had no qualms about dragging her back home.

"You won't leave," Olivia reached for Billie's hand, lending her strength in a comforting squeeze. "But if you ever do, I'll use every resource to find and help you." Billie nodded, satisfied with her godsister's answer.

I can do this. I chose to carry because I chose to stay. Billie felt the bands of generational trauma fall away.

"I'm going to be an amazing mother," Billie vowed. "I'll make them feel loved and safe and wanted. I'll let them spread their wings, so they won't feel stifled. We Vaux women need that, apparently."

That's what Billie's dad Mike had done. It was as if he'd known what she needed.

"Eh." She was her mother's daughter all along.

"C'mon," she said to Olivia. "Let's go back."

She wanted to get to know Bea, the beekeeper. And maybe one day, she'd let her meet her granddaughter.

"Don't forget to give Ama a hug."

Billie laughed at Olivia's joke. They both knew Ama would much prefer the words.

"What are you going to do about that cutie-pie neighbor?"

Olivia crossed her arms, looked at the water and smiled.

"The question is what is he going to do with me?"

EPILOGUE

A Home in Highland
October 2021

Garrett carried Olivia's suitcases out and packed them in her car. "I think that's everything." He yelled over his shoulder.

Mr. Whittingham stood by the door, ready to close up her home.

After a long thoughtful letter from Mr. Whittingham, she knew he'd meant no harm, nor did he mean to lie to Olivia. Looking back, it was clear that he wanted to ease her into getting to know her biological father. She was grateful for the stories. Charles wasn't the boogeyman or a heartless deserter. He was a very complicated man. At least, that's the impression she had from approximately thirty minutes in his presence.

She wanted to get to know him. And she would. She'd put her two-weeks' notice in at work but would give them a month more of remote work. Which she intended to spend at her father's estate in Highland Beach.

"We're going to miss you around here." Mr. Whittingham's voice was sad, yet proud. She imagined he used the same tone for his children when they left for college.

"I'll miss you, too."

"You've got to promise to come back to us." He wrapped his arm around her side, giving her a friendly squeeze.

"Of course. This is my home. And I have my business with Whitney and I'm Zora's godmother, too."

"That's right." He smiled. "You've got some roots here."

"You can come visit, too, you know. I'm sure Charles wouldn't mind."

"No, young lady. You need quality time with your *father*."

"Okay, but the offer still stands." She reached for his hand and squeezed. "Thank you for everything."

"You're welcome. I'll look out for the house while you're gone."

"It'll only be a month, max."

"Sure, it will." Mr. Whittingham smiled.

Ama had said something similar, but her tone had been more dreadful than Mr. Whittingham's hopeful tone.

"I've been to Highland Beach. Beautiful place. I can't say I like the people."

Olivia knew some of those people were *her* people, the Jones Family.

"Did I ever tell you the story of the two queen bees?"

Olivia shook her head, though Ama couldn't see her over the phone.

"Omar and I added another beehive to our property. A good friend who studied bees told us it was okay to keep them side by side. It didn't take long, maybe a few months, when the queen bee—the one who'd been there the longest—took her core worker bees and left the hive."

"Oh? Did you find them?" Olivia asked.

"No. They're gone and never coming back, but I learned a valuable lesson—two queen bees can't exist in the same space for long."

Olivia understood her warning. "Ama, I'm not a queen bee and—"

"Not yet, but Christine is. I know her and she knows me. So, if you run into any trouble on Highland Beach, you call me. Only one queen bee can survive, cher. Christine is no match for me."

Mr. Whittingham sighed, bringing Olivia back to the present.

"Go say goodbye to poor Garrett. Lord, that boy looks so long in the face."

Olivia hugged him again and then walked toward the door.

"Hey." She walked into Garrett's open arms.

"Call me when you arrive."

"I will."

"I want to see your face."

Olivia smiled into his chest. "I'll FaceTime you."

"Don't go replacing me as your favorite neighbor," he joked.

Olivia laughed. "I'll be too busy getting to know my father."

"Good." He opened the car door. "I want you to come back to me."

She wanted to return the promise, but she couldn't. She didn't want him to wait around for a woman who'd struggle to love herself.

"Garrett, I—"

"I know how you feel about me. I look forward to you realizing how you feel about me, too."

Olivia leaned in and hugged him tighter. "You're my favorite neighbor."

"Good. Now I want to be your favorite person."

Omar had been her favorite, then Ama. But Garrett had a strong shot, especially with his adorable little girl. She'd said her tearful goodbyes to Zora last night since she'd be leaving while Zora attended school.

"Bye for now." She lifted on her toes and kissed him. It was slow and sad and sweet.

She craved more, but she didn't go back for seconds. Not with two pairs of eyes on them.

She slid into the driver's seat.

"Ready?" she turned her attention to her mother.

Cindy shook her head. "No, but there's no way I'm letting you go by yourself. Not with Christine still around," she said with a determination Olivia had never heard.

"I must meet this grandmother of mine."

"Oh, you will. I'm sure it'll be memorable."

Olivia pressed the ignition, then waved goodbye to the two men she'd come to love.

The engine idled while she stared at them. Mr. Whittingham looked proud, yet melancholy.

Garrett didn't look at her, but off to the side, staring it seemed into nothingness. A slight wind picked up, the tails of his jacket danced in the air. He reminded her of a hero in classic literature— how'd she imagined Heathcliff standing on the moors.

She blew one last kiss, but not to them, to the house.

To Omar.

She had more than one father.

There was Chris Jones, the man who stepped in and loved her as his own.

Then, Omar Tanner, the man who took her to father-daughter dances. The first man to make her feel smart and beautiful.

Now she had Charles Jones. The man desperate to get to know his child, despite the risks to his career and life.

She was nervous about Charles, but she had six hours to settle the butterflies in her stomach.

"Here we go." She declared to herself and to the universe.

Thanks to Omar, she had everything she needed. She had good neighbors, good family, and a home. This wasn't goodbye to Sag Harbor, but a see you soon.

ACKNOWLEDGMENTS

Thank you, Sharina Harris, for helping me get this book across the finish line.

Thank you to my fearless editor and, dare I say, friend, Carrie Feron, who patiently waited for this book.

Thank you to my literary agent, Mel Berger, for believing I could do this and for always keeping me busy.

And finally to my Sag family—Raquel, Walter, Kim, Padel, KK, Teresa, Fred, Lindsey, Bibi, Slim, Pam, Kevin, Jeff, Peter, Robin, Adrienne, and all of those in the SANS community who welcome me onto Havens Beach every summer. See you at the Labor Day races.